PRAISE FOR THE NOVELS OF KAY KENYON:

MAXIMUM ICE

"Full-bodied characters, palpable environs, layered mystery and heady suspense combine like the many facets of 'Ice' in this sparkling SF novel. . . . Kenyon is a surprising new talent, and SF enthusiasts will appreciate her imaginative world and characters." —*Publishers Weekly*

"A vivid cast of characters, some interesting asides on religious authority, and the bleakly beautiful landscape make this a uniquely powerful tale reminiscent of Greg Bear." —*Booklist*

"*Maximum Ice* enhances Kay Kenyon's reputation as a strong new voice in SF. . . . In a stark and compelling story with a unique twist, Ms. Kenyon delivers a well-written, action-packed SF thriller." —*Romantic Times*

"Kenyon should be acknowledged by now as a master creator of realistic new worlds. She is also an aficionado of the fantastic, a weaver of fast and exciting stories, a writer capable of creating characters we recognize, characters whom we are happy to let into our hearts and minds. It's very simple: If you want to read an exciting, fast, and thoroughly involving novel, read *Maximum Ice*."
—*Statesman Journal*, Salem, OR

"Kenyon blends science, religion and the imperative to survive in an engaging tale." —*The Kansas City Star*

"A top-notch cyberfable that kept me turning pages into the wee hours. Powerful stuff." —Julian May

"Kay Kenyon is science fiction's newest master at creating worlds unlike any we've encountered before, but which are so deeply and convincingly portrayed that we wind up feeling as if we've actually set foot in them. *Maximum Ice* is her best yet, an adventure that's also a deep meditation on the interface between the strange and the familiar, and between shadowed pasts and unveiled futures." —K. W. Jeter

"Kay Kenyon's *Maximum Ice* is superb—an intriguing premise, strong characters, and a gripping plot kept me reading until dawn. I enjoyed it tremendously."
—Kathleen Ann Goonan

"A knockout adventure." —SciFi.com

TROPIC OF CREATION

"Kenyon's vision of a unique universe ranks with those of such science fiction greats as Frank Herbert and Orson Scott Card." —*Publishers Weekly* (starred review)

"A rich weaving of science, politics and mysticism. A believable, memorable story." —Brian Herbert

"Kenyon draws vivid characters you care about, both human and alien, striving on a harsh and memorable distant world." —David Brin

"More proof that Kay Kenyon is a major talent."
—Mike Resnick

"The real mystery in SF these days is why isn't Kay Kenyon better known? She writes beautifully, her characters are multilayered and complex, and her extrasolar worlds are real and nuanced, while at the same time truly alien. An exciting, fascinating, mind-blowing ride."
—Robert J. Sawyer

"Suspenseful and satisfying . . . a wholly worthwhile read."
—SciFi.com

RIFT

"A grand adventure filled with genuine surprise . . . rife with new ideas, delicious fears, and compelling events. It has pace, texture, excitement and rock-solid form. Put it at the top of your reading list."
—*Statesman Journal*, Salem, OR

"In a science fiction market where terraforming has gotten to be a tried-and-true setting, a planet that refuses to be subjugated by human science is a gift and a wonder."
—*Talebones*

"Kenyon has created a powerful book driven by characters with clear moral imperatives, and the stakes are survival of entire races." —Writers NW

"Kay Kenyon has done it again. Her third out-of-this-world science fiction novel confirms the quality of her writing skills and quantity of creative leaps of imagination."
—*The Third Age*

"A great, fast-paced read with all that I could ask of an SF novel." —Jacqueline Lichtenberg

ALSO BY KAY KENYON

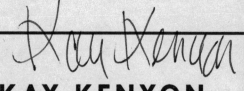

KAY KENYON

THE
BRAIDED
WORLD

BANTAM BOOKS

THE BRAIDED WORLD

A Bantam Spectra Book / February 2003

Published by
Bantam Dell
A Division of Random House, Inc.
New York, New York

ISBN 0-553-58379-4

Manufactured in the United States of America
Published simultaneously in Canada

OPM   10 9 8 7 6 5 4 3 2 1

For Robert Ray

ACKNOWLEDGMENTS

In writing this story I am indebted to a special group of people—friends who love science fiction and think that engaging, scientifically credible stories matter. My special thanks to Louise Marley for her valuable assistance with things musical and literary. I owe a great deal to Thomas P. Hopp for his patient review of the genetics issues in this book; his contributions were immensely helpful. Thanks also to my readers, Gary L. Nunn and David Hobby for their suggestions and corrections. I am indebted to Anne Lesley Groell for her thoughtful and meticulous editing, and to Donald Maass for his unique guidance. As always, I am deeply grateful to my husband, Thomas, for his advice and unwavering support.

All of my stories are the better for early lessons learned from writer, teacher, and friend Robert Ray, to whom this work is gratefully dedicated.

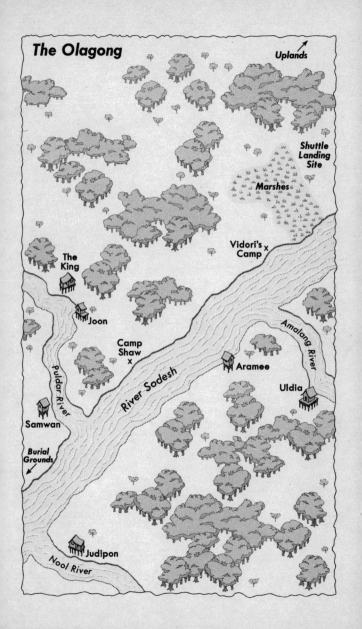

THE
BRAIDED
WORLD

THE MESSAGE

It was a time for turning inward, for licking wounds, for looking with suspicion on outsiders. Earth had been under siege from without, and from within. Under such circumstances, it was perhaps understandable that people closed their doors and drew the curtains. Especially if the outsiders weren't human.

It was a time of endemic disease. Despite all that biomolecular medicine could do, swiftly mutating microbes adapted easily to every treatment. Antibiotics and antivirals only spawned superresistant versions—genetic concoctions with conjugative sharing of resistance factors and virulence genes. Humanity was in thrall to pathogenic microbes, the invisible master race.

Thus it was that people greeted the Message with both hope and dread. Dread that the radio transmission from deep space was a snare set by the virulent universe; and hope that Earth's fortunes might improve. The doubters held that one's neighbors couldn't be trusted—especially if they lived thirty light-years away. After all, humanity's worst cataclysms had come from space: asteroids causing mass extinctions in prehuman times, and the Dark Cloud calamity in human memory: the killing time that left humanity a tenth of what it had been. The universe, they argued, was not a friendly place.

So, as for the Message, perhaps they shouldn't answer.

The Message implied the need for a long space voyage, not an appealing prospect to the World Council, despite a breakthrough in subspace tunneling as a path to the stars. With human civilization struggling to survive, why divert resources to a risky adventure of dubious value? If the beings who sent this message were so well-meaning, why did they hide themselves? No, the Council would not send out a starship.

But a private group would. One woman lavished her considerable fortune on the mission. She was a singer, a celebrity, but well past her performance years. And so, since she was old and up for a last adventure, she decided to go along for the ride. To bring back the promised thing: human genetic diversity.

For that was the promise of the alien message. *Come find what you have lost.*

In truth, it had *all* been lost.

The Dark Cloud had come into Earth's vicinity. Eventually, it departed. Between these two events, information leaked from the world and into the Cloud. Earth lost much of its electronically and biologically stored information. Insofar as human beings could be considered repositories of information—molecular, that is—they lost that information. In other words, they died.

This experience taught people that information can, under some circumstances, be considered a physical entity, subject to universal laws. Such as entropy. The Dark Cloud was deeply information-poor. When in proximity to galactic sites of rich information, the direction of information flow was inevitable—much as warm air moves into colder regions, and order to disorder. The Cloud read the information stored in electronic systems, and biological information in DNA. And in the process of reading it, transferred it to itself.

The Dark Cloud was a rogue structure of dark matter, a natural catastrophe—nothing planned, or intentionally sinister. Earth survived because of a last-ditch defense called Ice, a fast-spreading shield that protected humans and other information-rich systems from the Dark Cloud's predation.

Even so, the calamity had left too few survivors to sustain healthy populations of Homo sapiens. Lack of biodiversity lowered the immune system hurdles that disease pathogens must overcome. Humanity was a sitting duck floating on a shallow gene pool.

The astonishing claim of the Message was that someone had mined the Dark Cloud, salvaging the deep genetic pool and storing it as coded information. Because the Message was so brief, it contained no explanation, much less proof, of how such a thing could be done, or how it could benefit Earth. Implied was: *It can all be reclaimed.*

The skeptics balked. Suppose this was the very race that sent the Dark Cloud in the first place, who now meant to finish off what they started? *Nonsense,* said Bailey Shaw—for that was the name of the woman who was determined to go. *It's our last chance.*

Bailey Shaw supervised the building of the interstellar ship, calling it the *Restoration.* She believed in the power of a good name.

Most people called it *Shaw's Folly.*

PROLOGUE

Even from a distance, the planet looked like Earth: a dot of rare blue, embraced by a gauze of clouds. The ship could detect oceans, polar caps, magnetic fields, and an atmosphere with nitrogen, oxygen, water, and carbon dioxide. A close match to Earth, complete with stabilizing moon and ideal relation to its G5 star. But poisoning the crew's excitement was the growing sense that the planet was not—well, *probable*. Radio signals revealed that its inhabitants spoke a language suited to human articulation. *Improbable*, the biologists said. Then, upon closer approach, using laser imaging, the most startling view of all . . .

In her quarters aboard the *Restoration*, Bailey Shaw was enduring yet another sleepless night, a circumstance she blamed partly on old age and partly on the rough voyage. She rubbed at her sore eyes, myopic despite the ship's surgeon's offering a little corrective. At seventy-eight, Bailey was about done with self-improvement.

Her gaze went again and again to the view screen, displaying Earth's cousin, so far the only other water planet in the known universe. It was a world of scattered islands, with one forested landmass cinched in narrowly at the equator. Only this middle region gave evidence of civilization, one with limited radio technology and primitive dwellings clustered along a great river system. She blanked the screen, having seen enough, for now. It would all become clear on the ground mission, the expedition that would have been led by Captain Darrow, except that he was dying. Damn him anyway.

When the door chimed, she jumped. If they were disturbing her this late, there must be news. She swiveled her chair around, preparing herself.

On voice command, the door opened, revealing Ensign Petry, looking about sixteen years old. She couldn't remember hiring any sixteen-year-olds. Besides, they'd been in transit for three years, so he must be at least twenty. He stood stiffly, like a walk-on character in a cheap opera. "Ma'am," the youngster mumbled.

Bailey rose. "Go ahead, Petry. I'm not so frail that bad news will kill me outright."

He managed a miserable smile. Then, remembering what he came for, he sobered. "Mrs. Shaw, the captain is dead."

She thought he'd practiced that line on his way down from the medical suite. Like saying *The king is dead, Your Highness.* And not too far off, either. Captain Charlton Darrow was a formidable leader, the man she'd handpicked for the job of commanding a crew of forty for the six-year round trip, plus ground mission. Now what would they do?

The ensign looked like he might break down. "I'm sorry."

Oh, not as sorry as I am, she thought. The captain had been among the first to sicken, but Bailey had hoped he would pull through. After killing ten crew, the disease had run its course, knocked out by a drug they'd designed to stop viral replication. But it was too late to save Darrow. The irony was that, despite all their attempts at antisepsis, the virus had hitched a ride in the cleansing baths in which they stored their surgical tools. The damn thing had hidden there during the trip out, having gone into a kind of sporulation, toughening an unusual outer envelope around itself. It was disheartening to think how smart microbes were, little specks of living matter that never went to university.

She gave instructions, and Petry went off to prepare for the meeting.

The meeting at which she must appoint a new captain.

Pulling out a fresh uniform, she buttoned the green jumpsuit. *Not* her best color—but the uniform reflected the quasi-military organization aboard the craft and made packing easier, God knew. They needed a chain of command, being thirty light-years from home—as the crow flies. Using the stellar-mass Kardashev tunnel, the trip was a good deal shorter, or she wouldn't be the only elder on the mission.

Bailey headed down the corridor to the science deck, passing a few crew members, who, by their expressions, had heard the news. *Now what are we going to do?* seemed to be everyone's reactions, including hers.

By contract, Bailey reserved the right to choose the ship's leader. Because it was her mission. She had paid for every bolt, bucket of paint, and frozen dinner on board. One billion alone for the opto-crystalline tronic cubes. So yes, this mission was hers. Also hers was the duty to keep the faith, to bolster the crew's enthusiasm for the mission: pursuing an alien message, alien claims. And just how *could* DNA code be reanimated? Even supposing the lost codes of Earth were salvaged from the Dark Cloud, it was still only information, not life.

The crew could afford to be skeptical. Being young, they hadn't seen as much sorrow as she had: the loved ones dead, whole cities perishing. Perhaps they felt they could skip faith. And its corollary, penance.

She didn't blame crew members for their doubts. The brief, alien message held no proofs, only a claim: *Come find what you have lost. Salvaged from the dark structure, your genetic heritage is sequestered here.* Even if it was a ruse, curiosity alone would argue for a mission. And then, what if it was true?

People dithered about the Message for a hundred years. Before that, they weren't listening to space, being rather more preoccupied with reclaiming civilized life after the near extinction caused by the Dark Cloud. Once they *were* listening, they began analyzing the planet of origination; its presence could be discerned by the wobble of the parent star. The planet's edge-on alignment to Earth allowed astronomers to determine its atmospheric composition by identifying which wavelengths of starlight were dimmed by the atmosphere. The reason Bailey Shaw slapped her money down on the table was that the planet matched Earth. In such things as astronomical setting, mass, radius, and atmosphere, it was a perfect match. She had looked up at her staff—more accustomed to planning concerts and benefits than space voyages—and asked, *How much would it cost to go?*

It wasn't such a surprising move on her part. She would never sing again. Despite having a voice like the very angels, even now, in her eighth decade . . . So she was *looking* for something to do. And here it was.

The trouble began when they arrived in orbit and grabbed a close resolution of that boat traffic along the rivers. The readouts from three hundred kilometers overhead were blurred, but unmistakable. Those beings using boats on the rivers were human. As the science team fell into denial and the crew whispered apprehensively, Bailey had stormed around the ship, claiming victory. It's all here, she'd proclaimed, just as the Message promised.

And the sweetest utterance of all: I told you so.

Well, on this mission there were good days and bad. The present one, as Bailey stood in front of the doors to the conference deck, was definitely one of the latter. But she called up a confident smile. Anton Prados and Nick Venning stood as she entered the room, but she waved them back into their seats.

They looked uncomfortable, these two young men who'd shared quarters all the trip out, who'd been classmates at officer candidate school—who now were competitors. It was appalling to think of appointing one of these twenty-four-year-olds to captain a ship worth billions and to preside over an alien contact. But what choice did she have?

"Anton," Bailey said. "Nick." She found a seat and let the pause lengthen.

"I'm sorry, ma'am," Anton said.

No need to say what about.

Nick said, "He rallied for a bit yesterday. It's an ugly shock."

They were a study in opposites. Anton Prados was slim and black-haired, a handsome dark Russian look. A little serious. Young.

Nick Venning was a little shorter, more stocky, sandy-haired. Good with the crew. Quick-witted. Young.

They kept looking at the door, expecting to see Phillip Strahan join them. He wouldn't be. Strahan was a systems engineer, and would be staying on board to keep the ship and its science deck operational. Bailey had decided against appointing Strahan around midnight, before turning her attention to the remaining choices.

She voiced the wall screen forward, choosing a real-time view of the planet, now displaying the hemispheric ocean. If there was a highly advanced civilization here, perhaps it was underwater. But no, ground radar surveys found nothing that looked artificial. Yet, having captured one of the four orbiting satellites broadcasting the Message to Earth, they'd found the engineering so highly advanced it was incomprehensible. Furthermore, the satellite was composed of a material the science team called transuranic—something about its atomic number being, well, *astronomically* high. The thing was built to last forever, although it could be destroyed—as evidenced by the debris of one former satellite that had perhaps succumbed to meteor bombardment.

But where were the beings who'd created these things?

And if they had abandoned this planet, how long had they been gone? The materials of the satellite couldn't be dated by conventional means, since they didn't decay.

Bailey found herself asking the young men, "Do you think we've come here for nothing?"

Nick leaned forward. "That's what we'll go down to see."

"And you, Anton, what do you think?"

"If it's there, we'll find it." *It* referring to the code, to the vanished life of Earth.

Nick hastened to add, "Even if we have to run that ocean through a sieve."

The competition was heating up, the last thing she wanted. Especially since she'd already made up her mind.

"Bailey," Anton said. "May I say something?"

"No fair," Nick said, half joking. "No speeches."

He waved Nick off, looking at Bailey. Getting her permission, he said, "I never looked for this post, Bailey. Never thought in a million years that I'd be considered to captain the *Restoration*. I don't know why Commander Strahan isn't in here, but I assume you've given him the job. I figure that's fair. You don't need to explain. Maybe you shouldn't explain why you didn't pick us." He smiled. "For our morale."

Nick looked at Bailey, in surprise. "Commander Strahan doesn't have the time in service that either one of us do. He might be older, but that doesn't make him a better officer." He shifted uneasily in his chair.

Bailey held up her hands. "Don't jump to conclusions." She knew whom she would pick, but she dreaded making it final. Either one of them could take command. They'd been trained for command, an eventual one. They'd both served under an excellent officer, none better. Along with the entire crew, they had been studying the native language for two years, on the approach to Neshar, after the language program had cracked the translation and assembled a decent lexicon. They were both fluent. As model officers and good crewmates, they had dispatched themselves with equal ability. She liked them both.

But Anton was her favorite. He was not as decisive as Nick, nor as popular, though the crew liked him well enough. He kept himself the slightest bit apart. Of course, he was born to privilege, and it did show. She couldn't hold that against him, because in her classical singing career she had moved in wealthy circles. So, as for Anton's aristocratic bearing, Bailey thought she understood him. Nick, on the other hand, came from a humble background. He was book-smart if not wise, perhaps even impulsive. This quality made it easier for Nick to make a decision. So far, they'd all been good ones, but she'd only been watching him for three years.

She had to admit her choice wasn't entirely logical. The whole mission, for God's sake, was flying in the face of the *facts,* in favor of intuition.

"I've decided on Anton," she said. She let that hang in the air.

Anton swallowed, looking stuck to his chair.

Nick closed his eyes. When he opened them, he turned to Anton and offered his hand. "Congratulations, Anton." He smiled. "Captain."

"My God, Nick," Anton said. He took the hand. "Thank you." Turning to Bailey, he began, "But Strahan—"

She held him off. "Commander Strahan is needed up here for the engineering side of things. He was never in the equation." The other likely candidate, Lieutenant Brigid Dahlstrom, had succumbed to the virus two weeks ago.

Nick said, "Can I ask what you based your decision on?"

Bailey was grateful for the excuse that Anton had unwittingly provided. She said, "Perhaps *for the sake of morale,* I won't justify myself. Except to say this: Nick, you're the only anthropologist who isn't in the medical suite. You'll be on the ground mission, if the captain agrees." Anton looked as though he *should* be in the medical suite.

She went on, "You'll be busy, Nick. Whoever is down

there, whatever the nature of that culture, you'll be doing the analysis, making the interpretations. You'll be busy." Anton's specialty was astrophysics, a discipline not especially needed at this juncture. He could be spared to lead the most important endeavor in the history of the world.

Anton turned to Bailey. His dark eyes wavered. She wanted to comfort him, to tell him he was ready, although it wouldn't do to treat him like a grandson with a scraped knee. And she wasn't altogether sure he *was* ready, but the choices were few and time was wasting.

Nick clapped a hand on his friend's shoulder. "You'll do just fine, Anton. I'll be there to help you. OK?"

He got a smile in return. "I think I'm going to need it. Thanks."

Bailey rose. "This was a tough call, tough on all of us. Now, let's get some sleep, if we can." Before she turned to go, she paused long enough to say: "So, Anton, who's down there, then?" She tilted her head toward the wall screen, wondering what the *Restoration*'s new captain thought the mission was facing.

Anton's color had returned, and as he stood, he looked every bit a captain. "Humans," he said. "Strangers."

The concise summary gave her pause. This expedition would soon learn how human, how strange. She was more than ready to get on with it. To do, at the end of her life, one good thing. After a lifetime of self-indulgence, it was a nice plan.

Feeling energized, she decided to skip sleep and get her packing done instead. Time enough in the morning to inform Anton that she was going along on the ground mission.

He was the captain, now. He deserved to know.

I

MONARCH
OF THE
RIVERS

ONE

Deep in the night, the river flowed: a black, hot flood, here in this drowned world. Rain hurled down, peppering the thatch roof, filling the river ever higher. From the water's surface, wavering lights from electric lamps twisted back up, cut to ribbons.

Anton Prados sat outside the screened room where Nick Venning slept in his hammock. On the narrow walkway, with the river sliding under the stilted platform, Anton waited out his guard duty shift, a precaution in this land of disturbingly familiar beings. He thought he heard a small plop—a stone or a gecko falling into the river. His hand twitched on his empty holster, where his gun should have been. Confiscated by the monarch of the rivers. For the past two weeks, they'd been guests of the royal pavilion, taking the king's lavish meals, waited upon by his servants. Prisoners in silk, as Anton thought of it.

Still, it was a decent reception from a semi-industrial people with no concept of the galaxy, and no idea why the humans should think that anyone had called them. It could have been worse. Anton and his crew were rather like dinner guests arriving on the wrong night, on the wrong doorstep. The *Restoration* was lucky not to be turned away.

The shuttle had landed on a rock plateau in the middle of the populated delta lands. It was soon greeted by a throng of people arriving in skiffs, men and women with bronze skin and a range of weapons from digging tools to primitive pistols. Anton walked unarmed into their midst. It was a good tactic. Not that they were entirely surprised to see him. They had telescopes. They'd known visitors were here. Anton admired their poise, since his own crew continued to be dumbfounded by the presence of what looked like human beings thirty light-years from Earth.

Now, as he sat outside the monarch's palace, he watched the shadows of the residents pass to and fro behind the thin wall panels. The Dassa, as they called themselves. Descended, surely, from humans on Earth. Genetic diversity *sequestered*, as the Message said.

Though not always dark-eyed, they were bronze-skinned—altered or selected for the tropical environs, Zhen had guessed. Because they had to live in the hot latitudes of the planet. Because of how they reproduced.

Around him, the tiers of the royal compound stacked up to three stories, depending on the height of the foundation stilts. Under it all, the palace river turbines provided electricity. Across the small inlet, where the palace sprawled along the river, the women on the ground mission, Bailey and Zhen, were assigned quarters. Their light was out. Sleeping.

A gust of wind puffed at the woven reed wall, bearing pungent odors of bloated wood and mud. Dimly, he could make out small bridges here and there, inundated by water, arched wooden trestles protruding like the backs of sea monsters.

Geckos crawled freely up the stilts from the water to catch insects attracted to the lights. Anton watched them stalk their prey.

The geckos were genetically identical to those of Earth. Although microbiology, not zoology, was Zhen's field, she had research tools at her disposal; most of the shuttle cargo had been Zhen's lab equipment. In contrast to the geckos, however, some specimens of animal life had not made the transition from Earth in exact form. Or else they had evolved. The monkeys, for instance. The Dassa, for another.

Though the Dassa were not perfectly human, the women they called *hoda* likely were. Because the hoda could bear children, and proper Dassa did not. Not in the usual sense.

So the hoda represented potential breeding partners. From Zhen's analysis, their genotypes were incredibly diverse, a priceless reservoir of genetic diversity. But how could they be mates for those on Earth? Even supposing they were inclined to mix with their human cousins, how could they, given the space/time intervals—three real years, depending on the changing lattices of the tunnels. And, of course, the hoda were forbidden to bear young. So even now the solutions were not obvious.

Nothing was obvious. The civilization that created the satellites remained hidden. Dassa technology excelled in chemistry, especially for creating and molding superplastic ceramics using the local deposits of aluminum, magnesium, and zirconium. On a rainy excursion far up the Puldar River, Anton's team had seen the mill works, with its chemical labs and labor-intensive milling processes. But tronics and higher technologies were unknown to these people. The Dassa had not built the satellites.

The palace scholars and even the king himself, from what little contact they'd had with him, were not good sources of information, for they had no notion of *messages*. But if a signal was sent, it would have come, they said, from those known as the Quadi.

It was their belief that long ago the Quadi had created the people of this world. More than a creation myth, the belief was supported by evidence of tracings from stone carvings at a nearby site attributed to the Quadi. Among the pictographs of flora and fauna were those of *variums*, the shallow birthing pools, and the infants brought out from them. The ground team had seen these tracings, including indistinct renderings of what might have been the old race. Palace scholars said no, they were merely animals, or fantasies. "The Quadi are gone," they said, as though any likenesses of the Quadi would have fled with them.

Across the channel, a black gecko moved slowly up a post of the women's pavilion.

Anton rose. That was no gecko, to be seen at this distance. An empty skiff waited, tied to a pier. The black shape climbed toward Zhen and Bailey's room.

He was at Nick's side in two steps. "Someone's trying to break into Bailey's hut."

Nick came awake, managing to unravel himself from the sleeping hammock in one motion.

"Bring help," Anton said. "I'm going over."

Nick was instantly alert. "The guards won't let you."

"I know. Let's *move*."

Nick opened a screen, rousing the guards.

Anton had no intention of waiting for permission. He looked at the reed wall opposite the open screen where Nick argued with the guards. Then Anton plunged through the wall, taking splinters of reeds with him onto the deck.

He found himself on a narrow walkway with water sluicing by in a channel. Running along this walkway, he called to mind the layout—the maze—of the nearby quarters, with their catwalks, bridges, ramps, and huts.

His own hut was deliberately apart from the others, connected by a rope bridge that swayed now beneath his pounding feet, pitching wildly as he sprang onto a narrow ramp leading up. Dassa guards appeared from above, barring his way, drawing their single-shot pistols—primitive, but no less deadly.

"Soldiers," Anton said, pointing in the direction of the pavilion. In the crisis, he'd forgotten how to say *intruders* in the Dassa language. Well, *soldiers* would do. To his relief, the guards fell in with him, drawing pistols. "The hut of the hu-

man women," he told them as they ran along an extended
lanai, past screens now opening with curious Dassa, staring.
The guards led him at a fast clip into a snaking corridor inside the pavilion, through a gallery with burnished wooden
floors and then out, across a bridge spanning one of the
canals. They hailed guards on the other side, bringing them
into a line behind Anton and the king's guard.

They led him in a race up another ramp. The guards
then paused before one compartment and, raising their
long knives, sliced down each side of the mat wall, severing
the twine fastenings, and smashed past, into the interior.

In the darkness, figures moved. Anton shouted, in English: "Bailey, Zhen. Get down."

One figure remained upright, silhouetted against the
lights that now brightened outside.

Anton surged forward. The figure pushed open the reed
mat and jumped. The wall fell with him. Stepping to the
edge, a king's guardsman took aim with a pistol.

"Don't shoot," Anton said. "Capture him." But the
guard fired, and then again.

Bailey was at Anton's side. "Zhen's all right," she said.
"She was using the privy. All they found was me." As if to
confirm her statement, Zhen appeared at the open screen
amid the guards, her eyes wide.

Anton joined the guard at the edge of the hut and
looked into the water below. A black-clad figure floated,
facedown. A portion of the hut wall floated past him under
the pavilion.

There was just one body. The small dinghy could have
held only one, and no other craft were in view.

Nick was pushing through the crowd that had now
formed in the hut. He came to stand next to Anton. "You
went right through the wall, Captain," he said. "That seems
to have created more of a stir than the invasion."

"I needed a shortcut," Anton said. In the surrounding
ramble of the palace, people were gathered on walkways,
roofs, and bridges, or huddled under the long roof eaves.

Some held torches, despite the flammable pavilions, but the flames sputtered in the remains of the downpour. In the flickering light stood a silent assembly of guards and slaves, men and women of all Dassa ranks, the royal bureaucrats who took residence in the king's palace.

Anton mused, "I think they were after Zhen." Of course, Zhen had been controversial from the beginning, being *born to bear*. And, unlike Bailey, still able to do so.

Nick continued: "Right *through* the wall. Next time, try not to demolish palace property when you're in a hurry."

"Offer to fix it, then," Anton said. He watched the body floating below. The king had said there was resentment of the humans, and they must not go out, must give the Dassa time to adjust to them.

Nick turned away, annoyed. "These are cultural matters, Captain. They matter. Or why else am I on the ground mission?"

Anton looked at Nick, trying to bring his attention to wall screens and minor palace damage. Nick's face was hard and distant. It was an attitude Anton had seen in him over the two weeks they'd been groundside. A blameful look, as though Anton should not have risen so high. That might be true, but it hurt that Nick so often reminded him of it.

Below, the king's guard hauled the body into a narrow boat, bearing it underneath the stilted compound. With the spectacle over, people wandered back to their hammocks, but some still stared up at the hut where Anton stood. He felt their cool gaze. He wanted to answer them, to say everyone was all right.

But that was not entirely true, of course. A Dassa man had died tonight. And although the body was gone, an eddy of the river still bore a lingering, red tincture.

It had been raining for three weeks. Sometimes in thunderous downpours, sometimes in a sodden mist. Bailey was tired of it.

Now, at the first break in the weather, she was out of her quarters, looking to escape from the palace confines.

Give her something to *do,* by God. She never understood old people who preferred to sit and rock or nap. *Just shoot me when I start to fall asleep in company.* Even at seventy-eight, Bailey felt no older than a sprightly forty-five.

She was deep in the palace now, causing a bit of a stir among the nobles, who gave way before her with those polite smiles they had. Traversing the compound was not a simple matter. No single arcade was continuous, forcing one to ferret out bridge connections on one level, or follow ramps to other levels to pick up the thread again. The entire compound was badly in need of an engineer.

The aesthetics were another matter entirely. Woven reeds formed walls and roofs in an exquisite palette of neutral colors: browns, tans, yellows, and blacks. The floors, a burnished reddish wood, were the same color as the hair of these people, except for the slaves—the hoda—who were bald. The nobles all wore shifts of fabulous textured cloth, the slaves simpler fare—but lovely, as though the Dassa could not bear to be plain.

Someone drew a wall partition aside, and in climbed a young man from a boat anchored in the water below. It was unnerving how some screens could be doors and others were fixed. You never knew where, exactly, doors were.

She considered borrowing the young man's boat, but he might want it back. No matter. There were plenty of boats; it was a world of boats.

Anton had asked her not to mix with the Dassa without him. But what did he mean by *mix?* There were degrees of mixing. Bailey wasn't going to interfere with the king or with politics, especially now, with the attempt on Zhen's life last week and Zhen being under close guard. No, she would let Anton deal with the royals. In her life, she'd had her fill of important people.

Meanwhile, a little boat ride, to discover more fully who these people were. What they knew. How they could help.

Eyes on the prize, my dears. You didn't get to be diva of the Western world without focus.

Because it was all here, everything that the Message had promised. It was simply a matter of figuring it out. The answer lay with the hoda, surely. Unless she was just a very foolish old woman, lacking—as her detractors claimed— the sense and the loyalty to stay home and tend to the Earth. But of course this mission *was* her way of tending to the Earth, to restore what humanity used to have: vitality, immunity, depth.

They must hurry, though. Captain Darrow would have had them combing that Quadi archeological site by now, refusing to take no for an answer. He really should not have died. Not that Anton was botching the job. He had, after all, made a friend of this King Vidori, and they certainly had need of friends. But he might be carrying the niceties too far. Darrow was not one for niceties, nor was she. Case in point: When the virus broke out on board, the two of them agreed that the ground mission would go forward anyway. Despite the risk that inhabitants would be exposed to a human disease. They'd come thirty light-years, and those handy little black holes were a new concept. Who knew if they would even be there for any future expedition? Besides, the incubation period was safely past. They were clean.

She watched the hoda slaves as they milled in the palace byways, watched them very carefully. They were all women, of course. That was the definition of *hoda:* born to bear. But what sort of children did they bear? No one knew, for slaves were not allowed to bear children. The Dassa, unfortunately, had no concept of proper conjugal relations. Regrettably, they were a species that farmed its babies . . . in ponds. The term was *varium.* Where men and women swam, and the result was a very ex-uterine gestation and birth.

Once the crew had accepted how Dassa babies were brought into the world—once they fully absorbed this bizarre circumstance—then the whole Dassa culture became more disturbing. A varium birth wasn't a natural birth, nor a lab birth. Neither this nor that. So people on board the ship were upset—the very crew she'd picked for their tolerance of possible contact with alien cultures. But the Dassa weren't aliens. They were badly altered humans, and more disturbing in some ways than any exotic being could be. As though you could choose the aliens you got!

Dassa women passed her, sometimes with a child bundled on the back, peeking over the mother's shoulder. It seemed no one around here believed in day care; they took the infants with them everywhere, even though all mothers had slaves to assist them. Men were no use at all in helping to raise children since—given the nature of their "families"—men and women lived separately. And some women had many children, and sometimes several infants all at once. Although the variums were inefficient for reproduction, the Dassa did have the duty to swim every day. Babies resulted, and were welcomed by devoted mothers, aunts, grandmothers—and hoda.

Shim was standing before her. She was the king's chief of staff, or whatever the Dassa word was. A *viven*, a noble, palace-raised.

Shim had lovely reddish brown hair swept up into the most astonishing chignon. No hair out of place. Why the baby on her back didn't muss her hair was a question she really must ask one of these Dassa women.

"Shim-rah, thank you," Bailey said, using the standard pleasantry. Of course, one didn't shake hands, nor ever touch a Dassa's skin. Which was why they wore so many clothes in this hot climate—to prevent accidental touching. And not because they were so virtuous, either. Far from it. It was, in fact, a free-for-all, where the words for *sex* and *courtesy* were the same. It was just that their skin was considered highly sexual and an accidental touch might be more courtesy than you had in mind.

Shim said, "Oh, Bailey, thankfully I have found you."

The baby looked about a year old, with big blue eyes taking in everything in big gulps.

Bailey peeled off down a new walkway, leading out under yet another arcade. "Walk with me, Shim-rah, I have work to do."

Shim cocked her head. "Work? Oh Bailey, I will send for a hoda."

"No, no. I'm having fun."

Shim scurried behind her, and Bailey slowed her pace out of consideration for the small woman carrying a heavy baby. She was a noble, and the king's highest chancellor, or one of them. Bailey hadn't quite got the pecking order down. Nick had drawn all the ear ornaments—worn by both men and women—so one would know whether one was speaking to a very high pooh-bah, or a person of moderate standing, or someone lowly, and so forth. Shim wore the half-orb so typical of the king's court.

"Captain Anton sends for you," she said, mangling his name. "I can take you to him, thankfully."

"Oh yes," Bailey said without breaking her stride. They pronounced his name *Andon,* struggling with hard consonants. Only Bailey's name came easily.

They walked through an outside gallery that was several meters wide, with vendors on the pier and in boats in the water, selling food, textiles, animals in cages, and jewelry. She kept a lookout for an unoccupied skiff. A line of people waited for the "talk hut," the room with their ten or so communication devices: little ceramic telephones that made few connections and poor ones. Really, they might as well go in person to talk. But it was a novelty.

Shim, who was tense to be dealing with one of the humans, especially one who wasn't following suggestions, repeated her request. "Shall we attend Captain Anton?"

"Oh yes, but first . . ." Bailey noted that up ahead, where the inner pavilions gave way onto the big pond, many Dassa had gathered. "Let's see what's going on."

"Thankfully, that is just my point, Bailey. Anton and the king require your attendance for the ceremony."

Bailey approached the crowd milling on the pier. Surrounding the lake were the tiered compounds of the king, enclosing in this season what amounted to a grand, submerged plaza. Canals—formerly walkways—gave access onto the drowned plaza from three directions, and each of these was clogged now with boats paddling toward the middle.

"The uldia will present the babes," Shim said, referring to the order of women who presided over births. "But the king would have you watch from his veranda."

"It's too late now. If only I'd known sooner."

Bailey followed Shim's gaze up to the high deck of Vidori's quarters where his veranda fronted the plaza. As these quarters were the highest tier of the compound, the roof bore an imposing lightning rod here in this land of frequent rainstorms. On the veranda, she could make out his retinue. There, amid the plumage of state, she saw Anton's shabby green. Nick was at his side, the two of them like matching parrots, gone dull. Zhen might be there too, but was more likely hunched over her tronics than making small talk with the king. Bailey looked down at her own dreary jumpsuit, envying Shim's exquisite lavender and red ensemble.

Several nobles parted to allow Bailey and Shim a place in front. Bailey smiled at them, remembering not to show teeth. That close-lipped smile took some practice, and always made her feel like a cat with a mouthful of feathers.

Shim leaned in toward Bailey, murmuring, "See, by the flags there are eleven babes. The uldia have made a special display for so many babes. Most times they would not be in this place, but in the Amalang." Shim's face brightened as she pointed to one of the skiffs. "That's Deeva, my cousin's cousin. She'll have a nice fat baby girl, thanks be."

She nodded at the impressive barge in the middle of the pond. "Oleel is here, of course."

Bailey had heard of the woman. Very much a pooh-bah. At the back of the barge, iridescent cloth hung from a hoop like mosquito netting. Within, she could just see the form of a person sitting.

On the barge, women in robes handed bundles down to waiting skiffs. Those would be the babes. Women receiving their babies. Through it all, the head uldia, Oleel, stayed behind the curtains. What was the point, Bailey thought, of Oleel's attending if she wasn't even going to poke her nose out of the tent?

At last, the task of allotting babies to the women completed, the barge of the uldia departed, poled along by slaves and accompanied by a flotilla of small boats, including those of the women who were taking their infants to the family compounds. The fathers were irrelevant for a few more years, aside from having sired the whelps . . . And aside from tithing for the maintenance of women and children in general, the fathers would not know their children until adolescence. When the youngsters' scent developed.

These basic departures from normal human functions resulted in a distorted culture, one that elevated some family virtues and ignored others. No child went hungry, or so they claimed. Along with this happy fact was their casual practice of sexual liberty, even incest, for which they had no word. It was all so natural to them—as moral as sitting down to a good family meal.

Shim was waiting for Bailey under the roofed-in gallery.

"I hope I didn't get you in trouble, Shim-rah," Bailey said. "Tell them I saw the ceremony from down here. Very impressive. My compliments to Vidori."

"Oh Bailey, thankfully you didn't say so to the king. That was the uldia's ceremony, not the king's."

"Well, tell him it fell a bit flat, then."

Shim smiled hugely, but still no teeth. "Bailey makes a joke."

"Tell you what Bailey would really like," Bailey said. "I'd

like to borrow one of those skiffs and practice my boat-craft."

Shim looked blank.

"What do you say? Anybody here trust an old lady with a quick spin in their canoe?" Her plan was to paddle out of the submerged courtyard and explore the neighborhood. Right now, that neighborhood was a river. They called it the Puldar, one of the three great tributaries of the River Sodesh.

"Oh Bailey . . . ," Shim began. The Dassa loved to say her name, but it did get tedious after a while. "You may take a boat, certainly."

"Well then, fine. Whereabouts?"

"Bailey. Any boat. Anyone will be pleased to give you a boat. Just ask."

"How will I return it?"

"Oh Bailey, there are many boats. It doesn't matter where you leave the boat, but tie it to a pier."

Now it was Bailey's turn to look blank.

"They belong to everyone. No one has just one boat. One has all boats."

The light dawned on Bailey. "Oh. Well, then." Waving her good-bye to Shim, she made her way to the pier. A hoda was just tying up a skiff. "If you don't mind," Bailey said, "I'll take that." The hoda made a hand sign that Bailey thought was a *Yes ma'am*. Unfortunately, hoda couldn't speak out loud, so Anton had the crew furiously at work learning the hand sign they used. Bailey was a little behind in her studies.

The hoda vacated the skiff, pulling herself onto the dock with arms grown strong from labor. She held the rope to keep the boat close as Bailey contemplated how to descend into the thing.

It was not going to be easy, with the boat a full meter below the dock level. But it was at times like these that she saw the sense in wearing the military jumpsuit. Bailey sat on the dock, aiming her feet at the skiff. Then, with a little hop, she fell into it, tipping wildly to the side and nearly upending in the water.

Bailey smoothed her hair. Not very dignified. Around her, people in nearby skiffs had stopped all activity to watch this maneuver. They smiled when Bailey settled herself, kneeling, in the boat. Then they set up a patter of oars, slapping the water.

Applause. She accepted the paddle from the hoda on the quay and set off, determined to make a decent exit.

TWO

Anton watched from the king's balcony as the barge of the uldia receded. King Vidori had already turned away, to confer with his military chief, Romang, and a dozen nobles.

"She didn't come out," Nick said, watching the barge enter one of the canals, barely clearing the width of it. "That might have been lacking in respect to the First Dassa," he said, referring to one of the king's titles. The uldia and the judipon, the Second and Third Dassa, were the other great Powers of the region—in competition with the king, Nick had said, suggesting at the same time that Anton might play them off against each other. If the king still refused to allow access to the Quadi site.

"Maybe we should pay a social call on the woman," Nick said, keeping his voice low, referring to the Second Dassa, the person they called Oleel.

But Anton's goals at the moment were more narrow. The problem of Zhen, for instance. The problem of the confiscation of their weapons. "Vidori could interpret that as a threat," he said.

"Maybe that's a message he needs to get, Captain."

Anton knew Nick was itching to break free of the king's compound. They all were. But Vidori was asking for patience, to give the Dassa people time to get used to the idea of visitors. Especially visitors like them.

The king turned to them, motioning for them to join him inside. As Anton and Nick left the veranda, the servants closed the screens, finely woven, but sturdy. Outside, a light rain had resumed.

Anton noticed that the table had only two chairs drawn up. "I don't think you're invited, Nick," Anton said.

"Aristocrat to aristocrat, then," Nick said, grinning, making it hard to take offense. Anton remembered Nick saying he'd be here to help him, that day when Bailey named him captain. But from the first day, he and his friend had seen things differently. They were all second-guessing him, and no one more than Anton himself, who'd never looked for the job.

Nick left, along with Romang and the nobles. On a small stand was the king's private telephone, self-consciously placed within reach. It might have been a work of art, with its porcelain housing cast in a delicate pattern, typical of the miniature style the Dassa so prized. The voice box clicked now and then as though clearing its throat to say something.

Vidori was gesturing at the table. "We will present a meal," he said.

Facing the king, Anton wondered where to begin. It would be rude to come to the point. *Release Zhen. She'll stay with me, not in your prison.* They'd taken Zhen for her safety, Shim, the king's apologist, had said. *Strangling us with silk,* Anton thought again.

He waited for Vidori to lead off.

Like most Dassa men, Vidori wore his long hair clasped at the back of his head. It was slicked back so hard it shone. At his ears hung the crescent pendants, in black, the king's color, and at his waist, an intricately carved pistol, a reminder that this kingdom was at war. He was old enough to have a mature daughter, the Princess Joon, but was still re-markably handsome, with deeply bronze skin, always closely shaven. The women were often striking, yet they were not quite . . . feminine. Their bodies were trim and flat, almost boyish. Except for the hoda, some of whom appeared heavy-breasted and -hipped. The fact of *female* slaves was one of a long and growing list of issues that disturbed the crew and laced Anton's path with political and moral hazards.

Vidori began, "I regret that your Bailey could not be found." He spoke, as always, with a rich, though neutral voice.

"Bailey will join us next time, Vidori-rah. Along with Zhen, I hope."

The king let that lie. "Here is a meal," he said, gesturing to the table.

Indeed, food lay heaped on trays, with no utensils or plates. Anton took a chair as Vidori seated himself. There had been audiences with the king before, but never to share food. He wished there were not that additional array of protocol to navigate.

Vidori crossed his legs, sitting relaxed. "I have a report on your air barge, Anton. No one has tried approaching it. My guard keeps it secure."

The king was making a special effort to say his name correctly. He had given up on *Zhen*, referring to her as *Sen.*

"Thank you, rahi," Anton said, using the honorific. "After the attack on Zhen and Bailey, I am concerned about . . ." He searched for the Dassa word for *sabotage*, but settled for *mischief.*

Vidori waved this off. "The craft is secure."

Secure, yes. In the name of security, Vidori was holding them virtual prisoners. For their own sakes, or for some hidden reason? The king's motives were not the only thing hidden to him. This world, Neshar. This region of the rivers, the Olagong, as they called it. Where, in all this forest and river land, was what they had come for? Bailey continued to say it was the hoda; but the palace estimated their population at some twelve thousand individuals, too few to help the Earth reestablish a healthy population. Even—which was unthinkable, given the hoda role here—if they agreed to travel to Earth, and if enough ships could be provided for transport. No, the hoda were not the answer.

"The flooding continues," Anton said, pursuing his concern over the shuttle.

"Not enough to touch the craft. Nor will the rivers rise so high." The king looked in the direction of the flooded plaza. "When the Sodesh retreats, the Vol march. We have either flooding or battles. Which do you prefer, Anton?"

"I am more at home with battles, Vidori-rah."

Vidori seemed pleased at this. "A man like myself. With enemies." He gestured at the plate of food. "The guest eats first."

"Ah." Anton looked over the piles of garish fruit, choosing a piece of what he assumed was pineapple. Oddly, it *was* pineapple. On a planet where it should not be.

Through the wood floors a gush of water could be heard, evidence of the extensive plumbing system of the palace. The Dassa were fastidious about water. Half the energies of the palace seemed focused on repair and extensions of the ceramic pipe system, here in this society that had developed the river lands' rich clay deposits, with the harder-to-mine metals of the world a rarity. The fact that even their six-barrel pistols were partially composed of ceramics showed they had fairly well-developed ceramic alloy technology.

"What enemy tried to attack my crew, Vidori-rah?"

The king took a neon slice of fruit from the platter, chewing thoughtfully. "Someone who fears what you are: a powerful, far-traveling race who bear their young. The idea is abhorrent." He smiled. "I, however, am open-minded." He sipped from a cup of wine, a fine blue wine of the palace reserve. "I have enemies, too. There are barbarians who covet the Olagong, our braided lands. Their lands are cold, their children few."

To Vidori, it was self-evident that cold variums meant poor yields. A warm varium, the science team estimated, produced only one birth per thousand swims. Apparently, the Vol envied that number.

The king went on, "The barbarians would have what we have. That is the nature of our war. Your arrival coincides with this circumstance."

"Which circumstance, rahi?"

"Of the lowering of the Sodesh, and the advance of our enemies. Of course, there are many sizes of problems."

"I hope our arrival is not such a problem," Anton said.

"Some see that it is. I am not one of those." He reached for a handful of berries. "But the captain must learn to respect *walls*."

Nick was right. Smashing that screen had impressed the Dassa. They looked at him as though he might go plowing through a wall at any moment.

"We have caused you some inconvenience," Anton said. "Our arrival, and the attempt on Zhen's life . . ."

The king's pleasant expression fled, replaced with a neutral face.

Anton pushed on: "But I would welcome the opportunity to protect Zhen myself. If you would return her to my quarters and also my weapon and my crew's hand weapons." There, he'd gotten it all in. He locked gazes with Vidori, rude or not.

"Sen . . . ," the king said. "Thankfully, she was not murdered."

"We are grateful for the skill and bravery of your guards that night, Vidori-rah. However . . ."

"She is a hoda," the king said through a mouthful of food.

"She is a member of my crew. A valued chancellor. She is not a slave."

"She is born to bear." Vidori shrugged. "A hoda."

"My people bear children in our way. We have great

respect for Zhen, and that she is born to bear." It was necessary to make this point clear.

"Yes, but you are in the Olagong now, Captain."

"We are not Dassa."

"We did wonder what you are." He had, at their last meeting, been especially confused by the human concept of disease—of the humans' lack of *pri,* as Vidori had called it, which translated, Anton thought, to *life force.*

Vidori was watching him closely. "Captain, I will tell you a story. There is a bird of legend, called the ashi, with feathers the color of this meal you see before you. Long ago, before we had fallen into disrespect, the feathers were highly prized, and woven into fine clothes. The ashi cared for the chicks, flightless for the first weeks of life. Some years, if the river receded early, and the lands returned prematurely, the predators could walk the land bridges and ravage the young ashi. They cared little for the promise of the plumage, but devoured the chicks, just like this platter of food. These predators were vile creatures with no sense of beauty or respect. So the ashi prayed for high rivers, and so did the people who wished to see the ashi in flight." He paused. "Thus our expression, 'May the rivers swell.'"

Anton nodded. "The Vol are such vile creatures?"

"Problems come in all sizes. Some are Dassa." His dark eyes met Anton's, holding his gaze, then broke contact, signaling for the servants to remove the platter.

When the table was empty, Vidori stood and went to a corner of the room where a series of reed boxes lined the floor. He opened one, removing another, smaller reed box. He brought it back and set it in the middle of the table.

"You have studied the Olagong, thankfully," he said. "You know that we have three powers, and that among them are the Second Dassa and the Third Dassa—the uldia and the judipon."

Yes, Nick had pieced it together: The king presided over only one of the three realms. Each of the three powers claimed a river for its symbolic domain, and for its official palace. These rivers, the Puldar, Amalang, and Nool, flowed into the Sodesh, considered the braided sum of all rivers.

The king went on, "Together, the Three uphold the Olagong and all the traditional ways. But when the river recedes, there is a time when—problems—may occur."

If those problems were individual Dassa, they would likely be the uldia or the judipon. "Someone could take advantage of vulnerable times," Anton replied. "While the palace is preoccupied with the outside threat."

The king looked intently at him. "Thankfully, I have not said so."

But he *had* said so, between the lines, implying also the need for Anton's *security.*

The king was looking out the open veranda wall, where the rain had resumed its lush cascade. "Your chancellor Sen is in danger among us, among those Dassa less open-minded than I. But I will return her to you, since you wish it," he said. He glanced sharply back at Anton. "You will be responsible if she suffers harm. See that she is circumspect about being seen in the pavilion, and never alone."

"Thank you, Vidori-rah." It was a small victory, and a gratifying one.

The king turned his attention to the reed box. Unfastening the closure ring, the king opened the lid, revealing a liner of vibrant silk. Nested inside was Anton's side arm.

"For use against the enemies you can see. I return this to you, and you may wear it." His eyes flicked to Anton. "The rest I keep until such time as you choose to return to your great ship."

Anton had just been given Zhen, his weapon, and an assurance of his freedom to leave. It was all unexpected, and yet not all that he needed. "Vidori-rah," he pushed on, "I am not ungrateful. But as I have requested before, my people wish to view the Quadi site. The ruins."

Vidori paused. "I have said, this is on uldia land. The uldia would not welcome you there."

"It is necessary, rahi. For my mission."

"Give me time, Anton. I have said, the river is receding."
At Anton's frown, he added: "Perhaps I am not clear, Captain. The ruins are underwater just now, in flood season.
Did you know?"

Underwater. No, he hadn't known.

A swish of a wall opening. The two of them turned.

Standing in the opening was a woman of astonishing
beauty. She was dressed in a vibrant blue silk jacket and a
long skirt. The Princess Joon.

"Oh, you are busy, Father," she said. She looked at
Anton, smiling briefly. "Thank you, I will leave."

Vidori smiled broadly for the first time since Anton had
known him. "No, you must join us." He gestured her into
the room, with a sweep of his hand commanding her to
come forward.

After a moment's hesitation, she approached, her gown
rustling. She was tall, as tall as her father and Anton. She
looked at the pistol, lying there. "If it is war you speak of,
Father, I will have nothing to say. I will embarrass myself in
front of the captain."

"Thankfully, Joon, we are finished with the Vol for now."

"Thankfully," she repeated. She turned a bold gaze on
Anton.

He tried to keep from staring at her. He bowed.
"Princess Joon, my thanks."

She nodded, then turned to her father. "He speaks so
well, Vidori-rah!"

The king's retort was immediate: "He is the captain of a
great ship, Joon. Do not patronize."

Her face wavered. "I am sorry, Father."

Anton started to assure her that no offense had been
taken, but Joon was focused on her father.

Vidori softened. "No harm, no harm." His hand came
onto her shoulder. She stood before him, composing herself. She looked at her father, and the look seemed not quite
what it should be. Nor her father's look.

Anton turned from them to the open veranda, to the

drowned plaza outside, where the river system would soon retreat, leaving it and the Dassa lands clear—and perhaps more dangerous. He wished he did not know what he did about relations between some Dassa daughters and some fathers. Between some Dassa mothers and sons.

The fruit dinner sat uneasily in his stomach, one thing warring with another.

He accepted the weapon box from the king's hands.

Joon turned to him. "You must visit at my pavilion, Captain."

"I will, thank you, Lady."

Anton took his leave. He wasn't sure what would happen next between father and daughter, or even if anything *would*, but he judged it an excellent time to leave. Gripping the box, he departed the king's suite of rooms, more or less satisfied. He had the gun; he had Zhen. And the king had implied that they might visit the Quadi ruins when the rivers returned to their banks. Anton took that as a promise.

He walked away feeling as though he had just run an obstacle course, blindfolded. He thought Captain Darrow would have emerged from this meeting with more to show for himself. But the man was dead, damn him.

Nick Venning sat in the canoe, watching the paddles dip as the Dassa soldiers sped them along the middle of the river. All other craft gave way before them, and the current was with them, speeding their trip. Rain fell, denting the gray river to a swath of hammered steel. The canoe the king provided had a roof on it, supported by poles. They were all soaking wet anyway, but it kept the deluge off.

Behind him, Nick heard Zhen's complaints, though she was riding in a small screened-in cabin. She grumbled just loud enough for him to hear: ". . . cooped up for weeks in this stinking place and now can't see a stinking thing."

She hated going abroad covertly, and hated having Nick for an escort, although Anton had pushed hard for this trip to the shuttle for her to conduct diagnostics. He'd put Nick in charge, but without a side arm. Anton Prados kept their sole weapon for himself.

Nick turned halfway around. "Want me to continue my travelogue, or you just feel like venting?" He thought he'd done a good job describing what he saw of the submerged delta system: bits of bridges, trees, islets. But Zhen was in a mood.

"I want to vent."

"Fine, then. Knock yourself out."

He was tired of talking anyway, when there was so much to see. Through the downpour, he could just make out the larger world of Vidori's kingdom, his city called Lolo—although it was like no city he'd ever seen, and still wasn't *seeing*, it being seasonally drowned. Plying this tributary, the Puldar, were hundreds of skiffs and larger canoes, going about their business of trading and traveling, unfazed by the rain and the obstacle course of submerged objects.

In the prow of his canoe sat two other individuals: a Dassa noblewoman, back straight as a broom handle, and behind her a hoda, huddled and miserable. These would be Zhen's test subjects once they reached the shuttle. He was sure no one had bothered to tell the hoda woman where she was going and why. He would have done so, but he was separated from her by the three soldiers propelling the craft forward.

They passed a skiff laden with crates of fruit. On top of this cargo, a Dassa man and woman lay with each other, his hand roaming freely over her, and her moans carrying an unwelcome glimpse of high passion. Unwelcome, but Nick stared. It was difficult not to, though the crew had seen this kind of careless display before.

Zhen poked her head out of the tent. "Don't act like a country boy," she said, following his gaze.

"I'm not." But, the thing was, this Dassa man was bringing the woman to climax, it seemed, simply by touching her legs. No Dassa in the vicinity paid the slightest attention.

"You're staring," Zhen said. "Don't be an idiot."

The canoe was out of range now. *Thankfully,* Nick thought, picking up the Dassa saying. He truly would have chosen not to be confronted with Dassa intimate moments. But it wasn't as though the Dassa were looking for an audience; they simply had no boundaries. They were free of shame—and, some of the crew said, decency. Free as they were in this respect, the act of swimming in the variums— every morning, no less—had become so culturally charged that release was assured in those brief dips. It was intriguing. Disturbing. That the getting of children began in so stark, so lonely a manner.

Zhen growled, "I suppose you're in anthropological heaven."

He let that pass. Normally quiet and eerily focused on business, Zhen had a mean tongue when in a bad mood. He wondered that the old woman had chosen her for the mission. But Zhen was a big-time scholar, with a reputation in microbial biology.

"Goddamn muddy hells, answer me, Venning."

Cai Zhen called everyone by their last name, since she went by hers.

"Keep your nose in the tent," he answered. "I wouldn't want our crew virgin to get excited." He couldn't imagine Zhen doing it with anyone, publicly *or* privately.

"Up yours, Venning."

He let her have the last word, and that seemed to satisfy her for now.

The Puldar tributary—*braid* was a better translation from the Dassa—was here defined by huts hugging the banks, hundreds of houses on stilts, some leaning against each other for support, as though their legs had gone wobbly. Most were humble affairs, single-story huts that were not much more than boxes. Some were connected by rope bridges or continuous porches. Underneath them coursed the Puldar, still a full meter from the wood floors. It was at its zenith, the Dassa said, or they would not be so relaxed about the flooding. Carried along the current were masses of leaves, algae, dead birds, and limbs of trees, which the boaters nimbly dodged, nearly crashing into each other in the process. The middle of the river was for nobles, and in this trough Nick's canoe sped along.

The effortless movement of people and goods on the river system was just one example of the harmony and sustainability of the Olagong. Also, in Nick's view, there was the political stability of the Three Powers, the efficient distribution of wealth, the absence of poverty, the well-being of all children, and apparent freedom from disease. It was perhaps because of this ideal life that the concept of religion had never taken hold. The closest the Dassa came to worship was a sense of veneration for the rivers on which their lives depended. But even the rivers were not so much *sacred* as *treasured*. On the other side of the ledger, there was the chronic state of war, or at least unrest along the borders, and the fact that all this prosperity could in large part be attributed to slavery, an institution based on both race and gender in an inescapable linkage of social role and reproductive mode.

After a while Nick had the urge for company again, even Zhen's. "So what do you think you're going to find? With the imaging." He waited to see if Zhen would hurl a stone or just converse.

"I try not to *guess*, Venning. It's called science."

"Sure you do. It's called a hypothesis."

"OK, my *hypothesis* is that one of them has a uterus and one of them doesn't."

"Can't you tell by a, what is it—pelvic exam? You did those, right?"

"Yeeees," Zhen said, as though winding up.

"And you thought that the hoda, at least, has one."

"Need a visual to be sure."

A dead monkey floated by. Though it looked like an Earth monkey, it had broad webs of skin between its limbs, which served for brief glides in the tree canopy. Its arms were extraordinarily long, used for brachiating from limb to limb. A quasi-monkey, then. They'd also seen quasi–river rats, with eyes, ears, and nostrils on the top of their heads so they could swim while searching for food. However, other local specimens were dead-on for Earth counterparts: mangrove, palmyra, mahogany, banyan. This did tend to be the case with plants more than animals.

The ship's science team theorized that the animals, if raised up from genetic information taken from the Dark Cloud, were mutated. There would have been extensive damage to the data in the Cloud, perhaps from radiation. Some of those mutations would have been beneficial. Or they might have been intentional on the part of the beings who sent the Message. The old race, now vanished. The theory of the Quadi could be myth, but the team was treating it seriously. *Someone* had put satellites in orbit.

If these beings had raised up the creatures of this world—from DNA code—then they might also believe that humans could do so. So they might have preserved the code *as code.* Somewhere. Presumably they would also have provided the scientific knowledge to bring the code to life—perhaps by describing some version of the Dassa variums. This was the direction of the science team's current thinking. Of course, it would all be more simple if the hoda represented a people that could mix with Earth populations, which was why Bailey liked that theory.

"So," Nick continued, "if the hoda have uteruses . . . uteri?" Zhen didn't grace the question with a response. "If the hoda have them, then we might have hit the jackpot."

"Jackpot? You think you're going to marry a hoda and bring her back with you? Or load up the ark full of Vidori's personal slaves and take 'em home, like a cargo or something?"

"No, nothing like that . . ."

"Then how exactly might we have *hit the jackpot,* Lieutenant?"

"I hadn't thought that far. If we could reproduce with

the hoda, it would be a beginning, that's all. Instead of all the damn *endings* we've had on ship, at home, you name it. That's all I'm saying—I'm not trying to solve everything, or turn this into a goddamn kung fu match." He bit his tongue. Zhen loved to have people go off on her. It was what she lived for.

She peeked her head out of the curtain, her eyes as hard as ball bearings. "The Dassa won't let the hoda have babies, will they? It's against the goddamn law. *Forbidden.* If that's the jackpot, then we're shit out of luck." She yanked the curtain shut.

That was Zhen for you. The woman would never trade ideas with someone in the soft sciences. She was oriented to data, as he was to people, so she discounted him. Like Anton, lately. So changed from the days of studies and grueling preparation at the academy, when Anton coached him in math and Nick returned the favor in linguistics. Changed since the day the old lady handed Anton the position without giving Nick a chance to argue his qualifications. She couldn't get past his background—all blue-collar, no refinement.

Meanwhile Anton was right at home eating state dinners and hobnobbing with the privileged; it was the life he was born to before he finally severed the apron strings and struck out on his own. Now he'd gotten up a friendship with Vidori. Anton *would* start at the top of the power pyramid and work down; it was hard-wired into him, though Anton, despising his father as he did, would be the first to deny it and say he wanted to be just plain military. But *just plain military* would not by any stretch of the imagination describe Anton Prados.

It described Nick Venning, though.

They turned out of the Puldar byway into the great River Sodesh, where the sky and water blurred into one gray swath for as far as Nick could see. Here, the boats thinned out. Larger craft plied the giant waterway, barges and long canoes, many with thatch roofs held up by poles and bearing on top the cargoes of the braided lands. Some looked like they could not possibly remain upright, as tall and narrow as they were, but the Dassa were nothing if not water-born, and Nick gave up worrying they would tip over.

Nick saw that the hoda woman had laid out a small meal for her mistress, balancing the pink fruit on her knees to serve as a table. She leaned toward her mistress as the woman spoke to her, and then the hoda answered in sign, bringing a laugh from the noblewoman. It looked like the two might be friends on an outing. Except that one could not speak, and was a slave.

Nick wanted to know what the status of the hoda might be among the society of women known as the uldia. Slavery would be a complicated system; there would be factions and subtle differences in attitudes. The mission needed a captain with a wider perspective. Someone with a vision, who could see patterns and connections. That was what leaders did. It was what Captain Darrow would have done, God rest his soul.

The shuttle was intact, carefully guarded by a contingent of the king's guard. No doubt Vidori was eager to prevent it from falling into Vol hands.

It was eerie to be back in the shuttle after so long in the wood and water world of the Olagong. The noblewoman and the hoda stared around themselves at the metal environs, with its tangle of pipes and conduits.

Since Zhen wasn't yet a decent speaker of the Dassa language, she had Nick explain to the women what the procedure would be. He did his best, having memorized the anatomical terms in their language. Then Zhen took the women by the arm and led them into the exam room.

Nick sorted through his locker, cramming necessities into a stuff sack—at Anton's orders, leaving behind anything that was or might be construed as a weapon. That meant leaving behind the miniature scout drone. It operated within a limited range, anyway, its main utility being advance scouting in a combat situation. Vidori wouldn't be told about such a device, since they intended to steer clear of escalating the warfare here.

After an hour, Zhen emerged from the lab with the two Dassa women.

"Well?" he asked in English.

To his surprise, Zhen answered him simply, clinically. "The hoda has all her physiology intact." She glanced at the noblewoman. "The other has only a vestigial uterus. Nonfunctional."

So, then. The Dassa didn't reproduce—normally. They'd *said* they didn't. But this settled it. There were variums here, somewhere. Tended by the uldia. He realized that he'd been hoping it was a communication error or a myth.

Zhen was thinking out loud. "Question is, how do we get two types of Dassa?"

At Nick's blank look, she went on, "Some of the science team think it happened with a reversion mutation. Now that we know there are two kinds of Dassa reproduction, I think the hoda are definitely revertants. It's one way it could make sense."

"*Revertants?*"

Zhen was indulging him. "Yeah, revertants. The way that works is, the Dassa reproductive system is, let's say, controlled by a knockout gene that was inserted into the middle of a key gene that regulates uterus formation. So the varium gene can direct, and is compatible with, the whole Dassa reproductive strategy. But if the inserted DNA is naturally unstable to some extent, then it is occasionally excised back out of the gene by a reversion mutation, thus knocking out the first gene's function. Happens all the time in genetic research, where we can alter mice by inserting a gene and blocking its readout into protein, like if a genetically altered red-eyed fruit fly gives rise to an offspring that has the original black eyes."

Nick frowned. "I don't think *revertants* is a very good name, though. Sounds creepy."

"How about Homo sapiens, then? The hoda are Homo sapiens."

Nick's face must have showed how sweet that news sounded. "That's great," he said.

Zhen narrowed her eyes. "Don't applaud yet. We've still got a few problems." She moved to the hoda woman and took her by the arm, leading her to stand in front of Nick.

The hoda was staring up at Nick, as though she thought she'd done something wrong.

Zhen said, "Tell her to open her mouth."

"You tell her, Zhen—you're supposed to be learning Dassa."

Zhen turned to the hoda. "Open up the mouth."

The hoda did so, revealing a small mouth that was healthy in all respects save one. Instead of tapering, the end of her tongue was flat, where it had been sheared off. A puckered red line demarcated the fluted ridge where the incision had been made.

"That," Zhen said bitterly, "is what the Dassa think of people like us. So how much do you think they're going to care about our problems?"

Nick had seen enough. "You can close your mouth," he whispered to the hoda, and she did so, with a look of gratitude. It made him sick to see such a look on her face, when he'd done nothing for her, could do nothing for her.

Standing at the hatchway, and taking no notice of all this, the noblewoman was adjusting her auburn hair in her elaborate bun.

"We are *not* among friends here," Zhen said. "Of course, they only mutilate girls, so you don't have anything to worry about, Venning."

But Nick was plenty worried, even about Zhen. She had a wicked tongue. Sooner or later, someone in the Olagong was bound to notice.

THREE

Anton stood at the far end of the footbridge leading to the Lady Joon's pavilions. She had practically commanded him to call on her, and in fact he was eager to cultivate her as an information source. Shim had tried to talk him into a tunic and leggings in the Dassa style for his interview, and when this effort had failed, she'd looked worried about the impression he would make. She frowned now, as they crossed the covered bridge. Rain lashed down, sluicing in waterfalls off the thick roof matting.

They started across the bridge. Anton noticed Shim fidgeting as they walked. "What's the matter, rahi? You're fretting."

"But-tons," she said, using the human word. "Not expected."

Shim could not get over the buttons on his jumpsuit; it was not the first time Anton was bemused by what the Dassa focused on.

"Anything else I should know, besides that I look bad?" He threw her a smile, but the irony fell flat as she hurried to say, "Oh, Anton, thankfully I haven't said so."

Guards parted at the far end of the bridge, and Shim led the way along wood floors burnished to mirror-brightness. The odor of floral perfumes was stronger here than in the king's pavilions, and for a time the underlying smell of mildew gave way to a sweet, not unpleasant musk.

They paused at last in front of a wall of finely woven screens. Anton tried to guess which one would open.

He was wrong. The Lady Joon's chancellor, Gitam, slid open one of them and, smiling a greeting, waved him into the room, leaving Shim outside.

Joon's quarters were simple and fine, in the style of effortless beauty so typical of the Dassa. Lustrous black reeds formed lacquered screens framed in carmine wood, or what on Earth was mahogany. In the middle of the spacious room, a carved ladder led up to the ceiling, stopping at a closed door. A swag of woven cloth hung from the steps of the ladder. From behind this, the Lady Joon appeared.

"Captain Prados, thank you."

"Please, Lady, my name is Anton."

"Oh, now I will have to practice saying my *t*'s." Her smile was playful.

She beckoned him behind the tapestry, where chairs and couches, all without backs, formed a seating area. The beat of rain came softer in these quarters, and he suspected there was another level above this one.

The guest sits first, Shim had told him. He did so, finding the nearest chair.

Joon wore silver cloth, finely woven and without ornament except for a belt. The clasp bore what looked like a tiny portrait. She settled herself on a facing chair, more relaxed than she had been in her father's company.

"That is a lovely painting on your belt, Lady," he said.

"Oh yes, it is a favorite. My grandmother painted it for me. A portrait of *her* grandmother."

"In my world we have paintings, too."

"Similar. But different," Joon ventured.

It was a complicated thought. Anton wondered if Joon knew that the crew saw this world exactly in those terms.

"Your family is one of beautiful women," Anton said.

Joon responded, "Oh yes. And powerful. We are of the king's line." She regarded him with an unnerving glance. "Anton," she began carefully, "I will not compliment you on how well you speak our language, since I have been rebuked by my father for doing so."

After a pause to digest whether she had complimented him just now or not, Anton replied, "There was no offense taken, Lady. Not by me."

"Thankfully." Joon sat without any mannerisms or idle movements, a stillness that would have appeared stiff in someone less graceful. She might have been a predator ready to spring—or prey frozen in indecision.

Under the floor, pipes rattled with a pulse of water. Joon gazed at him, allowing the silence to lengthen.

"My people have returned from the—air craft, Lady," he said finally. There was no word for *shuttle*, or *space ship*, or even *humans*. "I have brought you a small token." Fishing in his pocket, Anton produced the thing he and Shim had agreed upon. Colored pencils. Suitably *useful*, Shim had pronounced, since nothing Anton had could be called *fine*.

He crossed over to her and handed her the gift, wrapped in a swath of Dassa cloth, taking care not to touch her.

Joon took out the pencils, examining them closely.

He sat again. "For drawing, Lady. You will need to cut them a little to keep them sharp."

"To make them bleed?"

"No . . ." He struggled to make sense of it, then had it: "No, they aren't paints. Not bright colors, but soft ones."

"Like ink pens." The Dassa had elaborate writing sets, with tubes supplying continuous ink. And every Dassa was literate, even the hoda, since they were schooled until adolescence. "I am thankful that you thought of drawing pens for me, amid all your troubles."

"Which troubles, rahi?" He certainly had his share, but she might know if he faced others he knew nothing of.

"Oh yes, the trouble with your great ship, where you do not thrive, and in your blue lands across the sky where you do not thrive, and then coming among us, so similar yet different." She paused, and he struggled not to show his surprise over her concise summary.

She went on. "The trouble with Sen, and with Bailey, and the small ship on the Sodesh which is resting on the lands of Huvai the reed merchant."

Sen—that would be Zhen—whose *trouble* was that she was female. And Bailey . . . but what could Joon know of his issues with Bailey Shaw?

"Rahi, you have a longer list than I do."

"It is a difficult list," she agreed.

"Is the shuttle on lands it should not be?"

Joon fingered the painted brooch, hesitating. Then she said, "Some do not approve of hoda with such privileges." She added, "Although hoda cannot be male, thankfully."

Anton said, "If humans are powerful, it implies the hoda are not well used. Is that right?" The rains faded into a light patter, and the room grew warmer.

"I do not say what is right, Anton. Only what is so." And he thought her eyes took on a more sorrowful cast.

"When we came here," he said, "we hoped to be free to come and go. To explore. But the king is cautious for our sakes."

"Hmm. *Cautious*. That is an interesting criticism."

"I mean no disrespect."

"But you wish to come and go."

"Yes. Since we are searching for something." He hesitated, but she rescued him.

"To thrive."

He nodded. To thrive, indeed. But the Olagong hid its secrets, and he thought the Dassa hid the Olagong. The *Restoration* was surveying the region from high altitudes, using a drone. It sent back real-time images of the delta lands.

They'd seen no archeological sites or evidence of buildings. The drone had lingered over the holdings of the Vol in the west, relaying views of a people even more primitive than the Dassa, living in tents and squalor. They used no radio— as did the Dassa—nor electricity. If the Quadi had left a prize on this world, Anton felt sure it was here, in the Olagong.

Pursuing this line, Anton said, "For instance, Lady, I have heard of the lands called cloud country. This is a place I would see firsthand."

"To search in it?" She seemed amused. "But Anton, there are only clouds and dirt paths. If there were Quadi secrets there, would not many generations of Dassa have found them?"

Nick said the region was a site of pilgrimage. Not sacred, in the Dassa's secular culture, but treasured, like the delta system. Like the variums. The custom was to go to cloud country for walking meditation. Nick thought this might be a vestigial practice with roots in a Quadi custom.

"Sometimes," Anton said, "a new set of eyes sees new things."

This brought a laugh. "Oh, Captain, I will have to remember such a saying." She rose. "Let us explore, then." She gestured to the ladder. "I will present my viewing room."

A servant appeared at some signal he'd missed, and ascended the ladder first, fastening back a trapdoor in the ceiling. At Joon's gesture, he followed the hoda, climbing up with Joon behind him.

He stepped onto a covered roof deck, bright in the vanishing rains, with the clouds grown thin as a fishing net.

The air sparkled with a faint mist, and stabs of sunshine gilded the wet timbers and eaves of the surrounding pavilion, brightening them from muddy brown to rosy tan.

They were high above the Puldar River, higher than any of the other rooms and levels, except for the king's pavilion, across the inlet. He stepped to the unfenced edge and looked out over a land suddenly filled with a gloaming light. The river appeared through tatters in the mist, like an unrolled bolt of silver brocade.

Joon spoke from close behind him. "It is beautiful?"

Anton turned to her. "Yes."

Her dark skin lent strength to the beauty of her face, and her half-circle earrings looked more like cutting blades than baubles. He knew that Joon was destined to be queen one day; then she would lead the army. She looked born to do so, as indeed she was.

She glanced past him, pointing at the river.

"There is your Bailey, of course."

Looking to where Joon pointed, he saw someone paddling alone in a small skiff, the only person in sight with short white hair. Boats parted before her as she headed out into the center of the Puldar. It seemed that Bailey had done what she pleased for so many decades that she took orders as merely suggestions.

"She seeks what you came for," Joon said. "Your lost pri. That the Quadi left behind."

"Yes."

"But what does this pri look like, Captain? We are confused about this."

"We don't know."

"Strange to search for something when you don't know what it resembles."

He smiled at the notion, because, stated that way, it *did* sound strange. "We do it all the time, in my culture," he said. They searched for the code. But there was, of course, the question of why, if the information was in coded form, the Quadi hadn't sent it to Earth with their original radio message. Anton thought that the reason was obvious. Who would believe such a thing, unless they had seen such code brought to life, in the hoda?

Joon looked back at the river as Bailey disappeared around a bend. "In my culture, the born to bear are not free to come and go like your Bailey."

"But the Dassa seem to tolerate old humans better than young ones."

"Some Dassa."

"But not the uldia."

"Do not think, Captain, that the uldia are separate from us. We are woven together, all of us, because of the rivers, the birth waters, and sarif. Every Dassa man and woman has two ties, thankfully. One to one's mother, the other to one's uldia of the birth waters. This tie is a birth tie, never broken."

A knowing came to Anton then. He had been thinking in terms of political factions and rivalries, but it was not so clear-cut. Kinship was the essence of it, and the uldia were, in a sense, kin to each babe they birthed. Nick had missed this; in carping about his restrictions, he'd ignored a thing any Dassa could have told him: Kinship was not just a matter of blood.

He thought, too, that Joon was warning him that Bailey was in danger. That they all were. That it was not just a group of traditionalists who feared outsiders.

She turned away from the edge of the deck, and as he followed her she said, "Oleel is my uldia."

"I didn't know."

Joon seated herself on a divan. "Oleel remained hidden on the barge that day because of you, Captain."

She *was* warning him. He thought of Bailey paddling blithely down the river, trying to make friends with people who might hide what they felt for the sake of courtesy.

Below the roof deck, the fog evaporated, and the angle of sunshine brought a blinding glare to the river. He and Joon turned away, to find seats under the awnings. Several hoda sat on the edge of the roof, legs dangling over, heedless of the heights, within earshot if Joon needed them. Their shaven heads made them look naked, compared with Joon's luxurious hair. And they were shorn of much else, of course, in the casual cruelty of the Dassa. He saw that the hoda chatted in sign language among themselves, and he let himself eavesdrop a moment, picking up phrases: gossip and mundane things. The Dassa didn't forbid the hoda their hand-signing. *Some* form of communication smoothed out the tasks of the day. So the taking of tongues was more an emblem of domination than a silencing effort. Indeed, the pervasive hoda silence said *submission* very well.

Joon, leaning back along the divan, stretched out a hand toward one of the servants, and the hoda hurried to her. The servant began to unfasten Joon's jacket. When it fell away, Joon's shoulders and arms were bare.

"I think, Captain," Joon said, "that humans are not woven together in the way of the Dassa. You are more separate among yourselves."

"I had not thought so," Anton said. Until today.

"We can learn from each other."

The servant removed Joon's woven reed sandals.

He wondered what it was she meant to teach him.

Ignoring the hoda's ministrations, Joon said, "My father is preoccupied in this season, Anton. He may need reminding that our guests came among us to search. I can remind him."

The woman did pay attention. She had discerned what he wanted rather faster than her father.

As the hoda retreated to the sidelines, Joon adjusted her position, causing her skirt to move up, revealing her lower legs.

Joon was gradually dispensing with clothes. What the devil was he supposed to do? He managed to say, "If the king would hear you without offense, I would be grateful to you."

Joon smiled. "I will risk offense."

"Do not, rahi."

"He will indulge me." That seemed the end of the conversation. She seemed so relaxed, and still guileless, looking at him with almost casual interest, as though he were just beginning to bore her. "Will you indulge me, Anton?"

Joon was offering sarif—courteous sex. It was the Dassa

way with each other. He hadn't considered until now that it would extend to him and his crew.

Slowly, he stood up. He had no idea what to do. Part of his mind wondered what article of clothing was coming off next. Another part wondered what Vidori would make of all this. "Lady," he said. "I can't stay. I'm a guest in your father's palace."

She didn't move, but kept regarding him with a calm expression. Then, in one graceful motion, she stood up, her feet quickly finding her slippers.

"I am sorry our meeting was not more cordial, Captain."

"It was a very courteous meeting, Lady. I do thank you."

"But Captain, it was not." In a bemused tone of voice, she said: "You have no sarif in your home lands."

"No. I fear not."

"Hmm. How do you care for one another, then?"

"In the human way. Similar to you."

"But different." She smiled.

He muttered further thanks and somehow managed to excuse himself, descending the ladder with a hoda following him down to show him out.

As he emerged from Joon's quarters, Shim was waiting in the corridor. Her expression quickly decayed into dismay, seeing his face.

"The interview did not go well, Anton?"

He glanced at her as they returned across the bridge.

"I have no bloody idea." He hoped that his behavior had not seemed terribly rude to Joon, but since sarif was, after all, only casual courtesy, he feared he had just insulted a princess.

Bailey's arms hurt from paddling, but she was pleased that she had the hang of it. She had even learned how to avoid dripping water on herself when she lifted the oar to the other side. The river had fallen a full meter in the last two days, since the rain had stopped, and it made the currents easier to navigate. Along this tributary of the Sodesh, she saw evidence of the land's returning, with hillocks of mud exposed, and bridges emerging between them. The islets, the ancestral farms, separated by streams, tributaries, and rivers. This is what the Dassa meant by braided lands. It was a hauntingly beautiful river world, one that almost brought her to song. Perhaps Puccini . . . But what was she thinking? Oh, it was a sly thing, that singing, always wanting to slip out. She pushed the song back. Pesky things.

Up ahead she saw the king's terraced pavilion, both lovely and forbidding. It looked taller than ever with more of the building piers showing. Squinting, she saw that someone in military uniform waited for her on the dock nearest the crew hut.

It was Anton, singled out by his black hair. She waved.

He didn't wave back. Oh damn, he was going to be in a mood.

She could justify her little excursion. She'd made friends at one of the compounds, one presided over by a Dassa woman named Samwan. Bailey was eager to convey what she'd learned, what Nick had failed to learn, since Anton had seen fit to keep the crew cooped up in the palace.

Incredibly, the woman had twenty-three children. In the Dassa scheme of things, Samwan was generously supplied by the tithes of men's labor: the produce, game meat, and coin that all fathers owed to all children. Rather than raise up children, some women might choose an occupation—some, indeed, were soldiers—but in this case, they too, tithed to the household compounds. Meticulous records of tithes were kept by the judipon, the men who formed the social service network and accounting system of the Dassa's economy. They came into the compounds bearing allotments of food and supplies, and distributing treats to hordes of children. Less cheerful tasks were to adjudicate disputes between households and to distribute hoda servants as the need presented itself. The third power of the Dassa exersized subtle control in the kingdom, apportioning wealth.

Yet the judipon, for all their influence, took a vow of *river hands:* passing wealth through themselves, keeping little.

It was a fine system, one that Bailey could thank God had never been thought of on Earth. One could never trust people to distribute money fairly, after all, and where was the challenge of beating out the competition if there essentially was none?

Next to the pier, she squinted up at him. "Anton, tie this thing, will you?" She threw the rope for him to secure. *Keep the man busy for a moment; men like that.* The rope slapped onto the dock, then slipped into the water.

Bailey poled off from the pier leggings with her paddle, trying to keep from bumping against it. She pulled the rope back into the boat. "Let's try this again, shall we?"

Anton watched her struggle with the skiff on the choppy current. "I would have thought you knew how to do this by now, Bailey."

"Usually there's someone helpful on the dock, though." She cast the line out again, and this time Anton caught it, tying it to a cleat. He reached down to hand her up, giving her a chance to climb up the crossbars on the pier.

He glanced at her hat.

It was a gift. When at Samwan's compound she'd mentioned the need of a hat to keep off the sun, and the mistress's hoda were set to devising a head-covering-with-brim. The first designs were hopeless, but she quite liked this one.

Bailey threw him a smile. "Like it?"

His hand came around her elbow. "Yes, it's smashing." He led her down the dock. "While you've been out trying on hats," he said, "the king's been looking for you."

"Whatever for?"

"Stick around and you'd know more." She could see that he was enjoying this, keeping her in the dark. Then he turned serious. "It's dangerous for you to be out there, on the river, alone. I'd like your support, Bailey. I'd like everyone's support, so that we're all . . . paddling in the same direction."

She pushed her hat more firmly on her head so as not to

lose it in the breakneck pace Anton was setting. "Where are we *paddling* at the moment, Captain? It would entirely help if I had the sense we were in fact going somewhere."

Anton kept his gaze straight ahead, maneuvering her to the left to ascend a long ramp. "To the plaza," he said.

"Oh dear, dressed like this?" But where they were headed at the moment was not the question she'd intended to ask, as Anton very well knew.

He said, "Vidori is taking a walk to view his plaza, and we're invited."

"Well, I saw it this morning, and I can tell you it's nothing but mud."

"You've been gone all morning or you'd know that about one hundred hoda have been in the square since dawn shoveling mud and washing the flagstones."

Bailey took advantage of his softening grip by pulling out of his reach and stopping in her tracks. "I've been *productive* this morning. I've been at Samwan's compound, and I've discovered some very interesting things that Nick, for all his training, has failed to notice." She had his attention. Those black eyes, so startling in a fair-skinned boy.

"For one thing," she went on, "the judipon. They have their fingers everywhere—knee-deep in family affairs, advising, cajoling, meeting in committees to decide disputes. They're inveterate busybodies, they know everyone's secrets, and yet the Dassa actually seem to *like* them. They're only males, by the way, as Nick guessed." She shrugged. "He gets some things right, Anton, but of course he's limited by the situation." The *situation* that Vidori kept them in the pavilion, and Anton complied. Of all the crew, only Bailey was welcomed abroad. Nick said it was out of respect for her age, and that she was beyond bearing years.

"So you don't need to worry about me. They're a peaceful people from what I've seen." After all, the little incident with that fellow breaking into their sleeping hut hadn't been repeated, had it?

But Anton wouldn't let it go. "We're dealing with a

brand-new culture, and you don't have the training, Bailey.
I'm afraid you're not being cautious."

She sighed. "Of course I'm not being cautious, you
ninny. Cautious is what's wrong with this expedition. Cautious is why it took me eight years to convince the authorities to even let our ship launch. Cautious is what's keeping
us cooped up in this house of cards. No, I'm not cautious.
Nor should you be, Anton Prados. How does it look to the
Dassa that an old woman's the only one with the guts to go
paddling on the river?"

She backed up a half-step at the look on his face. Oh
dear, she might have gone too far. She lifted her chin to
brazen it out.

His voice came more gently than she expected. "We *will*
go on the river. Soon."

They stared at each other, neither one giving in. She
hadn't quite seen this stubborn side of Anton before, back
an eternity ago when she made her impulsive choice for
captain. But it *was* her choice, for better or worse.

"I'm trying to befriend him, Bailey."

Vidori. The old fox who was playing political games, no
doubt.

"We depend on his support right now, and thank God
we're getting it. But he has to pick his way cautiously
among factions whose customs tell them people like us are
despicable. When I have his confidence, I will leave this
pavilion, with his blessing. Not without it. That is my plan.
It's proceeding faster than you may imagine, something you
can't know, since you're seldom here."

Bailey drew herself tall. She wasn't accustomed to back
talk from a twenty-four-year-old, captain or not. "Well,
then." She took off her hat and patted her hair. "In that case,
we'd better not keep his majesty waiting."

The plaza was still full of mud, but hoda continued their labor of shoveling and bearing out pallets of muck. The king

sloshed through the mud undeterred, ruining a fine pair of brocaded boots. The sun had cooked up the mud into a stew of rotting fish and jungle muck, creating a smell strong enough to singe nose hairs.

Out in the open square Bailey's hat drew a stare from Shim. *Skin cancer,* Bailey wanted to say, not that she knew how to say it in Dassa. *Wrinkles.*

From tiers of porches around the plaza, Dassa gathered to watch the king's retinue, all two dozen of them, including guards, the noble viven, the chancellors, and Anton, Nick, and herself. Zhen wasn't invited, and would have hated wasting the time, anyway. She was preoccupied, setting up a huge amount of equipment in the crew huts.

King Vidori was striking in his black and gray silk tunic and leggings. He had been most cordial to Bailey, complimenting her on her head-covering-with-brim. He spoke slowly, out of consideration for the language difficulties. Then he strolled farther into the plaza, nodding to viven on the high porches and conversing with Shim. The retinue walked behind, stopping when he stopped, proceeding at his whim.

She had to admit that the man was a formidable presence. Such people needed careful handling, as Anton was attempting to provide, of course. But she'd met heads of state and singers who considered themselves divas, and she knew how to accord respect in public and then do exactly as she wished in private. It required a delicate mixture of manners and villainy, something every starship captain certainly needed to master.

The retinue had stopped.

Two new people were standing in the center of the plaza. One woman, dressed in palace finery, stood next to another woman with hair flowing down her back—the first time Bailey had seen a Dassa woman's hair unbound. The sun lit copper threads in her hair, causing her shoulders and back to shimmer. As Bailey watched them, she saw that the long-haired woman was very young, a teenager. A terrified one.

An old man—a member of the judipon by his simple attire—joined the two, carrying a wire basket.

Vidori's procession now fanned out on either side of him, so that the group of three were in clear view of Bailey.

"Any clue?" Bailey asked Anton.

He shook his head.

The judipon official lifted the basket high and pulled it down over the girl's head. For a moment he obscured Bailey's view of the girl. When he stepped away, an assemblage in front of the basket had been inserted deep into the girl's mouth.

Bailey hoped that she wasn't going to witness what it seemed clear that she was.

Anton strode up to Shim, pulling her sleeve, and Bailey followed him. "Don't interfere," Bailey hissed at him.

Shim moved back from the king's side and spoke to Anton, saying something.

Bailey heard him say, ". . . do something."

In front, the king had moved forward to place something in the hands of the noblewoman, her face as placid as fired pottery. The woman then helped the girl to kneel. Something in the way she did so led Bailey to believe that she wished to be gentle with her.

Shim whispered to Anton, "The king pays the mother for her loss." She made a small smile. "It is a generous sum."

Anton made to push past Shim to reach Vidori, but Bailey surprised herself with how fast she latched onto his arm. "Don't be stupid, Anton. This is their custom. Don't be stupid."

Pulling away from her, he walked over to Vidori. He bent in toward the king, talking rapidly, and the king nodded, smiling. He wasn't listening, his attention focused on the basket. The girl was to be *clipped*, as they called it. Having reached adolescence, she had been revealed by her menses as born to bear. A hoda. A slave, from this time forward.

It was terrible, no doubt. But, after all, this was Dassa culture; you couldn't go barging in, imposing your own values. Anton was having words with the king, the young fool—and doing so *publicly* . . . It was so hot standing on the stone plaza. Sweat collected under her hatband, and her face seemed washed with a scrim of fire. The scene grew wobbly before her: young girl, wire basket, terror in the eyes. The judipon official raised his hand toward the device on the girl's head.

The girl's too young, Bailey thought, irrelevantly.

In the next moment, the old man slammed his fist down on a protruding flange—a little blade embedded in the cage. Bailey felt her own tongue convulse, her eyes flinching from the basket. For a moment the girl stood immobile as blood sluiced out of the wire mesh. Then she crumpled, pitching forward into the mud. The noblewoman watched her fall. It was the *mother,* Shim had said. Then the woman turned and left, payment in hand.

Bailey took off her hat, waving it in front of her face, but she was just stirring the hot air and it didn't help. She looked at the old man who had done the clipping. *If you figure out a penance,* she thought, *let me know.*

Meanwhile, the judipon was tending to the girl, removing the hood, inserting a pad to absorb the bleeding, wiping the mud from her face. It was almost tender, how he cleansed the face of this girl he had just mutilated. The girl moaned, and he made shushing sounds, as though consoling a child.

Anton was at Bailey's side again, still looking at the girl, who was stirring on the ground, a strange noise coming from her throat, like a moan she tried to conceal. "Such a peaceful people," Anton muttered.

Nick had joined them. "God," he said, "they cut off her tongue."

"I couldn't stop him," Anton said. "He wouldn't listen."

Shim approached them. "The king will resume his walk," she reported cheerfully.

"We are unable to accompany him," Anton said.

At Shim's confused look, Bailey hastened to add, "The sun," wiping her brow. "Anton will help me into the shade."

Several hoda were now assisting the injured girl to stand. Her sandals made two tracks in the mud as they half dragged her from the plaza. Left behind was the judipon, who stood holding the wire basket as though he were on his way to market.

To Shim, Anton said, "By your pardon, we will return to our quarters." He took Bailey's arm.

"Because of the heat," Bailey said, trying, still, to teach Anton a bit of diplomacy.

"Because of the blood," Anton said, and led her away, accompanied by Nick.

Oh, he was so young, not to understand that sometimes blood was the way of the world. Sometimes blood happened. And in those cases, you must make the best of it, because the world was not—would never be—a nice, safe place. It was because of these things that penance was so very necessary.

The king had turned to watch them leave.

Shim was left standing there to decide what to tell Vidori, whether it was the sun or the blood that drove them from the plaza.

"Lower your voices," Anton said. They'd just got back from the plaza, and now contained their conversation until they pulled the screen door shut.

Nick paced in the confines of their largest room, while Zhen continued her work in the corner, painstaking analyses of everything she could get her hands on, using her limited liquid spectroscopy tools. Thus engaged, she was only marginally watching the uproar. Bailey sat on the floor cross-legged, tucking frayed reed ends into her hat.

"Did you see the mother?" Nick said.

Yes, Anton remembered her face, cool as porcelain. More, he remembered the girl's face, locked in the terrible bridle, her eyes darting like trapped birds. And he could do nothing for her; the king had hardly listened to his protest.

Nick went on, "The woman took Vidori's money, and never batted an eye."

"What was she going to do in front of the king?" Anton asked. Sweat trickled down his face. He could open a wall to the river breeze, but there was no breeze, only the westering sun blasting directly against one wall of their hut.

"She might have asked for mercy," Nick said.

Bailey looked up from the floor. "Adolescent hodas don't get mercy."

"Did you see how she bled?" Nick shook his head as though he would fling the memory away. "And that—hood." Nick stopped his pacing, looking at Anton. "Did Vidori invite us so we could watch the bloodletting?"

Anton shook his head. "I think he just happened to be there." But now he was making excuses. He could see that Nick thought so, too. The king's standing there dispensing coins was almost more chilling than it would have been had Vidori done the deed himself. It was the custom to be cruel. Anton had seen such brutality before, in his own family. An image of his father came to mind. Now he struggled to reconcile two images of Vidori: the one who told folktales of plumed birds and wondered about Earth, and the one who could watch a young girl be mutilated.

Nick wiped his glossy forehead with his sleeve. "I thought maybe he wanted to intimidate us. Impress us with his power."

Bailey didn't look up from her task. "He doesn't need to impress us. Who do you think is in charge of this world?"

Nick frowned. "There are more powers here than the king, as I've said from the beginning."

Bailey sighed. "Yes, there's the judipon. Lovely folks, too."

"So much for the theory that they're just social work-ers," Anton said.

"They *are* social workers. It's just that they clip tongues, too."

This was too much for Nick, who stopped pacing long enough to stare at her. "You act like it's part of a job de-scription."

Bailey narrowed her eyes at him. "It *is*. The judipon job description. I'm not condoning, just describing." She yanked at a thread. "They used to euthanize hoda, long ago. Slavery's an improvement. They have this horror of a hoda passing for regular Dassa, so they want to make sure they're branded as such."

Nick snapped: "We all know the history, Bailey. But *see-ing* it . . ."

Anton leaned against the support beam anchoring one of the hut corners. In the last violent hours of the sun, the room took the full brunt of heat. He thought night would help to soothe all their nerves, if it would ever come. Fetid odors rose from the hut stilts where jungle greens clung, rotting one moment, baking the next. It smelled like tropi-cal Earth, felt like it. But this was the Olagong, as they had to keep reminding themselves.

Zhen looked up from her tronic screen. "Given how they do the clipping, I'm surprised more hoda don't die of infection."

"Maybe they do die," Nick muttered. "Don't assume they value the same things we do. For God's sake, sexual en-counters are as common as hellos. Mothers sleep with their sons, and the sons with their sisters. You can throw kinship charts out the window. When you come right down to it, what do we really know about these people?" He turned to face the bright western wall, staring at it like a blind man. "Not bloody much."

Zhen's voice came like the buzz of a gnat. "Who's sup-posed to be investigating that side of things?"

Nick turned slowly to face her, his jaw muscle quivering. "That judipon clipped the wrong tongue."

Zhen made a face and continued fiddling with slides. It left Nick's comment hanging heavy in the air, all the more ugly for going unanswered.

"Ease up, Nick," Anton said.

But Nick wasn't finished. "Permission to speak openly, Captain?"

Getting a nod, he said, "This place is twisting with factions. Let's try pulling on a different strand. We've seen what the male power structure is; let's delve into the other side of things, the uldia. Let me do it. Don't tie my hands."

Anton saw the sense of it, and the sense against it.

Nick continued, "Don't ask Vidori. Just do it. Face the music later, if he's unhappy. Act ignorant." He added, "Sir."

"It's not just a matter of the uldia," Anton said. "It's the whole issue of free access and exploration. We might win one interview, but lose the larger prize."

"But the prize is sinking away," Nick said. He gestured to the river outside the wall, his eyes lit by the setting sun. "Draining from us like the damn brown river out there. If we had the time to bring Vidori around, fine, but there isn't time. Let me act, Captain. Let me for God's sake *do* something."

"I'm not sure it'll be you who interviews the uldia, Lieutenant." He realized it was time to remind Nick that this wasn't a foregone conclusion. "There's plenty of investigation that can be done within the palace. The king hasn't set any limits on you here."

Nick swallowed, and the effort made it look like he had a gecko stuck in his throat. "Are you saying I'm not doing my job, Captain?"

"Everyone's doing their job," Anton said. "I'm just not assigning new ones."

"Keeping them for yourself, right?" The room grew silent as the two men faced each other.

Anton said, "My prerogative." He held Nick's gaze. "Captain's prerogative."

It had to be said. Nick was either a subordinate, or he was not. And that thought chilled him, because they were a long way from a higher authority. Nick had been a friend, and a good officer. He hoped he still was, at least the latter.

Finally Nick whispered, "Yes, sir."

Bailey stood, unbending herself in two stiff motions. "Well, if we're done with the pissing contest, I suggest dinner." Anton marveled at her resilience, that she could be hungry. The westering sun brought a fetid odor to the hut, spiked now and then by strong floral nectars from plants along the river.

Bailey caught Nick's eye. "So do we have to speak with hand sign at dinner tonight?" Nick knew the patois better than any of them so far.

"How else are we going to practice?" he asked.

She put on a bright smile. "Flash cards?"

But Nick was not going to be jollied along. "We have to learn the hoda language. They're an information source. They're human beings, for God's sake."

The radio hissed. An incoming call. Zhen moved to tune the frequency.

The radio hail came. *Sergeant Webb reporting. Come in, Camp Shaw.*

Zhen responded, "Got you, Sergeant. Stand by." She looked at Anton.

Anton spoke into the headset. "Captain Prados here, Sergeant."

The sergeant's voice sputtered into the hut: *We've got a bit of trouble, Captain. It's Commander Strahan. He's relieved himself from duty.* There was a pause. Anton guessed why, but waited, bracing for the news. *He's sick, Captain.*

Sick. The word struck like a gong. It always did. "Go on, Sergeant. What's it look like?"

It's a mutated strain, the medics are saying, sir. Two crew are down. It hits fast. Maybe there'll just be these two. But the thing is . . . As he paused, everyone in the hut was immobile, listening. *The thing is, it's already immune to the antiviral the med team designed this morning. It's like it was waiting for the vaccine; like it already knew.*

"Sergeant, what do the medics say?"

That's what they said. I'm telling you what they said. They're calling it a directed recombination. That means that instead of a random mutation, the virus chose the genetic segments that would get it past the vaccine we introduced. Sorry, sir. It's got us spooked, is all.

"How is Lieutenant Strahan? How bad is it?"

He's weak, sir. Like I said, it's fast. We've got him isolated, but that doesn't mean much up here. We're considering that it's an airborne virus. If it is, we're all exposed already. I'm acting on his behalf. With your permission.

"Permission granted, Sergeant." He looked around the room at Bailey, Zhen, and Nick, each absorbing the news.

As bad as the news was, it raised a further issue: that the four of them on ground mission might be reservoirs for the disease, exposing the Dassa. Anton closed his eyes, seeing visions of an epidemic among a population with no prior exposure.

"What are the first symptoms, Sergeant?"

Headache, fever. Strahan's temperature is one-oh-five. The thing is, our people are having trouble pinning down the virus. The rate of mutation is so high. They're talking about a nasty pool of genetic concoctions. Any one form might dominate at any particular time.

Zhen was nodding. Out of all of them listening to the transmission, she was the one to whom some of this made sense.

There was static for a few moments. Then Webb said, *People are afraid, Captain. We thought we had this licked. We don't.*

"I'm sorry I'm not there to help you," Anton murmured.

We don't want you here. We're infected, for God's sake . . . Sorry sir. Tempers are a little frayed tonight.

"Keep me posted, then, Sergeant." *Keep them loyal,* he wanted to say. Anton hoped Webb had it in him. He was a good man, middle-aged, a lifer in the service. He was also a long associate of Captain Darrow, and would have gone to the wall for him. But loyalties, Anton knew, didn't mutate as fast as microbes.

He put Zhen on the comm. She talked directly to the medical staff, and by her expression, learning more did not improve her mood.

Anton turned to his groundside crew. They all looked sober. The *Restoration* was now under the command of a sergeant. The virus was back, or one of its cousins. More virulent than before, more canny than before. Anton didn't want to think that the virus ravaging the ship wasn't done with them yet. But maybe it wouldn't be satisfied until it was the only living thing left on board. He stared at the floor. He and Phillip Strahan had played cards, been racquetball partners on board, been friends. They were all friends—all forty of them who set out on the mission, all thirty who remained. As Anton looked at the faces of the ground team, he felt a terrible helplessness. As captain, his job was to protect them. *Not doing my job,* he thought.

When Zhen joined them again, they considered their situation among the Dassa. Zhen looked bleak. "We could be exposing the Dassa," she said bluntly.

Bailey snapped, "We've been over this before. We're all showing negative for antibodies."

"The tests are meaningless," Zhen said, "if the virus is hiding in a reservoir in the body, or if it takes several weeks—which it could—for antibodies to develop."

Bailey sniffed. "We waited a decent interval to come down. We've done what we can. We're not even sure the Dassa are vulnerable to human diseases."

Anton saw the look on her face, the one that said, *It's already been decided.* "Zhen," Anton said, "we'll begin testing on a daily schedule."

Nick jumped in, asking, "What's this business about the virus being smart?"

"Nothing ludicrous, Venning." Zhen smirked. "Did you think viruses had little meetings to decide how to be nasty?" When he didn't rise to the bait, she went on, "We've seen this kind of thing before, back home. It's like the virus has its basic genetic material, kind of like a computer's data cube. Sometimes, a virus emerges that can scan the cube, turning off and on various genetic programs and databases. Or they can snatch information off of plasmids and transposons drifting by that carry bits of genetic data and programming. They turn stuff on and try it, and then try something else. It's faster than random mutations from reproduction." She shook her head at Nick, at the expression of bafflement on his face. "If this stuff was simple, would Earth be dying? Think about it, Venning."

He turned away. They had all grown silent.

Bailey stood in the center of the room. "I suggest we go easy on each other." She eyed Zhen and Nick. "All of us. We need to hold together, and bickering doesn't help. Carry on, Captain," she added. "I'm with you, of course."

It was a good speech, and Anton thanked her as the group dispersed, each member looking for time alone with his or her thoughts.

Anton judged that the sun was about to give up for the day, and he raised the blind, then ducked out for fresher air.

Nick stood behind him. "Captain, I'm sorry."

Anton turned to face him. "Forget it, Nick. I think we're going to need each other, more than ever. Can we put the past behind us?"

There was a lot of past involved. He wondered, if he was in Nick's place, how hard it would be to watch Nick take command and make judgments he would not make.

Nick nodded, making eye contact fleetingly, but making it. "Yes, sir."

It was the right thing to say. Anton didn't ask for enthusiasm, though it would have been nice. He just needed the

Yes, sir. That was how the military operated. Friendship had to fill in the spaces. Or not.

Left alone, Anton stared out at the burnished red of the river, dyed by the sunset. A thought that had been nagging at him now came into focus. If Webb hadn't initiated contact this evening, Anton would have. Because there was a task left uncompleted.

Back in communication with the ship, Anton asked Webb to bring in another satellite for inspection. There were four satellites, and so far the crew had taken apart just one. Duplicate satellites could have been used to assure that over thousands of years the broadcasting function would remain despite meteorite damage or system failure. Quite possibly all the units were the same, but Anton wanted to be sure.

Webb resisted the order. Crew were taxed too far as it was, he said, and there was no time or resources for extras. Eventually, under a direct order, he agreed, but Anton had not helped his relationship with the man.

It was time, though, to call in favors, to play his strongest cards. If the science team was under stress now, what would things be like if the contagion spread? He didn't want to think it, but it was conceivable that the ship and its crew might not have much time left.

Worst case, they had no time left at all.

FOUR

Before dawn, Anton slipped into the lagoon. This remote area of the palace grounds was deserted at this hour, a welcome relief after the long session on the radio with Sergeant Webb.

The banks of the pond were slick with mud, but erupting here and there with brassy green leaves, sprouting from rhizomes. It was a world returning from the flood. Swimming through the cool recesses of the cove, Anton submerged into the black waters. He felt his hair lifting in the water, his skin tightened to the cold plaits of the current. He surfaced, dove again, but his thoughts followed him.

He did have faith in the crew. The ship's science team was capable of powerful responses to infections, genetically designing many different classes of antivirals, engaging in the usual dance of drugs and resistance factors. Now, however, it seemed the microbes had learned some new steps . . .

Webb's desperate voice needled at him: *We don't want you here. We're infected, for God's sake.*

No one called it a plague ship. No one needed to. They

could turn around and go home, but what were the chances any of them would be left alive by the time they returned to Earth?

In the midst of this crisis, Webb kept up the reconnaissance flights, using the ship's atmospheric drone. They agreed on a sustained survey of the upcountry areas, the lands of canyons and clouds, but weather decreased the imaging success. Add to this the task of the capturing and reverse engineering of the second satellite, and the depleted crew would be very busy indeed. But better that way— keeping busy, fending off anxiety.

Anton let the black water take the night's work from his body, and from his mind.

Finding the bottom, he stood up in the rich muck, shoulders above the surface. He didn't know if this was a permanent lagoon, but by the position of the arched bridge nearby, he guessed there was at least a dry season stream here.

The dawn sifted into the palace compound with fingers of delicate light. But in this tucked-away place, surrounded by a screen of trees and far from the main byways, the night still clung.

Over the tops of the trees he could see the highest levels of the palace, looking like celestial floating cabanas, a dwelling place of the gods. Corrupt gods, certainly, strong on privilege and light on mercy. Much like his own family estate, with its hereditary wealth and power, where during one virulent outbreak of superresistant bacteria, his father had sent Anton's mother out the door in the estate wall. She never came back. It was only a week later that his sister also went through the little door in the wall. Anton stood in the garden, meeting her eyes. In that moment Anton's heart turned against his father, and years later, the day Anton left, he told his father why. They'd never spoken again.

The military had taken him in, and it became his home, Spartan and satisfying. Now, in this world of dynasty he was once again entwined with the aristocracy—as Nick was so swift to point out—those with the power to wear silk and clip tongues.

He swam to the bridge and under it, into the shadows. His hand touched something. It twitched. Recoiling, Anton found the bottom with his feet, and backed away.

Near the edge of the bridge, he saw a group of plants moving. They were like the other vines along the shore, but fleshy and swollen, with a vaselike structure opening up, peeling away. One of the pouches disgorged a tiny gecko. He'd seen such plants before, what the Dassa called *fulva,* varieties of birthing pouches, half vegetable, half animal. But it was always unnerving.

Some of the crew casually called this prevalent fulva mechanism a mutation. But the science team agreed it wasn't a random mutation. The birthing pouches of both humans and other animals were deliberate, an effective device to rapidly build populations. That was the prevailing theory. The Quadi had started with zero individuals, and had to bring the population to sizable numbers, including a rich genetic diversity. They'd altered the genomes, designing a reproductive process that could create a population virtually overnight. With plants, though, seeds could do that. It was just the animals that required modification.

The process was in some ways not so different from creating proteins as the bases of biotech drugs. Human technology could clone living gene sequences useful in treating disease, by growing them first in host cells and then in nutrient broths. The excruciating difference here was that the Quadi had begun with digital information, not a biologically active molecule. This old race could not only reproduce life, but create it.

He dove again, into the cleansing black waters, tunneling into the deepest part of the lagoon.

When he next broke the surface, he had company.

A Dassa woman stood on the bridge, looking at him. Except for her light-colored gown, he wouldn't have seen her in the shadows of this place. They stared at each other.

She approached, stepping off the bridge and picking her way down the muddy bank to stand by the water's edge.

"I am Maypong," the woman said. She bore a package in her arms, and now undid it—or rather, unfolded it, for it was a length of cloth. "Here is a cloth to dry yourself."

It was a polite command to get out of the water, but he saw no reason to jump to her command.

"I'm swimming," Anton said.

"Oh yes. But now I have found you before damage is done." She shook the towel at him.

"Does the cove belong to someone?"

"The king is happy to share his cove with you. But not for—swimming."

"I thought the Dassa swim every morning." From early dawn, the river was full of boats, men and women paddling to the variums of the uldia.

The woman frowned. "In the Olagong, we do not swim in the free waters. It is a private varium duty of procreation. To swim otherwise is exceedingly distasteful, if others should see you thus."

Distasteful to swim. Nick would love this: For all their sexual abandon, they were sensitive about the procreative act. Giving up on his swim, Anton moved to the bank and climbed out, where she wrapped a cloth around him.

As he dried himself, she went on, "The king has appointed me your chancellor, so future mistakes need not occur."

"*Chancellor?*" Anton said. "I'm no royal, to need a chancellor."

"No need? When you swim publicly? Offend the king? Go through walls of course?"

Someone was keeping lists. He wondered if buttons and failing to bed the princess were on her list as well.

He dressed as she watched him. "Shim has been advising me," he said.

Maypong brushed this aside. "Shim advises the king, and

has a babe on her back, Anton." She said his name better than other Dassa.

Looking up, he squinted at her in the semilight. If he was to have a personal attendant, perhaps it was a sign of the king's favor. If Maypong could help him, she would be very welcome. But if she was here to keep him from breaking the rules, by God, they might clash. "Maypong," he said, "if you're going to be my chancellor, I hope you'll teach me everything. Not just what you think I should know, but what *I* think I should know."

"A little of each, perhaps," she answered with a more pleasant tone. Folding the cloth he'd used for a towel, she watched with curiosity as he threaded laces through his shoes.

He smiled up at her. It was a fair thing to say.

"When you learn every needful thing, you will be fit to go among us."

Anton got to his feet. Was she saying he would be free to leave the palace? "In Lolo?" he asked.

"The Olagong is larger than Lolo. We would have you know we are not hiding things. Not hiding messages."

Nearer her now, he saw that she was shorter than he by a little. And that she looked familiar. He would have offered a hand to help her up the mud bank to the bridge, but of course one did not offer a hand to a Dassa.

The world turned gold and green as the sun infused the stand of trees. Maypong's gown caught the sun, becoming a pale lemon yellow. Her face was clear to him for the first time. And he knew the woman.

She turned and climbed the bank, stopping on the bridge. It had been scrubbed clean of mud, as had all of the king's pavilion, but her feet now left dark blotches on the decking. She turned to see if he was following her.

This was the woman in the plaza, the one with the unflappable demeanor. The one who watched her daughter being cut, who watched her daughter fall and bleed into the black mud. The woman without a heart. His skin, still wet from the swim, chilled in the breeze.

Maypong turned and walked slowly over the bridge. Her gown turned a garish color as the sun lit her fully.

Anton was acutely aware that he was making a choice. This woman might well be another silken noose devised by Vidori. Had the king deliberately chosen the one woman whom his crew would not accept? But how could Anton explain to Vidori that he deemed an obedient noblewoman unworthy? No, it couldn't be done.

At last, Anton followed her.

He was choosing, yet he had no choice. He thought that Nick would see this as another concession to royalty. But he hoped that Maypong would prove more than that, and indeed, his instinct told him she would. And in the Olagong, he knew, instinct sometimes served better than logic.

Every time she opened her eyes, the dream came back.

The dream that she was in a miserable slave hut, lying in a hammock, her mouth filled with pain.

Gilar resolved not to open her eyes. She would go back to sleep, to sleep in the comfort of her cool room by the river, with its song of water, her sheets like a silken river carrying her to another day. Oh yes, that place was within reach, just beneath this terrible dream. She would hold on to the brocaded corner of her bedclothes, while her body floated in this unreal world. The one that said she was a hoda.

She felt a pressure on her arm. Someone jiggling her, urging her to wake.

No, no. Mustn't open my eyes. There is a woman without a tongue out there.

But the jostling came again. The moment Gilar opened her eyes, the hoda signed to her:

>Welcome, Gilar.<

Here was a slave not using her honorific. She would have

this slave disciplined. But the place to do that was on the other side of the sheet, her home by the river.

Through the roof, imperfectly woven, panes of light slashed into the room, hurting her eyes along with her mouth. Something was dreadfully wrong with her mouth.

The hoda was signing again.

>Do you need more pain drink?<

Gilar nodded. She wanted a pain drink, even if this was only a dream. She sipped from a cup, then lay back again.

She opened her mouth to ask where she was, but when she did, out came an awful bray. Her throat convulsed, and a trickle down her throat tasted thick and wrong. She tried to speak again, and again came the squawk of a jiga bird. What was in her mouth? Gilar sat up, as hands came to restrain her. She brayed again and again. The pain dug down her throat like a shovel. The hoda held on to her, arms wrapped around Gilar's arms, pinning them to her side, as Gilar fought to stick her hand in her mouth, to take out the knife, to hit the hoda, and to fall through the sheet to a safe world.

Hmmm, hmmm, came the hoda's voice. The same sound her hoda slave had made when she was a child needing comfort. *Hmmm, hmmm.*

Hearing that old nurse's song, Gilar wept. Her face fell against the hoda's shoulder, against the rough cloth of her tunic. But her nurse was dead these three years past. Calming herself, she pulled away, looking at the slave in front of her, a young hoda.

The girl removed her hands from around Gilar, and signed to her:> Do not cry in front of Mistress Aramee. Be brave now, and cry with me later.<

Gilar hesitated to use slave language. In the palace she needed only to read what the hoda said, never needed to use hand sign herself. It was vulgar to wave hands. But she did so now, not wishing to bray. >Cry? Why am I crying?<

>You know why, my sister.<

Gilar reached up and wiped the water from her cheeks.

She knuckled at her eyes, but she kept her mouth firmly closed. No more braying sounds. >Where are my real clothes?< Gilar signed. This coarse tunic needed to be replaced at once.

>Maypong set them afloat in the Puldar.<

Gilar thought of her beautiful silk tunic, floating on the river like a sea serpent. She imagined Maypong setting the clothes there, after taking the coins from the king's hand, after turning her face. Away.

The sun had moved beyond the peak of the ceiling to slide down the steep roof. The day was aging. The sun moved in the heavens. She was truly and really here, then. In a dark realm.

The truth, when it settled upon her, made her feel as heavy as a stone settling into the river. The river took the bodies of those no one cared about. She didn't want to float long. She wanted, desperately, to find the bottom and have it over with.

>Maypong is not my mother,< Gilar signed.

>No. Not anymore.<

Outside Gilar heard voices. >What compound am I in?< Her fingers were more clumsy than those of this hoda, who had practice waving her fingers at people.

The hoda answered. >The Mistress Aramee's household.<

Gilar nodded.

She was fending off thinking about her mouth. If she thought about how her body had been ruined, it would drive her mad. She thought instead about Aramee, a woman with one of the best islets, right on the River Sodesh. A fine compound, so she had heard in the days before. But Maypong would hardly have known Aramee socially. Maypong was of the palace.

The hut door darkened. Inside stepped a woman of bearing. Her tightly wound hair glinted from sun leaking through the roof.

The hoda stood. Then, furtively, she signed to Gilar.
>Cry later.<

The Mistress Aramee approached the hammock where
Gilar reclined. She kneeled next to her with a pleasant expression on her face. "Open your mouth, Gilar."

The hoda urged Gilar with her eyes, pleading for her to
be obedient. Gilar opened her mouth to let Aramee inspect
her wound.

The mistress peered closely, her scent coming strong to
Gilar's nostrils. Aramee nodded and gestured to the slave,
who placed a cup in Aramee's hand.

"You are well enough to drink your cleansing broth."

Cleansing broth. It was the potion that all hoda drank, to
make them clean. Gilar's hand shook as she took the cup.
She paused. Perhaps she would hurl it in Aramee's face.
Perhaps she would spill it in her own lap. The moment
stretched.

Misunderstanding Gilar's pause, Aramee said, "It will
sting for a moment. Soon over." Her attempt at kindness
made Gilar's stomach sour. That she thought Gilar needed
kindness.

Tipping her head back, she swallowed the potion all at
once. She cared little for the medicine's effects. What was
left of her tongue burned molten as the liquid passed over
it. She gulped hugely, keeping her face calm. The potion
could have no effect on her whatsoever. Gilar was not born
to bear. Not.

Aramee took the empty cup, looking at it to be sure
nothing remained.

At the door the mistress turned around. Gilar raised her
chin, waiting for Aramee to give her some due, something
to recognize that she now had a slave who had been raised
in the palace.

But all she said was "It is a nice, straight cut. I will thank
the judipon for you."

Gilar stared at the doorway for a long while.

Beside her, the hoda signed, >My name is Bahn. Where you are now, so it was with me one year ago.<

Gilar hardly registered this information. >Take me to the door, Bahn, so I can look out.<

Bahn helped her rise and move to the doorway. Gilar moved as though she was underwater. Drugged.

Leaning against the post of the door, Gilar saw the wide mud yard, baked dry, the huts with neatly stacked equipment, children running, followed by their bald hoda nursemaids. In the rear, the sprawling hut of Aramee and her female kin.

>It is a fine compound, Gilar. Aramee is good, you will see.<

Gilar stared at Bahn. >But I am not a hoda.<

Bahn slapped her. Not hard, but the slave actually slapped her. The pain sent a wave of protest to the back of her skull.

>Never say that again.<

The blow calmed Gilar. She was now able to look at Bahn with patient hatred. Bahn who dared strike her. Bahn with her smooth skull. Someday, Gilar knew, she would look just like that, when the potion took her hair away. But inside, Gilar would never be a hoda.

She was palace-raised. These people would have to learn that.

FIVE

In the back of the skiff Nick peered out the gaps in the reed tent. The uldia hid him there, as eager as he was to keep this trip secret. This trip to Oleel's pavilion.

The view of the River Sodesh was altered from a week ago when he and Zhen had traveled to the shuttle landing site. Today the river flowed in a broad channel, and the land lay uncovered on either side, still swampy in places, but busy with farming activity.

It had been an instant's decision. Nick had been walking through a glade in the palace compound. A boat appeared from under a bridge, and an uldia asked him if now would suit him to interview the chief uldia. A boat was waiting, with a privacy cabin in the stern, and no one around to observe. He found himself in the skiff, crouching down to enter the reed enclosure. Perhaps his decision was propelled by the incident with the hoda and the wire cage, when Anton did nothing to prevent the mutilation, or perhaps it was the outbreak on the ship, or Maypong's new presence. He hesitated only a moment. He was convinced now that Anton wasn't competent. He'd hoped for Anton to succeed;

he'd tried to help him. But it was Nick who should have been awarded that post.

The skiff entered a narrow channel, a dark tunnel with overhanging tree branches. The splashes of paddling slowed, and the skiff bumped into what might have been a dock. A hoda removed the forward side of the tent and gestured him out of the craft and onto a ramp.

They were in the deep shade of a small pier—nothing like the grand entrance he'd expected at Oleel's pavilion. But of course they took him to a back entrance. Two uldia escorted him down a narrow corridor that smelled as if it had been underwater recently. At points along the corridor, electric lamps lent a murky glow.

They ascended stairs of white granite, quickly gaining height above the Amalang River. Emerging into a fine hall, Nick saw the first extensive use of stone that he'd observed among the Dassa. Through stone columns and open walls, Nick looked down on the jungle, pressing closer here than at Vidori's palace.

After crossing a roofed bridge and passing through a portico, Nick found himself on a mezzanine overlooking a central courtyard. Sounds of running water filled the place, compounded by those of a small stream set into the stone floor. Here and there water cascaded down the walls and emptied into the floor streams.

Despite the immense size of the pavilion, he saw only three people in it beside himself: his two escorts, and someone waiting for him on the mezzanine. She was a tall woman, dressed all in glittering gray.

"You are Venning," the woman said. She stood on the other side of the floor stream. And she was indeed a large woman, somewhat taller than himself. The size of her ear pendants were in ratio to her commanding face—the half-circles as usual, but inlaid with a milky white stone.

"Yes," he said, "Nick Venning." He didn't like their using the name that Zhen used, with those overtones of contempt. "Are you the Lady Oleel?"

"Did you think they lied, saying that we would meet?"

Nick looked at his escorts. "Not at all. My thanks to your people." He was conscious that the woman likely could smell him. Not just uldia, but all female Dassa had a strongly developed sense of smell—to identify parentage of infants. He took a seat so that Oleel could sit. She chose a riser on his side of the stream.

Behind her was a glass box inside which river plants undulated in the circulating waters. The tank was in fact connected by ceramic pipes to other water features on the mezzanine, so that it was all one system, or appeared to be.

"You were the captain's chancellor. Before Maypong took your place."

"She is helping us," he replied, but heat rose in his face, to think that was how people saw it.

"Oh yes, you would think so. I see it . . . with different eyes."

He was startled to hear her use a human idiom—an apt one. He realized they must learn to see things as the uldia did, if they wished to understand them, to calm their fears. Nick planned to address those fears—of why they had come, what they must do here, and if they offended, how they could be soon gone once their mission bore fruit. He would have Oleel understand their motives, and give her assurances that they would not linger to trouble her traditional view. This might win her support of their further access to the Olagong. Or at least remove her objections—to which he suspected Vidori catered.

She remained silent. His attention was taken by the glowing tank, with its pulses of green and purple photophorics that threw spots of odd color on Oleel's face. The plants might have been kelplike growths, except that they bulged in places.

"Do you like my fish, Venning?" Oleel gestured to her tank.

Nick had not quite seen fish there yet, but there was plenty of room for them to hide amid the plants.

"Very nice colors."

Oleel walked to the river side of the mezzanine, looking down. "And do you like your quarters with the king?"

"He gave us a roof when we needed shelter. Until our job is done and our visit is completed. But we meant no disrespect to—others."

"*Others* are upset." She sat down on a riser. Because of the rushing stream between them, Nick had to strain to hear her words.

"It is customary," she said, "when the chief judipon is infirm to allow the judipon to elect a younger man. Vidori does not allow such election. Thus the Third Power is weak, and the Olagong suffers."

"We know nothing of these things, Lady."

She went on, "It could be said that Vidori wishes to take another power, and that crippling the judipon with a man weak in pri makes them susceptible to royal commands."

"You think the king has plans to seize further power."

"I have not said so, Venning."

"We have no views on these things, Lady. We have our own goals: only to save our people and return to our home."

"How can you save them by being away from them?"

Nick took a slow breath. She didn't know their story. And she must learn it. It was the only way she could believe they did not come in conquest. "Lady, our people are sick and come in search of a promised cure." There was no Dassa word for *sick,* so he used their term, *weak in pri,* or life currents.

"We made no promises." Oleel's face was immobile. She had a way of speaking that used few muscles, giving the unsettling impression of ventriloquism. "We do not understand how a whole people can be *weak in pri.* Who can live without life current?"

"Someone did call us, Lady. Across the oceans of the sky. It came from those small moons." He pointed upward.

"Made from metal," Oleel murmured.

"Yes."

"Fashioned by a thinking race," she said.

"Is it wrong to think so?" But even the palace astronomers had long thought they were metal, not rock.

For a moment Oleel's face took on a gold tincture from the blooming of a biolume. "No, it is no sacrilege to think the Quadi could effect such wonders. They created the Olagong. And the Dassa. So your metal moons would not be so difficult." She put her hand in the stream running across the porch, trailing her fingers. The stream continued to the edge of the mezzanine and spilled over, forming a waterfall.

"You look for chemicals to save you. Medicinals?"

"No, we think not. But we don't know what form their gifts to us will take."

"Knowing so little, you chose to travel for years, far from home, perhaps to some disastrous end?"

He didn't like the sound of that last phrase, yet it was a fair summation. "We are that desperate."

"You would not like to stay and inhabit the Olagong. With all our pri?"

Nick swallowed. "It would not save our people. We don't come for just ourselves. We must go home. We *will* go home."

"I am glad to hear so."

"Then I promise." He thought this conversation was going very well. Oleel had just said she was glad. That was progress. If Anton had only seen how necessary it was to converse with the Dassa. All of the Dassa. Here was a woman concerned with possible expansionist motives of the newcomers. All very predictable.

"You think my pavilions fine, Venning?" Oleel had followed his gaze as he looked at the stone temple.

"I have seen nothing like it in Lolo."

"It is built in the way of the Quadi. Like their first pavilion." She rose, bidding him to follow her to the edge of the mezzanine.

Nick followed her lead, walking on his side of the floor stream, and looked down on the square below. No railings, in the customary Dassa building practice.

"See," Oleel said, pointing. "The streams of our courtyard depict the dry season beds of the great braids. My compound depicts the sacred Olagong, with the highlands over there, and the major islets as quarters for my ladies. All as in the original compound, which the river has claimed."

He nodded. "A fine layout. Very ingenious."

She ignored this. "You may notice, my people do not favor building with quarry rock. Yet here is a compound entirely of stone. It is in honor of the Quadi way of stone huts, where the Dassa were brought to life and where the Quadi themselves lived before their efforts were shamed by the manifestation of the degenerates. So you can see how hard it is for us to believe that the Quadi offered to help you when you are degenerates of the same template."

That was rather harsh, but it did not surprise Nick that she thought so—only that she had *said* so. "My lady—"

She cut him off. "You have in your midst a hoda raised up to high position. This would be the hoda Sen, who has, I have been told, a sharp tongue, and too much hair."

Even though he despised Zhen, Nick didn't like this insult. "We have no concept of *hoda*, Lady. We have abandoned slavery. Women are not slaves." He wanted to make that point clear in this society of women.

Oleel turned to watch the glass box of river plants. The ropy plantings were swaying with more agitation, as though nervous under her gaze.

"Sen is born to bear," Oleel said, her face in profile taking on a green tincture from the water plants, which were in turn infused with sunshine from the open walls. "She may, even now, be growing bodies inside of her. You had permission to bring four humans to the Olagong. But how many did you really bring? How many might Sen bear?"

"Oh, Zhen is not pregnant," Nick said, growing uncomfortable with the turn of the conversation.

"Do you promise?"

Nick opened his mouth to do so, then thought that it was unseemly for him to promise such a thing about Zhen, about any woman. And after all, he couldn't be absolutely sure of Zhen's sexual practices.

"I am sorry that you find Zhen disturbing. We keep her within the palace because of your wishes."

"*I* do not wish her to be in the palace, thankfully." Oleel had now turned from her tank and fixed him with a rock-hewn stare.

Oleel nodded to one of her attendants, and the woman came forward with a small bowl. From this, the attendant distributed a powder along the surface water of the tank, then withdrew several paces behind Nick.

As the powder settled into the water, all undulations of the river plants ceased.

"Does it occur to you, Venning, the difference between your people and mine? That we thrive and you do not? That you use your women for incubation and they produce offspring that do not thrive?"

"Well, that's not—"

"Have you considered how flawed is the human practice? Does this thought occur while you rush around looking for the long-departed Quadi to have left gifts for you?"

Nick struggled mightily with his temper. "We hold our women in more honor than you can imagine."

"You hold your women. That is my point. No one holds women in the Olagong."

"Except that the hoda are held," Nick said, locking cold gazes with the woman.

Oleel's mouth flickered with a smile. It was not attractive on such a stern face. But in the next moment, Nick's attention was diverted by the water tank. The bulges in the plants had taken on a blush of pink, faintly phosphorescent. Then the round growths began to split and disgorge a milky fluid. One after another, the pods expelled an effluvium bearing seeds, small tadpolelike shapes. The dark specks drifted to the surface, collecting in a putrid murk.

Oleel glanced at the tank and its ruined plantings. "In the case of these specimens, their pri was imperfect. It was better that they burst than bear life."

Nick was galled at her lecture, at her implied threats. He subdued his anger enough to murmur, "I regret we are not to have a proper conversation. Of respect."

Oleel paused. Perhaps she had not expected him to acknowledge her rudeness. "Do you think, Venning, that the royal pavilion respects you?"

"Under the surface, everyone thinks their own thoughts."

She nodded. "But few bring anger into a room? Which would you rather have, hidden or open?"

"Open anger can halt conversation, Lady."

"Hmmm. I had not realized this."

If she was playing with him again, he would surely leave.

"But now you know my heart," she said. "I would have nothing come between us, such as hiding of true heart. You know that I abhor what you are. Now we can move to other things."

"What other things?"

"Oh, whatever things you like." Oleel's attention drifted back to her tank, and she said in a low tone, "But now we must cleanse this tank. Yes, somehow it has become ruined."

As a hoda came to clean the tank, Oleel turned to him, saying, "Sometimes, it is possible for a degenerate to rise above shameful beginnings. Are you such a one, Venning?"

"I am what you see, Lady." It was all he could think of to say.

"Oh yes. I do see." She waved him away. "You will have more chances to rise. I will send for you."

At last the uldia led him away. Nick was in turmoil, not knowing whether to be elated or furious. But, aside from her bitter words, he had learned important facts today. And they would speak again, of *other things.*

He passed through a corridor where two uldia were embracing. His escort ignored them, but he frankly stared, as one woman put her mouth to the other's breast. There was no Dassa word for sex between two women, or two men. It was all the same, all sexual contact was sarif—the cordiality that bound them, and released them.

He tried to see it as social cohesion. But he was beginning to think he would never approve of it—not a value-neutral anthropological stance.

And now he was defying Anton. No, not neutral at all.

Anton was surprised at how fast Maypong could descend a steep ladder.

He hurried down corridors and ramps as fast as was seemly in the king's pavilion, and Maypong hurried to catch up. As he strode toward the great river steps forming the entrance to the king's pavilion from the Puldar, he tried to formulate a plan.

The king was boarding a lavish barge. Anton had seen this from a rooftop where he'd chanced to glimpse the preparations. If the king was going out, Anton was going with him. If Vidori wouldn't allow him to go abroad alone, then he'd go in good company, even if it wasn't polite or respectful—words that described the manner in which Vidori was controlling him.

"Anton, you are not dressed for noble company," Maypong said, finally catching up to him.

"Humans don't wear silk," he said, using an aphorism he made up on the spot.

"The king has not made us his guests for the river audience."

"Maybe he will when he sees me." He was counting on Vidori's unfailing courtesy.

They had entered the huge reception hall that fronted

the king's compound and was open to the river through thick wood columns. A crowd was gathering here—nobles, soldiers, hoda.

Maypong caught at his sleeve, jerking him enough to get his attention. "So what will you do? Stand at the top of the stairs and look lonely?" Still breathing heavily from the chase he'd led her, she fixed him with a dark stare.

"No. I'm going to ask him if I can go along." He turned and walked toward the porch.

"Which is very disrespectful."

He kept going. "Which I can't know because I'm a foreigner."

Anton approached the crowd. The wide expanse of stairs fell seven or eight steps straight into the river, as though made for a river god to ascend. The barge was drawn up, taking nobles on board, assisted by hoda.

As the crowd parted, Shim caught sight of him, eyes widening. She murmured in the king's ear, and Vidori turned to see Anton, who now stood with a considerable amount of empty space around him. Even Maypong had abandoned him.

He hadn't thought about what he would say, since he couldn't imagine what he would *need* to say. His only plan was to pretend that he thought he was invited. It was brazen to do so, but for the first time Anton relished the idea of using his ignorance in his favor.

"I'm sorry I'm not dressed for the occasion," he managed to say.

Vidori's forehead was wrinkled in some consternation. Waiting for some signal as to whether he was to be welcomed aboard or thrown into the river, Anton looked around as though admiring the barge.

Then the king smiled very broadly—his eyes not participating—and climbed a few stairs toward Anton. "You are late, Captain. Thankfully you have not missed us." He waved Anton forward.

As Anton descended the stairs, he saw that Maypong had

made her way down and was whispering to Shim, no doubt sorting out the protocols involved with this unexpected guest.

The sky was high and stacked with cumulus clouds, a searing white against the soft blue of the morning. Ghosts of the clouds shimmered in the water, magically keeping their position in the swift current.

In another moment Anton was enfolded by guards, nobles, and the general bustle as the congregation crossed a ramp and boarded the barge. The craft bore a tent in the middle, its fabric billowing. A line of soldiers held long poles at the ready.

Maypong was at his side. "Say little. Do nothing," she spat at him.

But he could hardly stay silent if the king spoke to him. "Think of it as a learning opportunity," he said. "You've said I need to learn."

Her face was calm, too calm. He knew he'd have to mend some rifts with the woman. And with Vidori. He needed to make a point, but keep a friend—if an alien monarch could be considered a *friend*. Nick wouldn't like to hear that word, but Nick was no politician. Anton had never realized that aspect of the captaincy, the push/pull of leadership and diplomacy. Well, today was *push*.

Without ceremony, the barge was under way, as the guards poled them off the sunken stairs. As they did so, Shim came toward them. "The king will have Anton sit near him," she said.

Maypong gave a lovely smile in response. As they rose she snarled at Anton, "Say little."

He looked from one woman to the other. They both looked calm and rattled at the same time. Shim, her round face very pretty indeed, and Maypong, more petite, thinner of face. But he didn't think her diminutive in any other sense.

The king sat among nobles in the front of the barge, with the smallest of platforms serving as chairs. Vidori sat with one leg crossed over his lap, the other outstretched. It seemed the only way to sit in long pants on the risers, so Anton did the same. The women, in tunics, sat sidesaddle. No one brought infants today.

As was his custom, the king wore black and gray, and went armed. That and the presence of many soldiers lent a more martial air to the outing than the otherwise festive mood would suggest. The nobles had grown very quiet as Anton took a place among them. He wondered if his presence was upsetting them and if any of them guessed that Vidori had not invited him. Among these nobles, Anton noted the androgynous beauty of the men. At times he had to take cues from the hairstyle to distinguish them from the women.

Maypong sat beside him, her upper lip sweating but her face studiously calm. The king glanced at her. It was only for a split second, but he thought Maypong faltered under that gaze. He'd exposed her to some displeasure, and was sorry for it.

But for now Vidori had assumed a casual demeanor, and was talking animatedly with a few of the viven, the palace-raised. Among them were relatives of the king, including numerous brothers who lived in the palace, and his sisters, some of whom attended on him. There were many cross ties and relationships here, and now Anton was in their midst, needing to make conversation, he thought, despite Maypong's warnings.

He turned to the nearest Dassa man. "A beautiful day to be on the river, rahi," he said.

The man looked startled to be spoken to. "It is the only day to be on the river."

Maypong leaned in to say, "The floods have receded, and this ceremony honors the season, Anton."

The viven had used no honorific. The Dassa never appended one to Anton's or his crews' names. Shim said it was because they were not Dassa. She smiled when she said it, but the crew knew an insult when they heard one.

The center of the Puldar was shallow enough to allow the crew to pole the craft, which they preferred to do rather than using the graceless barge engines, a recent technological development, and one seldom used because of the Dassa distaste for the noise and smoke that resulted from burning ethanol fuel. The current was in their favor, and the barge poled along with muffled splashes, nearly submerged under the clamor of the forest, the restless cries of the near-Earth creatures that called this place home.

The king was speaking to him. "We shall have silks made for you, Anton. For next time."

Maypong pounced. "Oh, rahi, humans do not ever wear silk, as the captain has said so many times."

"Ah." Vidori smiled at his companions as though to say, *Who knows what the humans do?* "But someday the green clothes will fall off." The group laughed at this.

"We have more green clothes where these came from, Vidori-rah," Anton said.

The smiles left the retinue. His remark had perhaps been clumsy, Anton realized. Into the silence, Maypong plunged: "But first the clothes will fall off, of course." She had made it clear that Anton had not contradicted the king about whether the clothes would rot off. It was not elegant, but the group's tension faded.

Maypong's upper lip glistened in the sun. Anton felt sorry for her, but he was rather enjoying himself. He had to admit it was glorious to be outside, with the rains gone, and to have made clear to the king that he was impatient to make progress.

Maypong begged permission from the king to stroll with Anton so that he could better view the river, and they began a slow pacing of the barge's perimeter. Maypong was calmer now, and they walked for a time without speaking. A few others walked as well, and from time to time entered the silken tent where platforms were set up for meal preparation.

The river was filling with boats that now followed the

barge, with much waving and calling back and forth. An iridescent bird skimmed over the water, scooping in its bill a load of water insects. Its sapphire plumage flashed in the sun, as achingly blue as Dassa silk, as Joon's gown the day he'd first seen her. Along the banks, woody vines plunged from trees into the river, like hoses sucking up water. Up and down them skittered beetles, reptiles, even monkeys, using the lianas as a pathway between river and canopy.

Maypong pointed ahead to the choppy waters where the Puldar poured its brown waters into the clearer, main river. "See," Maypong said, "there is the great Sodesh. Today is an auspicious day for river viewing, the first proper day for the king to view the braids."

Anton recited what he knew of the braids: "The Puldar, the Amalang, the Nool; tributaries of the Sodesh."

"Yes. Vidori has the Puldar. The Amalang is Oleel's, in her realm of the uldia. The judipon have their pavilion upon the Nool. All are braided together to form the Sodesh, our life river." She glanced at him as they walked. "That is the most you can know about us."

"I'm sure there is very much more."

"It is all there, Anton, in the braids."

"Sometimes," Anton ventured, "the rains make it all one river." And of course, the flooding brought with it the rich soils of the uplands to enrich their farmlands.

Maypong dipped her head, her acknowledgment that he had said something less than stupid. As she did so, her earrings swayed, showing off the exquisite miniature scene of a bird in flight.

"It renews us, and reminds us that we are not truly separate from each other."

They walked in silence for a time, past the kneeling hoda, facing inward toward the barge, waiting to be useful. As they walked, Anton saw that some of the viven had paired off, and were touching from time to time, in a casual but deliberate way, decidedly sexual. No one paid this the slightest attention.

He thought of the Princess Joon then, and as though reading his mind, Maypong said, "The Lady Joon would have come on the viewing today."

"Why didn't she?"

"Did you not see her at the top of the king's stairs?"

Anton had not, but his attention had been utterly focused on Vidori and himself.

"She attends her father on the first viewing of the season. But she declined, seeing you."

"Why?" He could imagine why. He hadn't seen her since their unsettling interview.

"Well, but she did not want to be seen with you, of course."

He paused, thinking that now he had the answer to Shim's question about how the interview went. "Does she believe I haven't shown her respect?"

"Have you not?" Maypong looked pointedly at him.

Anton took a deep breath. "She offered . . . cordiality . . . that I could not accept."

Maypong sighed. "Thankfully you have me as your chancellor at last." She gazed out as they moved into the Sodesh. "Also, Oleel would not like the lady to share a barge with you."

"Oleel is her uldia, and Oleel does not like humans. And," he added, guessing, "Joon is afraid of Oleel."

"Not afraid, but bound to her uldia because Joon's own mother is dead, and therefore her bond is all the stronger to her birth-water mother."

"So she can befriend me, but not in public."

"You begin to understand us, Anton."

"God, I hope so."

The barge continued its stately pace, gliding by the shoreline compounds, the poles rising glistening from the water and plunging down again. Near Anton, one of the poles rose from the water bearing a fulva husk, having speared a birth pouch of some creature—perhaps fish or fowl. It was jarring to remember that he was not in a normal place. That was Neshar: lulling, jarring.

Just as this thought came to him, the tent fabric blew away from one of its fasteners. Past the fluttering silk, Anton saw a Dassa couple lying on a raised platform. The woman's naked back arched at the pleasure her lover was giving her. Anton thought her partner was a man, but it was hard to tell with her knees in the way . . .

Turning from the view, Anton met Maypong's gaze.

She smiled. "Sarif."

"Right." He knew what it was. But in full sun, on the king's barge, it was unexpected. "So that"—he gestured at the tent—"is for privacy."

Maypong looked at him with a hint of amusement. "Certainly not. It is for shade, Anton. If one is going to remove one's clothes, of course."

"Of course." He wished she wouldn't smile that way, as though he still had not learned some simple lessons. The fact was, there was very little about Dassa sexuality that was simple. Joon—and her father—came suddenly to mind.

The fabric behind him whipped frantically, causing a hoda to come forward to secure it again against the struts.

A silence ensued. Poles dipped into the water. Curtains stayed tied down. He blurted out: "Joon and her father—are close?" Anton had been wanting to ask. Maypong was the only person he *could* ask.

She looked over at him, frowning. "The lady is his favorite, of course."

"Favorite what?"

"Favorite daughter. Oldest child. What else?"

"Well, there is physical closeness." The Dassa practiced incest, without any sense of shame. Even the women sought others in their compounds without regard to relation.

"This disturbs you," Maypong said.

He paused, but there was only one answer. "Yes."

"You must not think this way in the Olagong, Anton."

She stopped. "Why is a daughter pleasuring her father disturbing?"

He sighed. Where to begin? It wasn't, of course, a matter of inbreeding, since sex and reproduction weren't even linked here; that was where all the problems between Dassa and human began. But incest was also a matter of power and trust . . .

"It's complicated," he said.

"Not for us," she murmured.

The bargemen poled mightily to keep the barge from swooping into the center of the Sodesh, a wide, glossy corridor stretching for kilometers toward the mist-covered hills.

He couldn't argue from an interbreeding standpoint. It was enough that the uldia saw to it that the right Dassa swam in the right variums. He tried the viewpoint of the difference in power. A mother has power over her son, so that sarif, or cordial sex, might be coerced psychologically. And this was even truer between a king and his daughter . . .

When he finished explaining this, Maypong stared at him. "Why would someone coerce sarif? How can it be cordial, if it is forced?"

"Maybe someone wishes to . . ." He searched for the Dassa word for *dominate*, then settled on, "to win a bad kind of respect?"

"But Anton, how can it be winning respect to receive something that is so freely available?"

"Or maybe," he said, "someone doesn't wish to be—cordial, and the other person too strongly desires it?"

Maypong looked at him with troubled eyes. "Does this happen, among your people?"

"It is against our laws, but yes."

She shook her head. "Some laws you should not need."

How had she turned this into *human* moral lapse? They would never sort this out.

Anton saw Vidori standing in the prow, conferring with a bargeman. He could not admire him . . . and yet, somehow, he did. As he watched, he saw that the course was changed to make for the outlet of another river.

The viven had taken notice, and all attention was now focused on this new direction.

Maypong whispered to Anton, "It appears you will have your wish, after all." Her face had turned serious.

The king, however, seemed in an expansive mood. He announced to the viven, "We will present the . . ." Here he used a word that Anton didn't recognize. "My visitors are curious, and it has been long since I took the pleasure of viewing it."

"The ruins," Maypong whispered. "The ancient site. The king is granting your wish, Anton. I hope it is worth it to you, given the high price, and the fact that there is nothing there."

Anton watched as the barge approached the confluence with the Amalang River. Oleel's river.

Anton nodded to the king, making eye contact. Vidori smiled in ironic fashion, as though it were a game. But truly, Anton had no idea what Vidori's game was.

The barge navigated the currents with some difficulty, and then they were moving up the Amalang, a more narrow tributary, darker, greener than either the Sodesh or the Puldar. The waters cooled to turquoise under the cathedral branches of the trees, and the day faded to a golden green twilight. The viven were silent now, and the sound of the poles measured their progress with rhythmic splashes. The tent in the middle of the barge stood empty now, as the retinue grew somber and attentive in the realm of the uldia.

They passed the canoes of the uldia, women in gray tunics and sometimes robes who looked at them askance. And then the uldia fortress emerged in front of them, all in stone, and as large as the king's palace, though not as lovely. They quickly glided by the pavilion, not hailed or stopped by the gathering uldia who stared and pointed at them. The king looked steadfastly upriver, urging all speed on his barge captain.

They passed a large floating mat teeming with insects. "River ants," Maypong said.

The mat was composed of twigs and grasses, allowing, Maypong said, huge mounds of ants to scour the river surface for food. The ants were rather larger than Anton had ever seen, and he thought the river must feed them well.

It was an hour of steady poling, but they finally pulled up to shore, whereupon hoda stepped into the water to secure the barge with ropes.

Amid the flurry of activity, Anton asked Maypong, "What are the protocols, Chancellor?"

"Anton, you have asked to see this sunken place. Now you will see it."

"There are no taboos, or things I should avoid doing?" He meant to see it all, now that he was being given the chance. At her blank look, he added, "The site is not considered sacred?" He wished Nick were with him, to see with expert eyes what would be their first glimpse of Quadi leavings, aside from the satellites.

On the shore, hoda were cutting back the dense sprays of ferns next to the river, to allow passage on foot into the interior.

"We have said so before, Anton. The Quadi left us, long ago. But we do not raise up creatures to be objects of too much veneration, as the human custom is."

Worship. Gods. These were words she might have used, but didn't, there being none for these concepts in her language.

Vidori had already debarked, and was calling for Anton to join him on the shore.

He and Maypong did so, and they began a slow trek into the forest, the viven all following in a single line, stepping through thick mud but unconscious of the damage it did to brocaded boots. It was an outing, and their voices carried into the jungle, joining with the chatter of birds and hum of insects.

Once past the copious vegetation near the shore, they

made their way with less effort into the deep shade of the canopy. Like Earth's tropical forests, the Olagong harbored abundant species of trees, and they loomed tall, reaching for the sun.

Vidori led the group, just behind several large hoda who cleared away any obstacles. He turned slightly to Anton as he walked. "It is not far. The Quadi site is where the riverbank used to be, in ancient times."

"I thank you, rahi, for presenting these ruins. I take it as a special favor."

"Yes, Anton. I would have you understand we do not hide messages. If there are things the Olagong hides, it hides them from us all." He stepped over a fallen log. "Your air barges that always fly looking for things . . . they will have shown this as well, thankfully."

Anton masked his surprise. He had known that the king possessed telescopes. Apparently he used them to great advantage.

They hiked in silence for a time. The architectural summit of the forest, hidden visually, registered its populations by a cacophony of sound and the tremblings of the understory. A bird swooped into the darkened glade around them. As it lit on a branch, Anton thought it looked like a kingfisher, but as it turned its profile it revealed deep serrated edges along its beak. Similar, but different.

Joon's phrase did haunt him.

Now the ruins were in front of them. One moment there was only jungle, and then Anton saw slumping stone walls, nearly obscured by vines and roots. It was a ruin of large proportion, partly submerged in the muck of the clearing. His eyes tried to match it to what he'd glimpsed of Oleel's pavilion, said to be a replica. Yes, there were the same pillars, and their sizes did seem commensurate.

The roof was collapsed into the footprint of the building. Out of the center grew a gigantic tree, its muscular roots spreading in all directions, clasping the ruin in a woody embrace. The roots followed the form of the collapsed blocks of stone, in a solid flow of wood.

Viven began to pick their way through the pile of stones, and soon Dassa were exploring with as much curiosity as Anton. With Maypong at his side, Anton climbed through the jumble.

Underwater half of the year, this site lacked dense vegetation. Yet the river had leached and scoured it, leaving nothing but lumps where hewn stone had been. It was melting away. The Quadi had chosen an unfortunate building material: limestone.

Maypong sensed his disappointment. "You hoped it would be full of Quadi things."

Quadi things. Or Quadi meaning. But here was an edifice long erased. "I didn't know what it would be, Maypong-rah. I didn't think it would be so ravaged."

He bent down to inspect a fragment of wall. Something had been etched into it. Using one finger, he traced the pictograph—for that is what it was. The tracings in the king's archives had captured some of these drawings hundreds of years ago, perhaps thousands of years ago, before the river had carried the renderings away, a molecule at a time. He pocketed the fragment, for Zhen to analyze later.

Maypong said, "The first of the Dassa people drew these things. To record what they experienced."

Yes, Anton had seen those pictographs, of boats, jungle, and animals. And one fragment had shown what looked like hands: appendages that had six digits, two thumbs—clearly, two opposable thumbs. But that was the only surviving drawing of the Quadi form.

As Anton continued to search, the viven grew bored, and hoda brought out packages from the barge. Vidori's retinue lounged on fallen pillars and slabs of stone and took a leisurely meal.

After a time, Anton found himself sitting on a collapsed section of roof. Maypong sat beside him quietly, honoring his subdued mood.

"It doesn't make sense," Anton said.

"What does not, Anton?"

He picked up a shard of stone, crumbling it between his fingers. "The Quadi picked the worst possible building material. I'll bet they had a lot of choices." An understatement, surely, for a race that could *build* humans.

Maypong nodded. "Metal is best. But the mines are far away, and transport is always difficult."

He watched as a tree branch wiggled nearby. It was not a branch, however, but a snake hanging down, secured to a branch by its thicker back end. It was extremely long. Then, snapping its body toward a passing bird, it unhinged its jaw, caught its prey, and began swallowing it alive. Palace-born, Maypong seemed uneasy around the reptile, and they climbed down from their perch.

Anton murmured, half to himself, "It's as though they wished to remain unknown." He helped Maypong negotiate through a jumble of rocks, and their hands gripped for a moment. She smiled. He looked at her, thinking that she was very beautiful, and that he hadn't much noticed before.

"I think that is true, Anton. They left us nothing of themselves." She led him toward the place where the king was sitting. "If they had left many things, perhaps we would have made them revered beings. Instead of treasuring, as we do, the Olagong."

Revered beings. Perhaps the Quadi did not wish to become gods. It was true that there were some among the *Restoration* crew who thought it unnatural that the Dassa had no religion, but Anton thought the Dassa simply had their own way of revering the world.

Up ahead he saw that the king was talking to a group that had just emerged from the forest.

When Maypong and Anton joined Vidori, they were facing a contingent of uldia.

Leading them was an uldia of perhaps middle age—by the iron-gray hair wound tight on her head. By her sheer size and demeanor Anton thought he knew who it was: the chief of the uldia, Joon's uldia, and the king's nemesis.

Maypong began pulling on Anton, urging him into the background. Anton whispered to her, "Leave off, Maypong-rah. She and I would have to meet sometime."

Maypong looked at him. "You would rather not."

Vidori noticed Anton then, and gestured him forward. "I was just explaining to the Second Dassa your curiosity for this place, Anton. But she does prefer that we not linger." He looked to Shim. "That being the case, we must wind our way back to the river." Shim started to herd the viven down the path, but Oleel's voice stopped her.

"Oh this, then, is the visitor who demands to go here and there, without regard to whose land may be damaged." She wore a silver gown, hanging loose from her shoulders.

Vidori remained silent, making it necessary for Anton to answer. Maypong rushed in with, "My lord regrets any offense. Being a stranger, he may be excused at times."

Oleel turned to face Maypong. "Does your lord have a tongue?" Her face was unlined, but lacking the Dassa beauty, traded for heft and strength.

Maypong produced a smile that looked chipped out of rock. The viven stood like flamingos, waiting for something. Waiting, perhaps, for Oleel to go away, for the king to be delivered from this circumstance.

"I have a tongue, Lady," Anton said. "My people *keep* their tongues, although we do not always know what to say."

Vidori smiled the slightest bit. "I know what to say." He turned to Oleel. "I do beg your pardon, Lady. We will leave the ancient site to your care. It was full of mud, and has ruined a perfectly good pair of boots. But that is no one's fault but my own."

Oleel's deep voice answered him. "They are hoda, your visitors. Who keep their tongues. That is what is troubling, of course. Not boots."

"Yes, but it does not signify, since he can do no harm," Vidori said. "Anton is as empty of guile as the river."

Oleel smiled, showing teeth. "You are a poet, Vidori-rah."

"I am a soldier."

"Better to stay with arms than similes."

"When I can, I do."

"As to there being no harm, perhaps you did not know, Vidori-rah, being concerned with boots, that the visitor whom you call Sen is in a troubling state." At Vidori's quirked eyebrow, she continued, "Oh yes, we have heard that Sen is bearing inside her a human spawn."

Vidori's face darkened. "I do not think so, rahi."

Maypong whispered to Anton, "This is so?"

Anton thought Oleel was lying. He stepped forward. "Vidori-rah, this is not the case."

The viven around them were reacting with shocked looks and murmuring. Someone said, "Bearing? The creature bears?"

Oleel's voice rose above theirs. "Yes, you will see her stomach distend, and the thing will swell inside her, greedy for blood, making her sick. Somehow, the spawn will get outside. I do not speculate on how this happens, thankfully." She turned to the king. "It will be your problem when it occurs, I believe."

Anton was growing angrier, both at the lie and at Oleel's terrible description of pregnancy. But he had no time to argue with the woman, for Shim was propelling them down the path, herding the viven, and trying to change the topic, all at once.

Vidori was saying his good-byes, leaving the clot of uldia behind.

The group tromped back to the river, less carefree than they were on the hike in.

"She is determined to be my enemy," Anton said.

Maypong said, "Yes, because she is afraid of you. Because if it is proper to bear children of one's body, there is no need for the variums and the uldia." She lowered her voice. "But are you sure the thing about Sen is not true?"

He snapped at her, "No, damn it, it's not. No one is pregnant in my crew, on the ship or on the ground."

She seemed mollified by his answer. But Anton thought the damage had already been done. Just the rumor of a pregnancy was a very effective reminder to the Dassa that the humans were extremely different from them. And extremely repulsive.

From the looks the viven were casting him, he thought that any good impression he might have made on them today was ruined by Oleel.

Ruins, indeed.

SIX

Under a morning sun already molten, Samwan wel-comed Bailey at her dock. The mistress was dressed for la-bor, in simple pants and jacket, but even these were fine. Samwan was one of the lucky ones: a firstborn child who inherited an islet from her landed mother or father.

"Mistress Samwan," Bailey said as she relinquished her skiff to a hoda, "you look wonderful."

Samwan smiled. "Oh Bailey, one is dressed for labor." As she led Bailey into the compound, women waved—Samwan's half-sisters and full sisters, aunts, grandmothers. The compound filled with a chorus of Bailey's name, the human name without t's, k's, or, heaven forbid, zh's.

The grounds were baked hard, though the rainy season was only one week past. Under her hat, Bailey squinted into the glare of the day, wishing for sunglasses. Perhaps she would put the concept out and see what the industrious hoda might devise.

Amidst darting children, the yard teemed with work as women dug trenches to rebury ceramic water pipes ex-posed by the erosions of the river. In addition, Samwan was reconstructing her generator hut, where a new engine was being installed, driven by her household's hydrowheels in the Puldar, here in this land where people had no concept of public utilities.

As they approached the generator hut, Samwan cried out to one of the hoda workers. Frowning, she climbed a ladder, talking so fast Bailey couldn't keep up, but clearly showing the laborer how things should be done. Leaving Samwan to her construction project, Bailey wandered off, having grown more accepted in the compound, and hoping to see all sides of things, even things the Dassa did not wish seen—because of course everyone had something to hide. You didn't live to be seventy-eight without knowing that.

Proper Dassa and hoda alike worked in the long morning shadows of the huts or played with the dozens of children, here in this world of women's compounds and shared child-raising. Because so many female relatives chose to household with Samwan, the compound's allocation from the judipon was extensive, both in goods and slaves. Children nestled in hoda laps and mothers' laps, or rushed about in small gangs. Like the boys, the girls were lavishly tended, but unlike the boys, girls grew up and toward their sharply defined fates: to become proper Dassa or hoda. Bailey turned from those thoughts. It made her like Samwan less.

But every child here looked plump and healthy. Nick said that the adult-rich environment fostered a thriving, cooperative, child-rearing culture. Even the nonbreeding adults shared child-care duties, relegating kinship to a minor consideration. So Nick said, debriefing Bailey after each of her excursions, all the while resenting her freedom of movement, chafing at the restrictions the palace placed upon him. And then, yesterday, Anton had left Nick out of the trip to the ruins . . .

She passed two hoda who were caressing each other's arms, perhaps applying a lotion or salve—no, hands were straying under tunics and whatnot. In broad daylight. And worse, beside them two youngsters no more than five years old were mimicking them. Bailey turned away, appalled. She hoped that children's skin was not easily aroused. But then, why not really? They weren't human.

Toward the perimeter of the compound, Bailey found herself gazing at a piece of folk art called a *wallishen,* a "picture of one moment." It was one of those miniature stages that sprouted like altars in the compounds. Crouching down, Bailey saw stairs in front, replicating the entrance to the king's pavilion. And there, amidst the columns of the royal river room, were the viven, all dressed in robes of finest cloth, despite their diminutive size.

On the stage, one figure was dressed in black and gray, in fine brocade. That would be Vidori, of course. This figure knelt before a doll dressed in green, with black hair. Its face was a stark, unflattering white, and even in miniature, its expression was subtle and cruel, nothing like Anton Prados. On the steps of the river room were two dolls dressed in green with their heads removed.

Bailey stood, smoothing her clothes. A nasty little drama, so out of place in this tidy and friendly compound. If it *was* tidy and friendly . . .

She continued her rounds, feeling less buoyant. From the shade of a small hut came a sound. Something startling, almost improper. A sung melody.

An old hoda sat on a small riser, those ubiquitous stools that hung from pegs when not in use. She was crooning to an infant in her arms, spinning out a wordless hum, primitive and artless, perhaps, but arresting. Bailey hadn't prepared herself for this, least of all from the silent hoda. She hadn't heard music for three years. On the ship, when the crew played their appalling music in her presence, she retreated to privacy.

The hoda stopped her humming.

"Please continue," Bailey said, hoping to hear more. The old woman's fingers formed a response that looked like, *My pardon* or *Many pardons.* Bailey hadn't quite got the knack of looking at hands.

Samwan was at her side. "Oh, Bailey, please pardon us." Samwan's smile fell off her face as she glared at the hoda. The humming stopped. "This hoda is vulgar, naturally. Thankfully, you do not have to listen."

"I was enjoying it, Samwan-rah."

"Oh, Bailey, you're making a joke."

"Actually, I'm not." But to forestall further trouble for the hoda, Bailey turned away from her toward the shed under construction. "Samwan-rah, how is the new engine coming along?" The Dassa called all mechanical things *engines*. They would add new words, no doubt, as their nascent technology demanded it.

"Slowly, Bailey. The palace promised me an engineer today. But perhaps he is sleeping late."

Bailey knew the palace was the center for engineering. Dassa society parceled out the disciplines to the Three: the king oversaw engineering, astronomy, and history; the uldia chemistry, surgery, and biology; and the judipon numeration, dreamaturgy, and law. These disciplines in turn fit into the larger division of the realms, where the king was the guardian of the river and borders, the uldia presided over birthing, and the judipon oversaw society and wealth. There were missing disciplines. The geosciences seemed not to occur to the Dassa. Maps of the region and the world were poor to nonexistent. The only lands that mattered were those of the Olagong—where the fulva grew, and the variums thrived. Nowhere else so easily supported life. The latitude of the world in which the weather was conducive to the fulva was a narrow one.

Alone once again, Bailey felt the sun crushing down upon her, despite the shelter of her wide-brimmed hat. Near the perimeter of the compound, she was drawn toward a frondy wall of low-growing palms, with its promise of shade.

A path led into the thick underbrush, where the sweat on her skin immediately congealed. Breath came more easily. Branches rustled above, evidence of that canopy highway used by small mammals, some of whom never came to ground level, she'd heard.

She entered a tended field where the path was built up by layers of canes and woody stems. The byway was above the level of the plantings, the staple langva, an unusual, ruddy-hued plant with edible tubers and leaves. Hoda labor here was supplemented by the efforts of proper Dassa, both men and women, for the hoda population was not large enough to give the fields over entirely to slave labor. The hoda's primary task was directed to the most precious crop of the Dassa: their children.

Smiling and waving at field-workers, who murmured her name as she passed, she took a side path. The temperature was at least twenty degrees cooler in the deep shade. Up ahead was a fallen tree limb that would serve as a chair. It was quiet here, and shielded from the langva field by a line of trees. Bailey rested. A deep sigh came up through her body.

She hadn't realized until this moment that she was happy here, in this land of rivers and huts. Unaccustomed as she was to the outdoors, to forests, the beauty of it made her feel like singing.

Perhaps just one little song. After all, there was no one to hear. She opened her mouth. A few notes came out, and faded into the lush green foliage. Ah, Mozart. She began again. Stopped. Then she let it come out, a song she had sung many times, in an earlier age. The haunting "Vedrai, carino," from *Don Giovanni*.

Bailey held her throat. The gesture stopped her song. This was not what she should be doing. But wasn't it fine to spill notes into the air? And such notes: her beloved Mozart. She stood up, relaxing her diaphragm. She sang louder, oh, yes, *crescendo. Con bravura.*

Doloroso. The notes faded.

A green silence descended. She had forgotten her vow. The vow was important; it was penance.

She turned, hearing a noise. Several hoda were peering

at her from the bushes, their bald heads looking like the polished gourds of some strange tree. They wanted to hear. By their eyes they did want to hear. It was a group of a half-dozen hoda. An audience . . .

And so she sang again, for these women, these girls, remembering how far more satisfying it was to sing for someone other than yourself. She looked into the rapt faces of her audience. Some of them were so young. Like Remy, having died young. Her daughter. Or was it her sister?

Oh my girl, it is with your voice that I sing. But it's because of your voice that I must not sing . . .

Her voice trailed off. It was all so confusing. Standing, she said to them, "I don't sing." What a ridiculous thing to say, when she had just done that very thing. They kept gazing at her with those looks of surprise and admiration. "Please," she murmured, brushing the dust from her slacks, "please just go away. I'm terribly sorry, but I don't sing anymore." A mistake had been made. Worse, there were witnesses.

The hoda began moving forward, out of the trees, reassembling closer to her, waiting for another song. She waved them off, charging through the barrier of women, rushing down the path, away from them.

Those hoda with the enthralled expressions. People were so quick to admire, to confer celebrity. She had had enough—more than enough—admiration. One should have to earn such a thing. And she *would* earn it. It was what her whole mission was for. To do the one good thing.

If people would just leave her alone to get on with it.

Anton and Nick wound their way through the inner compound and across the east bridge over the inlet. Soldiers were moving in the palace, deploying to the border, to meet a Vol incursion. The king was leading the troops, as he did occasionally.

At the entrance to the baths, they found the communal

room empty. Nick and Anton judged that this time of the morning was the best time to clean up, when most Dassa were attending to their morning duty of the variums. The vaulted room held a large ceramic-lined pool with steps into the bath waters. Along the sides lay risers for sitting, and wooden scrapers to cleanse the skin.

Anton ditched his clothes and walked into the pool. The pipes feeding the bath passed over fragrant slabs of wood, infusing the room with a sandalwood scent. He submerged and came up streaming.

Nick sat on the edge of the pool, feet in the water. "She could have given us advance notice." He was still smarting over yesterday, when the king's barge left without him, and he somehow blamed Maypong for it.

Anton wiped the water from his hair. "I've said, Nick, that she didn't know." He looked at Nick directly. "And neither did I."

Nick's face flickered with reflected light from the bath. It was a face that had once been open to him, and too often now was flat or frowning. Nick's missing out on the trip to the Quadi ruins had formed a wedge between them. There'd been no time to find him as the party set out. Nick knew that, but it made no difference to him. Meanwhile, Zhen had dated the shards of rock at 10,500 years old, placing the Quadi intervention, if that's what it was, in the time frame of the Dark Cloud's passage through Earth's system.

But they had more to worry about than the ruins. The ship reported three more crew stricken with the new virus. So far, they were keeping them transfused, keeping them hydrated. And trying new serums. Which the pathogens easily mastered . . .

"I've been thinking about Homish," Nick said.

"The chief judipon," Anton said. "He's old and infirm, according to Vidori." Anton picked up a scraper lying on the pool's edge and began scraping his arms.

"Maybe old, but still powerful. We should give him some respect."

Anton waved the notion away. "Vidori has already said no to this, Lieutenant."

Nick bit the side of his cheek. "Of course he has. It's how he keeps things out of balance. The whole Olagong depends on the Three being equal. Homish is old and decrepit, time to be replaced. But Vidori won't allow the judipon to choose a new chief." He kicked at the water. "I've been investigating. It's widely known. Only the king can approve when a chief—of the other two powers—can be deposed. It adds stability. Vidori wants a weak judipon. That way his only obstacle to consolidation is Oleel."

Anton stopped scraping, trying to deal with this idea that Nick would not let go of, his theory of Vidori as a tyrant. "Keep your eye on our goals, Nick. In Vidori we have at least one powerful ally. Offend him, and we might have none."

But Nick was relentless. "But by befriending others, we could hedge our bets. Pay a call on Homish—make it clear where we stand."

"But it's *not* where we stand." They eyed each other, having come to the same chasm as before when Nick had been keen on reaching out to Oleel.

Nick said, "The judipon hoard the radio technology; they may know something."

"They don't hoard it. Radio is new to these people, that's all." The judipon used radio like a more reliable telephone, communicating tithe delivery times up and down the rivers so that the compounds would be ready to receive them. The broadcasts that the ship had picked up from space had been heavily laced with manifests, dates, and accounting details. The ship's language programs had pieced together a working vocabulary from these scraps, but it had been time-consuming. The judipon were no wizards of technology.

Anton went on, "I don't think anyone here is hiding information." He ignored Nick's little smile. "We have to get out and investigate, that's all. The drone has sent back visuals of an extensive pathway system in the uplands. That's where we'll go next."

"We could spend forever poking around, Captain. There's the whole planet. How many of us will be left in a week, in a month?"

It was the same question they were all asking themselves.

A rustle drew their attention. Both men looked up.

It was the Lady Joon. She stood framed in the morning sunshine of an open screen, accompanied by her chancellor, Gitam. "Oh," she exclaimed. "I did wonder why the bath was so silent."

She and Gitam approached the edge of the bath. Joon was dressed in an elaborate robe of pale blue with silver filigree.

Anton began moving toward the pool steps. "We will leave the baths for you, Lady. Pardon us."

Joon laughed, holding Anton's gaze. "No, but Nick may leave."

Nick exchanged glances with Anton. Joon was taking command of the baths, as was clear when Gitam came forward with Nick's clothes and a large drying cloth.

"You're on your own, Captain," Nick said. He hurriedly dressed, and then began backing up as Joon herded him out of the room with the skill of a sheepdog.

Anton was moving to get out of the bath, but Gitam blocked his way up the stairs.

Standing at the entryway, Nick said, "Will you be needing anything else, Captain? From me?" he added, with a smirk.

"No," Anton managed to say.

As Nick left, Joon breathed a satisfied sigh. "Anton," she said. "Now we have leisure to have conversation. Would you allow me to have conversation?"

He didn't think he should say no. And she was blocking the stairs. The moment stretched out, and neither of them moved. The sound of running water from the many pipes was the only other sound besides the distant chatter of birds in the trees outside.

Joon murmured, "I hope you will pardon that I have stumbled upon your luxury of private bathing."

Anton doubted that she had stumbled in here. "I will dress and we can talk, Lady," he said.

She stepped closer to the water's edge. "So we can be equal, as to being dressed or not? Is that the human convention?"

"Yes."

"Hmm. Then Gitam," she said, turning to her aide, "kindly remove this gown."

Gitam came forward and got busy at the fasteners in back of Joon's gown. For all the elaborations of her dress, it was quickly shed, and soon lay in a pile at Joon's feet. She stepped out, quite naked.

Her body commanded his attention. So much for Zhen's theory that the Dassa women had underdeveloped secondary sexual characteristics as a result of not bearing children. Joon was full-figured, superbly conditioned. Breathtaking.

"Now we are equal," Joon said. "Are we not?"

Anton tried to summon a response. Nothing came immediately to mind. There was nothing, in fact, on his mind but Joon standing naked.

"Equality," Joon said, "is something that I have thought on. It is what you have so much of, in your distant home, is it not?" She descended the steps until the water came up to her thighs. "Where you have no slaves, no removing of tongues."

"That is so," Anton said, watching the water level move up her body, trying to remember what Maypong had told him about male-female sexual relations. Not that he needed to know, he told himself. She was being friendly. It was only a bath, usually a quite communal event. But somehow, he doubted that anything communal was on her mind.

He summoned to mind: Dassa did not have . . . conventional sex. There was no penetration, for one thing. Not usually. This was considered a degenerate practice. But Maypong described a great variety of other ways of achieving "sexual closeness." Anton thought her lectures rather more detailed than the mission required, but Maypong could not be diverted from revealing the things she deemed it necessary he know in order to become civilized.

Joon dipped into the water, swimming to the middle of the expansive bath, keeping her head above water, not disturbing her hair. "Have you no high and low among humans, Captain?"

"We have rich and poor. But not a system to keep them so." He watched her deft strokes against the water, her dark arms flashing like burnished fish.

She swam back to him and sat on the steps, submerged to her shoulders. "Relax with me here, Anton," she said, noting his discomfort. "Soon enough, when my father returns, the palace will fill with soldiers. There is so little leisure to become friends." She looked up at him, and the middle of her brow furrowed. "Unless you do not wish to become friends?"

"Lady, I . . ."

Calmly, she waited, completely at ease, making him feel as if he was making something out of nothing, causing her concern for no reason.

He managed to say, "I don't know what you mean by *friends*. Friends do not bathe together."

"Hmm. But enemies do?"

He didn't bother to answer. She would have her way, and perhaps it would be merely a chance to talk of rich and poor, slaves and freedom.

The water shimmered around her, distorting the image of her body in its depths, but not enough to cloak its beauty.

"Tell me of Erth, Captain. I know nothing except of the Olagong, which I will one day hold in my protection. But all around me are enemies, the Vol and others. My education is incomplete. Compared to yours."

"What do you wish to know?"

"You have strange strengths and odd weakness. No slaves, but little pri."

She thought the absence of slaves was a strength. Perhaps her generation had more liberal ideas, certainly more liberal than Vidori's. He wondered what kind of queen she would be, when her time came. He would have liked to be here to see.

"On Earth, in my father's compound," Anton said, "we had no slaves, but my father left those people to starve who became stricken with illness . . . with lack of pri."

"You did not approve."

"No." He glanced up. They were alone. Gitam had left.

Joon murmured, "It is difficult to go against one's own powerful father." Her voice had a strange clarity here in this large pool.

"Yes, Lady."

She turned to him, stretching her legs along the submerged step. "Sometimes it is necessary to have different opinions than one's powerful father."

"Sometimes." It was strange to have such a discussion in a bath. It was all strange. He had a fancy to unhook her hair. He wondered if it came undone as simply as her robe. There were combs and twists, all very complicated.

Joon lay stretched out upon the stair, her legs almost but not quite touching him. "Lately I have been thinking that it is time for the hoda to be brought higher. In human ways. For the sake of equality. Would you agree, Captain?"

"Yes." She had finally asked a question he was sure about.

She smiled, keeping her lips together, but every expression was magnified on this woman of such calm demeanor. "Then we have a satisfying end to our conversation, yes?"

"If you say so, Lady."

"No, you must say so, Anton." She moved her legs aside, into the deeper water, gazing out into the middle, waiting for him.

What were they talking about? Anton had entirely lost track.

She kicked her feet under the water, causing ripples to course over Anton and her.

She was waiting for him. Waiting for him to say something, to do something. Her waiting was a powerful inducement. She left all the time in the world for him to say or do. He moved to her, as though commanded. He reached out, touching her face, turning her chin toward him.

"I say so," Anton said.

She moved into his arms, kneeling on the steps. He felt her breasts against his chest. Her piled-up hair must come down. He reached into it, plucking out the pins and combs. Anton felt her hair come down, surrounding them in a canopy. One of her combs floated beside them like a fabulous miniature skiff.

Joon was trembling as he touched her, her head thrown back onto the lip of the basin, her throat exposed. He caressed her neck. She reached for him under the water, and his hands roamed over her skin, slick and warm. Maypong's voice nagged at him. What was he supposed to do and not do? He ran his hand down her arms, and she arched her back and neck, causing her hair to trail into the water.

When he paused, she took his hand and stroked her shoulders with it, teaching him the extraordinary ways of her body, the skin that she kept so carefully covered, the body that hummed to his touch. And though he wasn't Dassa, she began to teach him the ways of his own skin.

She whispered, "Is it better to be cordial, Captain?"

"Yes," he said, pushing her back against the stairs, where her hair spread like ink through the water, curling around his arms.

He floated above her. She encircled him with her long legs, pulling him toward her. This course of things was taboo. But her heels pressed into his back, pulling him down. She couldn't be making a mistake, so deliberate she was. He pushed away from her for a moment, but her grip would not release him. And in truth, he hadn't tried very much to evade her.

His last thought before he entered her was: *Not her kind of sex.* But the heels in his back were insistent.

Mistress Aramee confronted Gilar, holding the offending discovery in her hand.

"Gilar, what is this that I have found?" Aramee stood beside a hot brazier, keeping her distance from the heat.

Beside Gilar, also kneeling, was Nuan, the chief hoda. Nuan poked at Gilar, commanding her to answer.

>My hair, Aramee-rah.<

Aramee glanced at Nuan, inviting another sharp poke to Gilar's ribs.

"No, Gilar," Aramee said, "this would not be your hair, thankfully."

Gilar glanced up at the mistress. Aramee knew very well it was Gilar's hair. Why would Gilar keep anyone else's hair? She had only been one week in servitude, not enough time for her hair to dissolve under the cleansing broth, so Nuan had shaved it off. Gilar had scooped up a thick lock of hair and hid it. Not well, apparently.

"What is this that I have found, then, Gilar?"

Nuan turned to Gilar. >You will say that it is the hair of a Dassa whom you no longer are.<

Not wanting a beating, Gilar signed, >It is someone's hair.<

They had taken everything from her: her hair, her clothes, her mother, her tongue. Truly, she was no longer a proper Dassa. But Gilar knew that she could never be silent and submissive, like the unctuous Nuan, like the relentlessly cheerful Bahn. She had figured out that some hoda were above others.

Some hoda commanded air ships and went where they pleased. These were called humans.

That was where the terrible mistake had been made,

that they thought Gilar was the other kind of hoda. There were high hoda and low hoda. Gilar knew which kind she was.

Satisfied that Gilar had repented, Aramee turned to leave. As she did, she dropped the offending lump of hair onto the brazier, filling the hut with an acrid smoke.

Gilar watched the strands curl and turn incandescent on the coals, keeping their shape for a moment before collapsing of too much brightness.

If the mistress hoped to intimidate Gilar, she had failed. That was the thing about hair.

It could grow back.

The hoda filled their pails with excrement at the sludge pit, humming and vocalizing as they worked, making jarring, vulgar sounds. At their sides, Gilar shoveled the stinking loads into her pail.

Bahn signed to her, >Fill the pail to the brim, Gilar, so we make better progress.<

Gilar looked at her, wondering how she could see buckets of excrement as progress. But she threw another dollop in her pail.

As they headed to the fields, Gilar hoped that—burdened by her pail—Bahn would shut up, but she managed to carry it in the crook of her arm and still harangue Gilar. She constantly chatted of the palace. Like most low hoda, she was dazzled by the nobles, always prating on about this noble or that one.

Gilar tuned out all this gossip of Dassa, who no longer held any interest for her. But when Bahn had news of the humans, Gilar paid attention.

Maypong had been appointed chancellor to the chief of the great air vessel. If Gilar were still of the palace, she would have seen this captain every day and talked of star barges with him, and they would have become friends, and then Gilar would have gone to Erth with the humans when they left, when they had found what they came for.

They had come, they said, on a great air barge that traveled the skies between stars, and they had come for help, being without pri, to the world of pri. But no one in the Olagong, not even Oleel, knew how to give pri to those without it.

This morning Bahn was full of the story of the human Bailey, of the pri of many years, and how she had sung in front of hoda, without shame. Many of the hoda at Aramee's compound gossiped about this, saying the humans were like them, being born to bear and liking to sing. Kea, walking in front on the path, had been one of those who heard Bailey sing. Now she was carrying her pail of dung and humming a new song.

Gilar dumped her bucket in the planting trench, and turned to go.

>Smooth out the sludge with the hoe,< Bahn signed. >It will ripen better if the air circulates freely through it.<

Gilar set her bucket down and eyed Bahn, the low hoda. >Why do you care how much air the dung gets?<

Bahn smiled. >Oh Gilar, the air cures the sludge, making it—<

Gilar interrupted. >But do you care for turds so much?<

Bahn raised her hands to reply, then dropped them, confused.

>If you want to be my associate, learn to talk of something less vulgar.< Gilar picked up her bucket and turned in the direction of the sludge pit. Bahn grabbed onto her arm, jerking it, and then dropped her hand away quickly so as not to arouse Gilar.

Bahn was standing on the path eye to eye with her. She signed, >Know, my sister, that I am assigned to your training. I would be tending the babes this morning, except that you must carry turds for a punishment. No one else wanted to train you, but I took pity on you.<

Gilar looked at her pail, stained with excrement. In an

awful, lucid moment she understood how she was perceived. They didn't regard her palace upbringing. They didn't think her fine or special. Even her own uldia no longer acknowledged her. She stood, bald-headed, on a path in the langva fields, carrying excrement. She looked just like Bahn. Just like all the slaves.

Turning from Bahn, Gilar walked swiftly back along the path. Tears gathered at her eyes; she blinked over and over to whip them away. How could she let Bahn's words cut her so? How could it matter what a low hoda thought?

Bahn was at her side, matching her stride, thankfully keeping quiet for once. Bahn didn't shame her by noticing her tears. But a hoda approaching from the opposite direction did notice. Meeting Gilar's eyes, she emitted a short bit of mewling song.

Turning to stare at the wretched hoda as the creature passed merrily along, Gilar thought she might hurl her pail at the woman.

Bahn urged Gilar off the path, into the undergrowth. >Do not,< Bahn signed.

>Do not what?<

>Do not anything.<

Gilar sat on the ground, holding herself rigid, holding herself back from flying at the hoda, flying at all of them, ripping pails from their hands, pushing them into the muck of the fields.

Bahn's hands moved. >That hoda said, "We cry with you, sister."<

Gilar signed, >That hoda said nothing to me.<

>She said, "We cry with you."<

Gilar looked back at the path. Hoda passed each other, nodding their greetings. Singing.

A long time passed as Gilar sat in the mud, with Bahn next to her. They watched the sun pierce the carmine trees and illumine the path now and then, as the wailing of the hoda stained the air in blotches.

Bahn hummed again. Then she interpreted. >I just said, "It is a language."<

>A language?<

Bahn hummed, then translated. >That is how you say, "Yes."<

Looking up at the path, Gilar began to see what no proper Dassa ever saw, that hoda were not so submissive as they seemed. That they had a secret language.

It was a vulgar language of tones. But it could be helpful to speak what the mistress could not understand.

Gilar signed to Bahn, >How do you sing, "I am human"?<

A tone came from Bahn.

And though Gilar had never in her life sung, never once, she opened her mouth and repeated Bahn's few notes.

Bahn regarded her with a sudden, close focus. >That was perfect, Gilar.<

Gilar sang it again.

>Perfect,< Bahn repeated. >You have tonal wisdom, my sister.<

But it was simple to copy Bahn, and the sound on her ears was not vulgar, but clear and sweet.

>Teach me another word.<

Bahn did, and then another. In the shade of the carmine trees, Bahn opened the realm of hoda song, and Gilar fled there.

SEVEN

The palace hydrologists and weather-mancers said that a storm was coming, and Nick believed it. The stupefying heat of the last few days could not go on without splitting open his head. He'd thought the pressure in his temples was the river stench, but now he suspected a weather front. They'd grown used to shipboard conditions; here, the weather staggered from one thing to the next, unsettling the body and the mind.

Inside the tent of the canoe, the heat nearly gagged him. Secrecy had its costs. "Hurry," he'd urged the hoda paddlers, but they kept their own rhythm.

He disliked this course of action: sneaking to the uldia pavilion, holding discourse with Oleel. It was insubordination, of course. Looking into Anton's face was the worst. Those black eyes knew him, but Anton said nothing. Damn, that the man made it necessary to lie and sneak. Damn, that Anton was so besotted by the king's daughter that every day he committed himself further to the king's cause. Even Bailey was starting to chafe. He'd heard them have words last night, when Bailey had accused Anton of badly judged entanglements. And now Strahan was dead.

God. Had they come thirty light-years just to die on this drowned world? Had they bucked their families, their friends, the opinion of Earth, for nothing? A suicide mission, people had called it; Shaw's Folly. To answer the summons of an alien signal, when the universe had dealt the Earth nothing but disaster. And, some said, when alien intent lay behind the imminent demise of Earth.

Alien intent. Was the very universe against them? The outbreak on board the ship was another instance of diabolically bad luck. Despite the preflight prophylactic measures, the virulent bacteria had hid on board in the least expected place, right in the antiseptic solutions designed to kill them.

Nick was dripping wet. His temples throbbed with the sheer heat. So it was with relief that he recognized the slowing of the canoe, signaling a turn into the hidden stream of Oleel's pavilion.

As before, they helped him onto the dock, which was shadowed by a thick stand of river trees, cloaking this access from Amalang River traffic. It wasn't really a stream here, but a lagoon, with brackish water slapping against the dock pilings. As the hoda ushered Nick into the doorway, he saw that the mangrove tree that sat astride the end of the lagoon was not solid, but hollow, as a skiff passed out from under it. Behind the skiff, the hole closed up again . . . but there was not time to watch, for two uldia were waiting for him just inside, taking over from the hoda, who stayed to secure the boat. They led him into the cool granite passageways, with their welcome chill.

Oleel waited for him at the head of a ramp, and led him to an area of the compound new to him: a large room housing long tables with ceramic and glass containers. A stew of chemicals hung in the air.

"My pavilion of medicinals," Oleel said without preamble. "You are interested, Venning?" Her face had a gray tincture, augmented by her silver tunic, which she wore over a long skirt. A fitted jacket kept her arms covered.

"Quite wonderful," Nick said. "If you're offering a tour, I accept."

The laboratory was like nothing he'd seen in Lolo. Here was an ordered, collective endeavor, with uldia hunched over pestles and tubes, glancing up warily at him. Braziers heated vessels and ceramic columns, releasing vapors, while tangles of ceramic pipes wound their way between valves and tanks. From nearby he heard the shudder of generators.

"You are not the only ones with mechanics and scientific understanding, Venning. Never think so."

He didn't think so; they'd all seen the rudimentary phones, the water turbines, the lightning rods, showing knowledge of electricity and electromagnetism. But here there was evidence of applications never guessed at: ceramic microscopes, and hints of chemical processes, though he could not imagine what their products were.

He leaned for a moment against the casement of a window. The normally open format of rooms in Oleel's stone retreat were here covered with shutters. As he leaned, he accidentally elbowed open one of the shutters, which fell wide on its hinges. Nick turned, surprised at the movement, as the shutter now sprawled open to reveal the tops of the trees, and a short distance farther, rectangles of water, like small pools.

Through the treetop canopy came the distinct wail of a baby. Somewhere out there were the variums, where babies were birthed. Where swimming was guaranteed to be orgasmic.

But they preferred that he not look at it. An uldia approached, reaching past him and closing the shutter. As open as the Dassa were about sex, it was odd that they cared if he saw the pools.

Oleel was saying, "Did you think us simple river people, Venning? Without engines and science?"

"No, Lady, but we haven't seen a chemical laboratory like this."

"Oh yes, chemicals. Whatever is needed for our industry and our ministrations. All are produced here."

They walked down the length of the tables, looking at tube stills, sedimentation tanks, drying screens, flasks. He couldn't keep from saying, "I thought you said your pri was too strong for illness."

She walked ahead of him, her gray bun swollen behind her head like a tree bole. "Even those of strong pri may be stung by an insect, for which we have salves and irrigations. The hoda require broths, of course. The bereaved must have tonics of mood. And of course, the surgeries. Any Dassa may take cuts, here and there." She spoke, as always, without moving much of her mouth. It was as though she couldn't bear to speak to him, and begrudged the movement it took.

They paused to watch a pulse from an inlet valve push reddish liquid into a deep ceramic cup set over a brazier.

"That is the distillate of langva, Venning, purged of impurities. The correct fractionation is a difficult art, but the residue is a powerful medicinal. It is the essence of pri."

"*Langva?*" It was the reddish tuber, the Dassa food staple.

"This is the source of pri, the gift of the Olagong, to those entrusted with its care." She turned to look at him. "You have no langva on your world."

Nick thought there was nothing like it that he'd heard of. The attending uldia tipped the cup, spilling the contents onto a tray for cooling. Oleel was still gazing at him. *No langva.* She was trying to tell him something. There was a thought clamoring for his attention. He turned away, looking over the tops of the tables, toward the shuttered windows, toward the outside world, where Dassa did not sicken, where no one faltered for lack of pri.

Immunity. These people had bolstered immunity. Strong pri, indeed. Beside him, Oleel was a specimen of strength. She looked like she could pole a barge entirely by herself. But it was not about Oleel.

It was about langva. Finally, the thought came loose.

Perhaps, just perhaps, the message they pursued—the meaning of that message—was not what they had assumed. Perhaps the "genetic heritage" was heightened immunity to disease. That was what could be recovered here, in the distillate of this red tuber.

Oleel produced a smile; you had to pay attention to see that it *was* one. She said, "Did you think that the Vol coveted our lands for the variums alone?"

A rhetorical question. It sent him deeper into his own revelation. The Vol wanted pri; they wanted the lands where the langva thrived. It fit.

His mouth went quite dry. He looked at the lab in frank wonder. Had he found the secret, that obvious thing, that the Quadi thought they would so easily find? Langva. The Dassa diet was based on this tuber. They baked it, mashed it, rolled it into dough. And it made them the healthiest people he'd ever seen. The Quadi, foreseeing what would befall humanity, had designed a solution, had given it to the Dassa.

His disobedience, his hunch—it was all worth it. It was just possible that he'd cracked the entire problem wide open. Instead of facing discipline for insubordination, he'd receive the thanks of a grateful crew.

He wanted to ask her for a sample of the residue on the tray. But by the look on her face, he thought she would say no. She wasn't a woman to give things away. Even as he felt grateful for what she had just told him, he also understood she would use the reddish substance as a bargaining chip.

She was leading him from the hall. Out on her mezzanine, they paused at the edge, looking into the courtyard below. Away from the chemical fumes, the fresher air eased his headache. The trickle of water from the floor streams and waterfalls of the courtyard screened away all other sounds.

At his side, he could barely hear Oleel as she murmured, "Tell me about your captain."

Glancing at her, he saw how it was. This was her payment. He gets something, then she gets something.

"Do you respect him, for example?"

Nick paused, though he shouldn't have. She noticed, damn her. "Yes," he said. "He's an honest man. We're friends."

"Hmm. To be obedient, is it necessary to become friends?"

But, of course, Nick wasn't obedient. Perhaps he wasn't even any longer a friend.

Her voice came more insistent. "Anton Prados was palace-born, and you were not." She was gazing down at the simulation of the Olagong on the floor below.

Palace-born. Perhaps that summed it up. But he would hear no criticism of Anton from this woman. Nick responded, "Palace-born, but rejecting the ease of the palace. He left his father to his wealth, joined the military. A man of simple tastes."

"Rejected his father, his heritage."

"Rejected the parts that exploited others."

"Others such as?"

Nick wondered at her surge of curiosity. It was not a good trend, her interest in Anton. She was probing for his weaknesses. Well, if she looked hard enough, she'd find them. Probably her birth-water daughter, Joon, could tell her plenty about Anton's weaknesses.

"Others?" Oleel repeated.

"Lack of pri is a scourage. It spreads among us. Some—pavilions—send these people away, no matter their relation. Such as Anton's mother, and sister."

"They lost their pri."

"Yes. They were sent out to starve."

Oleel watched the water fall from the mezzanine to the pool in the courtyard floor. "So he favors outcasts, then."

Nick wouldn't have said so. He would have said that he himself had more the viewpoint of the underdog. He was the one who had come to the society of women. Although, now that he'd seen more of it, he couldn't say that they were underlings. Perhaps, in some ways, they controlled more than Vidori did.

"Tell me what else a friend knows about Captain Prados."

She was compelling him to give secrets, and condemning him for it at the same time. He was torn, but then Nick did answer Oleel's questions, telling her about Anton Prados, giving her what a friend knows about his captain.

It was a small price to pay, however. Because of his revelation, perhaps the *Restoration* could restore them after all, could bring home their salvation. Now that he thought about it, he wondered why they hadn't seen it before. It was because they took the message literally: *What you have lost.* They kept thinking: *Genetic diversity.*

Wrong.

Anton sat by a canal deep in the king's pavilion. Under the overarching canopy of trees, the water sluiced by, gray in the morning shadows. Through the trees, he could hear someone playing a reed flute, a haunting sound that under other circumstances might have been sweet.

"Oh, I have found him."

Anton looked up to find Maypong standing nearby with a hoda. She stooped for a moment, and he could see that a child was with her, perhaps ten years old. She bid him good-bye and sent him off with the hoda. Anton knew that Maypong's remaining two children stayed in the compound of her sister, in order that Maypong could serve the king, but she visited them, and sometimes slept there.

She moved into the little clearing and settled herself next to Anton on the close-clipped grass. Watching the trickle of water, she said, "I am sorry that"—she struggled to say Lieutenant Strahan's name—"your friend has died. It is a hard thing. So young."

"Thank you, Maypong-rah."

"How will you bury him?"

"In the sky."

"Ah," she said, frowning at this concept of burial in the air.

Anton thought about all the zippered shrouds they had committed to deep space over the last months. Each one had been a little gouge out of his flesh. And now Strahan. In eight days, a strong man taken down. And three others stricken with the infection were following him, fast.

He turned to her. Her eyes were very light brown. Against the yellow of her yellow tunic, she looked like a golden sylph. "Maypong-rah, I need you to help me." She continued to watch him. He knew it was her duty to help him, but that duty was overshadowed by her service to Vidori. "Help me get out of the king's protection. My people are dying."

"Where would you go, then, Anton?"

"Everywhere. To see the judipon. To an audience with Oleel. To explore the Olagong. But to do so with the king's—permission."

"So, you will look for what we have hidden from you." She gazed at him with reproach.

"No, what the Quadi have hidden. There's no time anymore, Maypong-rah."

"Even though you will be easier to kill outside the king's palace? Especially Zhen?"

Anton knew it was a risk. Zhen knew. "Yes."

They sat without speaking for a time. He was glad of her company, and that she'd shared the burden of his news with him. Somehow he had grown easy with the woman, despite their conflicts. Though he couldn't remember exactly when or how it had happened, she had replaced Nick as his confidante.

Maypong spoke, finally. "What will happen to your Erth, Anton? We are confused about what will happen to you."

He thought he knew who she meant by *we*, she probably reported to him frequently. Still, he thought she was more than what Nick said, a spy. "My people will die. We have been dying. We have no future."

"You need our pri."

"No, we need what we have lost. Although maybe it's pri, as you say."

Maypong kept her eyes on the rushing water as it began to enliven, struck silver from the morning sun just now cresting the pavilion rooftops. With the sun came a searing heat, even filtered through branches. But the barometer was falling, and rain coming.

Maypong said, "If you take the hoda from us, how will we live?"

"That is not an option, to take the hoda."

"Thankfully."

"We're not an army. Our ship is not large. We might like to seek hoda as partners, that's true. But it's not our answer by itself." He tried to get her to look at him. "Will you help us, Maypong-rah?"

She kept her eyes averted. "I am the least of the king's chancellors, Anton. But I will see what is possible." She spoke with a sadness in her tone. He wondered if she had not been the least of his chancellors, if the king would have spared Gilar, her daughter. Or if it made any difference to her.

"What is a daughter to the Dassa, Maypong-rah? How did you bear—what happened?"

As he feared, raising the subject had offended her. She pulled her legs closer and sat stiffly. She responded, "How did your father give up his daughter?"

That jolted him. How did she know that?

Maypong went on, "And his wife, as you term it—how did he give her up as well?" She fixed him with her golden stare. "To keep you from harm, perhaps?"

The words nicked him. Maybe what his father did was to prevent an epidemic. But he never wavered, never grieved.

"Do the Dassa cry, Maypong?"

She rose, but remained staring at the canal. "No, of course." The music of the flute stopped in mid-melody. "It would mean that her fate was for nothing, instead of for the

Olagong. You saw that hoda who came here with me? Who would care for the children, who would help us harvest our lands quickly, when the rivers recede? And if the Olagong is weakened, will the Vol come down the Sodesh?"

He hadn't meant for the discussion to become blaming. Strahan's death and Maypong's sympathy over it had created a moment when he thought certain things could be said. But some things could never be.

The hoda had returned. With her was Zhen.

"Sorry, Captain," Zhen said. "I've been looking for you."

He stood. "Something?" By the look on her face it was not good news.

"Yes, Webb was on the comm. We need to get back in touch with him."

Maypong said, "I will leave you, Anton."

She turned, but before she could walk away, he said, "How did you know about my father?"

Maypong turned to him. "Oh, Bailey, certainly. She thought that the story might help me to understand you."

He watched her leave in the company of the hoda and her child. One of three. Not including Gilar, of course.

As he walked back to the crew hut with Zhen, he said, "What did Webb have to report?"

"He wouldn't say without you being there."

"Ask Nick and Bailey to join us."

"I can't find them."

"We need Nick there." Anton didn't want Nick to be left out again, not if he could help it.

"He's been gone for hours."

Where would he go? "Did you check the king's archives?"

Zhen looked stony. "That was the first place I looked."

"Right." They crossed an arched bridge, then went up a ramp into the main pavilion. He saw how tired she was, her hair plastered against her head, with no thought for a comb.

"Zhen, you can take a break, you know." Even early this morning when they'd heard the news about Strahan, Zhen had preferred to work at her bench than to sit with the others and absorb the news together. She'd said she'd rather "work it out." Meaning, literally, *work*. It wasn't healthy. "You knew Strahan, too. You've watched a lot of good people die, Zhen. There's no shame in grief."

She opened a sliding screen to the science hut. "I don't do group grief, Captain."

She was nothing if not frank. As was the whole team. He'd heard *Frankly, Captain,* more than enough, usually followed by advice someone thought he needed. Bailey, Nick, Sergeant Webb—they all had plenty of advice. Only Zhen withheld. He rather liked her for it.

When they hailed the ship, Webb was waiting for them.

"Zhen and I are here, Sergeant Webb. Go ahead."

Webb's voice came through a soft background fizz: *I thought I should get to you right away, sir, about what's going on. We've been working on that satellite, one of the others that we brought in.* He paused.

Some of it's what we expected, and . . . some of it isn't. So the part that isn't, we've been working on it. And the computer program says that it's a language, but we can't decipher it. Not yet, anyway.

"Slow down now, Webb. What language are you talking about?"

That's just it, sir. We don't know. Back when we came into orbit, we jumped to some conclusions. We were so focused on the Message, we assumed that the satellites were all broadcasting the same thing. And then we found debris from some of the satellites that had been destroyed by meteorites, and we thought that the remaining three satellites were simply redundant mechanisms to supplant any lost devices. Wrong assumption. Static filled his long pause.

"Go on, Sergeant."

Sir, this one satellite is broadcasting a code. It's not noise, like we thought, not a deteriorated satellite at all. Corporal Rodriguez has been running the data through our language program. It's a code. But not the same as the code that we were picking up on

Earth all those years. And its tight-beamed into a different quadrant of space. It's not even our solar system, Captain. We think it's aimed at a star called Gamma Crux, two hundred twenty light-years away.

Zhen and Anton glanced at each other, but neither one spoke.

Captain, are you still there?

"Still here, Sergeant. Fairly stunned, that's all. What else have you got?"

Not very much. Rodriguez says if it's a language, it'll be tough to crack. We've got no clues to go on, no context. This is going to be a language that doesn't even have roots in Earth languages. With the Dassa language, we had a lot of variety of text to piece together. But with this stuff, well, the message is short. Also . . .

Anton and Zhen just waited. Webb was going to tell this in his own time. *. . . also, a quick analysis of the broadcasts from the other satellites suggests that the static—what we thought was static—may be aimed at other stars. Different content, if Rodriguez has it right.*

"So you're saying it's not just one language. Not just one star receiving the broadcasts."

That's it. There are two other broadcasts besides the ones to Gamma Crux and Earth. But we're still working on it. Things have been busy up here, Captain. The funeral . . .

"No need to explain, Sergeant. Understood. Thank you."

But sir? Why would they be calling other places? We're all just wondering about that.

Zhen sighed. Anton murmured to her, off mike, "Because Earth wasn't the only planet depleted by the Dark Cloud."

"Right," she said. "Not the only inhabited planet."

Anton said to Webb, "Maybe they're getting the same message we got, Sergeant. You want a wild-ass guess, that would be mine."

Mine too, Captain. Just wondered how crazy I was getting.

Only, what's down there, on planet, then? We can't even find our own stuff, not to mention . . . other worlds. What if it's all a lie?

"Even crazier, what if it's all true? But right now, Sergeant, we're just gathering the facts. Keep going."

After the radio communication, Zhen and Anton stood silently in the hut. She raised the screen to let in a breeze, and blessedly, one came, bearing with it the smell of muddy water and rotting leaves.

"What is this place?" Zhen asked.

His very question. What was Neshar? And next, Where was the promised information stored? It must be someplace the Quadi considered obvious. They built no temples to withstand the ages, no prominent obelisks to house the secrets of the Dark Cloud. They wished to remain in the background, perhaps for the sake of the Dassa culture, to allow the civilization to rise without relation to an alien and advanced culture.

But what was the obvious thing Anton was overlooking?

"Neshar is the repository," Anton said, answering Zhen's question. "It's the holding pond of the Quadi. It's all here. That's what I think."

Zhen stood looking out on the Puldar. "What if other beings come here, like we have?"

In frustration, Anton muttered, "Then they can bloody well help us look."

EIGHT

Gilar could smell the storm approaching. She breathed the hot, moist air as the baby in her arms fretted. Gilar rocked her, this babe of Aramee's.

Here in the nursery hut, a half-dozen hoda tended to the infants, laughing with and humming at them. Bahn held a fat two-year-old, bouncing him while the child giggled.

In the corner, an old hoda was singing of the lands of the Vol, where hoda might have real lives. The Vol inducted the tongueless into their army, where they were equal to Vol warriors.

Bahn, thinking her a troublemaker, argued, but good-naturedly, that such hoda would just become slaves to poorer masters. Still, the old hoda said, we can be warriors in that land, and warriors have respect.

If Nuan had been here, Gilar was certain, she wouldn't have allowed the slaves to speak of this, it being disrespectful to Aramee, and dangerous. For this reason, Gilar knew, no one here dared to mention the truly dark thing: that some hoda managed to avoid the contraceptive drink, and sought to gestate babies within themselves because the Vol rewarded any hoda who came to them bearing a future warrior. In the land where children gew poorly. Gilar fended off the thought that humans also bore children of their bodies. It was a price she would pay if she had to.

Rocking the baby in her lap, she thought of a place where she could be a person of consequence: Erth. Often, looking into the night sky, she searched for the star that the palace astronomers identified as the Erth-star. Near to this star was a world where hoda—high hoda—reigned.

A wondrous sound broke into Gilar's reverie. It was not a hoda song, but something entirely different. Kea was singing something without sense.

Gilar turned to Bahn. >What is this she is saying?< Gilar didn't know the song language very well yet, and sometimes signed to Bahn to ask for translations.

>Oh Gilar, she is not saying anything. This is Bailey's song, which Kea heard in the forest.<

The notes went up and down and up in a pleasing sequence, one that fit into the mind as a pattern. A marvelous pattern.

When the woman had finished, Gilar signed, >Sing it again, sister.< She had never called a hoda *sister*, and it surprised her that she did so now. But she knew very few words, and Bahn made sure she knew that one.

The hoda repeated the song of the human woman.

Then, unbidden by anyone, Gilar sang the pattern. The notes were very difficult, after what they had done to her tongue. In the weeks since that terrible day, Gilar had not put her fingers inside her mouth. It was as though if she never tried to touch it, she had no proof it was gone.

As she sang, everyone stopped what they were doing to stare at Gilar. Even the babe in her lap blinked in surprise. Some of Bailey's notes were very high for the other hoda, but Gilar held on, because the high register was where she liked the sounds best.

Old Kea looked surprised. >You sound like Bailey.<

A rush of pleasure passed through Gilar. In a moment

the group had turned to other subjects: chores, projects, children. But Gilar was still imagining the song.

Bahn sat close beside her. >You have tonal wisdom, indeed, sister.< Her smile was tender. >Let me hear your voice again.<

Exulting in this melody, Gilar began again. Kea joined in, correcting her pattern of notes.

Then Bahn put her hand on Gilar's arm. >The babe is content,< she signed, urging her to put the infant in its hammock. The other hoda noticed the arm-touch, smiling, as Bahn led Gilar into the shadows in the corner of the hut.

Gilar followed Bahn, because her heart had lifted with a new hope. It had been weeks since she had had any closeness. No one dared approach her, and her scent said, *Stay away.* Until now.

She snuggled next to Bahn. I am human, she hummed.

Bahn rested her hand on Gilar's wrist. Whatever you are, you are sweet to me. Her fingers rippled lightly on Gilar's skin, setting it tingling.

Turning her hand over, Gilar opened her palm, that cup of tender skin, and received Bahn's finger strokes.

She held back for a while, because it was said that humans loved only one other, and if she must pick only one, it wouldn't be Bahn. But then Gilar abandoned her judgments of Bahn, because she was hungry to belong to someone, to belong to everyone. So, she had to admit, despite her humanness, the rivers ran true in her, in the way of the Olagong.

A storm is coming, Bahn sang.

Gilar smiled. Then take off your clothes, Bahn, and receive it.

Bahn did so, lying naked, and received Gilar's hands, taking sarif, and giving it.

However, as soon as the storm of their bodies had passed through, Gilar's mind was thinking of other things. Of meeting Bailey. Of giving her the proof. So that when the star barge left, Gilar would be on it.

*   *   *

Bailey had paddled far beyond Samwan's compound. Lost in thought, she now found herself on the Sodesh, having navigated the choppy confluence with hardly a pang of worry. Because all her worry was now focused on the *Restoration*.

She had no destination, her only goal being to propel her skiff, to tire her arms. Dassa in boats waved to her, yielded to her in the river, yet she hardly saw them.

Phillip Strahan was only thirty-six years old. If it hadn't been for Bailey, he might have lived to be her age. The ship crew were weakened by radiation, were susceptible to new viruses which themselves were only strengthened by the radiation, able to mutate faster and faster. Zhen said it was more complicated than that, but Bailey was never one to let the facts cloud her judgment. She was responsible. She felt like hell.

Shaw's Folly, they had all said. And would she be the last one left alive, the only one on board standing upright to steer the ship home? It wouldn't surprise her detractors, the ones who thought the Message was dangerous, mocking the *Restoration* with its old lady sponsor.

Her arms were tired, and she had still to manage the trip back. How far had she come? It was mid-morning. Anton would be looking for her. She wiped the sweat from her brow where it collected under her hat brim.

Yes, Anton Prados would be shaking his head about how she was always going off on her own. Anton Prados, who cavorted in the baths. Old Captain Darrow would never have compromised his dignity, would never have let that woman get his clothes off. Even Nick was starting to doubt that Anton had it in him to be captain. And just why was it that *she'd* thought so? She had trouble remembering the logic of it.

Stacked clouds floated through the sky, bringing her skiff in and out of shade, sending stabs of sunlight into her eyes just when she'd adjusted to the shade. They said the weather was about to change. Good.

A boat was approaching, down the middle of the Sodesh, heading toward her, not relinquishing right-of-way. It was paddled by a hoda.

Just as the other skiff came almost even with her, the hoda executed a smart maneuver and turned her boat completely around. She was now heading upriver side by side with Bailey.

It was a young woman. Had she seen this girl before? Something about the eyes . . .

The girl began to sing.

Now here was a strange thing: Bailey thought she knew that melody. It couldn't be, but it sounded like Mozart.

Bailey lost her composure for a moment, staring at the hoda. Responding, the hoda broke into a dazzling smile. Well, Bailey had not meant to encourage the girl, but she was fairly astonished to hear Mozart sung in this place.

They paddled together for a time. People in passing skiffs noted them together, and turned to watch as the hoda attacked "Vedrai, carino" from *Don Giovanni*. She must have heard Bailey that day at Samwan's, but it was astonishing that she'd picked it up on one hearing, even if she did sing right through the rests. No, it was not well done. Still, the girl had a decent, if untrained, voice.

Now the hoda was missing the accidentals that come in the last section of the piece. Really, if one couldn't get it right, best not to sing in public. Bailey broke in, and sang it as it should be sung. She knew she shouldn't do it, but it was quite unbearable to hear Mozart done badly.

As Bailey sang, she avoided eye contact with the girl, who was watching her every movement as though stage-struck. They paddled into the shade of a vast cloud. The two skiffs sliced the water, the paddles dipping and tapping the rhythm. An easy joy rode the river, along with muted sun and glassy water. The girl at her side picked up the corrections, and they sang together, but of course the hoda had no Italian; had no words at all.

Soon the hard brightness of the day returned, knocking the song out of the air, bringing Bailey back to her senses. *Why do songs come up,* she thought, *when I'm trying so hard to be good?*

She turned to the hoda. "That's enough," she said. "Nicely done, to be sure, but run along now, Bailey has errands to do." She pulled a deeper stroke on the paddle, attempting to move forward of the other skiff. The girl looked stricken.

And in that moment, Bailey recognized the girl from the plaza, the too-young girl in the wire cage.

Bailey stopped paddling, drifting back on the current. It was the girl who bled in the cage. *Stay away from me,* Bailey thought. *I can't help you, I can't save you.* "I can't," she said aloud.

But the hoda had come abreast of Bailey's skiff again, singing still.

Bailey began paddling wildly, sending splashes in all directions, with the result that the boat made no progress at all. "Enough, I said. Run along now."

The hoda put her paddle across the gunwales and signed to Bailey.

It was hard to make out what the girl was saying. But she kept repeating it, and finally Bailey comprehended. She was saying, *I am human. Take me with you.*

"No. No, you aren't. Please go away. Please."

>I sing like you do,< the girl signed, her face overeager.

Bailey fixed the hoda with her best cold stare. "Not in your wildest dreams do you sing like Bailey Shaw." Noting the girl's distress, she added, to soften her criticism, "Keep to hoda songs, my dear. That would be best."

She managed to turn her skiff around, which she should have done an hour ago, and now her new course, with the river current, was twice as easy. Glancing behind her, she saw that the hoda was watching her like a dog that had just dropped a bone in the water.

Bailey pulled hard on the paddle, getting some distance from the girl. *Take me with you,* indeed. That they were going back to Earth was not a rumor Bailey wanted Vidori—or Oleel—to hear. She had to be stern with the child; it could all blow up, become an incident. There could be more blood. Bailey wouldn't be responsible for that.

Her arms were so very tired. She set her paddle across the gunwales and drifted for a few minutes. Just ahead was the Amalang confluence, the river of the uldia. Bailey's attention was caught by dark shapes in the trees.

Oh, dear. Bailey was drawing closer, seeing the shapes for what they were. Bodies in the trees. Several women hung upside down from tree branches, roped by their ankles.

Eight hoda, hung up in the trees.

Near Bailey, skiffs were treading the current, watching this display. Bailey beckoned one of the Dassa, a woman, to paddle closer to her. "What has happened?"

The woman was reluctant, but Bailey urged her on. Finally the Dassa said, "Oleel hung them up. They sang the human song."

Bailey closed her eyes. *Bad things happen when you sing.* She, of all people, should have known this. Her skiff was moving past the hanging bundles.

"Bailey," the woman asked. "Shall I help you?"

They knew who she was. Everyone knew who she was. Just not *what* she was.

"Oh yes, please. I have come too far."

With surprising agility, the woman managed to transfer herself to Bailey's skiff, then secured her own to trail behind. As she did so, Bailey saw that the young hoda who had followed her was staring toward shore. Surely she was no longer interested in Mozart. That was Bailey's fervent hope.

*   *   *

Viven clustered as usual outside Vidori's apartments, awaiting the king. This afternoon they left a wide berth around Anton and Maypong, now that there had been hoda killings, killings associated with Bailey. Anton assumed he would have to answer for Bailey, although everyone seemed to know more about the events than he did.

According to Maypong, the uldia had killed several slaves caught singing a human song that Oleel judged degenerate. It seemed they had learned the song from Bailey, who, incredibly, had been singing in the forest. But, Anton reasoned, Bailey never sang. And now she was supposed to have sung in the forest?

And then a badly shaken Bailey had come paddling home, spilling out everything: that she had seen eight hoda hung by their ankles from trees along the Sodesh. And that a hoda had approached her on the river, a person she thought was Maypong's daughter. They had sung together, "for only a few bars," and then Bailey's common sense took over, and she'd put a stop to it. Anton and Bailey had further words, and he left her, hurrying to see Vidori.

Outside the king's apartments, Maypong looked ashamed. She whispered, so that the nearby viven wouldn't hear: "That hoda bothered Bailey with rude singing. I am sorry, Anton."

Anton whispered back, "That hoda is your daughter, Maypong-rah."

The day had grown darker with storm clouds, and Maypong's gown looked sallow. "You are confused, Anton."

But he was not confused. Never clearer. "She wants to go somewhere where she can be happy."

"Thankfully," Maypong said, "she can be happy in the Olagong." She held a palm up to stop his response. "The Dassa girl who cannot be happy as a servant is dead." Her voice swam at him through the saturated air.

"Her heart isn't dead," Anton said. "Only broken."

Maypong glanced toward the king's apartments, perhaps hoping he would come and rescue her from this conversation.

Anton went on, "Doesn't her father care? Doesn't anyone?"

"Certainly her father was sorry to learn she was a hoda." *Sorry for his reputation* was the implication. Well, paternal ties were often weak here, Nick had said.

Viven watched the two of them with sidelong glances. Anton tried to summon his thoughts for the upcoming meeting with Vidori. He would say nothing of the satellite broadcasts. He needed time to sort through the implications. With tensions already high in the Olagong, mentioning the alien signals could be disruptive—perhaps dangerously so. Who knew what Oleel would make of such intelligence? Or who Maypong would tell if he confided in her. Not for the first time, he wondered how much she could be trusted.

"I need you to help me, Maypong-rah," he murmured. "I would be happy to think I had your full loyalty."

"Do you not?"

He paused, then plunged in. "You could counsel me about the Lady Joon, for one thing."

"But what counsel is needed?"

He regretted that afternoon in the baths. The woman had pursued him, even to the point of breaking sexual taboos. She wanted to please him because she wanted something from him, perhaps to align him with her political agenda, one that was entirely unclear to him. Still, he had to admit that he was just as responsible for that episode. And Nick had wasted no time in telling Bailey and Zhen, naturally.

"Did you know that Joon . . . wishes to be cordial with me?"

Her eyes flashed in some anger. "How can I know what the princess intends, Anton, or that you do not welcome her?"

"You could pay attention, Maypong." He left off the honorific to add weight to his words.

That got her attention. She stopped and turned to look at him, her light brown eyes steady, raised to meet his. "Now, Anton, I will tell you directly what I thought you knew. You are signaling to all the palace that you have sexual interest, yet declining to be cordial with your Dassa hosts. The princess was only responding to you as a Dassa does."

He stared at her. "*Signaling?*"

Her eyes turned hard. "I have said we catch the scent of moods."

"I thought it was a traditional saying."

"Oh, yes, and also factual. Would you lie to me and claim that you are not sexually interested?"

Anton looked down the corridor, summoning patience. Good Lord, was his every thought open to these people?

Maypong was relentless. "If you didn't want cordiality with Joon, why have you not lain with me, as I have suggested?"

People were taking notice of their argument. Anton tried to soften the conversation, which was growing more hostile with every moment. "Maypong-rah," he said, "please understand, cordiality among humans means more than what it means here."

"*Means more?*"

"It means affection. Love."

"And it does not here?" She was standing her ground, looking unhappier than ever.

"Among my people, such expressions are saved for . . ." He thought it not entirely true, but he finished, ". . . special people. People whom one loves." That wasn't what he meant to say. Indeed, he had demonstrated with Joon just how little humans *saved* such expressions.

But she was already pouncing on his words. "So you withhold affection from some people."

He paused, sticking to his story. "Yes."

She snorted, turning back to watch for the king. "No wonder you people get sick and die."

Shim emerged from the king's apartment, her baby slung on her back, chattering, and led Anton to his interview, leaving Maypong behind. The clot of viven eyed him resentfully as it became clear they would have even longer to wait.

Vidori was bent over a table with a soldier, and they looked up as he entered. Romang, Vidori's chief of arms, began gathering scrolled documents, and, handing them off to an adjutant, swept past Anton with a curt nod.

The king was dressed in a gold and brown robe with black trim at the hem and cuffs, a more relaxed attire than Anton had ever seen him in. Vidori flicked his hand at the hoda attendants and guards, and Shim ushered them out, closing the hall screen with a soft swoosh.

"Sit, Anton," Vidori said. "This will be my last pleasant moment of the day." His ear ornaments flashed with an obsidian glint. For the first time, Anton saw that they were etched with a miniature scene, of braided streams and a boat.

Anton relaxed a little, hearing the king's mood. Perhaps his mission was not going to be blamed for the massacre.

Vidori stared out at the Puldar, a broad path of gray under the clouds. "The rivers have receded, Anton."

The floods were past. It was a dangerous time, Vidori had said before.

He turned somewhat, to catch Anton's eye. "There are two edges to my battles now. One is on the eastern border, far up the Sodesh where the Vol test our strength."

He left unsaid, *The other is up the Amalang.*

Vidori had just returned from the Vol engagement. Perhaps he'd already seen what Oleel had hung in the trees to welcome him. But other deaths were foremost in his mind.

"There was a battle yesterday, Anton. We died, some of us."

Anton hadn't heard of this; but skirmishes with the Vol were not uncommon now. "Was it a hard loss?"

"No. But they were stronger than I thought." His eyes met Anton's. "Hoda. Hoda were among them, fighting us. That is a hard thing, to be slain by a hoda."

Or to be killed for singing, Anton thought, but didn't say.

Even with the veranda screens open wide, there was not the slightest breeze. The day hung heavy over them, squeezing flat all movement and sound. Even the forest birds and insects seemed to have suspended activities, waiting for the storm.

The king motioned for him to come onto the veranda. There was no relief from the heat, but it felt better than sticking to the chair.

The Puldar was full of boats—thousands of skiffs, with people returning from the variums, their daily obligation of procreation at the temple of the uldia. Below them, a great barge bore judipon down the Puldar, along with crates of goods.

The king looked tired. His profile, as he gazed out, was chiseled and fine, but his complexion was grayed a little. Anton guessed he had not slept last night.

"My people are obedient," Vidori said as he watched the river traffic. "They have their duty of the variums, and their duty of tithing and rearing strong children."

He turned to face Anton. "Even so, times are fragile. My duty is to keep the ways of the braid, to assure that the hoda bend to their tasks so that the Olagong may thrive. Bailey should not embolden the hoda by approving their habit of song, when we deem it vulgar, and when some songs are judged impudent by the Second Dassa. Emboldened, the hoda run to swell the ranks of the Vol, and then my soldiers are killed at the hands of slaves." Vidori fixed a studiously netural gaze on him. "It will not suit, Anton. It will not."

If Anton was going to incur the king's displeasure, it wouldn't be over singing. "Perhaps it's time for Bailey to leave," he told Vidori.

"No, Captain. I hope that is not your decision."

"What, then?"

Vidori moved to the edge of the veranda. As usual in the pavilions, there was no railing, making such movements seem reckless. The king squinted into the distance, watching the Puldar, perhaps seeing things that Anton could not yet see, or never would.

"My wish," Vidori said, "is for Bailey to remain among us. The people see that she does no harm, and that humans are good on the river. She is an acceptable ambassador for you. Wearing a hat. The people like this Bailey, and that is helpful to me. As long as she is respectful."

Vidori stood with his hands behind his back, watching the boats keeping the ways of the braid. Out of nowhere he said, "You think I am harsh, Captain."

"Regarding the hoda?" Anton hesitated, then said, "It is true that Dassa ways are hard for us to approve."

Vidori turned toward Anton, locking gazes with him. "But do you think me harsh?"

"I had not thought so, Vidori-rah. But we hold human life higher. All human life. It's our way, but not yours."

"So Joon has told me."

"Joon?" He had hoped her name would not come up. He was not a rival with Vidori for Joon's affection. Or was he? The event might well mean nothing to Vidori. It might well mean nothing to Joon. He wished it had not happened, and planned that it would not again, even as extraordinary as it was . . .

The king continued, "Yes, she has told me that you think it is time for the hoda to be brought higher."

Anton felt the ground becoming unsteady. Was Joon purposely undermining him? "I believe that is what Joon herself said. I haven't expressed an opinion."

Vidori frowned. "You do not believe such?"

"I don't say everything I think. Not here." And what did that make him, then?

"That would be helpful. For you not to say so."

Anton murmured, "You walk a fine line, and so must I."

"*Line?*"

"A saying among us. That you must not swerve to one side or the other. To satisfy many points of view." Politics. Anton decided he hated politics.

Vidori regarded him. "You do understand me, I sometimes think. But you do not approve of me."

"Rahi, I—"

He held up a hand. "Not a fair question. You are my guest." He nodded at the river. "Do you see how many boats there are, Captain? Do you think I steer them from my veranda with my hand?" He glanced at Anton. "Or with my devotion?"

Anton saw how the boats made their way, thousands of them, in chaotic harmony, threading their way here to there. He thought that he knew what the king was saying, that he could not, by himself alone, alter the braided lands.

The king went on, "But if I thought no change could come, I would not sit the throne, just to observe the River Days, the ceremonies. I would leave that to Joon. But my sight goes farther than the Sodesh. Beyond the Vol. I have Romang to command the army, and none better for the fight. But for other things I need time, Anton. I know that you would leave the palace, and make your searches freely. But I have said, I need time."

"Rahi, I have no time. My people are dying."

"Just a little time."

He said this so casually, with a king's assumption of privilege. Anton looked at Vidori, wondering if anyone at any time had ever said *no* to the man. If it was time for him to say no.

Anton said, "I must search further, rahi, beyond what you have shown me. There is something buried in this land, I am convinced of it."

"Buried?"

"Stored. Both obvious and hidden." Something that a newcomer might see immediately.

Vidori sighed. "So then, you would set out, offending Oleel, and she will say that I have given you leave. You can see, from the heavy fruit of the trees along the Sodesh, that no good can come of it."

Now the man had assembled an argument that suggested Anton would be responsible for any retaliations that Oleel might devise. The tone was condescending, and it grated. He had to break free of the man.

"Do you think, Vidori-rah, that I am less devoted to my people than you to yours?"

The king's face became stony. "You are a long way away from the people you claim to cherish."

It stung. Whether he meant Earth, or the ship.

Then their attention was drawn by a commotion on the river, and Anton saw the thing that Vidori had been watching: a barge lined with soldiers.

"The barge of the dead," Vidori murmured. "From the fighting up the Sodesh. Here are those soldiers fallen at the hands of the hoda who call themselves Vol."

He continued, "On their way to the burial lands down the Puldar. Other of my fallen soldiers will not lie on the same barge."

Even in death, the distinctions remained. "I think, rahi, that the Olagong will never accept me and my mission. Since we are born to bear. It will not change." That being the case, there was no longer a reason to remain chained to the palace, however silken the cords.

"I am sorry that you think so, Captain. It is not my vision."

But as had been made abundantly clear, they saw things with very different eyes.

NINE

Every screen in Zhen's hut was thrown wide open, sup-plicating the air for a breeze. Bailey sat nearby, watching Zhen, feeling as listless as Anton in the oppressive air.

Anton leaned against a corner post, observing Zhen's methodical movements with her botany samples. Her fingers were short, but incredibly flexible, as she maneuvered her slices and powders onto slides, peering at them. Her attentions had turned from the Dassa genome to analysis of the local food staple, a reddish brown tuber called the *langva*. It was Nick's suggestion, since he felt that the regional myths of the plants might hide deeper significance.

"Zhen, you can take a break," Anton said. Her hair stuck to her skull, as though her work—as sedentary as it was—made her hotter.

Without looking up from the ocular of the scope, she said, "Is that an order?"

"No."

Her face looked stuck to her microscope.

"Finding anything interesting?" he asked her.

"Yes. It's all interesting. There are interesting proteins,

for one thing. These langva have at least one hundred kinds of endotoxin receptors. It's like they have a hundred different ways to detect flagellin from bacteria."

"Meaning?"

Zhen looked up, frowning. "Meaning it's interesting."

Bailey said, "Well, I haven't seen a sick Dassa on this planet yet. Make us a tonic, Zhen," she said.

Zhen closed her eyes, not getting the humor. "This is enough work for a whole gaggle of researchers. That's why I don't take breaks."

Noise in the corridor outside. Hurrying feet. Someone running. Nick poked his head into Zhen's sanctum. "Captain."

Following Nick into the central crew hut, Anton found the main hall screen thrown wide, revealing a mass of people rushing in one direction: toward the river.

Nick reported, "Something about the king leaving."

Anton got Bailey's attention. "Stay with Zhen," he ordered. Then he and Nick melted into the general rush, a controlled stampede, here where running was so rare.

As they approached the king's river room, they saw that a throng had already gathered, some hugging the perimeter and others milling in the center with equipment and loud voices.

Viven were shouting for hoda to fetch equipment, amid a general push for the river stairs. Men and women were armed with short swords, and though it all looked very martial, the expressions on their faces were too eager and cheerful for a battle. Banners came out, hoisted and unfurled by assistants, revealing colors and symbols Anton hadn't seen before. Nick had turned to one of the viven to make inquiries.

But then all heads turned, noting Vidori's entrance into the hall. He received the bows and greetings of his nobles, then spied Anton. He hailed him.

A path cleared between the two men, and Anton walked

down it. Vidori turned to Shim. "My guest will come with us, Shim-rah. Make him ready."

Nick murmured to Anton, "It's something about a hunt. A celebration of sorts."

The king turned to Anton, saying merrily, "You consent to come in my war canoes?"

Someone murmured, "An-ton will paddle that hoda," and nearby viven broke into titters.

"Will you come?" Vidori repeated.

"Of course, Vidori-rah. But where are we going?"

At the king's side, one of the viven said, "We don't know. That's the game."

Turning away, the king strode to the steps, commanding, "Someone give the captain a short sword, or how can he play?"

That left Anton in a knot of viven, all of whom—or none of whom—were tasked with giving the human something of theirs. They eyed him with distress. Finally, Nidhe—one of the king's brothers—drew his sword from his belt and pointed it at Anton, business end forward. "Captain, I present a sword."

He presented a difficulty. Anton could not grasp the handle without inadvertently touching Nidhe. The blade looked sharp. Now several of the palace-born turned to watch, a sly humor coming into their faces, some more delighted than others.

Maypong was at his side, coming out of nowhere. "Oh, Nidhe-rah, thankfully you are so generous."

Flicking open the wide sash around her waist, she used it to take the blade end of the sword in her hands. She turned the hilt to Anton, smiling brightly, a line of moisture on her upper lip. She must have run to get next to him during this exchange.

Anton took the sword, noting that its wooden hilt was carved and bore short tassels of blue and gray, as though the weapon was decked out for ceremony.

"Maypong to the rescue," Nick remarked. "Have a nice hunt, Captain."

"What kind of hunt?" Anton wanted to know.

Nick shrugged. "Don't know, Captain, but you're about to find out."

Maypong pushed Anton forward with the slightest pressure on his elbow, a maneuver she had perfected so as to avoid touching him anywhere more personal.

Nidhe stomped ahead of Anton toward the river, his hodas bearing a standard, also blue and gray.

The king was already boarding a canoe, and the other viven boisterously followed.

It did not seem a good day for an excursion. The palace was preparing for the storm, bringing in skiffs and loading them inside the pavilion and battening down some of the larger screened porches. But the dark clouds were still distant, towering far away up the Sodesh, against the hills. Lightning flickered there, little worms of fire.

"Anton," Maypong said, "this is a great honor from the king, for you to join in the hunt." Her eyes were bright and hard. "You must smile very much around the viven." She glanced at him. "Even when we catch her. Do you understand?"

She herded him down the steps, commandeering a canoe in which three viven were already ensconced, by their faces hoping for more conducive company. As Maypong clambered into the canoe, Anton noted that she wore leggings and a simple tunic, along with businesslike boots. She helped him in as the craft rocked, and they were off. Anton turned around just enough to snap at Maypong, "Tell me what the hell is going on, Chancellor."

Maypong's smile was as phony as his own. "Oh yes, Anton. This is to bring down the hoda who is . . . Do you know the word?" Indeed, she had used a word that he did not know. Then she said, "This hoda is bearing young inside her body, by your pardon."

The hoda rowers guided them out into the center of the

Puldar, where the king's lead canoe had already set out. They jockeyed the craft carefully to avoid the general crush as viven waited their turn to enter single file. Anton's boat was just one boat back from Vidori's.

Anton was absorbing this news of a pregnant hoda. "She has run away?"

"Of course. She will flee west, to the Vol, but we will overtake her, thankfully."

One of the viven in the back of the canoe said, "And we shall paddle her, Captain."

Laughter greeted this remark, but Anton was filled with foreboding, made worse by the atmosphere of merriment.

A canoe sped past him, propelled by slaves with a cargo of several cages. As it passed, he caught sight of a large bird with a hooked beak. The canoe raced to catch up to the lead canoe.

The river ran gray and flat, like an ironed sheet, and few boats plied its waters. With the approaching storm, a hush had fallen on the Olagong. The only sound was the slap, slap of the paddles and the occasional shout of a viven. Common folk stood watching on the banks and on docks, some shouting encouragements, as children ran alongside the river, trying to keep up with the canoes. In the distance, thunder rumbled in muted quakes.

"Maypong," Anton said, "how does it happen that a hoda taking contraceptive drinks becomes . . . bears young?"

As he turned to ask his question, she made a face at him, reminding him to smile.

"She will have shaved her head to escape notice, having taken a lover who . . ." She hesitated. "Who penetrated her. Because the hoda only pretended to take her cleansing broth. Her mistress will undergo reprimand."

"What will happen to this hoda?"

Maypong crept close to him, saying in an undertone, "Now, Anton, you will for one time listen to your chancellor. I am going to tell you what will happen to her, and you will smile and act as the viven are acting. Do not shame the king."

She plopped herself back into position in her seat, and said, rather more loudly than necessary, "What will happen to her, Anton, is that she will be pierced with a sharp sword. That sword will have honor. May it be your sword, Captain."

"And so goes the braid," one of the viven said, behind her.

Slap, slap went the paddles. The hoda drove the canoe forward, heedless of the discussion of the killing of their fellow slave.

In front, he saw the king in the lead boat. On his wrist sat a falcon, feathers rippling in the wind. The king's arm came up, and the bird launched. It flapped hard, keeping abreast of the canoe, then climbed, gaining altitude over the Puldar, and banking north to a distant copse.

The hunt was on.

The air was sour with ozone, and Anton's stomach clenched. The line of canoes in front and behind carried the colorful privileged, out for some fun. Even the commoners gathered for the spectacle, cheering on the viven and their outing. Another bird launched off the king's wrist, hailed by cheers and the slapping of paddles. The clouds rolled down the sky, following the river, straight into Lolo, where the war party slopped happily along, where a pregnant woman fled through the copses.

Anton stood up in the canoe, no small feat. Behind, he heard Maypong call to him to sit down, and in front he drew the attention of Vidori, who waved. Anton didn't know what he would do, perhaps jump into the water . . . Maypong was standing then, just behind him. "You disturb the paddlers, Anton. Is it a human custom to stand in boats?"

He was aware that he looked ridiculous and that he had no plan. "It isn't a human custom to hunt people."

"You cannot prevent this hunt. So then, please sit, since if you fall, you will embarrass the king."

He was beyond concern about embarrassing the king. How could he have thought that Vidori was in any way admirable, that he would support Anton's mission?

"Sit, Anton. I beg you." Maypong's voice was as shaky as he'd ever heard it.

Everyone was now looking at them, and the hoda in his boat were paddling ever so gently, keeping the canoe stable, as other canoes came abreast, their occupants staring.

"Why did he invite me?" Anton asked, still looking upriver at the towering black clouds, wishing they would hurry their pace and create havoc in the river.

"He needs you to prove yourself to the palace-raised, so that his reign is secure, and not toppled by having you as a guest."

She stood behind him, still trying to civilize him. Of all that she said, what got through was *so that his reign is secure*. Anton had no business shoring up the king's reign, not by any means, especially not by hunting down a pregnant woman. Vidori had just crossed the line.

The king was watching him, looking troubled. But Anton was thinking about the Dassa woman they pursued and how she should be surrounded by loving family and friends and thinking of a proper name for her child. Instead, this nightmare. He wondered what desperation could have driven her to break the ultimate taboo.

"Please, Anton," came Maypong's voice. "Sit."

He did so. There was nothing else to do. The viven murmured remarks about standing up in canoes. Maypong laughed and said that it was a human joke, to stand in boats.

A few drops of rain plopped into the canoe. A purple drape was moving across the sky, carrying its saturated load. The line of canoes turned into the Sodesh, the hoda paddling furiously in the ragged confluence. Out in the main river the wind came upon them in cold wads, forcing the hoda to contend with both current and wind. The viven

shouted for more speed as the slaves dug their paddles in—
uselessly, for a time. They treaded water, as in a dream,
working hard, getting nowhere. Then they began to move,
to the cheers of the viven.

In the distance, the falcon circled. Someone pointed, and
the canoes turned toward the northern shore, Vidori's in
the lead.

As they approached the river's edge, Anton saw that it
wasn't land, but marsh grass growing out of the water.
They plunged directly into the waving grasses, following a
channel barely one canoe wide. Now Anton could see nothing but the canoe directly ahead of him, and a saffron world
of tassel-topped grasses. He heard a flap of wings, and then
the king's bird flew low over his boat, nearly swiping
Anton's head before veering away.

The canoes peeled off at a junction of canals, slicing into
an even narrower passage, where the grasses bent toward
the boats, whipping them in the wind.

Then lightning spun out of the sky, almost searing the
eyes, turning the marsh to a land of golden spikes. The
viven fell flat into the canoes, leaving the hoda upright to
take any hits. Up ahead, Anton saw Vidori standing, peering
over the marshlands, heedless of the crackling of lightning
and, now, of the bone-splitting roar of thunder.

Maypong commanded the hoda to pull to shore, and the
slaves shoved the canoe into a tuft of grasses, driving the canoe onto a sandbar. The other canoes were following suit.
Exiting the canoe, Anton could see that Vidori was rushing
ahead, in the company of several viven.

Nobles pressed around Anton. One of the women
pointed with her sword toward the treetops, where a raptor
was spiraling in place. As though her blade had cut a hole in
the sky, the rains came all at once, deafeningly.

As the hunting party plunged forward, Anton stayed behind. His sword was missing from his belt. He looked about
in the grasses, but it was hard to see in the downpour. Only
in the intermittent lightning could Anton discern the

general direction of the stampede of nobles. Maypong was gone. He was alone on an islet, as the waters of the canals rose.

He had no wish to join the frenzy. He'd let them rush onward to their kill. The rain fell like stones, washing away sight, filling his ears. For the first time since he'd come to this world, he was cold.

Now and then he thought he might have heard a shout. But then the lightning came again, and the thunder, so close it numbed his ears. He kicked at the grasses, looking for Nidhe's sword. He walked back to the canoe, but it was floating down the blackened surface of the canal, like a horse let loose and grazing.

He walked into the tall grasses, kicking them aside. No sword. But here—a shadow, a movement. He thought it was a large beast, there and then not there.

In a lightning flash, before him stood a woman. No noble costume, and no hair. She looked at him, her eyes filled with electricity, then turned and fled, almost galloping away, splashing across a canal. For some reason, he shouted, "Wait!" But of course, she would not wait. He was of the palace, and she was fleeing for her life, and the life of the life within her. Anton staggered forward. "Wait!" he yelled again, but thunder swallowed his cry.

Then he was running after her, scanning the marsh, looking for her, a single figure scampering and crouching. If he could find her first, before the king, before Nidhe, before . . .

He plowed through a canal, coming up to his thighs in water, feet sticking in mud, pulling them out furiously, clambering up onto the next hump of land. He saw her again, far off. She was fast, a strong runner. She had to be. He plunged after, but he seemed to drive her before him, instead of coaxing her to remain. It was wrong, all wrong, but he ran.

The rain eased, and into the void poured a low cloud,

grabbing sight, sucking up sound. Anton stopped, closed his eyes, listening.

A shout in the distance, then another from the opposite direction. He was gaining on the hunting party. He had got turned around, but thought he knew the direction the hoda had gone. He raced that way. There were crashings at his side. It was Nidhe. Now Anton played dumb, turning in another direction so that Nidhe would go awry, but the man did not, instead pointing true, urging Anton on. Anton went with him.

Together, they pummeled the grasses down, rushing headlong as though they knew where they were going. Anton worried that perhaps Nidhe *did* know. They approached a stand of trees, almost slamming into a trunk in the thick fog.

Maypong was there. "Anton," she gasped, as though desperately relieved to see him.

"This way," she said, and both he and Nidhe followed her. They batted their way through vines and aerial roots, plowing their way into a clearing surrounded by squat, frondy trees.

She was there: their prey.

Already down, the sword still in her, she lay dead. Viven in a circle around her, not looking triumphant, but only confused. A girl, barely a woman.

Anton thought of his father. The old man, so like these viven—the privileged, the brutal. *This is how the world is, boy. Better get used to it.*

The king stepped forward. "Who takes the honor?" No one answered.

The girl still bled, but her blood was all watery on the ground.

"Whose honor?" the king repeated. The viven stood with drooping standards, the hoda behind them looking at the fallen girl, their normal silence deeper yet.

Nidhe stepped forward, frowning, and crouched beside the slain hoda. "This is my sword, rahi."

The king nodded. "Then you have the honors today."

Nidhe stood. "But I did not catch her." He rounded on Anton, lifting his chin to summon Anton's explanation.

"Nor did I," Anton said.

The noble party looked uneasy, and then grew sullen. Who would they celebrate? Who was spoiling their game?

As they argued among themselves, Maypong grabbed hold of Anton's hand. The gesture was startling, and he bent toward her, toward her urgent pull. "Anton, the law says that the person whose sword takes the hoda may have a fine gift of the king. Even a piece of land." She turned fiercely to look into his eyes. "Away from the palace, if you wish."

The king was happier than his courtiers. He turned to Anton. "My guest, we will present a fine gift, even if you do not admit your accomplishment."

Nidhe stepped forward again and retrieved his sword, wiping it on the moss of the nearest tree, amid a renewed downpour.

In that interval, Anton knew that he had waited long enough. "Vidori-rah, may I choose a gift?" At the king's nod, Anton said, "A piece of land."

As Anton spoke, Vidori's face slowly subsided from pleasure to neutrality.

"Big enough to accommodate my crew. All four of us. With a hut." He felt his words parcel out until there were no more of them. He'd played his hand, a short one.

Now the clot of viven stood unmoving and silent in the relentless rain.

Anton didn't wait for Vidori to speak. He was looking at the girl, curled up, arms locked around her belly. When he looked back at the king, he saw him as a stranger.

His voice cold, Anton asked, "Will you grant the gift?"

There was a mutter of astonishment from the nobles. One of the Dassa women hissed, "A degenerate. With land."

"It is the law," the king said. He let a feral smile claim the moment, but his eyes were hard as fused glass. He turned to

Maypong. "Tell him that it is granted." And then he strode from the clearing. Slowly, the viven followed.

Anton watched Vidori go. Well, it was over then, their friendship. He and his crew would be outside the palace now, under Anton's authority. Now that the king's authority was intolerable. So be it.

He realized he was still gripping Maypong's hand. Her face was so pale it looked as if she were wearing a mask of silver, but it was only the rain. He released her hand, realizing with an odd emptiness that she had at last become his true chancellor.

When all the viven had left, Maypong and Anton followed. They were not to bury the hoda. Anton would not be allowed to so much as cover her body. Even the hoda would not allow it.

As they left the enclosure of the trees, the king's raptor came flapping into the marshes, flying to Vidori's wrist, obedient.

Behind Anton, from the clearing, he heard the slaves singing, but softly.

II

DOMINION
OF
CLOUDS

TEN

In the mist, the sun sat hazy and low in the sky, like melting butter. Standing on the island of land the mission claimed as its own, Nick watched the sunset with mixed feelings. There was so much beauty here. But a few meters away, the rotting carcass of a quasi-monkey lay tangled in floating tree branches, another marker of the great storm that had wreaked such havoc on the Olagong.

This world had two faces. It was an almost happy land of palace-raised and slave-raised. And Nick was split in two as well: He thought he'd cracked the world's secret, with the discovery of the immune-boosting langva; on the other hand he was dying.

Of the same thing they were all going to die of. Oh, death was afoot, and now it had kicked him in the gut. The little rosy growths on his skin were just showing below the cuff of his shirt. He pulled the cuff down.

He didn't want to die. God, life was more precious than ever. He didn't want to die at twenty-four, before he'd made his life worth something. As a test subject for what langva could do. For humanity's pri. All he had were a few hints from Oleel. But in this land of hints and innuendo, this world of deep jungle and murky waters, he may have made a breakthrough.

The sun was going down fast, as it did in this part of the world. He welcomed it, knowing he looked bad in daylight, and needing just a little more time. Zhen still took the daily blood samples, popping them into the rack for analysis, but he had no worry on that score. He'd reconfigured the program to read Anton's blood sample twice, in place of one for Nick Venning. Anton had been pronounced clean. So had Nick.

It was poetic justice, that Anton should provide cover for Nick. Anton had made his own shipmate irrelevant, traded the mission's anthropologist for the native one, Maypong. Nick was an appendage, good for errands and construction projects, but not vital anymore. Because Anton couldn't stand to take advice, couldn't stand to be wrong.

Water formed at the corners of his eyes. The Olagong was so lovely, even though the glare of the sunset deepened his headache.

He noticed every small pain from his body, wondering if it was the infection. He was exhausted, yet tense. He had a light case of diarrhea, despite Oleel's infusions. Or maybe *because* of her infusions. He accepted that there might be side effects. But so far, there was just a slight fever, and unlike Strahan and the others, he was still on his feet a week after the first symptoms.

He mused that he might feel healthier if his dose were stronger—especially since he'd given half his most recent dose to Zhen to analyze. He'd made up a story for her, that he'd persuaded an old Dassa man to give him some, that he'd even tried a taste and it had made him feel energetic.

"You tried a local medicine?" Zhen said, incredulous. But it was a plausible story, because Zhen thought he was stupid anyway. He pulled his cuff down again, over the spot on his wrist. He disguised a similar spot on his cheek with a stubby growth of beard. People noticed he didn't look well, but ascribed it to the Dassa potion.

Nick walked out onto the small dock he and Anton had built. At his hip was the mission's one side arm—loaded, in case anyone threatened Zhen. Anton judged that the king would allow them to protect Zhen with force. Nick hoped he wouldn't be asked to kill a Dassa for the sake of someone like Zhen. But he kept an eye out for trouble, all the while searching the Puldar upriver for both Bailey's and Anton's skiffs, which should be returning soon. Bailey was at Samwan's compound. Maypong and Anton were off trying for an interview with the judipon.

The judipon. It took a murdered pregnant hoda to do it, but at last Anton had heeded Nick's advice and reached out to the other powers. Easier to do, now that Vidori was off this past week leading a sortie along the border. Anton was fond of the easy route—when what they needed was the *fast route*. For the crew's sake. Sergeant Webb was scared; Nick could hear it in his voice. In two weeks, the new outbreak had killed eight crew members—a 90 percent fatality rate, leaving the crew numbers badly depleted at twenty-two. And some of those were sick. Odd. Usually virulent strains weren't fast. The microbes had no future if they killed off all the hosts. Well, maybe for the next go-round, the virus would learn to go easy. Of course, by then, there'd be no crew left.

Zhen's shadow moved against the wall of her work hut. She was always working, oblivious to the fact that one side arm was little protection from fanatics. Zhen's lab was the first thing they'd built, a sturdy hut protecting her equipment that Vidori had summarily dumped in the center of the islet. Next came construction of the elaborate composting toilet system and a bartered-for water pump and generator. Then, having assured herself that the river laws were being followed, Maypong finally approved the building of sleeping huts.

Nick made his way to the crew hut, sitting on the steps,

and turned on his tronic notepad. Every time he saw the uldia, he added to his schematic of Oleel's pavilion. He
thought there might be something to learn, maybe even
something hidden by the ancient race itself. Oleel said the
uldia's compound was built as a replica of the original stone
home of the Quadi. Which, in turn, was a replica of the
Olagong. There were the river courses set into the floor of
the courtyard. Different rooms were islets—or islets as they
once were, before the shifting erosion of the river. There
were river steps, where all of the floor streams spilled out
again into the Amalang River, just as the Sodesh poured into
the great world ocean.

Who, in God's name, were the Quadi? How advanced
might they be? And why had they abandoned this world
without a trace of themselves? Perhaps, as Anton said, they
didn't wish to be known, or it was of no cultural value to
them, so they turned their backs on Neshar as if it were
some minor feat. And yet they called to four distant stars,
saying, *Come to Neshar, come see what we have wrought* . . .
What the messages actually said, the science team didn't
know.

The alien radio messages troubled him. How could the
langva plant contain compounds suitable for other races,
life-forms that might be based on entirely different chemical
and DNA architecture? However, the newly found messages
didn't invalidate his theory. Whatever benefits Neshar offered alien civilizations, this planet was clearly about *human*
needs, and *Earthly* life. Where else in the universe would
there be Dassa? And pineapples?

A boat that he'd had his eye on for a little while was now
clearly making for the dock. He slapped the notepad shut.

Walking down to the river, hand on his side arm, but not
drawing it, he watched the craft approach. Not a skiff; it was
too fine to be a commoner's boat. For a moment he worried
that Oleel was going to openly visit him here. She was hard
to control, but seemed to want secrecy as much as he did.

He'd meant to tell Anton about Oleel. And he would, when he was sure of his breakthrough.

Watching the canoe approach, he squinted as the black waters threw shadows up into the faces of the passengers. But even in the growing dusk, he knew it wasn't Anton or Bailey.

It was the Princess Joon.

The canoe made straight for the islet. Hoda paddlers brought the canoe next to the dock, and one jumped out to help Joon debark.

She did so, standing in the dusk, her gown looking like congealed moonlight. She stood as still as a chess piece.

"Lady Joon, thank you," Nick said in greeting.

She didn't answer him, but looked past him to the huts. The hoda climbed back into the canoe and sat with the three others, all of them unmoving, like pawns.

Now she approached him. "I think you are the one called Nick." She couldn't say his name, of course, mangling it into *Nid*.

"Yes, rahi."

Stopping a few paces away from him, Joon seemed content to be quiet, not announcing her purpose or explaining anything. "Oh, you have three huts," she said, scanning their handiwork. "And they have not fallen down, either."

"Maypong was a good teacher," he said, hoping to cut her, though it was only a hunch.

"Yes, Maypong is good with her hands."

As she turned her profile to him, he frankly stared at her. The blue of her pendant ear ornaments brought out the dark hues of her skin, making her look like a fabulous queen. Her beauty stirred him. The idea that Anton had been intimate with her filled him with depression.

She turned back, looking closely at him for the first time. "You are here alone?" She saw a shadow on the hut walls. "Except for Sen?"

"Yes." There was a sudden rush of hope that she had come now because Anton was gone. Come to deal with a more receptive human. Perhaps Oleel had said that Nick was such a man.

She said, "Do you worry that the captain is abroad so late? My royal father would not want him to be in jeopardy."

"He is well, I'm sure, Lady."

"And you, Nick. Are you well?"

It was then that he saw her nostrils flare. She could smell him. His illness. It mortified him, that he might smell foul.

"I hope to be well" was all he could manage.

She smiled. "Do you bar my way?"

She was asking him if he meant to prevent her from leaving the dock. He moved to the side, and she went past.

His illness meant nothing to her. She was looking for Anton. Her hair, so perfect; her gown, barely rustling with her smooth movements. He had an urge to muss her, to shatter the placidity.

"And Bailey," Joon said, "the old woman is still paddling so late?" When he didn't answer, she said, "We are all fond of Bailey, so she will be watched over, thankfully."

"Anton, though, can be difficult," Nick said, thinking she might open to him. Anton had told him that Joon was concerned for the plight of the hoda, that she didn't share all her father's views. He felt some attraction to her, a woman who dared to have contrary opinions.

"Anton speaks with my father's voice."

Nick frowned. Was that good or bad, in her view? Bad, he decided. He replied, "Not everyone here feels the same about the hoda."

"Oh yes, I have been learning about this *equality* of yours. Perhaps Anton turns away from hoda suffering, now that he has killed one. Even now, her bones lie like carrion in the grasses. Does this sadden you, Nick? You seem to be sad."

He swallowed. It had been a long while since anyone had noticed how he felt. Joon was dangerous, yet appealing. And if Vidori were killed in battle, the mission would be dealing with a new ruler, one who thought of *hoda*, and *sad*, in the same breath.

"Does it sadden *you*, Lady?" He was surprised he had voiced this question.

She turned an appraising gaze at him. "If I am saddened, it would be for what is coming, what I cannot prevent."

"What, Lady?" But she wouldn't talk to him, was in fact already turning away, leaving him where he stood, helpless and sick, wanting to reach out to her. She'd come here for Anton; she would have talked to Anton. What could such a strong woman see in so weak a man? An ally for the hoda, for whom she had some unusual sympathy?

He followed her to the dock, where her servants waited to help her into the boat.

Standing on the wooden platform in the dusk, Nick wondered about her comment, that something was coming which she couldn't prevent. "What is coming, rahi?"

She looked past his shoulder to the huts they had built, and it seemed to Nick that rather than contempt, her eyes held melancholy. "I can help you," he said, not knowing if he could, but meaning to try if she'd let him.

A spark of ridicule came back to her voice. "But of course, the damage has been done."

"Let me help," he repeated.

She raised her chin, and her face became queenly again, strong and dark and impervious. Turning to step into the canoe, she said, "Perhaps all that can be done is to look at things with new eyes." Her servant handed her down to her seat. "It is a fine saying. One that Anton taught me."

The hoda paddlers sent the boat gliding into the Puldar, setting up a gentle wake that rocked their skiffs, tied up nearby. The musk of the river ran strong, with the Puldar's deep juices enriched by animal carcasses from the storm.

From behind him he saw that Zhen had joined him on the dock.

"You toady," she said. "That was a sweet little conversation with the palace slut."

He looked at her with loathing. "Is eavesdropping the best you can do for company these days, Zhen?"

She smirked. "Yes. Science is a lonely calling."

They watched the canoe disappear into a soft mist feathering off the river.

"This immunity you're so interested in, Venning. I don't think the langva are the whole answer."

She could switch moods faster than Anton could go through walls. The wake of Joon's boat was just visible, a slash on the river, from which the last of the sun welled up.

"A big factor is the profound diversity of their genomes. It's why the Dassa aren't really at risk for our viruses. The Dassa are descended from at least forty genetically significant human populations of Earth. They might have naïve immune systems, from the standpoint of human disease, but they're equipped to handle them."

"I'm not worried about the Dassa. They're strong as oxen."

Zhen snorted. "Glad to hear you're not worried. That means a lot. Howwwwever," she said, stretching out the word, winding up, "a big question is why their immune responses would be strong. When you look at historical plagues of high virulence—the American Indians with measles and smallpox, for instance—you can see that their small gene pool is what allowed sixty million of them to die in the western hemisphere. The microbes were able to adapt swiftly to the very narrow set of homogeneous barriers before them. The Dassa, though, present a maze of genomes for any virus to negotiate." She shrugged. "So, though the langva have some immune-boosting properties, it's not what's going on here, in the main."

Nick wasn't listening. "Just keep looking, that's all."

Zhen muttered, "Pedaling as fast as I can, Lieutenant. It would help if there were a few more hands to pitch in. Next time we'll bring scientists on the ground mission instead of cultural types." As she turned to go, she said, "You still drawing little pictures in your notepad?"

Unconsciously, his hand was resting on his side arm. He moved his hand, lest he be tempted to put her out of her misery.

"Yes," he said. "Still drawing little pictures."

Gilar's hands were white and puffy from handling the chemistries. She had learned by smell which vials held the worst corrosives, but her hands were shredding. Little hunks of skin hung from her fingers, tormenting every movement.

Everything in Oleel's pavilion was hard-edged and bright. Gilar had never been in a stone house. Her feet ached from the unforgiving floor, and her eyes from the awful whiteness of the place. After two days as Oleel's slave, she thought she had fallen as far as one could. But remembering what hung from the trees along the river that day, she reflected that perhaps she had not.

Mim worked at her side, signing, >Pay attention. You may drop the vial, and have punishment.< From the scars on her face, she was one who'd had *punishments*. They were alone in the scullery, but Mim didn't speak in song, only in hand sign. Oleel favored quiet.

At Aramee's compound, the uldia had come for Gilar without warning. One moment she was working on a burst water pipe, and the next everyone was staring at the pier, where Aramee was standing, welcoming a barge of uldia.

Then someone was walking toward them. It was Nuan.

>Stand up, Gilar,<Nuah had signed.

When Gilar did so, she saw that Aramee, across the yard, was gazing at her. She was in the company of several uldia.

Nuan looked stricken, and Gilar guessed that she had broken yet another rule. Although why Nuan should care what happened to the compound's chief troublemaker, Gilar had no idea.

>Now you will have reason to believe in Aramee's goodness< was all she signed.

Bahn came running up, alarm in her face.

It was over within moments. Aramee had coins in her hand, and the uldia commanded Gilar to enter their barge.

Aramee had sold her to the uldia. Now, however, the mistress looked doubtful, even worried. But didn't they know no one could hurt her anymore? Didn't they know that—despite Bailey's rejection—somehow she was going to Erth?

She passed a hoda who signed, >Oh Gilar, our sister.<

And then Bahn: >The river bears you, my friend. Remember the river bears you.<

And, indeed, the river had borne her to a place of implacable stone. In the pavilion of the big woman, Gilar had lost every outward trace of herself. She was bald and ugly now, and like every other hoda, she no longer had to shave her head. One morning she had awakened and the stubble from her recent growth of hair lay in the hammock like a secret code of lines. But inside herself, nothing had changed.

Sometimes Oleel looked at her sideways, intently, as though she knew Gilar's secret hopes, and meant to ruin them.

Now, Gilar found herself alone in the scullery, with Mim on some errand. She let the cool water spill over her hands, cleansing what was left of them. In a faint voice, she hummed a tiny length of melody, the Bailey song. To her amazement, the sound was larger here in the rock palace. She piped out a high note, and another. Truly, stone made for very good sounds.

That was when she discovered that she had not yet fallen very far.

A thumping noise came from nearby. Someone was running up the stone steps. Several uldia appeared in the doorway.

The women hurried her downstairs, not gently, and marched her forward to the very middle of the courtyard, where the large woman sat among her senior uldia.

She looked like a lumpish statue carved right from granite. Her robes covered massive thighs, but her sandals peeked out at the hem, sandals as large as any man ever wore. Gilar was staring at the woman's feet, reluctant to engage her eyes.

The voice came loud, though the large woman didn't shout. Her voice was naturally robust, and could always be distinguished from other uldias', even at a distance.

"Did you bring a vulgar sound to my home?" Oleel asked.

>No, but I sang,< Gilar saw herself sign to the woman with life-and-death power over her. It came out naturally. She'd never learned the things Bahn hoped she would, like how to cower in front of proper Dassa.

Gilar braced herself for the blow. But it was a long time coming, if it was going to. Oleel nodded at one of her attendants, who left, then returned with a small plate.

The uldia with the plate commanded Gilar to open her mouth.

Oh, not my mouth, Gilar thought. *I don't open my mouth.*

But she did open it, because the uldia could force her to. The uldia took a small round ball from the plate. As she brought it close to Gilar, Gilar could smell something foul. With shock, she realized it was excrement.

"Open," the uldia commanded again.

Mother of rivers, Gilar thought, falling deep inside herself. *No, no.*

And then the uldia placed the ball of excrement just behind her teeth, in that part of her mouth where her tongue . . . where her tongue . . .

"Now close your mouth," the uldia said.

Saliva came flooding into Gilar's mouth, in an attempt to fend off the invasion, but in fact it made the ball taste worse. Gilar's stomach rolled and jumped.

"If she spits it away, take out her eyes," Oleel said. Then she turned from the girl, the plate, the horror, and continued her conversation with the other women.

Gilar watched her turn. With the revolting morsel in her mouth, Gilar watched the large woman, and she saw how it would be. She and this woman were like fire and water, like flood and drought.

One of them would have to die.

ELEVEN

Approaching Samwan's compound, Bailey could see a great barge pulled up, and a flurry of action on the dock. She stopped paddling long enough to scout the situation.

Dozens of judipon were crawling around the barge and dock, carrying baskets, lockers, and bales into the yard. It was tithe-day, then. It was beyond her why they chose the hottest part of the day to haul goods.

Patting her hat on more firmly, she resumed her progress toward the shore, wary of any hodas in skiffs who might accost her and expect a song. There would be no more singing, by anyone. How swift the retribution had come, for that one small song in the forest. Anton tried to soften it, saying that Oleel would have found some other pretense to clamp down on the hoda, but still, Bailey knew it was retribution for her lapse. How many more girls would die because of her? None, she resolved. Never again.

Samwan's hoda rushed down to the water's edge to help Bailey debark. They handed her up from her skiff onto the dock. She could hardly meet their eyes, both for her own lapse and Anton's, that he had allegedly killed a pregnant slave on the king's big hunt, and got a nice piece of land in exchange—despite the fact that he *hadn't* killed her, thank God.

Onto the pier ran a pack of children, shouting her name and chanting the Dassa word for singing, while the hoda hushed them, sharply. God in heaven, had everyone heard about one song offered up in the depths of the jungle?

Across the yard, Samwan waved at her, having learned that waving could be a proper greeting, and now using it to her advantage, because she had a dockful of judipon and piles of hemp, animal kill, dried fruit, and langva tubers lying about and needing disposition, and no time to play hostess to Bailey. Her sisters rushed about, giving directions, looking over the records with the judipon, who crouched on stools, sharing out the record plates. Bailey didn't know the word for the judipon accounting system, but physically they were stacks of circular papers collected on tall spindles, with raised bumps denoting the indecipherable numbering system, tallying the convoluted dole.

It wasn't all festive. The huts were hung with fresh palm leaves, the custom in honoring the dead, needful these last weeks because the compound had lost a ten-year-old boy in the big storm, and he was presumed dead.

Bailey had paid her condolences to Samwan's sister Irran, but the woman seemed inconsolable and was taking grief potions from her uldia. Bailey would like to know what magic potion *that* might be. Perhaps Nick was right to give some of it a try, though lately he was barely dragging himself out of bed, having made himself ill with the local concoctions. There was apparently no end to the foolishness of twenty-four-year-olds.

She sat down on a stool, feeling tired herself. She had been here late last night, taking a meal with Samwan's household—a sprawling, lengthy affair that seemed to never end, not even providing her a proper moment to slip out.

As she sat watching the happy mayhem of tithe-day, she noticed a wallishen, the dramatic folk art of the compounds. Bailey scanned it, hoping it had no green-draped figures. No, this one wasn't about humans.

It was about Irran. Bailey felt inordinately pleased—she actually thought she had this one figured out. Someone was pulling a child from the river, and someone else was pulling palm fronds off huts . . . which would mean that Irran's boy had been found alive. Ah. A nice wallishen, for once.

Bailey looked beyond the wallishen to Samwan's engine hut—only half completed, and without the new river engine the mistress had been expecting. With an inner wince, Bailey remembered that this was Samwan's punishment for allowing Bailey to sing in front of the hoda, though Samwan didn't know about it until afterward.

A shrill voice broke her reverie. Looking up, Bailey saw Samwan in deep dispute with a judipon. He was an old man, but his voice matched Samwan's in volume. In keeping with the judipon vow of river hands, he was dressed in a plain tunic and leggings. As they argued over the tithe, some of the paper rounds slipped, scattering on the ground. The judipon scrambled to respindle his precious records, but at that moment, shouts from near the river caught everyone's attention.

Samwan turned from the judipon, hurrying toward the dock, with Bailey in close pursuit.

A skiff was pulling up to the pier, paddled by two men bearing a bundle between them. They brought it onto the dock as a wail went up nearby.

Irran struggled forward, even at the same moment that a flap of cloth fell away from what the Dassa men were lugging, and Bailey saw that it was a young child, terribly bloated, dead long enough to turn the color of the river.

Irran fell to her knees on the pier, reaching for the pitiful bundle, holding out her arms, crying, insistent on having the body. The Dassa men looked to Samwan for direction. She nodded. And though Bailey could smell the rot of the body from where she stood, the men gently laid it in its mother's arms. Then Irran began to rock and moan. All the women took up her dirge; it was quite alarming, the volume of the cries.

Finally Irran stopped wailing, and peeled back the blanket in which her son was wrapped, looking at the awful ruin as though it were the sweetest sight, as tears flowed down her face.

Bailey felt her own eyes heat up, her throat thicken. She shook it off. For heaven's sake, children died all the time, didn't they? Always running off in storms. Always . . .

Bailey turned away. She was going to lose control. It would be unthinkable to cry in front of all these people, and she wouldn't, certainly not. But the tears started from her eyes nonetheless. She stalked away from the crowd, along the riverbank, where a narrow beach allowed her to walk free of the welter of vegetation.

Around a bend in the islet, she sat on a tree trunk beached by the storm. Hugging herself, she felt tears moving through her body, upward, to her face. Didn't she know that nothing good came from crying? It spoiled one's makeup, and puffed up one's eyes, ruined the voice . . .

And it accomplished nothing. She would have cried for her sister, or her daughter, or whatever you called a clone. But it wouldn't have accomplished anything; she was still dead. Dead of infection following surgery.

She wiped her eyes furiously, but still the damn tears.

Setting aside her hat, Bailey knelt by the river and washed her face. The water was cool, despite the torrid heat of the day. After a time she found herself sitting in the mud of the river, letting her face dry, letting the sun fall on it. She closed her eyes.

Her parents had developed the clone as soon as it became clear that Bailey had the voice of an angel. Bailey lived with the knowledge that someday, when she began to age, the clone's larynx would be hers. Her parents had died by the time Bailey started having trouble hitting the high notes.

It was always the clone's fate; it was why Bailey and she never met. Her parents had paid well to keep Remy comfortable. Remy, she was called by her caretakers—although until recently Bailey hadn't known her name. Her parents had explained that the girl would just lose her voice, that was all—but the infection took her. And Bailey, also undergoing surgery, for the implantation, didn't hear about the death until later. All this in strictest secrecy, to forestall adverse publicity. By the time she learned of the clone's death, crying would have done no good whatsoever.

So even in her advanced years Bailey still had the voice of an angel—to the consternation of her enemies. And then, after a few more years of a remarkable career, she decided that she was tired. Tired in body, tired of the stage, tired of working nights.

By then she knew that she had committed a crime. Simple people would have figured it out right away, but Bailey was a grand dame of the stage, and she was by no means simple. So at last, when she was retired and had the leisure to have a conscience, she had had a rather large attack of it.

She would never sing again. That took care of further profits from her dead sister, daughter, clone.

And then there was reparation. The one good thing.

It was still worth doing.

She stood up, a little wobbly. By God, it *was* worth doing.

A litter carried by judipon came through the assembly room, bearing Homish. And although Anton and Maypong had been waiting all night for an interview with the head judipon, they bore the litter past the two of them and set it into a canoe, where they began paddling swiftly down the Nool River. Homish was going for his obligatory sexual swim, Maypong said, although the old man was beyond a proper contribution.

Now the sun came up over the roof of the judipon pavilion, charging the river with molten light. The already oppressive heat notched up. Even so the river room was filling with Dassa, seeking advice, asking judgments, telling dreams, and receiving interpretations. It was a baffling subculture, one that Maypong had drilled him in for this private interview—if it ever came. The judipon said that Anton must go alone, an unwelcome restriction.

Maypong would know what to say and not say. He trusted her, since that day of the storm, when she'd stood by his side and dared oppose the king. In token of her allegiance, he had shared with her the information about the Quadi satellites, that the old race was calling more than humans to this world. She was not shocked. To her, it was natural to think the cosmos housed other beings. There were the Quadi, of course. There were humans. If other beings came, they could be no worse than the humans had been, she'd said with a straight face.

And so, with Homish gone, they waited. Anton tried to think through what he would say to this judipon, if he was allowed to see him. But his thoughts instead turned to a vision of last week's hunt. The day was seared into his memory. The dead woman—barely a woman, yet bearing a child, and dead because of it. He had tried to save her—though he'd had no hope of doing so. His borrowed knife had killed her. And he'd profited from that, achieving his goal of freedom from the palace. So he was just like his father, profiting from a world he didn't create, but must condone. It was a muddy world when it came to ethics.

He was finally saved from these thoughts by Homish's return. The judipon loaded him off the barge, and he looked better. Some color was in his face. He pointed at Anton.

"Oh, here he is at last. Nirimol," he said to his chancellor, "look who has paddled over to see me." The judipon motioned for Anton to follow as Homish was borne along on his litter. Nirimol was at his side, the tallest of them, as thin as the spindles on which they kept their records.

Anton glanced at Maypong, who smiled at him. "You are ready, Anton. Remember my lessons."

Homish's high-pitched voice echoed down the corridors as his bearers hurried onward. "What do you think, Nirimol? Anoon has finally come to give us respect. We rise, we rise!" A series of barks finally registered with Anton as laughter. So far Homish was the only Dassa besides children that he'd heard laugh out loud. He wasn't sure this was a good sign.

The pavilion was not so grand as Vidori's. In fact, as Anton passed through the woody corridors, he found them faded and in disrepair. Screens sagged in places, and little cocoons of water beetles nestled in the corners.

Nirimol led the way, his tunic ill-fitting, as if the hoda tailors could not bring themselves to craft so tall a garment. His hair was worn in a bun on top of his head, not the fine roll of the Dassa women, but a functional knot that only added to his height. *A powerful man,* Maypong had called him.

The old man was saying, "Even the big woman dreams, Nirimol, she told me so, as I swam. Oh yes, it was a good dream, too! She dreamed of fire ants swarming. Mark that down, Nirimol: fire ants!"

Nirimol flicked a wrist at a hoda who brought him one of the elaborate writing contraptions they used, a hookah-like instrument, with which Nirimol made notes on a round disk of paper, even as he walked.

They passed rooms where judipon, singly or in groups, bent over papers and stacked spindles, or spun them around, feeling the surfaces, calling out numbers to others who recorded the numerations of the Dassa. It was beyond Anton's vocabulary to know what sums they discussed.

Entering Homish's apartments, Anton reeled from the ghastly odor that filled the room. The hoda carried the old man forward, carefully arranging him on a sleeping platform amid a jumble of brocaded blankets. On the floor surrounding the bed were jars and bottles and ceramic vases that likely were Homish's medicinals. Already a chancellor was spooning a syrup into Homish's mouth, dabbing at the sides of his mouth, where as much dribbled out as went in.

Homish shoved the chancellor away, coughing. "Enough," he croaked, slapping at the insistent hands. He looked up at Nirimol with eyes awash in rheum. "Make them stop, Niri," he said, like a small child begging a favor.

Nirimol glared at the attendants, who slunk away, but remained hovering.

With a sinking feeling Anton saw that he would have at least thirty witnesses for his interview, when he had hoped for privacy.

"Homish-rah," Anton said when the attendants quieted, "thank you."

The old man looked startled. "And who are you?"

Nirimol bent low as though to explain, but again the thin arm came out with a slapping action. "No, let him say."

"I am Anton Prados, a guest in your land, rahi."

"Oh, Anoon, is it? Finally come to give respects?" The potentate smiled, showing bad teeth. Even with good teeth, the gesture would have boded ill. "After you've spent your respects with my family, I'm surprised you have anything left for an old man like me."

Anton saw it was to be a bad interview. Maypong had said that Homish liked to call Vidori and Oleel *family,* and not always sincerely, either.

"Your pardon, rahi, if I am unschooled in your ways. I hope for your indulgence."

The voice was like cracking eggs. "Begs my pardon, Nirimol. You heard."

"Yes, rahi," the chancellor muttered. He then put on a pair of mitts, and to Anton's amazement began to massage Homish's left hand. Restoring circulation, Anton guessed. Homish was the first Dassa individual he'd seen who looked ill. But then again, Homish did not so much look unwell as infirm from age. Maypong said that Homish had "pri of many years," and as she said it she looked regretful, as though pri ran out eventually.

One of the slaves came forward to the side of the bed that Anton couldn't see. She pulled back the covers. There was a hose and nozzle, and much fumbling about. Homish groaned, but didn't slap the hoda away.

That procedure accomplished, the old man summoned a backrest, and settled against it. He fixed Anton with a direct stare. "So the big woman sent you, did she?"

Anton thought that likely to be Oleel. "No one sent me, by your pardon, rahi. I've come for your help, by myself."

Homish pounced. "Oh, count again, young hoda. How many people came in the skiff today, Nirimol?"

"Two, rahi."

"Can you count, Captain Anoon?" Homish asked. "Did you come alone?"

"As you see, I am alone before you. But I wish Maypong were here to help me."

Homish's eyes stopped wandering and locked in on him. "Finally, the truth. Hmm. Maybe you are harmless. Coming in a skiff, not a barge—no pretensions. But leaving the king's pavilion, how do you explain that, when the king makes you his guest, and then you turn from him. Why?" Without waiting for Anton to answer, the old man plunged on: "The king is my friend, yes, we were born on the same day, the day of all braids, and have a dozen children, each of us. Can you say the same?"

"I have no children, rahi, regrettably."

Not only Homish, but all the judipon looked startled at this pronouncement.

"Well, that is a lie," Homish said. His eyes swam in their sallow orbs, as though tainted with urine.

Anton was losing the thread of this conversation.

"King Anaar and I . . ." Homish faltered as though he also was loosing the topic. "But that was his father." He pursed his lips. "It's Vidori, now, isn't it?"

Anton said, "Yes, rahi, Vidori is king, and I must ask his pardon for leaving his palace, but my mission is desperate, and I must seek help where I can."

Homish yanked his hand away from Nirimol's ministrations. "With the big woman, even?" Homish asked. His voice wavered, but he was very much paying attention.

"No, rahi." The old man was keeping track of who paid

respects to whom. So Anton was glad to say he'd visited *here* before *there*.

From the tube that ran under the covers, a trickling sound issued, and then with a foul smell something splashed into a ceramic urn, clarifying the tube's purpose.

"Sometimes the truth, sometimes lies," Homish muttered. "What am I to make of this hoda, Nirimol?"

"Ask him a dream, my lord," Nirimol murmured. The chancellor turned to Anton, regarding him for the first time. His eyes were pale, giving him a hollow look. Anton did not think the man wanted this interview to occur.

"A dream!" Homish cawed. "Yes, we'll have a dream. Do you dream, Anoon?"

"I would rather suffer for what I do than for what I dream, rahi." Anton would not step into the minefield of dream interpretation. *Maypong,* he thought, *what now?*

"*Suffer,*" Homish repeated. "He is afraid of me. Good." He took a sip of a proffered broth. For a moment his eyelids fell halfway down, and Anton thought he might sleep. But Homish's voice came softly: "I used to be a Power to fear. Now I am surrounded by bottles and poisons." He looked directly at Anton, and his voice was soft but firm. "I would die, if they would let me. I spit out the medicinals at night. Save them up in my cheeks and spit them out, but they know my tricks." He glanced at Nirimol, not unkindly.

"Rahi," Anton said, "I am sorry for your troubles, truly. I also have troubles, and would ask your help. I have waited all night to ask your help."

"All night? They kept you waiting?" Homish sighed. "Then ask, Anoon, since you waited all night. Ask me your questions." Homish closed his eyes, either to sleep or to better concentrate.

"Rahi, long ago the Quadi put spheres in the sky, and used them to send messages. The Quadi had great powers, as you know. Their powers might help my people, who suffer far away. When we came here, the king told me he knew nothing about messages, and now I come searching everywhere in the Olagong to find out more."

Homish's eyes snapped open. "Messages. Oh yes, I've heard about your messages." He gestured at a chancellor, who looked confused. "Messages," Homish spat at him. "The spindle, you fool, the spindle." The attendant fled the room.

"Now we come to the subject," Homish said. Nirimol helped him to sit up straighter, as the attendant returned with a tall sheaf of spindled papers. The spindle was set upon the floor at the old man's elbow.

Homish's hands were trembling as he reached for the middle of the spindle, pulling at several paper rounds that came loose, having slits through the radius on one side. "Here, here . . ." Homish was fumbling with two of the plates, but one of them slipped to the floor. His fingers traced the ridges upon the paper, trembling in his excitement.

Anton stepped forward, astonished at the flurry of activity, hoping for something from this decayed Third Power of the Olagong.

With surprising vigor, Homish waved a paper round at Anton. "You came to the Sodesh in your air barge—that is the first river, but the tenth day. Ten and one accumulate to eleven, as any numerator can tell you. Eleven! But the year is 5042—that is eleven again. There is a message for you, if you were wise, Anoon. But a man who flees a king's hospitality is not wise. That is one reason we know that you are not true-born."

Homish fluttered his hands at Nirimol, who withdrew another paper round from the spindle, handing it to his chief. Now, with a paper in each hand, Homish waved them at Anton, looking like a skinny bird trying to take off.

"The Sodesh, I say! Landing right on Huvai's isle, the twenty-first isle, in the records. Now that is one short of double your number." Here Homish looked slyly at Anton, as if checking to see if he had guessed the significance.

Anton had not.

"But Huvai's birth number is ten, and that equals one. Twenty-one and one arrives at twenty-two! You see?"

Clearly, the old man thought this was a triumph of numeration. Anton felt he should respond. "Very interesting, rahi. Please tell me, by your pardon, how my number of eleven can help me."

Homish's face collapsed into a deep grimace, and he licked his lips. "How? How?" Slowly, his face relaxed into confusion. He turned to Nirimol, clutching at his chancellor's tunic. "How was it, Nirimol? Eleven and eleven, because Huvai's birth number . . ."

Nirimol bent close to Homish's ear and said, "Because eleven is the climbing number, my lord." He straightened up, but Homish still looked unhappy. The chancellor bent down again. "The cloud country, my lord."

Homish's face flared to understanding. "Yes, the cloud country! The numbers say you must climb, Anoon, and walk the upper regions, just like any novice judipon. You are no better! All must walk among the clouds and from walking learn the wisdom of the land. All wisdom is in the land, Anoon, all wisdom."

Homish slapped the papers off his bed. "We record everything. It gives us something to do." He glared at the attendants clustered around the room. "They are all useless old men frittering away their pri-less years on numeration and dreams. But wisdom is in the land . . ."

"What is in the cloud country, rahi?" Anton had come close to the bedside, despite the disapproving looks of Nirimol. "What should we look for?"

Homish regarded the paper round in his hand. He traced his fingers over the bumps. Then he grabbed Anton's hand. The old man's fingers were as cold as granite, and as strong. "You will pardon my touch, Anoon," he whispered. "An old man can offer no sarif, and a young man wants none from such as me."

Then, feathering Anton's fingers along the paper,

Homish crooned, "Yes, yes, feel the numerations of the land. But you must be blind to feel them . . ."

The ridges and humps of the paper pressed into Anton's fingertips, like a language impossibly foreign. But it was not the paper that Homish wanted him to read. It was the land . . .

"What is it, rahi? Help me."

But Homish dropped his hands, exhausted.

Nirimol motioned a hoda to remove the backrest. "Sleep now, Homish-rah," he said.

"No, no. No potions," Homish pleaded. He fought to sit up without the backrest, and succeeded, despite several chancellors' coming forward with broths and blankets. He looked at Anton, as though Anton might save him. Indeed, Anton wanted to clear the room, open the windows, and pull out the tubes. But Nirimol was in charge, and Nirimol said his lord must sleep.

Pushing the others away, he said, "Take the hose, take it, damn you all." A hoda came forward and, pulling the covers to one side, removed the tube, even as Homish struggled to stand. Nirimol steadied him.

Homish came up only to Anton's chest. His feet were bare, his toenails so long they curled like sheep horns.

"Now that you have spurned the king, where do you live, Anoon?" came the quavering voice.

"On the islet the king gave me, rahi."

Homish nodded. "Oh yes, *the king gave you*, because you tricked him. Does a guest trick a host? Does he?"

"I was told it was the law, rahi."

"The law!" Homish turned to Nirimol. "He talks of the law to the law keepers!" Nirimol's reaction was contemptuous.

"I am the law," Homish croaked. "In the Olagong, all come to the Third Dassa for the law, as you do not. But if we talk of the law, then I will tell you the law says that hoda may not own the isles, nor any handful of soil." He advanced on Anton, pointing at him. "You are hoda, all of you; though you sail through the air, and some of you are not female, yet you are degenerate. You pollute the rivers if you stand on the isle in ownership." He staggered forward, forcing Anton to back up. "Pollution. That is what you are." When Anton didn't react, Homish lost control. "Get out, get out!" Supported on Nirimol's arm, the old man got up an alarming head of steam, driving Anton to the apartment entrance.

"Rahi, my pardon," Anton was saying, but Homish went on.

"I dreamed that you died, you and your hoda crew, and your body was cast into the river. All bodies cast into the river. Yes, a true dream."

Nirimol motioned a hoda to help him get Homish back into bed, but still Homish fought him. Finally he turned on Nirimol. "Let go of me, you river turd."

Slowly, Nirimol released his grip, his eyes like weathered bone.

Swaying, the old man looked utterly incapable of standing unsupported. But he did stand, and more, taking a few rigid steps toward Anton. His eyes were pleading, and Anton closed the distance between them, unsure whether the old man would beat him or hug him.

Homish pulled on Anton's sleeve, pulling Anton's face down to his lips. He whispered in his ear, his breath a fetid inundation. "Don't trust them," he whispered.

"Who?" Anton whispered back.

"The judipon," Homish said, barely audible. "River hands will pull you under."

He released his grip on Anton's sleeve. Then, pulling himself as tall as his stature allowed, Homish raised his hand in an imperious gesture.

"Get out, I say!"

Anton locked gazes with the old man, half addled, but only half. Then turned and strode from the bedchamber, sucking in a deep breath of river air, discharging the medicinal fumes from his lungs.

TWELVE

"Let me paddle, Maypong-rah."

"No, Anton," she said, "but you may bring out the meal I have prepared." She looked back from her paddling, eyeing a small bundle.

Turning out of the Nool River into the Sodesh, they had left Homish's pavilion. The river was milky in the morning light.

A river rat swam by, its top-of-the-head eyes swiveling to note the skiff. Anton had yet to see a crocodile or any venomous snakes. Perhaps the Quadi judged them dispensable—this being one of a thousand questions regarding what the Quadi did, and why. *All wisdom is in the land*, Homish had said. A nice folk saying, but Anton was already formulating a plan to hike to the canyon lands, as the old man had urged. Maypong thought it decidedly too dangerous, being so far from Vidori's protection and given that it was nothing but a place of superstition.

As Anton unwrapped the meal of figs and cooked roots, he asked her, "If Homish believes the canyon lands confer wisdom, maybe it's something concealed in jungle growth—in ruins or caves."

"Anton," she had responded, "would I have kept such knowledge from you? Do you think I am so bad a chancellor?"

"I know you'd tell me what you know. I'm looking for what you *don't* know."

"If I don't know, how can it be possible for me to tell you?" She turned a brief smile on him. "You will have to help me to eat, since I am paddling, Anton." She was challenging him to feed her while she sped their skiff over the water.

He leaned forward and held out a piece of fruit. She turned toward him, and he placed it in her mouth, but in the chop of the current, he touched her lips. The intimacy of the touch took him by surprise.

She made eye contact, then. He was the first to break it. So she had said she was willing, and he had said no thanks. They were getting good at communication.

"Anton, we are alone on the Sodesh. We could find shelter here. I know many places."

"Maypong-rah. We are . . . you are my advisor. Appointed by the king. It is a serious role."

"Thankfully, yes. You have said so many times. But I think now we may also be friends."

Her paddle dipped and pulled, never dripping on her tunic. She was deft on the river, deft at most things. But he would rather have her a friend than a lover. It might be best not to have any lover at all, as Bailey had sternly advised him.

He continued, "We have a different way of looking at it, Maypong-rah. Humans would think if all friends have sex together, then sex is trivial."

"How peculiar that you should think so, Anton."

"Sometimes humans are bothered if sex doesn't mean anything." Although that afternoon with Joon had been hardly more than lust.

"Oh, it means everything," Maypong said. "Where would the Olagong be if people had sarif with only this person or that one, and our bonds were so few? How would we care for each other throughout the braided world, if we had not touched each other? Where would we drown our desire for each other? Sarif is the river of our hearts. *Trivial* is not the right word."

"No, your pardon, Maypong-rah."

"But you must let me know when you decide to change your mind," she said cheerfully.

They continued to share their small meal, Maypong paddling with relentless rhythm, Anton parceling out the food. In the still air, the river's surface held a reflected world of rippled forest, made of sunlight. His heart lifted to be on the river with her, on such a day. Boats and barges passed them on both sides, the occupants gazing at them directly or furtively. A few waved, no doubt having picked up the gesture from Bailey.

On the shoreline Anton noted yet another war barge, tied up to a pier, with its cargo of fallen soldiers from the latest border skirmish. *Killed by hoda,* some of them, the hoda that were swelling the ranks of the Vol. The Vol were certainly not Quadi. Anton had persuaded the king to allow the ground mission to examine a Vol cadaver. Zhen's genetic analysis showed that the individual was closely related to the Dassa.

"Anton." Maypong was alert, straining to look upriver, but still paddling steadily.

In the distance, a barge now commanded the middle portion of the Sodesh.

"The Princess Joon," Maypong said.

He watched the poles flash up and down in unison, like the segmented legs of a giant water insect. Somehow he hoped she would pass them by.

"She will have you on her barge," Maypong said, paddling still.

He thought that likely if Joon had her way. And he didn't

want to offend Joon, both for her own sake and for her political position. "Shall I go with her, Maypong-rah? Tell me the proper thing."

"She will expect it."

"What does she want?" The craft grew larger, coming on.

Maypong lay the paddle over the gunwales, gaining time, letting their skiff move backward on the current. "To be queen," she said.

Anton swallowed, seeing the house of cards take on another story. That was the politics of it, of course: that tryst with Joon, her pursuit of him, and now, coming down the river. What a fool he'd been.

"How am I a part of her plan?"

"Perhaps she wishes to use you—your high armament. I can't say what her schemes all are. But you must choose, Anton."

"Choose?"

"Yes, to go or not. You chose once, did you not?"

By the tone of her voice, Anton wondered if Maypong was jealous of what had transpired between him and Joon. But no; Nick had said there was no such thing as sexual jealousy here. It would be like taking it amiss if one's lover shook hands with someone else.

Maypong had turned around and was now facing him, waiting. Waiting for him to choose.

Only a couple of hundred meters away, poles began retracting. He saw a woman in vivid blue standing at the side of the barge, surrounded by many hoda.

Maypong locked gazes with him. "Refuse her," she said.

"I will," he answered.

She frowned, her upper lip beaded with perspiration. "The difficulty is that you will offend her and she will be disgraced in public." Maypong had withdrawn her knife from her belt. "Unfortunately, we are having an accident." She plunged her knife into the reed bottom of the skiff, and then again.

As Anton watched her in amazement, the boat began taking on water, rapidly soaking his boots, then suddenly swamping the entire skiff, leaving them floundering in the cool river. Maypong managed to say to him, "Having swum in the river, you have been vulgar, therefore being cordial is not acceptable today."

A shout went up from the barge, and several hoda jumped in to help them.

Surrounded by hoda, he swam with Maypong to the barge, where servants pulled them out of the river. They were now sitting in a puddle of water, like fishing catches.

When he looked up at Joon, he found her gazing at him with an intensity that made him uneasy. He stood to face her, as hoda assisted Maypong to rise.

"A poorly made skiff," Joon said. "Did you make it yourself?"

Well, that rather settled the matter of what her mood would be. "Your pardon, Lady" was all he could think of to say.

The blue of her gown cast a stormy glow into her cheeks. "Thankfully we happened by at the very moment your boat gave up." She turned knowing eyes on Maypong.

"Rahi, thank you," Maypong said, looking innocent.

"How is my brother Lord Homish, Captain?" Joon asked, switching gears.

Homish was not her brother, but it was a convention to call him that. And apparently it was also a convention to spy upon Anton. "He did not look well, Lady."

"He does not thrive," she observed, without sympathy.

The expression called to mind their conversation on her roof deck, and the formidable intelligence of the woman. Someday she would have the royal pavilion, and her ideas about equality—if sincere—might mature. But she was not queen yet.

At a command, brocaded cloth was brought forward and draped over his and Maypong's shoulders.

Joon said, "While you were rushing out to meetings,

there have been occurrences, Captain. For instance, the hoda Gilar now enjoys the hospitality of the Second Dassa." Joon flicked her eyes at Maypong, and then back at Anton. "You will recall that this hoda was one whose tongue clipping you observed in my father's plaza."

"I know who Gilar is," Anton said coldly.

"Yes, this hoda is one who has already offended my uldia. Thankfully, Oleel will teach her proper respect, such as she somehow has never learned."

Maypong was shivering, eyes averted. This was ill news about Gilar, that Oleel had taken control of her. Anton wanted to comfort Maypong, but knew that must wait.

Joon turned from them, watching as several hoda dragged the ruined skiff onto the barge. Walking over to the craft, full of river weeds and trailing sticks, Joon remarked, "Oh, see how poorly this skiff is constructed, with two very bad holes in the bottom. It is a wonder it didn't sink sooner."

She turned back to the two of them. "We have heard how difficult Gilar is to train. It was necessary to put a ball of human soil into her mouth until it melted." She looked at Maypong. "Are you warm enough, Maypong-rah? You do shake."

Maypong's voice was small. "Yes, rahi, my thanks." Her hair had fallen from her chignon, and fell about her face, hiding her expression.

But Anton was gathering a temper. "So much for our talk of equality, Lady. It meant less than I hoped."

Joon's composure ruffled for a moment. Perhaps she wasn't used to directness. "My pardon, Captain. I only report what I have heard, not what I have done, or *would have done*."

Suddenly he was weary—of the politics, of Joon. "Rahi, I will need a skiff. My duties call me, though I thank you for your help."

Joon held him a moment longer with her eyes. She seemed on the verge of something more, perhaps something more tender than she had shown in this exchange. But then she motioned to a hoda, and soon a good skiff was brought from aft stowage. They lowered it to the water.

Anton climbed in front and took the paddle. As they pushed off from the barge, he took the cloth from his shoulders and tucked it around Maypong, who was shivering.

The many poles of Joon's barge crashed down all at once, launching them in earnest downriver, setting up a wake that crested the skiff's gunwale, soaking Anton and Maypong again.

He set the paddle into the river and drew strongly on it, fueled by a simmering anger. "I'm very sorry, Maypong," he said, forgetting the honorific.

After a moment her voice came: "No, Anton, I am sorry." She went on, "Oleel uses Gilar against you. Because of me. I am sorry to cause you such trouble."

"Oleel is trying to provoke me. Because you and I are close."

Her silence was his confirmation. He jammed the paddle into the water, drawing hard, thinking of the uldia, whose ambitions against the king included torture of youngsters. And he must not interfere, or give Oleel any reason to condemn him. Already, Bailey had given the uldia reason to complain. But that was only singing, and Bailey's popularity was not much tarnished. His own status was rather less secure.

He propelled the boat in the direction of his islet, hauling with the paddle until his arms grew weary. In the silence of the remaining trip, he had time to grow puzzled. Puzzled why Oleel thought that someone in his position—depending on the king—would react foolishly to cruelties against a hoda. How did she guess that his first inclination would be to interfere?

He let that question simmer, while the image came vividly to mind of a young woman with her mouth full of dung.

*   *   *

Rain lashed at the hut roof, making the radio hard to hear. The garble of sounds hurt Nick's ears: the noise of the rain, the noise of the river, the noise of the forest. In all this cacophony and in the dead middle of the night, he knew someone should be on guard, but they were all huddled around the radio, listening.

Zhen hunkered over the comm unit, adjusting the pickup, getting nowhere.

She'd been on guard duty when the transmission came in, but by the time she got Anton to the science hut, Sergeant Webb's voice had drifted into static.

Now all five of them sat along the hut perimeter, looking worried. He feared it was more bad news, since Webb wouldn't have called during their sleep period if it wasn't important. Nick had the sickening feeling the whole mission was starting to slide downhill. He carried it in his stomach, the shock and dismay of the last few weeks.

And then Oleel had dumped him.

She'd promised him the langva distillate, *promised* him. Guinea pig, for the mission. His big discovery, maybe. But now she'd cut him off, wouldn't see him. And the things she'd *said* . . .

Maypong was sitting there so calmly, smoothing her tunic. Oh, Maypong was happy. Going off on high-level meetings with Anton, living with them as though she were—well, human. And next to her, Bailey, trying her hand at a little Dassa weaving project, as Maypong helped her. Bailey looked ridiculous.

They had sat for the past hour, talk drifting to this thing and that, but mostly of Anton's meeting with Homish and the planned expedition to the uplands. But Nick could tell them it didn't matter, that the answer was right here underneath their noses, in the chemistry. He would have told them, but now his proof was slipping through his fingers— he had no medicines; he was getting worse. Oleel had suckered him, dragged all she wanted out of him, promising him life itself. And, perhaps better, *honor*. With an effort, Nick swallowed, his throat a tube of sores. He would have died for his people, would have died in honor. Now he would just die.

It was still possible that Zhen would find something. People would remember that it was Nick Venning who'd zeroed in on the langva and its immunological essences, Nick Venning who'd snatched the sample from Oleel. If that too were not just a sham.

Bailey looked up from her handwork. "Nick, go to bed. You look awful."

Anton turned to Nick, looking at him with a fresh, almost startled, gaze. "Get some sleep, Lieutenant." He smiled. "Permission to take it easy."

Take it easy. Nick could have struck him. Sweat poured down his face. Despite the storm, the night was ungodly hot.

"No thanks, Captain," he managed to say.

Without looking up, Zhen fired off a shot: "That's what happens when you drink the local hooch."

Before Nick could take the audio cables and strangle the woman, the radio whistled and gargled, drawing their attention.

"They're still sending," Zhen said, though it was all noise.

Nick said, "When the message comes in, I think we ought to keep it among ourselves." He flicked his eyes toward Maypong.

"Oh for heaven's sake," Bailey said, pulling at a knot. "If Maypong were going to kill us in our beds, she's had plenty of chances before now."

Nick observed that the captain let that be, let Bailey support Maypong, so he didn't have to, didn't have to stand up for his latest concubine. Though he wasn't completely certain she was.

Bailey grimaced as she yanked at a thread. "Damn this

stuff, anyway." She shoved the mangled braid at Maypong, who looked bemused at the tangle. Patiently, she began to pick at first one thread, then another. It made Nick edgy to watch such fiddling with string. Then his mind brought Oleel around again, like a nightmare carousel. Each time she came around, she said, *No pri can save you. You are dead already.* She swung off on the circle, her hair bun coiling like a snake. Then she was coming round again. *No pri can save you. Save you. Dead already.*

The way she said it made it sound like it hardly mattered. So alone. Those who had been friends no longer were. Those who were against him smirked at his downfall. He wanted someone—maybe Bailey, maybe Anton—to say, *Nick, I need you to help me. God, man, are you feeling OK?* Just the little human things that were not happening on this mission from hell.

Now Anton was seeking out the Three Powers, finally, but not including Nick. They might even go up-country. And guess who wouldn't be going along?

A voice filled the cabin: . . . *check, over.* Restoration *calling Camp Shaw, over.*

Zhen was on it. "We hear you, *Restoration.* Spill it—we have a storm here, bad reception, over."

This is Sergeant Webb, are you present, Captain? Webb's voice was so clear for a moment that he seemed to be hovering in the middle of the room.

Anton came forward. "I'm here, Sergeant, go ahead."

Captain, this is for your ears only, over.

Anton paused for a moment, then turned to survey his small group. "I'm going to have you all stay."

Nick tried to restrain his incredulity. "Captain, respectfully, just the crew, no others." He looked over at Maypong, who was studiously untangling knots.

"She's my chancellor, Lieutenant. It's a matter of trust."

Nick stood up, dizzy, holding on to the corner post of the hut. "Damn right it's a matter of trust! I don't trust her, and maybe others don't." He looked around, but no one met his eyes. "As for chancellor, don't make me laugh. What are we, going native? She's Vidori's minion, for God sakes."

Maypong rose. "I must excuse myself for a private thing." Catching Anton's eye, she said, "My pardon."

OK, Nick thought. *The woman knows when to take a potty break, give her that.* With Maypong out of the room, he sat down again, under Anton's dark stare.

Anton turned back to the radio. "Proceed, Sergeant. I'm listening."

The unit coughed, and then homed in on the signal. *Captain, the crew—nineteen of them—without me, and without my knowledge, have presented a majority petition.* The noise that followed sounded like a chorus of nonsense.

"Repeat, Sergeant, couldn't hear. What kind of petition, over?"

. . . go home, Captain. The crew voted to go home. They want to go now." After a pause he added, *"They're young and dumb, sir. I'd lock 'em all up, but who'd run the ship?*

"Understood, Sergeant. How serious is it, Webb? Do they make demands?"

No, sir, just saying the mission isn't working, and to go home. It's ugly, Captain. Hasn't come to arms yet, but some of the lads are sick; you know which ones. Some of 'em aren't holding steady anymore.

Nick watched as Anton struggled to digest this blow. The mission was sliding downhill, oh yes, and it wasn't just Nick who thought so. He'd wondered how long they'd hold on with the virus passing among them like a hot rumor. They didn't want to die in the subzero universe, far from home.

"Sergeant. We're making some headway. I'm going up-country in a couple of days, pursuing a lead from the chief judipon. Maybe we can see something under all that cloud cover. Tell them, Sergeant, that we're making progress."

I'll tell them, Captain.

Anton caught Bailey's eye. She had dropped the needle-work. Standing, she walked over to him, motioning for the hand mike. "If it's a mutiny, perhaps I might be allowed a word with the young criminals?"

"That's not a word I'd use," Anton said. "Don't call it mutiny. Not yet."

A half-smile stabbed her cheek. "I'll leave such things to you, but let me speak to Sergeant Webb."

She put her mouth to the mike. "Now, Ethan," she began, calling the sergeant by his first name, "I want you to tell the boys and girls that there's a very good chance we'll all go home heroes. This is no time to get cold feet. The genetic codes are here, I'm sure of it."

Webb answered, *Yes, ma'am. But what the crew is afraid of is they'll all be dead by the time you find them, begging your pardon.*

"This was always a dangerous mission. Did I promise you anything different?" Without waiting for a reply, she continued, "Remind them, if you would, that I have no intention of being held hostage by my own employees."

Bailey had a glint in her eye that Nick had seen only once before, when someone had put on a recording of her voice over the ship's systems, as a birthday surprise. She had stalked to the console and yanked the tronic wafer out of its slot as if pulling a bad tooth. Never said a word about it then or ever again.

"Remind them, if you would," Bailey said, "that this isn't a union ship. We don't whine, and we don't vote." She thrust the mike back to Anton, as though it were his turn to sing.

"Sergeant," Anton said. "I leave it to you what to say to them. You're in charge up there. But tell them I'm asking them to hold on."

Yes, sir. But . . .

"Go ahead, Sergeant."

Sorry, Captain, but they're giving you one week. Then they're firing up the ship and going home. Even if it's over my dead body, which it will be, by God.

Anton still held the mike, struggling with what to say. Then: "Thank you, Sergeant. Message received."

Nick looked at Anton with the first surge of compassion he'd felt for the man in weeks. The crew deserved to be shot for treason.

But then, they were dying anyway.

THIRTEEN

Anton watched as Maypong expertly paddled the skiff, navigating the hugely crowded Puldar, rife with barges, canoes, and skiffs, each one packed with Dassa and slaves. A light rain pitted the river, but rain would not keep the people from welcoming their king home from battle. Behind Anton, Bailey sat, wearing her hat which served her well for an umbrella.

Vidori's war canoes had come down the Sodesh early in the morning. In his wake, every boat in Lolo followed, heading to the palace river steps.

Maypong maneuvered around a skiff overloaded with young Dassa women, boisterous with the prospect of a palace gathering.

Anton hoped that he could get the king's ear for at least a moment. He hadn't spoken to him since the awful hunt, but Anton wanted to give Vidori the news himself, that he was going up-country. He was chasing shadows, perhaps. But here in the Olagong it was all shadows and submerged promises. And he had six days left. He hadn't much doubt that his desperate crew would abandon the mission.

In the distance, the palace bulked up against the sky, towering over the trees and the flat valley lands. Anton saw Vidori's quarters, the topmost level, decked with colored banners of his loyal viven, and nearby, the almost-as-high pavilion of Joon, hung with blue. He wondered if the lady was standing there, watching him approach.

She had pretended to be interested in the conditions of the hoda. To encourage Anton to expose his ideology, so that Oleel could use it against him, to accuse him of encouraging rebellion of the hoda, and their mass escapes to the Vol. If that was the lady's plan, he had sorely disappointed her.

Near the river stairs, the crowd of boats jostled as close to one another as paving bricks, but somehow the water craft managed to snug up, creating a narrow channel for his skiff to pass through. As he approached the stairs, Anton could see Vidori standing at the top of the steps, and there, as Maypong had led him to expect, stood Oleel as well. And Nirimol, although not Homish himself.

Anton clambered out of the boat to assist Bailey onto the river steps, where her jumpsuit got soaked to her knees.

She scolded Anton: "If you'd let us wear palace silks, it wouldn't take eight hours to dry off."

"I could carry you," he said, needling her. Bailey would certainly never make an entrance in that manner. Her sidelong stare only broadened his smile. He led Bailey up to the river room, with Maypong close behind. Or he thought that Maypong was close behind. Sensing her absence, he turned around, and found her pausing at the lower steps. She was looking at someone in the river room.

It was Gilar, standing among Oleel's attendants. Bailey said, "Oh dear. Anton, it's the girl again."

Anton walked back down the steps toward Maypong, wanting to take her arm, or her hand. He caught her eye instead. She had grown very calm. Then, because Vidori was standing at the head of the stairs and had to be greeted, he and Maypong approached him. Vidori wore a fine uniform of gray padded silk. Despite a deep-set fatigue around his eyes, his movements were confident, his smiles frequent. But when he glimpsed Anton his expression hardened, and Anton knew their rift was not forgotten.

"So," Vidori said, nodding at him. "Your duties permit a visit, I see."

"A visit *is* my duty, Vidori-rah, and my pleasure." He turned to Oleel. "My respects, to the Second Dassa, and to the judipon," he said, acknowledging Nirimol as well. Those were the two lines he'd memorized from Maypong, to get a start on the protocols. At his side, she ignored Gilar as best she could.

Vidori looked past him to Bailey. "Ah, the lady of the hats."

Oleel's voice came like a deep gong. "And of the singing, so we have learned."

Bailey made a curtsy. "A bad reputation is better than none at all, Oleel-rah."

Servants brought a plate of food for the king, and Oleel took a morsel from it, and then the viven were helping themselves, and soon the plate was handed down the steps, making the rounds of the commoners gathered there. Anton waited until Oleel's attention was diverted elsewhere, then moved through the viven to the king's side.

"Vidori-rah, a brief moment, if you will walk a pace or two with me."

The king murmured, "I will find you later." Anton nodded and retreated, but as he did so, he found Gilar blocking his way.

She looked at Maypong, standing next to Anton. Her eyes raked over her mother, intensely enough to leave scratches. Then she raised her eyes to Anton, a clear look of such yearning that Anton's heart contracted.

At that moment, Oleel's voice, unmistakably strong, rang out: "Your pardon, Anton, that this hoda blocks you." Oleel was rounding on the girl. "Still no deportment, despite my lessons."

Gilar bent low. Seeing the fire in Oleel's eyes, she went further: She went to her knees, and then onto all fours like a dog.

Oleel stood before them, next to Gilar. She was taller than Anton by a few centimeters, and must have weighed a good bit more, though she wasn't obese. Her bearing was one of a warrior who knew her strength.

Maypong jumped in, "No offense is taken, Oleel-rah. Please allow us to celebrate this day further."

"Yes," Oleel said, "celebrate that the king has returned safely from the wars now waged by hoda with spears. We do celebrate. And grieve. Do you not grieve, Maypong-rah?"

Maypong's voice swam through the clotted air. "I celebrate today, for the king's sake."

Oleel paid no attention to this answer, but called an uldia to her side, whispering. In another moment, the assistant left, then returned with a basket. A wire basket.

"Gilar," Oleel said, "you see how the hoda Bailey wears a hat. You will also wear a hat today." She thrust the cage down to Gilar. "Put it on."

Gilar stared at the basket. People turned to watch the incident unfold, freezing the river room in a tableau of nobles, colors, and Powers—with a young girl on her hands and knees staring at a wire cage.

Anton felt the heat rise in his chest and face. He locked his muscles, his body into place with great effort.

Gilar held out her hand and took the cage from Oleel. She raised it up and slowly brought it down over her head.

"Now," Oleel said, "insert the mouth funnel."

Again, Gilar paused.

"Young hoda," Maypong said, "do not shame your training." Her face was calm, waiting for Gilar to be obedient.

The mouthpiece went in. The little knife was no danger, because her tongue was not thrust through the flange, there being no tongue to do the duty.

Anton met Oleel's eyes. Perhaps she hoped he would do something foolish. Perhaps the viven also hoped that he would. Their eyes were greedy; but he would give them nothing. That light in their eyes alerted him not to indulge himself—by taking the basket and pulling it over Oleel's head.

He found himself crouching down next to the girl. The face in the cage regarded him with clear, amber eyes. "Gilar," he whispered to her, "forgive me." He didn't know what he meant, or what he hoped Gilar would take from his words. It was little; it was nothing. She looked at him with a strange and even fearful intensity. He hoped it wasn't hate. But he didn't blame her if it was.

He stood tall again, and forced himself to walk away. The party resumed as though nothing had happened. Gilar faded into the crowd.

Maypong stood at Anton's side. Composed, accepting. "Do not be distressed, Anton," she said. "The viven watch you."

Anton gazed at the palace nobles, hating them, hating their world.

In the king's river room, the celebration was still under way. Gilar faded into the background, and then—knowing the palace so well—she took the back corridors and side ramps, having cast the wire cage in the river.

The king's roof was slippery in the rain. Gilar flattened herself out and dragged herself toward the top, one hand-hold after another, slowly, slowly. She must make no noise, not yet.

Trickles of water streamed through the thatch before her eyes, separating into strands, then combining in larger channels. Keeping her face down, she scuttled upward, determined not to fall from the steep incline, not to die that inglorious way, by falling into the courtyard.

She pulled harder, hoisting herself ever closer to the lightning rod.

*   *   *

Eventually, Vidori approached Anton. Vidori, the monarch who presided over it all.

They gazed at each other, Vidori's light brown eyes against Anton's black. "Vidori-rah," Anton said, "my mission takes me into upland country tomorrow. I leave with Maypong at dawn, to see if there is anything to be learned in the canyons."

"There is nothing but canyons in the canyons."

"Still, as strangers, we may see what others miss, after long acquaintance."

Vidori nodded, his face smeared from his journey, but still royal, somehow. "Go armed, then."

"I will, rahi."

Vidori made to turn back to his retinue, but paused. "That is all you have to say?"

Anton thought of several things that might be said, such as, *There are those in the braided lands in need of your devotion.*

Vidori seemed to hope for something from him, and not a rebuke, either. Perhaps he wanted some sign that Anton regretted leaving the pavilion.

But Anton answered that *no,* he had nothing more to say.

And on that note, Vidori turned away. Until the clamor began.

Tearing her tunic into nice long strips, Gilar set about binding herself to the rod. Even if they shot her, they'd have to come up to get her. She thought these things with calm resolve. Once you were ready to die, the penalty lost its terror.

When she'd been inside the wire basket in the river room, her vision had cleared. She saw that the big woman had wanted the captain to intervene, to seem to be against the kingdom. Gilar had gone to her knees, hoping to mollify her tormentor, but still, the cage came down. Inside the mask, she saw that Oleel controlled her utterly, prodding her to ruin the human captain.

But then he could never take her to Erth. As he wanted to do.

I'm sorry, he'd said. Maypong had stood by his side, the one who should have said those words, but who would never be forgiven, never, so long as the river ran. Maypong had her palace duties, her chancellorship to the Erth captain. She had her tongue. Gilar, sold for six coins, was no longer her daughter. So the captain was her only hope.

She tightened the knots.

From below the roofline came a voice, calling her. Someone was on the lower story.

Gilar, sang the voice.

It was Bahn.

Go away.

Gilar, come down, I beg you.

The voice seemed to come from another world. It had no body, no reality. There was another world below, a world of people with simple happiness. But it was another country, not Gilar's country. She tied another strip around herself and the rod.

Oh sister, they will kill you.

Leave. Before you die, too.

Gilar, they will punish all of us. This is so wrong, and will bring us suffering. Is that what you want?

Yes. Perhaps it was even true. Perhaps it would shut Bahn up.

After a very long pause, Bahn sang, Then you are no sister to me.

Wasn't the hoda gone yet? From below, she heard Bahn's noisy descent. Gilar sang, Find yourself a lightning rod, Bahn.

With Bahn's retreat, the other world faded. From her perch Gilar could see over the palace, over the plaza, now empty in the rain. She could see over the Puldar River, and into the foggy distance. Above her, but hidden, were the stars. This might be the closest she ever came to them.

She began to sing.

*   *   *

Anton, Bailey, and Maypong hurried along an outside walkway and down a ramp, rushing to the plaza along with other palace denizens, Dassa and hoda alike.

As they emerged onto the covered lower gallery that looked out onto the plaza, they found Vidori standing with Shim and other viven.

Anton went to the king, murmuring something. Then he turned back to Maypong. "It's Gilar," he said, his voice gentle. "She's bound herself to the lightning rod."

Bailey looked at Maypong. She was the *mother*, she should *do* something. But the woman's face was blank as she gazed toward the roof.

Then Bailey heard it. A strain of melody . . . a familiar five notes . . . of Mozart. In an instant, she had the piece—yes, it was "Vedrai, carino." Eerily, the song seemed to come from heaven, from a distance, yet close to hand. The child was singing opera on the king's roof. *Oh dear, oh dear, oh dear.* Now they would shoot her for Mozart's sake. And Bailey was complicit, somehow. *Oh dear God . . . if I had kept my mouth shut, for once.*

Maypong and Anton huddled together, amid the confusion of guards rushing about and uldia gathering in the square. No one noticed as Bailey wound her way into the plaza.

From the first, clear joy of the notes, Gilar knew that song was a form of sarif. She sang with her whole body, trembling with the power of it, knowing that it touched people in intimate ways. The music was strange, and that was part of its allure. It was Erth music, the music she was born to sing. You could no more silence it than you could forbid sarif, the love that bound Dassa to Dassa and hoda to hoda. It was more than sarif. It could enthrall a whole compound, touch many at once, Dassa as well as hoda.

So she sang, full-throated and with abandon, even as the thuds of people climbing the roof came to her ears. It was the commotion of the lower world. It couldn't touch her here. Not before she sang for Captain Anton.

Though the rain threw down a gray curtain, Bailey had a clear view of the child. She was bound to the lightning rod, on the rooftop. Singing.

They would kill her now. Suddenly, she couldn't breathe. She pulled in a breath, but it didn't help; she was suffocating. A nearby viven said, "Bailey, are you well?" He took her arm as though she were about to fall, but she pulled away. "I killed her," she said, to the nobleman's consternation. Then, in her own tongue she repeated, "I killed her." The girl. For her voice.

The voice . . . Gilar's song hovered over the crowd. Soldiers were running up the ramp, climbing from three directions. They seemed not to hear the remarkable voice, the voice of a natural soprano, doing theme and variation on a ten-thousand-year-old song from a different world. No, they couldn't hear it. All they heard was defiance.

Bailey looked toward the king, standing with his retinue. He was conferring with Romang, his war chief, and then Romang was rushing across the plaza as the uldia gave way before him, even Oleel, who stood in the center of the square, looking up.

A head popped up over the edge of the roof. The lower world was here, after all. Gilar saw the soldier's grim expression, his eagerness to lay hands on her. She renewed her song, that small and strange melody that she took for hers, that gift of Erth.

Gilar looked up to the sky, hoping for a brief moment that lightning would come to the metal pole, and take her

away to its realm. She would rather that Captain Anton
come to rescue her. But if not, lightning might do.

Then the soldier had her by the leg, hoisting himself up
at her expense, hauling dreadfully on her, until he too stood
at the roof peak, balancing beside her. He would throw her
down now. She saw how he looked to the plaza, where
massed many soldiers, and, among them, the big woman.

The singing stopped. Instead of Mozart, there was only the
patter of rain. Bailey waited for the girl to cry out, waited
for it to be over. There was nothing she could do; these people would extract their horrible punishment—one from
among their considerable repertoire.

On the second-story roof, she saw movement. Soldiers.
They were bringing the girl down. They tossed Gilar off the
roof of the first-floor gallery, a drop of a few meters, and
then other soldiers caught her like a duffel bag. Romang
was there, arguing with the uldia. The women appeared to
win the argument, because the girl was given over to them.
They brought her forward to face Oleel.

Bailey looked back toward the king, toward Anton and
Maypong, and saw them milling there, under cover, out of
the rain, out of the conflict. She didn't blame them for being
safe and dry. There was nothing to be done. Gilar's fate was
as inevitable as the direction of the Puldar. All downhill.

She could walk away, but wasn't that what she had done
last time? It would be more comfortable just to not watch,
and Bailey had always chosen comfort. She was a selfish old
woman, and she had been a selfish young one.

Deliberately, she moved toward the center of the plaza,
pushing past uldia, and proper Dassa, and soldiers. They
parted for her—even the grim soldiers, even the unbending
uldia. Now, with a front-row position, Bailey watched one
of Oleel's minions bend her ear toward her leader.

*   *   *

Gilar tried to walk independently, but the soldiers yanked her along, hardly letting her feet touch the ground. The rain had washed her clean of fear. Back in the lower world again, she found she cared less than she'd thought about her fate here.

Yet she looked to the place where the king stood, because at his side might be Captain Anton. But there was a great crowd there, and all she could see was . . .

Bailey.

The old woman stood at the edge of the clearing, opposite Oleel. The old woman was watching her. Her posture was stiff. Her eyes said, *See how brave you can be. Be an Erth woman.*

And so she would.

They pulled her down until she was on hands and knees. She saw the knife. They were going to take something.

Ah. Her hand.

Bailey was the only human in the circle.

It was none of her business. It was her business. Things twisted together, and could not be sorted logically. She must stay and watch, be present. It was necessary to be present, and not say that because she wasn't there she wasn't responsible.

I am monstrous, came the thought. *I am not forgiven.*

The uldia splayed Gilar's fingers on the stone paving. Gilar remembered that if they took her whole hand, she would be cast into the river. But if they took only three fingers, she could still be an effective slave. *Take the hand,* she urged them.

The pain, when it came, was like a slap, nothing more. It jolted her arm; her body flinched. Around her, the world cooled.

Then the stumps of her three vanished fingers seemed to curl in pain.

*   *   *

Bailey saw the blade stab toward the ground. She saw the blood swirl into the rain-soaked stone, in rosy pools.

Rosy pools.

There was a commotion around her. The rain fell in gentle needles, running down her neck and face. People were moving, vacating the plaza. Show over.

Rosy pools. The blood drained north, toward the king's rooms, toward the compass point of the lightning rod. It all meant something. There were omens in entrails. She staggered forward, staring at the crimson eddies.

Only one other person remained in the circle. The uldia Oleel. She eyed Bailey with curiosity, and for a moment her nostrils flared, as though smelling the telltale stench of history.

Then she turned away.

Bailey said, loud enough for her to hear: "You forgot the fingers, Oleel. They're yours now. They'll always be your work."

Oleel stopped cold, her body bulked into a sodden wave of gown and bun. "I bequeath them to you, old hoda," she said, not turning around.

As the uldia departed, Bailey found herself saying, "If you ever decide to get a decent seamstress, do let me know. Those shapeless robes are really quite dreadful."

But Oleel merely retreated from the plaza, leaving Bailey with the blood and entrails.

Then Anton was at her side. He had a blanket, and laid it across her shoulders, saying gently, "Let's go home, Bailey."

"My fault," she whispered.

"No, no, Bailey. We couldn't stop them."

He thought she was talking about Gilar. But didn't he know she was talking about Remy? She looked at Anton. "It doesn't help not to sing. That's not the atonement."

But she knew what was.

FOURTEEN

Anton's boat slipped into the Puldar two hours before
dawn, in silence, without lights. Maypong insisted on the
precautions. Their craft was only slightly larger than ordinary, to accommodate food and gear and the travelers:
Anton, Maypong, and a hoda to paddle.

There was a tension between Anton and Maypong, because of what happened yesterday to Gilar. If he hadn't
pleaded with Vidori, the girl would be dead. But now
Maypong's cool detachment troubled him. It was the same
look he'd seen in his father's eyes when he'd sent Anton's
mother outside the compound: cold, walled-up. *She's con-
taminated, boy. You want to die?* Yes, was the answer. At the
time, he would rather have died than say good-bye . . .

As they loaded the skiff, Nick had been strangely silent.
"You're in charge, Lieutenant," Anton had said, "if anything
happens to me."

Nick's face was dark. He was still sick, and Anton was
worried he had poisoned himself more severely than they'd
thought. His tests had come back negative for the virus, and
besides, his symptoms didn't match. Zhen had tested for a

wide range of infections, and found nothing wrong with him. "Take care of yourself, Nick," he said. "I need you."

"Do you?"

Anton couldn't risk losing both officers at once, and as ever, he feared leaving Zhen alone.

"I've said I need you, Nick. Stand by me, man." But he knew the two men's solidarity was long over.

"For as long as I can, Captain."

The words trailed after Anton as they entered the Puldar. *For as long as I can.* And just how long was that?

Now, in the black waters near the shore, they skimmed along, the hoda paddling softly, expertly, under Maypong's instruction to make no sound.

She was a big woman, this hoda named Reen, apparently chosen by Maypong for her strength, to help carry supplies when they left the rivers and began to climb. They'd be gone three days—half the time allotted by the ship's crew. The shuttle would have saved time . . . but Anton had decided against risking the craft in the rugged uplands, and leaving it unguarded and subject to ransacking from Vol—or, Anton thought, uldia.

For it was clear now that Oleel meant to use their mission as ammunition against Vidori. And though Anton was no admirer of the king, he thought Oleel a worse alternative for the Olagong. She would tip the balance, erase the king's power. Become the One Power. But to accomplish that goal she needed the populace on her side, needed the Dassa to hate what the humans were, and the *threat* of what they were: free beings, born to bear. Some of the Dassa needed no prodding.

Now, as they turned out onto the River Sodesh, with its clearer view of the night sky, Anton could see one bright star rising just ahead of the sun, the morning star called Quadi's Lantern. They paddled toward it, trying to get far past the Amalang tributary—Oleel's tributary—before first light. In the profound night, the river's presence was sound alone: the rush of river over stone and branch, the rustle of paddle on water. Under the weight of their skiff, they cut a vanishing passage through the water's ink.

Alert for enemies, Anton thought he would relish a meeting with Oleel; a chance to take her down, on a dark river, without politics and tradition to protect her. Without ten thousand Dassa standing behind her, as she mutilated young girls.

In the tepid light of the approaching dawn, Anton saw Maypong in the prow, her back straight and still. One of the ten thousand Dassa who supported Oleel.

Maypong and Reen had spent an hour camouflaging the boat, until it looked like a knot of tangled branches from the last flood.

Anton distributed the gear into three packs. It was slow going, a noisy, crashing effort of finding passage through undergrowth and, worse, over the tumultuous roots of the shallow-rooted jungle trees that, having given up on soil, grew from the sides of the trees downward to whatever nutrients they could find. Away from the cultivated islets of the Dassa, the jungle reverted to its indigenous ways, with wild vines and thickets, the foliage heavy with flowers, dripping colorful sap. Amid the rank plant growth were the ubiquitous gourds large and small, the birthing pouches of the planet's fauna, or quasi-fauna. Part vegetable, part animal . . . the distinctions were not the same as on earth, Zhen said. They grew from the soil on viny umbilical cords, the seams that would split at maturity evident from the petal-shaped scars. But the gourds were as hard as rock. *They soften,* Maypong had told him, *when it is time.*

Under Maypong's lead, they traveled north, away from the river to the hills. His ears were stuffed with the unceasing jungle clatter, the chirps and scuttling, and the background chitter of insects. It was like the static of the radio when, early that morning, he'd tried to pick out Sergeant Webb's voice, tried to make out the words and the man underneath the words. He didn't know if Webb could speak frankly if there were others with him on the bridge. Anton tried not to take the threatened mutiny as a colossal failure on his part. It could easily have been Captain Darrow in the same position. Couldn't it?

Ahead, he heard Reen splashing through a stream, one of many that had been keeping their boots thoroughly wet. Approaching the stream, Maypong kicked a large branch into the water, using it for a bridge. This action disrupted the nearby jungle growth, setting up a squalling of monkeys, who hurled something at them, pods the size of lemons. Anton saw one creature peering at him from among the tangled roots of a banyan tree. Its face was alight with a vicious intelligence; its ears drooped like mud flaps. A not-quite-monkey. A variety of monkey, brought to this planet the same as the Dassa—imperfectly.

He heard Maypong's voice from up the trail. "I know why you are so quiet, Anton. You are thinking that I am a bad chancellor." As she disappeared down into a gully, he heard her add: "And a bad mother."

Anton crested the hill, noting that Reen was already climbing the next hillside. He wasn't going to touch the subject of *mother*. Nerves were frayed thin enough.

Carefully, he replied, "*Good mother* here is different than where I come from." And *good father, good daughter.*

As they began to climb, the conversation lapsed. The flat river lands had given way to the low hills of the valley wall. After pausing for a silent midday meal, the three of them continued their climb, slick with sweat and now battling an envelope of gnats, like a new layer of skin.

Maypong stopped to confer with Reen, and then to Anton's astonishment they proceeded to strap Maypong's pack onto Reen's already heavy one. Maypong left to reconnoiter their trail, which would soon split into east and west passages over the valley escarpment.

"Let's wait here, Reen," he said. The woman could not possibly shoulder that mountainous pack.

>Maypong-rah says we must hurry,< Reen signed. >To make a camp before sunset.< She signed quickly, challenging his fluency. But Nick's lessons paid off, and he kept up. The woman hoisted the double pack onto her thigh, then bent into the straps, and somehow stood tall. Anton watched her as she set out, a towering backpack obscuring its bearer.

They were following a ridgeline up into more jagged hills. Down in the gully to one side came a rustling movement. Reen had stopped, watching, and Anton, behind her, followed her gaze. A circular portion of the jungle floor trembled, setting up a rustling of fronds and vines.

Reen signed, >Woor. The fulva are in woor.<

Peering closer, Anton saw the fulva gourds. They were twitching and bulging on their stems. A snapping noise issued from the circle, and then another, as several of the gourds split. Soon all of them were erupting as the cracks spit out a slick jelly.

Reen signed, >They all come at once. Those who eat them can't take them all. Some will escape.<

The first newborn emerged, kicking its back legs free of the gourd. It was a wild pig, with black hairs matted against pink skin. At once, it wobbled to its feet, shaking itself free of the gooey strands. Little teeth glistened in its mouth. It staggered off into the brush, wisely distancing itself from the noisy birthings. No mother to suckle it; therefore the early teeth . . .

Reen urged Anton to leave before predators converged. Large cats, for instance, by her description.

As they continued up the path, Anton heard the cracking and splitting sounds of birth sacs for several minutes. He tried not to imagine a similar scene with Dassa babies, but the vision came anyway. It was a thought he'd kept at bay for as long as possible. But wasn't it all a matter of familiarity, and custom? What in nature could be so foul that a scientific mind could not accept it?

Plenty, Anton thought, swiping at gnats and hurrying to put the scene behind him.

By late afternoon they had climbed high enough to leave the heat and gnats behind. Here, in a region of steep, green hills, Maypong thought it safe to follow the well-beaten trails. Anton found it a relief to be on a clear trail free of undergrowth, as the three of them walked single file along sinuous paths worn from millennia of Dassa seekers.

They left the wide trees of the lower slopes and entered a land of squat, frondy bushes and mosses. They could see across the narrow valley to the side of the next hill, lush with green.

Following the switchbacks along the mountainside, they soon brought out warmer clothes, then climbed toward clouds hugging unseen peaks. Now fully enveloped in the fog, Anton could see no farther than Reen, who followed Maypong.

At a switchback bend, he found Maypong sitting on the trail. She was taking off her boots.

They had hardly spoken for hours. It was a bad silence, and one Anton both wanted and didn't want to repair. He watched as she handed her boots to Reen, who strapped them onto Maypong's pack.

"Maypong-rah?"

She rose, lifting an eyebrow at him.

"Why are you taking off your boots?" The trail was rock-strewn, and he hoped her boots weren't a bad fit, because she would need them.

"To walk barefoot," she answered, slipping her arms into her pack and shouldering it.

"Barefoot? The path is rough, Maypong-rah."

Reen was watching them from the lead position, frowning at Anton. They were both frowning at him. Just what wasn't he getting here? "Maypong-rah, is there something wrong with your boots?"

"No."

"Then why aren't you wearing them?"

"One doesn't, in cloud country."

Anton quelled a growing sense of annoyance, trying to keep a reasonable tone. "I am wearing boots; Reen is wearing boots. One *does*."

Finally, Maypong met his gaze. "Not if one is seeking . . . peace, you might say."

"*Peace?*"

"Yes. A peaceful heart." She noted his look of consternation, and added: "Seekers who come here with a storm inside will walk cloud country without boots. It is our custom, Anton."

He gazed at her, sorting it. "Storm . . ."

"My daughter," she whispered.

They faced each other on the path. Words came to mind, and evaporated. She couldn't walk the path barefoot, not carrying a heavy pack, perhaps not at all.

He was looking at her, trying to sort his emotions. The one clearest to him was relief. The woman felt something.

"Maypong . . ."

She stopped him, shaking her head. "This is what I will do. Since we come to cloud country, I must." Her eyes glittered with flat light reflected from the haze. "For Gilar, yes?"

"I shouldn't have criticized."

"It is not for you, Anton. It is for me."

The import of this was now becoming clear. He turned to Reen. "Put your pack down, Reen, please. We're not moving for now."

He was blocking Maypong's path. Her feet were bound in woven stockings. They wouldn't last ten minutes. "Maypong-rah, Gilar's circumstance isn't your fault. There's nothing you can change."

"No. But when my feet bleed, I will be able to cry."

Looking into her eyes, he saw how her placid face held a lock on tears. He should have known why it had to in the

Olagong. Gently, he said, "Maypong-rah, why didn't you tell me what you planned to do?"

She blinked, saying, "Would you have taken me up-country, if you had known?" When he hesitated, she said, "Then you would never get here. Taking the hidden ways, the side ways, was necessary. Who knew the route—who that you could trust?"

He took a deep breath. He turned to look at Reen, who was still watching him. "What will persuade her, Reen?"

Reen softened a notch, signing, >Nothing.<

He turned back to Maypong. His heart felt like it was developing a cleft, a ravine. He must turn back, for her sake. But he couldn't, for the mission's sake.

Seeming to read his mind, she said, "I will walk on with you or not with you, Anton."

He knew that look in her eyes, and didn't doubt her. "Take off your pack then, Maypong-rah."

To his surprise, she obeyed, lowering the burden to the ground. Anton looked up at Reen, who was already coming forward. The hoda knelt on the trail and started removing the pack's contents, distributing things into the two remaining packs. That done, Reen hid the empty pack in a mass of vines.

"Maypong," Anton said, forgetting the honorific, forgetting his recent bitterness toward her. "I'm sorry that I thought you hard."

She stood before him. "I *am* hard."

As they started forward again, Maypong in the center, he could only watch her bare feet, and wince as she kept pace with Reen.

That night, the three of them huddled together on a small ledge some distance from the trail. Anton kept guard, thankful for his weapon, but knowing it might mean little against greater numbers. Occasionally Maypong, her feet torn and swollen, moaned softly, despite the healing mud that Reen spread on them. With the moon new, darkness was absolute, but he could feel the fog against his face.

At dawn, after a cold meal, they climbed back to the path and trekked on. Whatever clues or ruins Anton hoped for were—if present—doubly obscured, first by clinging vegetation and second by fog as thick as burrs. If there were caves they would be invisible, unless the *Restoration*'s laser survey revealed some promising site. At last radio contact, it had not.

As they resumed their hike, Maypong's feet blistered and broke. She hobbled, but silently. They were all silent now, speaking when necessary in sign language. Above them, the path switchbacked to the crest and then down again, Maypong signed, forming a nonending path throughout the maze of the uplands. Below them, down a hugely steep ravine, the sound of a stream gurgled at them. At one point they passed a rope bridge that spanned the near gorge, a spider's thread gluing one hill to the other.

Rounding a switchback, he saw Maypong pointing down the valley, where a tear in the fog revealed a patch of neon green on a hill where the sun set the hillside alight. As Anton squinted, he saw a line of people winding their way up a switchback trail. They were uldia, by their dress. Fog re-formed under their path, making it look as if they were treading clouds, gray angels in an altered heaven.

>Walking meditation,< Maypong signed.

The line of women snaked along the path, barely an undulating ribbon at this distance. If it was wisdom they wanted, Anton figured they'd be walking a long time. Seeing them put him more on edge. Maypong had said there would be other travelers here, and that some might not be seeking wisdom.

As they ascended their own path, he tried not to stare at Maypong's feet. She allowed one blister, the worst one, to be bound with a cloth, but now the cloth fluttered free, useless. Tearing his eyes from the sight of her bare feet, he squinted at the hillside. It was furry with green; there was nothing but green, though he scanned every hump and protrusion for signs of a vanished race. He conjured up every manner of thing—phantoms of mausoleums, stone tablets, hidden doors—only to find, when sweeping the moss away, that what he had uncovered was yet another branch or rock. There was nothing here. He queried Maypong and Reen. *Are there features here, something notable, perhaps named among the Dassa? No, it is all the cloud hills, Anton. Are there caves? No, only cloud hills. What is the bridge called? Cloud bridge.*

There was blood on the path in places. >Maypong-rah,< he signed several times, >go back. Reen and I will do this trek.<

Always her answer was the same: nothing. Tied to Reen's pack, Maypong's leather boots flopped in the swaying gait of the hoda. It was awful, and inevitable. He felt so ignorant of the Dassa, and their predecessors, these Quadi who left no footprints.

The sound, when it came, was like a stone dropped onto porcelain.

There was a large arrow embedded in Reen's temple. She lay sprawled on the path, twitching.

Anton was crouching, swinging his pistol up and down the path. Maypong whispered, "Below us."

He heard the cracking of branches. People climbing toward them. "This way," Maypong whispered, urging him down the path, the way they had come. "The bridge." He glanced down at Reen, now lying still. Blood streamed out where the arrowhead exited the right eye. He squatted and, snapping the ties, yanked Maypong's boots from the pack. Then he rushed to join Maypong, who was already sliding down the hillside. She had left the path, heading into the rear flank of their pursuers.

Voices on the slope. The close-packed flora distorted distance—the voices sounded as if they were a hand's breadth away. Maypong was moving fast, trading silence for speed, and Anton followed, gun at his hip, needing both hands to grasp roots and vines as he went down, unless he wanted a much faster descent. She waited for him in a little gully, lying in the mud, pressed close to the hillside.

He lay on top of her, concealing her brighter garment with his green fatigues.

She whispered next to his face, "I'll lead them away. Go down the trail, cross the bridge, and then bear southeast as much as the hills allow. Thankfully, you will find the Sodesh."

"No. You're coming with me."

"We have no time, Anton. Cross the bridge, now."

"No." He held her firmly, making his point with the tension of his body. "I'm not going without you."

She nodded then. They began to descend again, riding on their backs part of the time when it was so steep they were practically standing up. Then, skidding onto the trail, they rushed down it, with the noise of their pursuers still bright in the foliage. Anton ran with his pistol drawn, as Maypong rushed headlong in front of him.

The rope bridge was much farther than he remembered. Shouts rang out behind them. He guessed there were about a dozen of them, and there were men among them, not just uldia, or so he guessed from their voices. Maypong ran, heedless of her torn feet, and dangerously, with her long knife drawn, ready to turn and fight. At the next bend she pointed with her knife toward the gorge, but it was so full of fog, he couldn't see anything. She had seen the bridge, however, and now they ran faster, just centimeters from the steep plunge to the river.

It was then that a hole appeared in the clouds, and he glimpsed the bridge: a filament in midair.

Maypong led him down a side path where they came upon the near end of the bridge, anchored by great spikes in a rare use of metal. The ropes were frayed and rotten; Anton thought the bridge had long been abandoned.

"Hope for clouds," Maypong whispered, staring at the bridge.

"They'll follow us," Anton said, turning sideways to listen to the voices, coming faint and loud as the canyons echoed and disguised sounds.

"Hope for clouds," she repeated.

They crouched, looking down a three-hundred-meter drop graced with jagged rocks and seeping water. Behind them, they heard voices. Maypong stiffened. Dassa were coming down the path, having figured out where their prey had fled.

"Clouds, clouds," Maypong whispered, like a prayer, from a woman who never prayed, who never conceived of such a thing. *Clouds, clouds.* Anton took up the chant in his mind. He didn't think the bridge could hold one person's weight, much less two.

A branch snapped nearby. Anton caught sight of hair caught up in a disheveled bun, its red tint flashing in the tatters of the sun . . . His heart thrummed in his chest, his hand gripped the pistol, safety off. Beside him, Maypong didn't breathe or tremble. The Dassa passed within two meters of them, then responded to a hail from the path and crashed away.

It was then that the cloud country returned to its usual form and the fog closed all gaps, rolling up from the gorge, swirling over the world.

They went for the bridge.

Anton held Maypong firmly by the elbow, forcing her ahead of him to forestall the plan he knew was in her mind: to make him cross alone. The thought nagged that he should let her save him, that it wasn't merely his life that mattered, it was the mission, and he was all that held it together, with Nick faltering, and Zhen a lousy leader in every way, and Sergeant Webb in over his head. He could accept Maypong's allegiance. He had accepted it; had let her step into danger as his chancellor, making her daughter a pawn in Oleel's hands. He had let her suffer in every way, and never questioned that it was his due, treating her as a servant, because he needed her; the mission needed her. He needed her to remain on this side of the span, so that the fraying bridge could hold.

But he pushed her forward onto the bridge.

The bridge consisted of two thick ropes forming the main girders and rope sections connecting them, to walk on. Despite the rope railing on both sides, the entire construct was more air than substance. He stepped forward, off the ledge of ground, onto the cloud bridge, blocking Maypong from moving past him. With little choice, she moved out farther onto the squeaking net of the bridge. To better distribute their weight, he followed some meters behind her.

The fog was so thick he could see nothing but his hand on the rope. The squeak of the rigging—the only sound except for the distant hiss of the river—scratched loudly in his ears. Maypong had disappeared ahead of him, but he sensed her by the quivering strands of ropes, the interplay of his footsteps and hers, seesawing the bridge. Then, for a moment, he thought he discerned the buttery yellow of her jacket, like a flame in front of him, and he set his eyes on that, feeling with his feet for the next rope to stand on.

A mist fell on his face. He had become an initiate, traversing the air into a country of clouds. There might be answers where they were going, or death, or nothing at all. But suspended here, over the gorge, there was only Maypong, a melting golden spot before him. He followed her, leading with his heart. How wrong he'd been if he'd thought that he was fated to love the king's daughter. All along, it was to be a woman more common than that, yet more noble. And he thought that it was not a matter of chancellor and captain for Maypong, and never had been. Vidori hadn't commanded her to die for him, just to teach him.

The rope split beneath his foot.

He plunged down, through the hole, his hand slipping from the rope railing, holding on now by his fists, grabbing one of the great ropes. His feet dangled into the valley, kicking air.

Slowly, he raised his knees and bent his body, forcing his legs over the great rope, one of the large ones. If it broke, it would bring the whole bridge down. Grappling, he hoisted himself forward, until he lay prone on the sideways ladder, his heart thudding enough to vibrate the web of the woven bridge.

"Anton?" came her voice, full of fear.

"I'm all right," he said. His stomach was still flailing down into the chasm, but the rest of him abided. "Keep going." He pulled himself upright.

Staggering on, one rope at a time, he could see Maypong, far ahead of him, dancing from one rope to the next.

Oh, that was bad. He could see her.

The clouds had begun to evaporate.

A shout went up from the hillside behind them. Anton rushed forward, heedless of footholds. He heard Maypong urging him on, and then the report of a gun. The attackers had abandoned the silence of arrows.

There was yet a third of the way to the end of the bridge. Maypong was almost completely across, rushing wildly, the ropes swaying . . .

"Anton!" cried Maypong. "They are cutting the bridge!"

He sped onward, claiming the rope rungs with feet that calculated the intervals, thinking that if the bridge gave way on one side, he'd become a wrecking ball on the end of a crashing pendulum, smashing into the hillside.

Maypong was on the hillside now, reaching out for him, to help him if he got close enough.

"Get down," he shouted, as bullets sliced by.

And then one of the great ropes gave way, and the pathway skewed to one side. He now clung to the side railing, one foot on the remaining great rope. He turned sideways, creeping along the remaining strand, as the day brightened around him, and the hole in the clouds seemed to follow him like a spotlight.

Her hands were three meters away. She stood in the rain of bullets, reaching for him.

The bridge fell.

As he felt it give way, he leapt forward, propelling himself headlong toward the valley side. And she caught him, hands latched onto one forearm, dragging him as he scrambled against the crumbling hillside.

And then he was next to her, lying on the solid ground, the bridge dangling down the steamy gorge.

He laughed. Holding on to Maypong, he laughed. She pulled him into the cover of the undergrowth.

"There is something funny, Anton?" she asked irritably. A bullet sliced into the mud nearby.

He nodded. "Yeah, there is." As she helped him sit up, he said, "They just shot themselves in the foot."

"How do you know whose feet are shot?"

"Never mind. I just mean they can't follow us now."

"That's very true." She looked over at him. "Maybe that is funny, as you said."

"Well, let's get out of here." They climbed up to the path, the ever-looping path of the region. The gunfire now fell well short of them, and they rested a moment.

"One thing, though, Anton." She was looking across the valley. "Did you see who is following us?"

Yes, a group of men, about ten of them. He stopped to squint across the gorge, just thickening again with fog. On that far hill he saw a very tall man with a bun on top of his head. Surrounded by men in tunics. Not uldia. They were judipon.

So, he wondered, *did you come with or without Homish's knowledge?* He waved.

Nirimol was staring in his direction, but didn't acknowledge.

Anton turned back to his companion. "Here, take these," he said. "They almost strangled me." He handed Maypong the boots that he'd tied around his neck for the climb across the bridge.

Maypong gazed at them.

"We're going home now, Maypong. I can't get there if you're going to fall down on the job." She frowned at the dropped honorific. "Can I just use your name? If I love you, can I call you Maypong?"

Her eyes softened. After a pause, she said, "If you want."

"I want."

She nodded like a queen granting a momentous favor. Then she sat on the muddy hill and strapped on her boots.

.

FIFTEEN

Bailey had never in her life felt less like going to a party.
She sat in the great canoe as it sped down the Puldar, rowed
by the king's servants, following a golden path lit by the setting sun.

Shim had come an hour ago to request Bailey's presence
at the king's festivities. Incredibly, and despite all that had
happened, the king had summoned her to the palace to
sing.

No, she'd told Shim.

Shim had blinked. *"No?"*

It was too soon to sing. She hadn't finished studying the
file. Sergeant Webb had sent it to her only two days ago, and
she had to finish reading it, every word.

"I don't perform any longer," Bailey said, trying to smile
politely. "Too old, and besides, my agent arranges these
things. He's terribly difficult to reach these days."

Nick came forward, taking Bailey by the arm, whispering to her. "Don't be stupid. Go and sing, for God's sake."

Bailey raised an eyebrow at this impertinence. "I don't
feel like it," she said. "I'm out of practice."

Nick looked dreadful. The poisons from that devil's brew that he'd drunk made him look half dead. He hissed at her, "It's politics, Bailey. Maybe Vidori is trying to soften things for that poor hoda, trying to say singing isn't so bad. Try to think of someone besides yourself."

Bailey looked over at Shim, who was starting to look hopeful.

Damn and damn.

Calling up a rather good smile, she strode back to the chancellor. "Well, perhaps a song will do no harm."

Oh, but song had done a world of harm, in her world and here. Yet *not* singing wasn't the answer, and never had been. Instead, she must face things squarely. So she'd sent for the file, the file she'd carried with her for twenty years but never read. It wasn't a long record—terribly brief, in fact. The short history of her mirror image, the sister—daughter—clone . . . *person* for whose death she was responsible. *Why bother? Why wallow?* The old lies still had life. *Because not knowing doesn't save you. It kills you.*

Now, on the river, heading to the king's party, Bailey watched the Olagong, the braided lands, pass by. She had spent decades pushing the world away, rushing from one engagement to the next. Even this mission, her one good thing, was a gig. But the Olagong had pulled on her, taking her down into itself, where young girls lay in rosy pools, and the thread of your heart could fray and then reweave.

And so she would perform, at last. It was a good day for it: high and bright, and with Anton out on that expedition, and everything going in the right direction, finally. The young pup was proving more canny than she'd thought. She had to admit he was starting to get his sea legs. He had defied the king, and here came Vidori's invitation in spite of that.

As the king's palace hove into view, she reviewed her repertoire: Mozart, perhaps Puccini, or there was that Rossini she'd always loved. But then again, such fast coloratura . . . perhaps it was best to stay with the lyric repertoire. *My goodness.* How desperately she *did* want to sing!

Even from this distance she could see that the palace was brimming with Dassa. Well, then, a good crowd. It surprised her that she cared.

Bailey leaned forward. "Shim-rah, take me in the back way."

Shim twisted around to look at Bailey. "Everyone will expect you to come to the river stairs."

"Then we'll surprise them, won't we?"

Shim ordered the rowers to change their course slightly.

"And Shim-rah, I'll need to borrow some clothes." She added: "Something showy but tasteful. Think you can find an extra gown?"

Now Shim brightened. "Oh, Bailey, thankfully I have many showy and tasteful things."

"My kind of girl," Bailey said, starting to go into performance mode.

Teetering along on the high-soled sandals, Bailey walked slowly toward the river room.

"Hurry, Bailey," Shim urged. "We are already later than the king wishes."

Bailey held up the brocaded skirt with one hand to keep from tripping on it. "It'll be worth the wait, my dear. An audience never grows old, only more eager." The ensemble was a gorgeous peachy-gold with rose trim and a golden insert around the neck. But the damn thing was heavy and just a little too long.

As they proceeded down the hall, hoda and Dassa alike stopped to frankly stare. Bailey hoped that she was creating the right impression, and didn't look like a horse in a petticoat. "Are you sure this gown is the right one?"

"Oh, Bailey, it is the most showy I have."

"Yes, but how do I look?" Damn, all she needed was a little reassurance. She had sung so little recently—could she command her voice now? How would she do in that middle register?

"Like . . ." Shim faltered. "Like . . ."

"Oh never mind," Bailey snapped. She nodded to an old viven hurrying toward the great hall, and the Dassa actually smiled at her.

"Shim-rah," Bailey said, "tell me again why Vidori wants me to sing."

"Because the people love you, Bailey."

"Yes, but why does he want me to sing?"

"To make the people happy, Bailey."

Bailey snorted. It was nothing of the sort. It was a political maneuver. Nick was right—the king was making an effort for the hoda. But why, when he had never cared before?

Ahead, the crowded hall loomed. A few Dassa saw her coming, and made a clear passage for her.

She held her head high and glided into the crowd.

As she moved into the hall, she saw the king standing near the steps, amid the press of viven. People turned to her on every side, and all conversation vanished in a moment. She approached Vidori, still furiously debating whether a curtsy would suit or not, and if she would bloody well topple over.

As he nodded to her, she took a sweeping curtsy as far to the floor as her ridiculous shoes would allow. "Your Majesty," she said, smiling. It had the desired effect: People gaped at her and made her the absolute center of attention.

"Ah, Bailey," Vidori said, beaming. "May you never wear green again."

She sparkled at him. In her element now, she was soaring, ready to sing, the devil take her doubts. She had always sung with *nerve*, her critics said. Well, she'd lean on that now.

The king turned to the throng, raising his voice. "I have commanded a song to be sung in my palace. I have a mind to enjoy singing, and you must all enjoy the singing along with me. That is my pleasure."

At this strange speech, Bailey nodded to him, then turned back to assume command of the river room, even as a wave of voices swelled around her, people murmuring *song,* and *Bailey . . .*

She drew her gaze around the crowd, silencing them.

She knew that the song must be in Italian, since she couldn't translate on the fly. And there were only a few candidate arias for this performance. It must be a celebrity aria, with range and depth. She chose "Sempre libera" from *La Traviata,* because, though it was coloratura, and challenging in its register, it spoke of being finally free . . . and went with the gown.

She began. The opening notes filled the hall, and to her surprise, she realized that the place had marvelous acoustics, magnifying her voice, which emerged rich and full. Annoyingly, a murmur came from the crowd, but she sang over it, as people turned to each other and whispered. There were uldia present, and they frowned, but the majority of the audience looked more surprised by her gifts than anything.

She spun out the melody, singing well, even without an orchestra, allowing the notes to command the very air. Soon the crowd grew silent again, and with relief she continued, allowing the emotion to charge her performance, attacking the top notes without reaching, yes, and no wobble, either. Watching the king, she thought him entranced, though the old fox knew how to act as much as she did. She looked over the heads of the audience, to the river, now deepening from rose to blue as evening came on. It was about time, far past time, that the Puldar heard a fine song.

So, Gilar, my dear, a corner of her mind said, *this is for you.*

Beyond the throng of viven, the common Dassa were listening, out there in their skiffs, and she sang most of all for them, hoping that they liked it. In the end, that was what her career, her signature performance, came down to: *Did you like it, did it move you, did it take you and make you whole?*

The song was over. The last note hung for a moment. All

in all, it had been an exciting performance, and the little flaws had probably gone unnoticed. However, the crowd was not clapping. Oh dear, she knew she'd gone a bit stiff in that middle register. But Dassa didn't *ever* clap, she remembered with relief. The whole room was frozen. She knew she really must do something.

She swept toward the king, curtsying again. "I hope the song pleased you, rahi."

Vidori said nothing, but turned to the throng outside, gathered on the river. "And did Bailey please you?" he asked, in a heart-stopping maneuver that Bailey thought very ill-advised.

She had a clear view down the steps now, as viven stepped aside and gazed out at the skiffs gathered there.

Dassa rocked in their boats, all looking up the steps at Bailey and Vidori. Then a woman in a skiff near the steps slapped the water with her paddle. And again. She was a big woman, of an age to command attention. Nearby, someone else slapped a paddle. Then, from the fleet of skiffs came the clatter of paddles beating on the water, the sweetest applause Bailey had ever heard.

She took this excellent moment to make another, very deep curtsy.

The crowd erupted. People cried out and more paddles hit the river, as fists of water rose up and showers flew in all directions.

Then the viven on the steps were cheering, and the cry was taken up deep into the river room. The king looked around approvingly. At last a quiet descended as Vidori stepped down a stair or two. He spoke to the assembled Dassa, to those in the skiffs. He was no fool—he knew where his power came from.

"Since you have approved, I also approve, and say that singing will be good. All may sing, Dassa and hoda alike."

The king was a gambler, she realized. He had used her popularity to bring song to the river lands, to approve the hoda in an indirect way, to reproach Oleel by raising a hoda custom high. But not, of course, unless the crowd approved.

Bailey saw that here was a man very much pleased with himself. And relieved, if she was any judge of expressions.

He turned to her, bowing slightly, then spoke to the crowd: "Bailey has brought a fine gift to the Olagong, and I thank her for it."

At this, the paddles hit the river again, and there was a general commotion, and before long, the idea came forward—Bailey couldn't remember just how—for another song to be sung. And so she agreed to an encore.

Perhaps something a bit more dramatic this time . . .

She moved to the center of the hall.

Maypong leaned heavily on Anton throughout the day, but by afternoon they collapsed into a makeshift camp. Her feet had swollen so badly she had to cut part of her boots away. After a simple meal of peeled roots that Maypong had managed to gather, they huddled together, exhausted.

As he held her, she finally cried. The release took her body, shook it hard. Still in jeopardy as they were, she cried silently, and whispered Gilar's name. He knew why she'd had to mutilate her feet in order to grieve. Crying implied rejection of everything she believed in, even herself. Anton held her tighter, opening to her as he hadn't been able to before.

Finally, she was quiet, and he left her to rest, climbing a nearby outcropping to try for a quick view of their surroundings before dusk obscured the forest.

He thought the judipon had lost their trail, but he kept guard nonetheless. Maypong said that Nirimol had acted without Homish's knowledge, and that Nirimol was no friend to the king, or to the king's human friends. If he and Oleel were allies, he might attempt to prove his worth by carrying out the judgment of Olagong law on the humans. Anton decided against contacting Nick for backup. His tronic notepad could bounce a signal to the ship for relay. But he felt their camp was safe for tonight.

Night fell, fueling the animal cries—the celebrations, signals, and laments of the quasi-Earth creatures.

He was going to be calling the ship's bluff, whether they would abandon him here. Because he wasn't going back without the cargo. Whatever that cargo was.

He looked up at the patch of night sky that he could see through the trees. The small moon was just rising over the emergent trees of the canopy, its sliver not stealing much of the stars' glory, that of one star in particular—the *Restoration,* a fast-moving speck, three hundred kilometers high.

Hold on, Sergeant, Anton thought. Were he looking down at the planet now, Anton knew, Sergeant Webb would see nothing here, with the hemisphere inked out in night. *Hold on, Sergeant.*

Back in camp, he found Maypong awake, sitting up. "Did you see anything?"

"Stars."

"You've seen many stars in your lifetime, Anton. That is a fine thing."

He thought he might have seen more than he ever wanted to, but he smiled at her. In the slight chill of the night, he sat next to her, wrapping his arm around her.

"Are you tired, Anton?"

"I don't know." He was exhausted. And wide awake.

"I hope not." She moved closer to him. Her feet were bare, peeking out from her leggings. The sight stirred him. Well, he was an easy mark, alone with the woman he loved in the privacy of the forest.

But he had avoided her for many weeks, and for good reason. Now he couldn't tell a good reason from a bad one. "Maypong, I love you," he said.

"Yes, and we could also lie together."

"Is it your duty to offer?" He still wasn't clear about the obligations of cordiality.

"I lie with whom I will, and none other."

Not a comforting thought, but she was trying. "I wouldn't want you to lie with others." He thought he might be asking for her not to have sarif with anyone else. He told himself earlier that he wouldn't, there being no way she could do so and still honor who she was. But here he had said it.

"For how long should I not have sarif, Anton?" She was holding both his hands, looking at him, being both earnest and tender.

"Forever," he said.

"That is a long time not to be cordial."

It would not be settled tonight. And he wanted her, badly. He began to pull open the fasteners on her shirt. "How about one week, then?"

"Yes," she whispered, unbuckling his belt.

They made a pile of their clothes and he lowered her onto them, trying to remember what he should and should not do.

She made it easy for him. "Anton," she whispered, "lie with me in your custom. Teach me the human way. I would have you that way first." She smiled. "And then my way."

He commanded himself to go slowly, and he had to. In a way, she was a virgin. The idea so overwhelmed him that he nearly lost himself on her belly. Then he began teaching her his customs, some of which he made up on the spot.

Afterward, they lay on their backs, entwined, covered with sweat. Maypong rose and collected stream water in a gourd, splashing it over them both.

"Come back," Anton said, "I'm not done with you."

She sat on top of him, challenging him to begin again.

"But rest first," he said, letting her win. She toppled over into his arms, and they lay still, letting the breeze wick over them. He gazed at her, this woman of such dark and profound loveliness. "Tell me you love me, Maypong."

"I love you, Anton." Spoken tenderly, though on request.

He didn't bother to wonder what it meant. She had no concept of exclusivity. She loved many people. The word for *love* in Dassa meant *care*. But he liked hearing her say it, and liked that she knew what he hoped she meant by it. All so complicated, and irrelevant at the moment.

He focused on the corral of stars in the gap above them. It was like looking at a fire—one could never tire of looking. He remembered the ship glinting overhead . . .

Then he sat up, leaning on his elbows.

"Anton?" Maypong said.

He was on his feet, then. He pulled his trousers on, thrust his hand into his pocket. His notepad was still there.

Maypong was dressing. "Do you hear something?"

"No. But I saw something." The image of the ship. Its systems couldn't view him at this distance, but they weren't blind.

He turned to her. "Maypong, what if the ship can see something we can't? All that canyon country. What if the whole area means something?"

"With respect, how can a canyon mean something, Anton?"

He ran his hands through his hair, thinking. "Your traditions say there is wisdom in the canyons. What if the wisdom—of the Quadi—is contained in its layout, as seen from above? Nick heard that Oleel's pavilion was built as a model of the original Quadi site. Is that right?"

"That is our legend."

"He also heard that it's laid out in the pattern of the Olagong itself, that the palace is a map of the Olagong."

She paused, frowning. "You think the canyons are a map?" Her voice turned doubtful. "That is not highly believable, Anton. Who could draw a map in the land?"

"The same ones who created the Dassa. They somehow replicated the human pattern here. That's why we're so alike though we were born so far apart. Normally, that wouldn't be highly believable." Glancing up at the night sky, he added, "I'm going to contact the ship. It can't hurt to ask." He voiced a command that brought an immediate connection.

The officer of the watch responded. The corporal thought it might take him a while to find an overflight image of the uplands that wasn't obscured by clouds.

While they waited, Maypong asked, "Why, if the cloud country is a map, would the Quadi urge us to walk, when we cannot see the canyon pattern just by walking?"

"I don't know why your custom is to walk." He sat with her now, the notepad balanced on his knee. "Maybe the Quadi knew that someday you *would* see it. They knew that human missions would see it, if we ever came here. Maybe they knew you would be curious when you attained space flight, and you would look down and discern the pattern. Maybe walking meditation is a misinterpretation."

Maypong's voice was distant. "We will have space flight? Do you think this will ever be so?"

"Someday you will. Just as someday the hoda will be free. Things change, sometimes even for the better." He held her close, feeling on the verge of something, though it was just a hunch.

"I would like to go into space. With you, Anton."

He drew back, smiling. "What about all your other lovers?"

"Perhaps just a cordial hug now and then," she murmured.

Well, she was trying. Things change, he'd told her. Maybe *he* would have to change.

They waited, each letting their imagination play against the dark jungle.

The picture, when it came, was blurry from a haze of clouds. The small screen in the notepad showed an image, green on green, of the canyon lands, not a pattern at all, much less one that told a story. They stared at it. Anton turned the screen in one direction and then the other. He saved the image. Thanked the corporal.

"Anton . . ." Maypong took the handheld device. "Look

at it this way." She turned the notepad around again. Pointing, she said, "The stem." Anton squinted. "The outer leaf, the tuber." Maypong nodded soberly. "I know this pattern."

"It's a plant?" He took the screen from her and focused on it.

"Oh yes. An easy one to know. It is the langva plant, our food of the river lands."

He held the screen at arm's length, finally seeing the pattern. It wasn't a map. It was a simple image. If he tried, he could see a langva plant. He didn't think he was just convincing himself. His excitement mounted. Langva, the plant. But why?

Maypong whispered, awe and skepticism in her voice, "How could they shape the canyons thus?"

Anton paused, looking around the small clearing. "Maybe they created the world, too."

SIXTEEN

In the first light of dawn, Nick paddled on the Sodesh, his skiff one of thousands. As they did every morning, Dassa men and women traveled to and from the uldia pavilion to fulfill their duty of the variums: to swim, to procreate. He was conspicuous, he realized, but he might draw less attention when the rivers were crowded with morning traffic. He would insist that Oleel see him. And in case she turned ugly, he'd left word in his notepad where he'd gone—and why.

Nearby, a group of women, probably sisters, happily paddled, chatting and sharing breakfast on the river. They paid no attention to him. Perhaps he was growing invisible as he began to die.

Although Oleel claimed that nothing could save him, Nick believed that langva heightened the human immune response. Other than inducing a pronounced nausea, the langva extract had helped him at first, giving fuel to his breakthrough idea: that the chemical properties of the langva were the reason the Quadi had called them to Neshar.

Still nagging at him was the question of why the Quadi wouldn't have sent the chemical formula as information in the message to Earth. The crew had asked that same question from the beginning, about the genetic code itself. For some reason, the Quadi wanted humans to come here. *Come find what you have lost.*

This trial of the langva extract, although clumsy, even reckless, had to continue. Before the *Restoration* stole away, abandoning them here. What Oleel seemed not to realize was that they could take the langva anytime they wished, wresting its chemical secrets eventually. So withholding the distillation gave her no advantage, and it could well kill her only human friend. Whatever game she was playing with him, she had miscalculated the cards he held.

Paddling close to the bank, he struggled to identify the back way to Oleel's keep. When ferrying him to meetings, the uldia had always kept him under a covering. But he thought he knew the way.

And here it was. Marked by a fallen banyan tree, draped into the river, the one with roots jutting upward like octopus arms. Steering the boat through a wall of vines, he found the inlet leading to the dark realm of the uldia.

Seeing the little dock deserted, he paddled quietly by the stone entryway to the wooden one. The passage under the great mangrove tree formed a gate to the compound, where, during one of his visits, he'd seen a canoe of uldia pass through. As he approached the tree, he saw that the passageway was solid with roots. A camouflage, he knew.

Sitting in his skiff before the mass of roots, he tugged on them. The roots had the feel of wood, slippery with moss. He groped at them and yanked, then pulled his skiff to the far end and pulled again. This time the roots came open, on a simple hinge.

So the uldia didn't lock their doors. Perhaps they thought they had no worries, no competitors. They didn't reckon with Nick Venning.

Under the huge tree, he floated in watery darkness.

Little frazzles of light danced in the cracks of the tree, making the passage oddly more blind. He felt like he was moving from one world to the next, through a birth canal, into the realm of the uldia, masters of birthing.

Pushing on the opposite door of roots, he peeked out. Morning sun slashed at his eyes, driving a needle of pain into his head. He closed his eyes, struggling for control. When he opened them again, he saw that before him lay a winding water path overhung with moss. He pushed out.

It was a green tunnel, incandescent in the sun, filled with the smells of growing things, dying things. No breeze stirred to freshen the air. Penetrating deeper, he came upon a view of the stone pavilion, bulking up among the trees. He would have to leave the skiff, and creep toward—

An infant's cry broke the stillness.

He found himself floating in the direction of the cry. As he peered out of his cloaked passageway, he saw, some meters away, Dassa heading in several directions, no doubt toward the pools. How many variums were there to accommodate the vast population of Lolo? The land here must be all variums, thousands of them, with their communal secretions . . . He tried not to feel disgust. But it was all so impersonal, and at the same time, so public.

More baby cries. The jungle was a nest of babies.

How did the infants get born, anyway? They came, he knew, from fulva, the great, loaded casings. Gestating in water, like the human uterus, and then . . . what? Crew had speculated. Dassa had described it: The uldia tend the variums. The egg and sperm find each other—not that easy, or efficient, except for the sheer numbers of swimmers. When the uldia deem it needful, they close the varium, and the pool brings its contents to maturity.

Just beyond the cloaking branches, one such varium was active. There, an uldia waded in a small lagoon.

He could see the sunlight firing the water surface, and the uldia moving around, but for a better view he climbed out of his skiff, securing it next to him with vines. Creeping up the embankment, he parted the undergrowth for a clear view.

It was a varium, one of the closed ones. At a distance, Dassa voices filtered through the jungle. No one swam here except for the young uldia, her robes floating around her as she stood waist-high in water, holding something. Around the pool, the moss and vines of the islet screened it from its surroundings.

He hardly breathed. It was a birth.

The uldia bent over a floating gourd and sniffed deeply, over and over again. He could detect an odor, a warm, yeasty smell, not entirely pleasant, but one that probably masked his own smell from the uldia.

The gourd bounced in the water probably because the uldia was pushing it down. But no, the fulva was bouncing on its own, shaking with some internal commotion. Part of him didn't want to see this—if the babies came out of the vessel like an animal from an egg, it would be an ugly sight. But still he watched.

The egg was enormous, the size of a woman's uterus. How did it float? This question was answered as the fulva squirmed and dipped once more, turning to the side and revealing that, underneath, it was held aloft by a tremendous stalk.

A coarse, cracking sound disturbed the tranquil scene, followed by a more robust ripping noise.

The sack began parting along what appeared to be seams as the gourd oozed a cloudy, thick jelly. The uldia bent low again.

And lapped at the jelly.

Nick's stomach recoiled. He turned onto the muddy bank, struggling not to make a sound as his insides roiled and then vomit surged up his throat. Fortunately, the cracking sound came louder from behind him, masking his wretched noise.

He reached down for water, wiping his chin clean, and moved back into position, forcing himself to continue what he'd started. Sweat chilled him. *Get a grip.* What did he think Dassa birth was? He knew; the whole crew knew. But seeing changed everything. He resumed his position, staring helplessly.

In the varium, the egg discharged its load. As sections peeled back, the gourd spewed out a curdled pulp. In the midst of this an infant squirmed, its head gleaming brownish red in a stray dollop of sun. The uldia pushed aside the jelly, driving her hands into the egg, and pulled the baby free of its capsule, accompanied by a sucking noise as the gourd released its burden.

Attached to the baby at its stomach was a small cord. The uldia bent forward and bit the thing in two.

The creature she had brought forth was covered in slime, eyes closed but mouth open, crying. Nick had time to wonder how it managed not to choke on the jelly now cascading from its flesh. The newborn was a biological nightmare, half animal, half vegetable . . . a travesty of birth, a dreadful variation of the human.

Just as the Dassa were a dreadful variation of the human. It was why they held no life sacred, why they mutilated their daughters, why sexuality was so twisted. They were nothing like humans. How could they be, when this was their beginning?

He slunk away, and tears popped out of his eyes as he struggled to quiet his stomach. He skidded down the bank, managing to climb into his skiff and propel himself down the green canal, its greenish gold light a mirror of his bilious stomach. Desperate for fresh air, he had the strength only to pull his boat along, hand over hand, using vines to propel himself and his craft.

God in heaven, he thought. Did God approve of this nightmare? No, this was nothing divine or natural. The Quadi had taken what was human and made it revolting. People had warned them, people of Earth had known: The universe is loathsome; don't go looking for horrors.

But they had gone looking. And found them.

*   *   *

Gilar watched from an upper level of the stone house as people wound through the birthlands, seeking the proper variums. At each varium an uldia monitored which Dassa swam where and which Dassa, by virtue of too-close relation, was sent on to a different birth pool to avoid inbreeding. So the uldia were busy this time of the morning. It was the best time of day for mischief.

Pain swelled down her arm, collecting in her hand. Even though she had lost three fingers, it had been worth it. The king had noticed her, and had proclaimed singing favored by the court. Her triumph must have been noticed by Anton Prados, by Bailey. And Oleel had not dared to kill her. Gilar had tweaked the big woman's nose, and lived to remember it.

Heady triumphs, but for now, she needed drugs. She knew where to find pain distillates: in the labs. Perhaps the labs would be empty for just a moment.

Hurrying down the stone stairwell, she found old Mim blocking her way.

>You have business here?< Mim signed.

Gilar's hand language was severely limited now, but she managed, >I have errands.<

Mim smiled crookedly. >Like stealing this?< She held up a vial of brown liquid. Then she handed it to Gilar. >Take some, before you fall over.<

Grabbing the bottle, Gilar pulled out the stopper and slugged back the liquid, emptying half of it. The glorious drink cooled her throat; it was the same medicinal they'd given her for her mouth in Aramee's compound, in a gentler place.

Mim was holding out her hand for the bottle. >You need no more for now.<

Gilar squinted at the old woman. >What if the uldia catch you?<

Mim grinned so broadly that her cropped tongue

showed in her mouth. She turned, pointing down the stairwell.

There, a group of hoda were just now crowding in from the landing. Among them was Eshi, one of her new friends.

Signing for Gilar to follow, the women moved down the stairs.

If the uldia caught them gathering like this, she knew, punishments would follow, but the medicinal buoyed her. *Let them fuss.* She handed the vial back to Mim and followed the group, cupping her right hand in her left, cushioning the jarring motion of movement.

Descending to the bottom floor, they hurried through the narrow passage and into a sleeping chamber. There Mim kneeled down to remove a block of stone, and then another. The old hoda slipped through the resulting hole, and the group held back, waiting to see if Gilar would follow.

But of course.

Gilar, on her hands and knees and unable to lean on her right hand, made only slow progress through the dirt tunnel. But eventually she clambered out of a hole into the outside air. Here, a woody tunnel bored through an arch of tree roots. She hunkered under the low ceiling and followed Mim into a ravine, which at last opened into a sunken clearing, out of sight of the pavilion. She sucked in the smells of the redolent forest, and stood tall.

A dozen hoda, many of them older, stood in the hollow, feet sunk into the water collected there.

Gilar turned to Mim, and sang, because it was easier than using hand sign, Why are we here?

Mim sang back, Because Fazza has come.

She knew no *Fazza*—an outlandish name.

The other hoda gathered here were unfamiliar to her, except for Nuan, of Aramee's compound, who greeted her with a barely suppressed smile. Then the women began ducking down under an enormous hardole tree, its buttress roots forming an arched doorway. Gilar followed, and soon found herself in a cozy tree room. Someone brought bio-lumes.

Do the uldia come here? Gilar sang to Mim.

Sometimes. But we have lookouts posted.

Gilar looked at Mim, old, scarred, and seemingly obedient. And Nuan, whom she'd thought Aramee's devoted slave. She wondered who else pretended to serve, and conspired to gather in secret. The thought that people were fighting back filled her with a strange exaltation.

Now a new arrival filled the entranceway. A stranger.

His clothes, sewn pelts of animals, were not proper Dassa dress. At his belt hung two metal knives, one long, one short. He turned to watch Gilar and Mim approach.

"So," his voice boomed in the dusky chamber, "this is the girl that sings?" He looked at her with a glint of intelligence and humor.

Mim urged Gilar forward. >This is Fazza.<

"Sing for me, child," he said. "I understand you sing loud and strangely. I would hear such a thing."

>You would wait a long time, then.< Gilar raised her chin and frankly appraised him. He smelled as though he hadn't cleaned himself in a long while.

His eyes narrowed. "No offense meant. You do what you like." He looked around the chamber. "Whatever you like. Fazza will indulge you."

As the man surveyed the group, he said, "Here you see a young girl who dares to go against the king. Though she won't sing for us"—he looked at Gilar, and bowed slightly—"she has already done more than ten generations of slaves have done." He rested his hand on one of his knives, standing with an easy warrior's grace that Gilar had to admire. He was one who didn't cower.

Fazza went on, "You meet me here under the big tree, and I thank you. Someday, a meeting like this will happen in the sun. Hoda will gather in compounds of their own, and in palaces without shame. And with their tongues." He turned to Gilar. "If you think you can sing *now,* a tongue would make you even better." He looked at the women, nodding to those who seemed to know him. "The Vol take no tongues, Gilar."

Ah. He was a barbarian, then.

Fazza continued, "The Vol are friends to you who are born to bear. We have no slaves, no punishments. All we ask is for sisters in arms. Against the masters of the wire cage. Some of you have come to us, and some of you have killed the soldiers that serve the king, sending their bodies down the Sodesh as a message." He paused, looking at the gathering. "Now is the time for the river to bear a stronger message."

Eshi's hands flashed. >No hoda ever come back to say if the Vol keep them as slaves or not.<

Some of the hoda smirked in agreement.

Fazza drew himself up. "Once a hoda comes among us, who would want to come back and be a slave?" After a pause he went on, "Only a few have dared to come. But if you leave in groups, you will have strength. Leave your mistresses of the wire cages helpless to care for themselves. Run to join us. Dare to be what Gilar is." He pointed a hairy arm at Gilar.

Mim and Eshi looked at her, as they all did. In dismay, Gilar realized that she was supposed to say something, to judge Fazza. But why her? Was it true that no hoda in ten generations had ever publicly defied the king? She had never thought about history or how the hoda would view her. Only how the humans would view her.

There, in the cavern, the understanding came to her, stark and clean: Humans didn't view her at all. They never had, and they never would. To them, she was nothing.

Nuan looked up as a new hoda ducked through the opening to join them. It was Bahn.

She stared at Fazza, sniffing contemptuously. Then she turned to Gilar. >We were sisters, once.<

Gilar nodded. >I remember what we were.<

Bahn gestured at Fazza. >Send this barbarian away,

Gilar. When the Vol come down the Sodesh, they will sweep our compounds away and destroy our fields, and us with them. All that we have will be gone. The peace of our lives will be gone.< She looked down at Gilar's hand. >See how your peace is already destroyed.<

Gilar looked at the white claw of her hand. Then she regarded the women huddling under this great tree. She wasn't the only one who had been mutilated. They stood in front of her, scarred, hobbled, and mute. They were all part of the grand mutilation, the thing that made them sisters. She was no sister to Bailey, or to Anton Prados. So, if the hoda wanted her opinion, they'd have it.

>Go away, Fazza,< she signed.

At his startled look, she continued, >I think the Vol are no better than Dassa. Our rebellion, if it comes, will be against everyone who despises us. When we rule the Olagong, will you still be a friend? When we are strong, we will meet you again. Then we will see.<

Nuan's hands repeated the notion. >When we are strong, we will see.<

Fazza shook his head. "You will never be strong without the Vol. You need our iron." His hand was on the hilt of his knife.

Gilar frowned. He smelled of power and violence. No different than the uldia. >Everyone thinks they know what we need. I don't think you care about what we need, but only about what the Vol need: the Olagong.<

Fazza saw that the women were listening to her. "Someday we will take the Olagong," he said. "We would have spared the hoda; you would have been proper Dassa. Otherwise you are the king's spawn, and will eat our iron."

She held his gaze, grown flat and hard. >Go back, Fazza. I say we don't need you.<

An old hoda began to lead him away, directing him to the bright light of the door. He turned back to the group. "We are warriors. You are slaves, only slaves."

That was enough. Gilar threw back at him: >We rise up,

Fazza. We rise up—without you.< It was bold to say, and she wasn't sure it was true. But this Fazza was only another master, and a lying one, she thought.

Another hoda came to assist the first in ushering him out of the chamber. He raised his voice, saying, "I will remember you, Gilar. Look for me."

When he was gone, Gilar was left facing off with Bahn. Bahn's face, once so eager and sweet, was pinched. She had once been Gilar's sister, but only on her terms. The terms of obedience.

But, in Gilar's early days at Aramee's compound, Bahn had been good to her, had taught her the song-speech. Gilar sang: Rise up someday, Bahn. My sister.

Rise up, a few hoda sang, passing the chant among themselves.

Hearing this, Bahn turned and left the woody cave, not looking back. But the gathering held firm.

Now, with Fazza's two hoda escorts returned, the circle of women looked again at Gilar. She knew she should have something clever to say. A plan. But she had nothing at that moment but a hope, small and unfamiliar.

It begins with a song, Gilar sang. When we sing, we rise. She didn't know how, but she thought song was a beginning.

Someone sang out, What if they punish us, take our fingers?

Gilar looked at the hoda who'd asked the question. She didn't blame her for being afraid. The forest rustled with the sound of wind blowing through leaves. It was a percussive music, a cleansing sound. It didn't matter what happened now, or later. Gilar's path was set. She could never be obedient.

Looking around the circle, she held her white claw over her head. Who is willing to sacrifice fingers?

Mim raised her hand. She looked like she couldn't knock down an uldia, much less a king's soldier. But she was smiling. Then, one at a time, other hands went up. Eshi, and Nuan, and the other hoda leaders. The circle spiked with raised hands, making all the women look twice as tall as before.

Rise up, my sisters, Gilar thought. Somehow, they would rise. And if they did, they wouldn't need the Vol—or the humans.

Still filthy from the long trek, Anton stood in the doorway to the sleeping hut and looked down at Nick Venning, lying asleep. He tossed in the hammock, grinding words out of his mouth, frantic and indistinct.

"We had to sedate him," Bailey said. "Zhen and I were worried he would hurt himself." She was wearing a Dassa tunic and pants, in a rich brocaded fabric. *From Shim,* Bailey had said. Anton had heard about her recital, but he'd had little time to think about how Vidori's new politics of song fit in with the king's ambitions. Such things would have to wait.

He saw clearly Nick's deterioration. His skin was pale, a stubble of a beard looking like a pox on his face. He'd lost weight. *The poison,* Zhen had said. *It attacked his digestive functions. He can hardly eat.*

Meanwhile, Maypong was resting in the women's hut.

"What happened to her feet, anyway?" Bailey asked.

He gave the simple answer. "She lost her boots—for a while."

"We think he's trying out Dassa medicines," Bailey said, going back to the subject of Nick. "He disappeared yesterday for several hours."

"He left the islet? Where did he go?"

"He ran into some trouble. Came back muttering about how ugly the Dassa were, and how we couldn't trust them." Bailey shook her head. "You never know which ones are going to crack, do you? He's definitely fraying at the edges.

Best send him to the ship, since he's not much use down here anyway."

From the hammock Nick muttered, "No use . . ."

After showering and checking on Maypong, Anton met with Zhen and Bailey. He quickly summarized his findings from the upland trip, and his escape from Nirimol—perhaps a rogue judipon, or else Homish's henchman.

Bailey was watching him with bright eyes. "You found something up there, didn't you?"

"Yes. I might have."

Zhen frowned. "*Might have?*"

He nodded. "I went looking for artifacts, repositories, technology. I didn't find any." Then he smiled. "But I have a lead."

Suddenly the two women were paying very close attention.

Anton removed the notepad from his pocket. "Unless I'm seeing things that aren't there." Voicing it on, he brought up the image sent him by the *Restoration*. "This image is a scan from an overflight of the drone. Over the canyon lands."

Bailey frowned. "I thought they didn't find anything on those surveys."

"They didn't recognize what they found." Anton handed the screen to Zhen. "But Maypong recognized it."

Zhen pursed her lips and squinted. "Looks like eroded valleys. Am I missing the big Quadi encampment or something?" She handed the screen to Bailey, who peered at it.

Anton replied, "They left us an indicator, but it was too big to see." He took the screen back from Bailey, turning it toward them so they could both view it at once. "It's in the shape of a langva plant. The canyons are modeled on that shape. But you need to be far enough above it to discern the pattern."

Zhen snatched the view screen again. She peered closely

as understanding crept into her face. "Could beeeee," she murmured. "Maybe."

Bailey looked skeptical. "Why would the canyons take that form? *How* could they?"

Anton said, "Maybe the Quadi modified the canyons."

Zhen shrugged. "Or the plant was engineered to fit that image."

"Or this is a grand inkblot test," Bailey said, "and we're seeing what we want to."

Zhen said, "That's a lot of trouble to go to. Why didn't they leave us a nice diamond tablet with the directions in big print? Something, say, in the middle of the ocean, that the Dassa wouldn't be likely to find?"

Anton had been building some theories. "Maybe they thought they did. Maybe, to them, the whole thing was obvious. Given their goal, if it was a goal, not to leave artifacts."

"Ah yes," Zhen said, screwing her lips into her default expression: skepticism. "The theory of not messing with the Dassa culture. These Quadi were so scrupulous."

Bailey murmured, "Why, I wonder?"

"Maybe bad things happened when they encountered other cultures. Cultural erosion or implosion." Anton waved that aside. "But let's assume for a moment that this is a clue, a clue so large we couldn't even see it."

Zhen said, "A clue about the langva." She looked at Anton. "Well, I hate to admit this, but Venning has always thought the langva are important. That the plant holds chemical properties that accounted for Dassa immunological strengths."

Bailey smoothed her brocaded tunic. "So," she offered, "Nick ingested some of the local medicines to prove his point."

"Yeah," Zhen snickered. "And look what happened. Damn near killed himself." She looked over at the sleeping hut, as though expecting Nick to come rushing in to justify himself. Then, keeping her voice low, she said, "I analyzed the langva, testing it for immune-boosting properties. I think Nick's right, that it has them. But they're useless to us. Humans don't have the proper receptor sites." She shrugged. "Venning strikes out again."

Bailey said, "Maybe it's trying to tell us to look in the lands where the langva grow. They don't grow everywhere—that's why the Vol are always trying to crash in."

Anton shook his head. "The Olagong is the place we've *been* looking. We hardly need a clue to go in that direction."

Zhen stood up. "OK," she said. She put up her hands, gesturing for silence. The great Zhen was thinking. Anton was more than willing to give her silence to do the thing they'd brought her here for: think.

"Oooookaay," she said, "it's not in the chemistry. But it's in the biology, maybe."

Anton and Bailey waited, afraid to disturb her.

Then Zhen swore under her breath and glared at them—surrogates for herself, and for the foolish thing she had done. "I never sequenced the genome. I was looking at the chemistry."

They sat silently for a time. Finally Bailey said, "Or maybe the langva is a fertility drug. If we all had more children, that would be useful."

Zhen looked at her with incredulity. Bailey was off the subject. Anton gestured for the old woman to be quiet.

Looking over their heads, Zhen said, "It's in the DNA. It's coded into the DNA of the langva."

Bailey blurted out, "But isn't the plant's DNA for the plant?"

"Not all of it. I need to look," Zhen said, turning away to her plant samples and her computer nodes, already having forgotten the others.

A movement in the doorway. "No, don't look." Nick stood there, leaning against the post of the door. Standing up, he looked much worse than when he'd been asleep and covered with blankets.

He nodded at Anton, attempting a smile that came out as a feral grin. "Don't open the box, my friend."

"Nick," Anton said. "You shouldn't be up. You look . . ."

"Sick? Think I look sick?" Nick swaggered into the room. "Nah. Just a little sick to my stomach, is all. Maybe we should all be a little sick to our stomachs." He pulled down the cuffs of his shirtsleeves and shuffled into the center of the room, eyeing the screen and its canyon pattern. "Clues, is it? Think the Dassa gave you clues?" His body shook with a laugh that was more like a coughing fit. "Here's the big clue for you: the hoda. That's what the Dassa think of humans. To them, we're only fit to be slaves. Didn't you figure it out yet, how they mean to use us?"

Anton exchanged looks with Bailey. She rose. "Nick, let's hold this conversation for later, when you're feeling better."

"*Later?*" Nick turned to face Bailey. As he stood next to the old woman, the comparison between them was remarkable. Nick looked older than Bailey, more frail, more unstable. "I'm not sure we've *got* a later. *I* don't, anyway."

He gestured at Zhen, already hunched over her sequencer. "Hidden DNA? Pictures in the canyons? You people are grasping at straws. The truth's right under your goddamn noses. It's between two competing races of humans. The Dassa don't want competition. They lured us here, don't you see? *Come find what you've lost.* The old bait and switch, old as the hills—promise one thing, deliver another." He started to sway, and Anton leapt up to grab him.

Nick went down on one knee, struggled to rise. "Wake up and smell the stench, Anton. Bait and switch, don't you see? Send the message, get us to come, reveal where we live . . ." He fell again.

Bailey was standing at the doorway, looking out. "Oh dear," she said.

Anton let go of Nick, leaving him on the floor. "What?"

She turned. "Those dreadful women in robes."

Anton rushed to her side. There, on the dock stood dozens of uldia.

Among them was Oleel.

He turned back to Zhen. "Tie him up. And gag him." Zhen turned to follow orders as Anton strode out into the harsh afternoon sun. The uldia were pushing onto the islet from the dock, Oleel in the lead.

She stopped as Anton approached.

"Your visit is unexpected, Lady," he said, looking in alarm as her cohorts spread through the property.

"So has yours been," Oleel answered. "But now, thankfully, it is over."

"This is my land, rahi. And I will ask you to keep your people back."

Oleel looked at him for a long time before answering in a firm but low voice, "Anton Prados, you will leave the Olagong, now! You have brought enough ruin, you and your people without pri." Her attention went past him then, to someone standing in the door of the crew hut. Zhen.

Oleel whispered, "We should have killed her that night. That night you went through Vidori's walls." Anton's hand came to his holstered gun as Oleel turned back to him, her voice dropping into a deep register. "Because of you, the hoda no longer know how to serve their masters. Because of you, the king no longer knows how to serve his people. The king may claim singing is good. But it is the anthem of rebellion. You say that lost things are hidden here. But there is only the Olagong. Will you pick it apart, piece by piece, before you are satisfied?"

A movement at his side caught Anton's attention. Turning, he saw several uldia pulling Maypong toward the dock. Anton rushed forward. "Let go of her."

A dozen uldia stood in his way.

Anton surged forward, yanking one of the uldia away from Maypong. Suddenly a blow crashed across the back of his head. He staggered, losing his balance, as he heard Bailey shouting from behind.

Maypong was at his side. "Anton, use no violence here. Please."

He struggled to rise, clutching at her, getting only a handful of her gown, which was ripped from his fingers. "Maypong . . ." He staggered to his feet, finding Bailey by his side. As his head cleared, he saw them shoving Maypong across the dock and into one of the boats.

Running down to the water, he encountered a solid mass of women between him and Maypong. Oleel stood above him, on the dock. As Anton looked beyond her, he saw that the Puldar was full of boats, carrying Dassa. Some of them held torches.

The woman said, "One thing we will investigate is whether Maypong is the subject of a terrible error. We will investigate whether Maypong is a hoda who has escaped our notice." Oleel stared down at Anton, making sure she had his complete attention. "Yes, we have been worried such a mistake was made."

She produced a smile that barely dented her cheeks. "We shall see. If you are soon gone, then perhaps she is not a hoda."

Anton drew his gun from its holster and aimed it directly at Oleel's forehead. It would be so easy to kill her. In his mind he saw her falling heavily onto the dock, saw himself rushing past her to the boat, grabbing Maypong . . . "Release her, Oleel. The king said I can protect my people."

She didn't falter. "Yes, the king has allowed you a gun to protect your people. But Maypong is not one of your people. The law says I can hold her." Anton held the gun steady, and just as steady, Oleel stared back at it.

From the end of the dock, he heard Maypong call to him. "Anton, do not use a gun on the uldia. As you value your mission, do not."

"Maypong . . . ," he called.

"No, Anton. It will ruin you."

No, it would not help to kill Oleel—they had Maypong. Slowly, he lowered the weapon.

Oleel said, "This dock is not worthy of the Puldar." She turned to an uldia standing next to her. "Burn it." Then Oleel strode off, descending into one of the canoes. The uldia followed her, emptying the islet, the dock, paddling swiftly away.

A torch fell onto the deck. And then another. Anton ran up, kicking the torches into the water. But a hail of flaming brands came at him from the skiffs that still surrounded his island. Zhen and Bailey succeeded in pulling him back from the pier, as the flames finally caught.

The people in the remaining boats were not uldia, but ordinary Dassa, the ones who supported Oleel, the ones he'd been ignoring, seeing the Olagong as the king's land. It had never been the king who ruled, but the Three Powers, closely bound. The flames spread, jumping to Anton's skiff. Then Dassa began hurling torches at the huts. Anton and the two women kicked dirt over them, but the reed matting took fire.

"The lab," Zhen shouted, and they abandoned the sleeping huts to the flames, concentrating on the lab hut. But the fire leapt onto the wood structure, and soon they were hauling equipment out and piling it at the water's edge. Nick sat, bound and useless, among the salvage.

The four of them watched as the flames consumed their camp, finally guttering out in the surrounding moist vegetation.

Turning toward the river, Anton looked for any more torches among the boats, but the skiffs had fled, along with the canoes of the uldia, bearing Maypong away.

III

KINGDOM

OF

RIVERS

SEVENTEEN

Gilar and Mim scrubbed the ceramic pestles, waiting for the signal. Nearby, an uldia bent over a microscope, while others labeled herbs and compounds, in the industrious labs. Although she worked one-handed, Gilar's finger stumps still ached as the uldia weaned her from pain tonics.

From the corridor, a hoda flashed a hand sign as she passed by. Responding, Gilar wiped her wet hand on her apron and, catching Mim's eyes, began stacking the pestles to carry to the storage room. From there she slipped out the back way into the main corridor. Here were hoda, casually yet strategically positioned, to keep watch along the hall. Eshi emerged from the back stairwell, clearing her throat. At this signal, Gilar slipped into the stairway and hurried down. She passed another sister, one of two dozen hoda comprising the secret chain of movement throughout the compound. The hoda used the chain for minor disobedience such as allowing an injured sister to rest, or permitting sarif during chore times.

Today the chain cleared a path straight to Maypong, in her cell. Gilar scurried down the stairs, entering the lower region of the pavilion, wrapped in the twilight of a few luminaries.

When she reached the cell, a hoda passed by, signing, >Not long, sister.<

Gilar looked through the bars. Inside, the prisoner looked up, startled. "Gilar?" She came to the bars, peering through.

>No honorific, Maypong-rah? Was it you who removed my honors, then?<

Maypong had the grace to look away. "Yes, my daughter. But I had the help of the Olagong and the Three." When she looked back at Gilar, she said, "You are grown, all at once."

Was it so? It had been only two months since her palace days, with her fine clothes, and her tongue. Did she look so different? Certainly Maypong looked different. Her long hair clumped in dirty strands, and her gold tunic was torn and smudged.

>Maypong, you have become old.<

She smiled. "Oh, yes, Gilar, and wise, I hope." Her feet were bound in cloth, treated with pungent salves. Had the uldia beaten her? Well, she must get used to that now.

Maypong glanced at Gilar's own bandage. "Let me see your hand." When Gilar didn't respond, Maypong said, "Unguent of nisda will help."

But it was too late to be a mother. >I have all the help I need these days.<

"Oh, but you do not, Gilar, my child of the lightning rod." No trace of mockery lay in her words, or Gilar would have struck her. "I beg you, don't allow the stone woman to ruin you."

Gilar felt a smile cut across her face. >You think I am not already ruined?<

Maypong's eyes glittered in the faint light of the luminaries. "Yes, my daughter. I think you are not ruined, despite all that Oleel has done."

>Good, then that's settled. You're content with my sta-

tus. And I'm content with yours.< If Maypong would just stop being perfect, Gilar mused, she might soften toward her. If ever there was a *stone woman*, it was Maypong.

"You think I am content, Gilar? Is that what you think of me?"

Gilar looked at her mother's proud face, regal even as dirty as it was. >No, of course you're not content to be Oleel's prisoner. You must miss the king's company, and Captain Anton, and the freedom of the river.<

"I have not been free on the river, Gilar. I have been bound by the braid, the same as you."

Oh, this was too much to bear. Gilar's hands flew up to respond. >The same? The same?< She opened her mouth very wide, the first time she had done so since *that day*. She stretched out her tongue as far as the root muscle would allow. >Tell me. Are we the same?<

Maypong looked at Gilar's hands as they signed. Then, slowly, her eyes came up to focus on Gilar's mouth. As she looked, her eyes filled with tears, but, in her composure, nothing escaped from them. At last she said, in a whisper, "No. Not the same."

Gilar found herself gripping the bars of the cell with her good hand. But this woman was not worth her anger, was not worth calling forth any more sorrow.

A hoda passed behind in the hall, making the sign for *uldia*.

Gilar signed, >My sister says our time is up.<

Seeing the signal pass between the two, Maypong frowned. "Be careful, my daughter. These hoda—some of them are traitors to the king. Did they persuade you to sing on the roof? Did you know that Anton Prados begged for your life?"

>He did nothing for me. I climbed high. And I will go higher still.<

Maypong clung to the bars. "Gilar, I fear for you, for what you may do . . ."

>And you don't fear for yourself, Maypong? You should worry about yourself.<

Maypong's intolerable lecture continued unabated. "Watch and wait, Gilar. Someday the hoda will be free; it is the way of things to change. Do not so easily give away your life."

Gilar gazed at the woman in disbelief. Gilar was no longer her child, to be given advice. The law said she was no longer Maypong's child, and Maypong had confirmed this when she'd set her clothes into the Puldar.

Maypong was still talking. "Someday our people will climb into the air, Gilar, and travel as the humans do. Anton has said this."

Gilar paused. Her dream of Erth stirred for a moment, a powerful dream. A dead one.

"Perhaps I will travel there with Anton," Maypong said.

The words hit hard: Maypong, not Gilar. But it wasn't true. >Anton will leave without you, Maypong. He doesn't want you, he only uses you.<

Maypong waited, watching Gilar carefully.

Then Gilar began to sign what she had come here to tell Maypong. >Change is in fact coming. In three days' time, Oleel will crown you with the metal basket. That's what will change, Maypong.< There, she had said it. The moment of triumph, when this woman learned that she would fall from her high place.

Maypong closed her eyes, murmuring, "So that is the way of the braid . . ." When she opened her eyes, she said, "Three days—you are sure?"

What difference did it make when? But Gilar nodded.

"And she will announce this publicly?"

>Oleel's chancellor has already gone to tell the king.<

Maypong whispered, "On that day, Gilar, we will be sisters."

Gilar's throat constricted. It was true. They would be . . . sisters, then. For a split second she thought that she didn't want to watch the crowning, though until this moment she had relished the prospect. She turned away, sickened.

Mim was approaching, and signed to her, >Uldia on the south steps—take the middle staircase.<

Gilar hurried to follow Mim down the corridor. Behind her, she heard Maypong's voice, small and resonant in the stone cell. "Gilar, my daughter. Forgive me." Gilar rushed on, her eyes burning. The voice pursued her: "For all that I have done against you, and failed to do. Forgive me."

Gilar couldn't forgive her. But no one should wear the wire crown, not ever again. Not even Maypong.

Anton replaced the mike in its cradle. Despite the sun's having gone down, the heat lingered. Heavy air tunneled into his lungs as he sighed. Tomorrow his seven days were up. Webb had said, *I don't know what the crew will do. They're not thinking clearly.*

Anton had pleaded, "Give us a few more days, for God's sake."

The crew members were aware of his discovery in the canyons. Maybe it would stay their plans, if they were *thinking clearly.* Perhaps, too, they should be thinking about what reception would await them on Earth for abandoning the mission.

I've asked, Webb had said. *I don't know what they'll do.*

A new vaccine had stopped transmission of the virus, and the remaining stricken crew were recovering, with no new cases reported for the past five days. This round might be over.

Bailey opened a screen. "Come have your dinner, my dear." She'd been very gentle with him the last two days, since Maypong's detention.

He followed her to the table, where a meal of dried meat and fruit waited. Along with a small package.

"Joon came by," Bailey said as she ate a bit of roasted meat.

Tearing open the cloth wrapping, Anton found a pile of broken sticks. Bailey leaned over the low table, frowning.

"Pencils," Anton said.

"Colored pencils," Bailey mused. "But they're all broken."

"It was a gift," Anton said, thinking the relationship, like the pencils, was beyond repair.

Whatever opinion Bailey held about the broken pencils, she kept it to herself. She poured from a carafe of fruit juice. "Are you going to send Nick up?"

Anton stared at his food, thinking. Nick was critically ill, they knew that now, after Zhen had figured out he'd been switching the blood test results. He'd hidden his condition in a desperate bid to avoid the *death ship*, as he called it. Anton set the bundle of pencils aside.

"Yes," he answered, "as soon as I can arrange it."

One of the screens opened. It was Shim. "The king consents to see you now, Anton," she said.

Bailey raised an eyebrow at Anton. "Need any help?"

He smiled at her. "Yes, lots." But he left her to finish her dinner.

As Shim led Anton through the pavilion, the corridors became ever darker, until they could barely see their way. "Why are the lights out, Shim-rah?" Anton asked.

"The king has darkened the palace to view the stars, Anton."

They climbed a ladder onto a roof walkway, catching a hot breeze from the river. Shim's baby was on her back, wrapped tightly against his mother. The infant pointed behind them at the river, saying, "Uldia." He had a tie to his uldia of the birth waters, never to be broken. Like Joon to Oleel. Joon—doing Oleel's bidding, goading Anton to stumble. Perhaps Joon's interest in hoda equality had been false from the beginning. Somehow, though, it was difficult to imagine the Lady Joon doing anyone's *bidding*. Even her father's.

Shim was climbing another ladder, surefooted and with

an unerring step despite the blackness. "Over there," she said, gesturing at several people moving in the shadows at the edge of the roof.

"Why are we meeting here?" Anton asked her.

"Oh, Captain, perhaps there are not so many ears on the roof."

Anton's eyes were adjusting to the darkness. He recognized Vidori, by his dress and bearing. Attending the king were three people Anton hadn't met, along with an array of instruments that he took for telescopes, by Shim's remark. The instrumentation was emitting a low whining noise, as of moving parts, or perhaps a nearby generator.

The king nodded to him. "Yes, Anton." He gestured to his instruments. "My astronomers say that your ship can see the stars better from so high. Is this true? That the stars shine better for you?"

"Yes, rahi. Above the atmosphere, the view is better."

Vidori bent over to look into the eyepiece of one of the telescopes as an astronomer adjusted it for him. "You must have seen a wonder or two, Anton. With your fine telescopes. Better than ours. Higher than ours." The king turned a small knob on the scope, still watching the sky. When he stood upright, he nodded at the others, who left with Shim, leaving the two of them alone.

"I was hoping to have word of Maypong, rahi, with your pardon."

A silence came between them. "How is it that Maypong comes to mind when you are thinking of leaving, and will no longer see her in that case?"

"Have I said I will leave, rahi, or do you say I must?"

"I have not said so, Anton. But you have your answers, you said. If so, then you will travel home." Anton had told him all that had transpired on the trip up-country. Vidori seemed genuinely surprised by the langva theory—but not by Nirimol's attack. Well, he had said, *Go armed*.

"We haven't found what we need. Not yet."

"But when you do, you will leave?"

"Yes, rahi. But Maypong is a matter by itself. She shouldn't suffer for my sake."

Vidori turned and walked to the edge of the roof, looking down on the river, where lights lit its bank, describing its course all the way to the junction with the Sodesh. It was the only light Anton could see, except for Joon's pavilion in the distance, brightly lit, as though in defiance of her father's habit of stargazing.

"And you," Vidori said, "should not be seen to leave because the Second Dassa demands it."

Maypong was a hostage, that much was clear to both men. But Anton suspected that to Vidori, Maypong was expendable in the larger political arena.

"And you, rahi, shouldn't allow the Second Dassa to flaunt your authority."

"Oh yes, my authority." Vidori turned back to him. His face was very dark, his expressions masked even more than usual in the night. "But you have not forgotten there are three authorities in the Olagong?"

"No, rahi. I have not forgotten. Nor have I forgotten that one of them arranged an assassin to try to kill Zhen in this very palace." Vidori had heard that Oleel admitted it. Anton went on, pressing home his point, "The same authority that now holds Maypong. Your enemies are very bold. How long will you tolerate it?"

"Not long," the king murmured. "She is an excellent chancellor."

"She is my particular and cherished . . . friend."

"Ah." Whatever Vidori made of that comment, Anton had no idea. "Thankfully, Oleel will not keep her, Anton. I have said this."

"Or harm her?"

"Will not keep her, I have said." Vidori's tone grew strained.

But then, the conversation had been stilted from the beginning, their former easy conversations long passed. To Vidori's credit, however, he'd taken them in after the burning of their islet had made it clear they were unwelcome on the Puldar.

After a moment, the king gestured toward his telescope. "I will present my stars, Anton."

Anton realized he was being invited to look into the contraption, a large assemblage firmly bolted on ceramic mountings. Anton walked over to the telescope as Vidori indicated the eyepiece into which he should look.

Bending over it, Anton could at first see nothing but a blur of light. Vidori's hand came over his, guiding his hand to the tuning knob. After a moment of adjustment, something came into view. It was the ship. The telescope was tracking it, in synchronous motion.

Anton stood up from the eyepiece. "Rahi, you are not stargazing, you are shipgazing."

"That is true. It is a fine sight, this ship that flies among the heavens." He murmured, "I told you that my sight went farther than the Olagong."

It was not a particularly welcome thought. Not for the first time, Anton wondered if Vidori wished for the technology that Anton could offer. So far, the king had not broached that subject.

"What do you see then, rahi?"

Vidori's voice came low, and urgent. "I see that Oleel wishes to unravel the braid, to usurp the powers, to keep the Olagong from changing."

Anton said, "And *is* it changing?"

The king almost smiled. "There is singing where there was none before."

Anton considered this. Was Vidori's ploy with Bailey to warm the Dassa to his human allies? Or to the hoda? But even Joon did not think the king sought betterment for the slaves.

Vidori continued, "Oleel unravels things under cover of night. I would flush her into the open. Before she grows strong, you understand."

"Many Dassa are already with her, so it seems to me, rahi."

"Oh yes, but not as many as are with me. I know this, because they paddled the river when Bailey gave us her song. They are still with me." Vidori's voice became more personal, more urgent.

"Stay with us, Anton. Force her to reveal her treachery. She cannot abide you and what you are. This will force her to move against me when she is not strong." He lowered his voice still further. "And before the death of Homish, who is loyal."

It took Anton a moment to piece it together. The king wanted Anton and his mission as a thorn in Oleel's side, to precipitate an action on her part so that the king could move against her. Before Nirimol brought the judipon over to Oleel's side. He planned a peremptory strike against the threat of her revolt. It wasn't at all that Anton had arrived at a bad time. He had arrived at a perfect time. He had always been a tool that Vidori meant to use. There was little Anton would have put past Vidori, but his cunning was more convoluted than Anton had guessed.

"Deliver Maypong from Oleel, and I'll stay a little longer." There, now he was playing the same game as Vidori. Lies and politics. Perhaps he would have done well to have played it from the beginning.

"Yes" was all Vidori said.

So, now he had reason to believe that Vidori would keep his word. Because he wanted something from Anton in return. But if the *Restoration* abandoned him, he had no doubt he would be of little value to Vidori.

The king was silent now, as though he too saw that their footing had changed. He seemed more cynical. And more honest.

The meeting was over, but Anton stayed. Now that they were being honest, there was something he wanted to know. "Who killed that pregnant woman, rahi? When you hunted her, did you kill her with my knife so that I could have a piece of land and incite Oleel according to your timetable?" Vidori was silent, but Anton wasn't going to let him stay that way. "Was it all part of your plan?"

"I didn't kill the hoda."

"But you ordered it."

"Yes." He glanced around to be sure his attendants were out of hearing range. "I instructed Maypong to slay the hoda, using the knife of Nidhe's that was in your keeping."

Maypong. She had been gone from his side that day for a little while. She had disappeared in the rainstorm. Then reappeared by the hoda's body. He remembered thinking, *My true chancellor, at last.* But no, she was the king's.

Vidori nodded at Anton. "You wanted to leave the palace. Thankfully, I arranged it."

"I think, rahi, that you arranged exactly what you wanted." Anton didn't like the thoughts he was having, didn't like to think that Maypong was the king's pawn. But of course she was, of course she must follow his orders. He wondered just how much the king had ordered her to do. His heart turned dark. Had everyone used him?

"I take my leave, rahi," Anton murmured, sick to death of the conversation.

"There is the matter of your lieutenant, however."

Anton turned back. "Nick? Lieutenant Venning?"

"Yes. He has not been a good chancellor to you, Anton, I think you know."

"Hasn't he?" Was there more that Vidori had orchestrated, had hidden?

After a pause, Vidori said, "He has been on the Amalang, but hidden."

The Amalang. Oleel's river. "Hidden?"

"Oleel has set him to spy on you. He has spent many hours in her company." Vidori shook his head. "Not a good chancellor."

Anton stared at the king, ready to refute this. But in his heart, Anton knew that Nick was capable of it. Anton had never been his captain, only his competitor. "How long?"

"Since you came among us. Weeks." After a pause, Vidori said, "You didn't know, then. Good. I had hoped that you didn't know."

Anton didn't try to hide the bitterness. "Hoped that I was loyal?"

After a beat, Vidori said, simply, "Yes."

"You might have told me sooner."

"I walk the narrow line, Anton."

Anton's own phrase, the idiom he had taught the king, back when there'd been time for wordplay and room for trust. *The fine line* between what one could say in the Olagong, and what one could not.

Anton turned away then, and without pleasantries left. In the shadows, Shim waited for him, to lead him through the maze of roofs.

EIGHTEEN

The records referred to her as Remy. No last name, though of course it was Shaw.

All that remained of her now were medical records and stray notes from caretakers, recording things they thought important: test scores, treatments for infections—oh, the health records *were* important—and sometimes an entry about a birthday or holiday. Through a succession of caretakers, a patchwork history emerged.

She was fond of softball, with a good arm and a tendency to hit to right field. She was good at spelling and math; had little interest in science. She read books, not always good ones, but lots of them. And, oh yes, she could sing.

How much did her caretakers guess about the place; so far removed, home to pampered but undereducated children? Somehow the enterprise evaded government raids. Perhaps the story was that the children's families were being hunted by gangs and the children must be separated from their parents. Or that they had a rare infection needing isolation and study. That would explain why their health was such an emphasis. And there *was* a rare health threat: Their wealthy counterparts would by and by harvest them for needed parts.

Bailey went back to her reading:

Remy broke a toe in a fall at age fourteen. She was a bad patient, played softball anyway, was grounded. Ignored the grounding. Result: The toe healed imperfectly; caretaker dismissed.

As though any caretaker could prevent a Shaw girl from doing exactly as she pleased. Bailey shook her head. *Play softball, my dear . . .*

She read pulp fiction, especially sports fantasy stories. Young girl from backwoods hits the big time. Remy liked to sing. She was good at it.

Bailey closed her eyes, rubbing them. To imagine a life from the piecemeal entries required concentration. It required a vivid imagination to fill in the blanks.

She concentrated on the screen again. She must continue, no matter how hard it was. You had to know what you did, in order to repent it.

Sometime during this session, and without directly thinking about it, Bailey decided not to go back to Earth. Whether the mission succeeded or failed, they didn't need her any longer for inspiration, for patronage. They needed Anton. Despite a shaky start, Anton Prados had grown into a fine captain. He'd handle the rest of it. But as for the rest of *her* life, it wouldn't be spent back on Earth. She was too old for long trips. She was staying, and that was the end of it. Perhaps she'd known it would come to this when she'd accepted Shim's clothes as a gift. Anton didn't like the costume, but in his heart, he must have known she was staying.

If not, she'd certainly have to tell him . . .

A hall screen opened. Zhen stood there.

"Where's Captain Prados?"

"Good evening, Zhen." Bailey blanked the screen, then looked up at the woman. Her hair was pressed down as though she hadn't combed it today. It had been two days since Zhen had poked her nose out of the science lab—the little room down the hall where they'd put all the scientific equipment that had been salvaged off the islet. "He's with the king." Bailey waved in the direction of the king's quarters.

"When did he leave?" Zhen looked around the room as though Anton might be hiding from her.

Bailey tucked a wisp of hair into her new upswept hairdo. These people had never heard of bobby pins. You just took your meter-long hair, twisted it several times, and dug in combs the size of daggers.

"I don't know. Some time ago, I think; I've been busy."

"Why is it so dark?"

"Is it?" Bailey looked out into the corridor. It was a bit shadowy.

Zhen looked at her in consternation. "I have to find him. Don't you pay attention to *anything*?"

Bailey raised an eyebrow. "If it's my business, I pay attention." Zhen looked distracted, even alarmed.

"Can I help, Zhen?"

But the woman had already fled down the dark corridor.

Bailey tapped the screen, bringing the records back. *Sixteenth birthday. A cake, chocolate. A box of books, autographed . . .*

Anton slapped the screen aside and strode into Nick's sleeping hut. The king had given them an extra space as a sickroom for Nick. But it was empty, the bedclothes twisted and heaped, pots of moldy food scattered around.

As he turned from the doorway, he collided with a hoda. He recognized her as the woman assigned to administer to Nick. "Where is he?" Anton demanded.

Her face froze. >Oh, he is wandering, but will return now and then.<

"Wandering where?"

>He goes everywhere, since he cannot rest.<

Anton took her arm to make her pay attention. "I said, *Where?*" A look of confusion came into her face. Realizing he had just made an unintentional sexual advance, he released her. She *would* be surprised that a human chose a hoda as a sexual partner, when the whole palace was at his disposal. A surge of frustration went through him, at the bizarre rules of Dassa intimacy, at the easy betrayal by his own crew. It was all twisted here from the way things *should* be.

Leaving the hoda, he strode to his quarters to ask Bailey about Nick's whereabouts, but she was gone. As a last resort he checked in on Zhen, only to find her screen left wide open and the lab empty. Papers covered her workbench, full of scrawl, some pasted to the wall screens and stirring in the breeze through the slightly open river screen. He turned on his heel and plunged into the corridor again, his anger mounting.

Nick had been subverting him from the very beginning. He hadn't even waited to lose confidence, he'd just tossed it out right away. It had been all jealousy and resentment from the day that Bailey had chosen him over Nick. It was from that day that Nick's eyes had grown cold.

Anton found one of the king's brothers lounging on the deck off the plaza. Had he seen the lieutenant? *The one without pri?* That was what they called Nick. Anton almost said, *No, the one without honor.*

Yes, he'd seen Nick near the baths not long past . . .

Anton took the ramp into the lamp-lit gardens. He stopped a hoda he recognized and asked again, but she pointed in the direction he'd just come from.

Taking a deep breath, Anton paused. He was standing on the very bridge where he'd first spoken with Maypong, the woman he'd thought was without a heart. And now, in this moment, he realized that it wasn't Nick who'd driven him to this frenzy. He'd already known that Nick had turned from him; it was one reason he gave him nothing important to do. No, he was frantic at the thought that Maypong had betrayed him, that she'd done everything for the king's sake, that it had all been duty to her, never love, or what passed for it here. He would have taken such love as she could give. Because she was Dassa, he would have taken her on her terms. The terms of this world, where she was perfectly adapted and full of grace.

And standing on that bridge, he believed her. She hadn't betrayed him; she had managed to hold her loyalty to her king and to him in the same strong arms. She'd done both. He believed that. So when it came to betrayal, it was human betrayal that took the prize.

Someone was standing at the foot of the bridge, looking up at him where he stood. It was Nick.

"I heard you were looking for me, Captain." His voice was reedy. The polyps in his throat were rampant now.

Anton turned to face him. "No, Nick. I was looking for the man you used to be."

Nick started to laugh, then coughed instead. "If you find him, let me know. I liked him better."

"So did I."

Nick swayed a little, bracing his hand on the bridge railing. "Sick people make you nervous, Captain? Afraid I'll contaminate you?"

Anton let that lie. If Nick wanted the moral high ground, he'd have to come up with a better excuse than that. "Who do you take orders from these days? Just so I know."

"I was looking for a captain." The voice was small and simple.

"And I wasn't it," Anton finished for him. "So you chose Oleel."

Anton approached him, walking down the slope of the bridge. As he did so, Nick swung away from him, heading down the path, staggering, but somehow staying upright. He was thin, his fatigues hanging on his frame.

Nick's voice came back to him as he wobbled on: "Didn't choose her, no. Never went that far." He turned around, almost tripping over his own feet. "Think I'm a traitor? Of course I didn't *choose* her." He resumed his headlong rush down the path. "Talked to her, though. Like you should have done."

Anton caught up to him, jerked his arm to stop him, bringing him around to face him. "I should have had concourse with a woman who hates us?"

"Yes."

Anton's stomach rose. "You bastard. You lying bastard. You're up on charges, Nick. I don't care if you live to see them, but I'll have your commission for this."

Nick's eyes brightened. "Oh, a court-martial is a good idea. I hope I live to have one—it'll be a hoot. We can talk about how you cozied up to the king and screwed his daughter while the ship went to hell and the Dassa—"

Anton struck him. He pulled back enough that he only clipped him on the chin, but it was sufficient to send Nick rolling down a slope next to the path. Anton stood there, fist still clenched, ready for Nick to come back at him. But he could barely gather himself into a crouch, much less rise.

"Good hit, Anton." Nick said, struggling to rise. "Good one, Captain."

Anton felt like an ass. He would have welcomed a retaliating blow from Nick Venning, but the man could barely walk, let alone fight. It was a damn shame.

Instead of rising, Nick seemed to give up on the maneuver and just drew his knees up, then sat and gazed at the narrow canal nearby. Anton found himself walking down the slope and sitting next to Nick.

His sweat mixed with drops of water condensed out of the air, but as wet as he was, it was still damn hot for the middle of the night. What was Nick doing out here, anyway? Why did he roam?

When Nick began to talk, it was in a conversational tone, as though that was all he could muster.

"I was going to tell you. But I got sidetracked with the medicinals. I knew you wouldn't let me test them on myself, but I knew you'd like me to, as long as you didn't have to approve it." He nodded over and over. "I did that for you, Anton, so you could keep your nice, soft hands clean."

Anton had known about that; they'd all known he was taking drugs. They just hadn't known he'd got them from Oleel.

"It didn't work." Nick pulled his sleeves up and gazed at the purple welts on his lower arms. "But that's how I found out the truth, so I guess it doesn't matter because eventually I found out."

A couple of viven walked by, glancing at them.

Nick turned around, staring at the two Dassa men. "Look normal, don't they? See, that's your problem, Anton. You got all tangled up with them, with the king, with Joon, with Maypong. You couldn't keep perspective anymore. You took them as human." He glanced over at Anton. "They're not."

"You should have talked with me, Nick. You've been spinning theories, but all by yourself. You could have talked to me."

"Yeah, I did talk with you. I begged you to get on with it. If you'd listened to me, you'd have been to the big stone place, seen the variums, seen how they hatch . . ."

"The variums?" Oh, Nick had been busy indeed.

After a pause, Nick said. "Yes. Variums." He was trying to swallow, and it sounded like he was strangling. Finally, he said, "When the eggs split open, a white gruel comes out. It's not full of blood, like a natural birth. The creatures don't live in blood, they live in a white sap. That's why they're so cruel. No blood. I guess they get up blood in their veins, but by then it's too late." Now that he was good and warmed up, the words poured out of him. "See, if you're raised up in a pond, kept inside an egg, the whole reality of your being is animal, not human. So if a child dies, it's like an animal sniffing, feeling a loss, and then rutting again to pass along the genes. They don't love anybody. They can't love. All they can do is be animals. And hate the women who bear—and for the same reasons."

"We know all this, Nick. It's never been a secret, how they bear, that they distrust us. That some of them hate us."

Nick's voice cracked. "But you didn't *see* it. The baby coming out of the fulva." He turned to Anton, grabbing onto his sleeve. "The uldia was there, sucking out the fluid. The hatchling came out, looking like a ghoul, dripping with the stuff, no mother to hold out her arms in welcome, just the witch. And the smell . . . oh God, the smell of it . . ." His face had contorted, and his eyes were bright, seeking Anton's, but somehow looking past them. "They'll kill what we are, they'll change us into something we don't want to be. If you'd seen . . . if you'd tried to see . . . but you never did, Anton. You never wanted to think what we'd become if we mixed with them. Whatever they are, we should run from them. Run hard."

"So now you think they want to conquer us?" Nick had said he did, the day they took Maypong.

Nick pushed Anton away, staggering to his feet. "You think I've lost it. You're not listening. Maybe before, when I was in a fever, I said some things . . . I was still trying to figure it out. Maybe they're not going to enslave us . . . but see, they don't need to. All they need to do is *absorb* us. Same deal. We'll become Dassa. Some of us will be monsters, some of us will be slaves. Just like them. Me, I'd rather be a hoda." He started climbing the bank. "Of course, guys can't be hoda, so . . ." He was muttering as he hurried over the bridge, with Anton following him.

Anton caught up to Nick and tried to steady him. "Calm down, Nick. Don't you see this is just what happens to people when things look their worst?"

"Yeah, they see the truth."

"No, they start looking for easy answers, absolutes. Scapegoats. I never took you for xenophobic. Your psych scores were good. But now you're turning out to be just like all the doubters back home. 'The universe is out to get us; stay home, be safe . . .'"

Nick had calmed, in fact. He was breathing deeply, regularly. "Captain, one last thing? Can I tell you one last thing before you throw me in a cell?"

Anton nodded.

Nick looked around. "But we'll need to go up on the roof. That OK?"

He took Anton by the arm and started pushing him down the bridge ramp onto a path that cut over toward the king's river room.

"Where are you going, Nick?"

He waved the question away. "I've been gathering evidence."

They were on the roof, having taken the same route that Shim and Anton had just a couple of hours ago. A thin layer of clouds had netted over the night sky, and must have driven the astronomers from the roof, along with Vidori, because the observing platform was empty.

They approached the instruments. Nick whispered, "I've been here before, some nights. Did you know the king had telescopes?"

"Yes."

"Have you looked through them?" Nick ran his hand along the ceramic tube of one of them.

"I've seen him tracking the ship, Nick. He's just curious. It's no threat to us."

Nick snorted. "No threat to us. Not as such." He uncapped the lens of the nearest scope and swirled it around to aim away from the sky. Into the king's compound. Kneeling down, Nick unscrewed something from the base of the instrument, holding it up. Anton couldn't see what it was, but Nick announced: "Erecting eyepiece. For terrestrial viewing. So the view isn't upside down. The view is better when it's right side up."

Nick screwed the eyepiece in, his hand shaking, and almost dropped it. "Oops," he said. "Don't want to break it. Crack it like an egg . . ."

A breeze from the river carried the fetid smell of rot as the heat evaporated the water and left ooze on the banks to ferment. Anton was getting impatient with Nick; he'd let him go too far. It was part of the problem, indulging the man all this time.

"Look, Anton." Nick had stepped away from the scope.

Anton sighed. He stepped forward, bending down to the eyepiece. "So you've been spying, then."

"Yeah. Somebody had to."

The lens showed nothing but a garden, lit now from the compound lights that had brightened since the king left the roof. There was a large pond, a bridge in the distance. All empty.

Anton said, "Well, what now?"

"We wait."

Anton stood up impatiently. "Nick, what have you seen? You can tell me."

"Oh, I don't think so. Nothing like the real thing." He fixed Anton with an odd little stare. "Not in a hurry, are you?"

He wasn't. So they waited, silently. There was nothing left to say. Nick felt no sense of shame. It was all justified. By the variums. And by the garden, and what it contained.

Nick kept ducking over to the scope and checking out the view.

After some time, his frantic checkups paid off. "Oh, yes," he said. "Now here we go."

He practically pushed Anton down to look.

A man was standing by the pond, alone. He wore black and silver, and stood gazing out with a composed manner. He looked up into the scope's lens . . . no, up into the sky.

Stargazing again.

After a time, a figure approached from the back of the garden. Someone dressed in dark clothing. Well, dressed in blue, with a silver inset at the neck. Her ear ornaments glinted in the light from the lantern near the pond.

He heard Nick's voice behind him. "Adjust the focus, Captain."

The focus, though, was perfect. Perfect enough to see that Joon was now dispensing with her tight jacket and underblouse. Her dark skin took on a bronze luster in the light that fell on the pond water and bounced back on her. Her movements were all silent, as though this was some netherworld that had never had sound, only calm, deliberate action.

Then, perhaps not wanting to soil her narrow skirt, she stepped out of it, and cast it onto the lawn.

Anton started to withdraw, to stand up, but Nick's hand was on his head, pushing him down again, to the eyepiece. *We knew*, Anton told himself. *We knew. Everybody knows, everybody does it . . .*

Nick's voice was in his ear, whispering, as though their voices might disturb the scene before them, right within arm's reach, though hundreds of meters away. "This is your high king and his fine daughter. The one you fucked. They do this right in the open. The garden can be viewed from lots of porches. No reason to hide . . ."

Vidori was still gazing into the sky, as though his interest were really there and not in the little garden. It was a lovely little garden, with tended plants and a perfect, oval pond. His beloved daughter was sharing the fine evening with him. And was about to share more.

Then Vidori turned to her. All in silent, slow motion, she went to her knees in front of him. She parted the brocade that hung from his waist.

Anton pulled back from the telescope, sickened. Then Nick was grappling with him, trying to force him back.

He laughed at the expression on Anton's face. "They won't mind if you watch, Anton . . . It's all in a day's work. I've watched lots of times. Which way are they doing it this time?" His voice was high-pitched, too loud. He grabbed Anton's shoulder, swirling him to face him. "Human, you think? Is this what you want with *your* daughter, if you and

Maypong have one? Or just imagine if you have a *son*—him and Maypong . . ."

"Stop it!" Anton growled. "Be quiet." He lurched away, stalking off, toward the ladder.

Nick's voice followed him. "Oh, *quiet*. Of course. I forgot, we're supposed to pretend. The captain of pretending . . ."

Anton was fleeing the roof, the garden scene, Nick's voice.

Nick called to him, "How do you like your King Vidori now?"

Anton hurried on, his stomach knotted, his mind roiling. He despised Vidori. Oh yes, they'd known, they'd all known about this. But they hadn't seen it. He never wanted to see it.

And maybe that was the problem, just like Nick said.

Mim found Gilar in the langva fields in back of the pavilion. >Maypong swims,< she signed.

Gilar nodded, thanking her. It was impossible to get near Maypong's cell now, with her uldia guards strengthened against some action of the king's. And Gilar did want to see Maypong. To tell her, *I would not wish the crowning on you.* And then, the thing she'd never thought she would say: *It was never your fault.*

She followed Mim out of the field as the sun rose in full force. The weather-mancers said this would be the hottest day of the year. Her skull still not hardened against the sun, Gilar unconsciously covered the back of her head with her hand.

With Maypong in the varium, they would have privacy to talk. Here was proof that Oleel knew Maypong wasn't a hoda. Hoda didn't swim. But there would be no witnesses, other than uldia. Oleel would make sure the varium was far removed from the usual sites, so that no viven saw Maypong accorded the rights of a proper Dassa.

Gilar and Mim carried stacks of brocaded towels into

the forest, to justify their presence. As they passed other hoda, eyes met, and songs conveyed needful information. Oleel swims in the upper variums. She has just entered the pool.

The stone woman was always the most watchful, following Gilar especially. But lately, with Maypong, she had another creature to torture. And today she swam in distant parts.

Mim led Gilar down a narrow path into the river-side variums, which were less used. Then they departed from the path, slipping through dense undergrowth, in absolute quiet. Water trickled and splashed as, nearby, Dassa swam.

Mim pointed to one side and waited behind as Gilar slunk forward on hands and knees, parting the foliage.

At the edge of the varium, Maypong sat in her dirty tunic and leggings. One leg was bent under her, the other outstretched in a graceful pose, as though she were attending on the king.

Gilar tossed a small stone into the pond.

Maypong turned in surprise, seeing her. Shadows deepened her eyes, as though she hadn't slept. "It is dangerous for you to be here, my daughter."

Hearing herself called *daughter*, Gilar let her mouth soften into a smile. >Everything is dangerous in the stone pavilion.<

Maypong's face bore a line of perspiration on her upper lip, though it was cool in this shady place. She looked out into the shallow pond, but made no move to undress. "I will have no more children," she said.

Well, if Oleel said for her to swim, she must swim. There would be no choices about that, didn't Maypong know?

Maypong went on, her voice small and lost. "I'm sorry that I couldn't save you."

Since Maypong was facing away from her, Gilar maneuvered around to the side, where her hand sign could be seen.

>I will save myself, Mother.< There. She had said the word.

But Maypong was strangely preoccupied. "Oh yes, Gilar, please do so. You have been my favorite, always. Your siblings are dear to me, but you are my best child, my beloved daughter." The rising sun slashed into the pond through changing pathways, hitting the surface like the flash of fish gills. Maypong went on, as though speaking to the water, not to Gilar. "The hoda have a long river journey, I believe. I would not have you throw away your life for the sake of despair. If you sacrifice your life, it must only be for love. When there is something you love above all else."

>But what can that be?<

"I hope you never find such a terrible thing." Her eyes met Gilar's, a gaze so open that Gilar thought she could see straight into her.

"I will swim now," Maypong said.

It was proper for Gilar to leave. She backed up. But then she caught sight of a different sort of light, something Maypong had in her hand.

Gilar crawled back to the water's edge. >Mother, what do you have?<

Maypong looked over at her as she stepped out of her tunic. "Oh, it is only a small blade."

A blade? >You shouldn't swim with a knife, Mother.< Something was wrong, strangely wrong . . .

Maypong said, walking into the pond, "Somehow my uldia has given me one, though."

Her uldia. *By the braid, Maypong's own uldia had given her a knife.*

"She thinks to save me from public disgrace, but I would be honored to join you, Gilar. Never think otherwise. But this is for Anton. For love, you understand."

Gilar spoke. She did the thing no hoda ever did, forcing words up, words that came out misshapen and awful. "No, Mother, no," she garbled out, unable to articulate the real word, except with the back of her tongue. Gilar rose to her feet, stumbling forward, splashing into the varium, trying to stop what was coming.

But Maypong lay forward, on the water, as though beginning her swim. Her arms, however, were under the water, and they jerked toward her stomach, and then Gilar knew that her mother had slashed herself. Maypong curled in on herself as blood welled up to surround her. Gilar splashed forward, too late. Moans came from her throat, but it was too late. Maypong jerked again, and the knife must have drawn sideways, as she did the unthinkable damage.

Mim was at Gilar's side, as Gilar groaned, "No, no, no." Mim's hand came up over Gilar's mouth, dragging her out of the varium, onto the bank. Gilar fought her off and turned back to the water.

The pond was still again. Maypong lay facedown, floating quietly. At the pond's edge, her yellow skirt draped into the water, ballooning in the wind, sparkling in the morning light.

As Gilar moaned, Mim shushed her. There, there, my sister, she sang. Let her swim now, in peace.

Swimming in blood. *Mother* . . .

Mim led Gilar away as the sun turned brittle on the forest leaves, hurting Gilar's eyes. Tears came. Mim held her, crying too.

Behind them, a shout went up. They had discovered Maypong and her desecration of the varium. Everything was twisted here, in the stone woman's pavilion. Twisted and ruined.

A boat, Gilar sang.

Uldia were running up the paths, some armed.

Gilar stared at the jungle floor, not seeing the tangled roots. Her mother was dead. And why? So that Oleel couldn't force the human captain to leave—for Maypong's sake. Maypong had struck against Oleel. So brave, so cruel.

Find me a boat, Mim, Gilar sang.

At Mim's alarmed look, Gilar sang, I am leaving.

NINETEEN

The warm trickle down his throat was blood. Weak gums. Nick's whole body felt like a sack of wounded flesh. Even so, Anton had judged it necessary to shackle him to the room's main timber, where he could go no farther than the makeshift latrine. The Dassa were so fastidious. Didn't Anton know how it made humans look, to piss into a jar?

With the dawn firing up the woven screens, it was already hellishly hot, cooking the slime in the river and in the latrine to a poisonous stench. From time to time a hoda came in and tried to get him to drink. Once, Bailey looked in on him, shaking her head. *Made a mess, haven't you,* she said.

As the sun brightened the hut, the shimmering form came back, the one in the corner. Captain Darrow. The old man, in full insignia. By his expression, he was distressed at what they'd done to Nick.

"We'll get you out of this, Lieutenant," he said. "Hold tight, now."

"All those notes on Zhen's wall . . . ," Nick began. Zhen had tacked sections of tronic printout on the walls. He'd scanned them late last night, before his run-in with Anton.

"Yes, I know, son. Quadi propaganda. I've seen it."

Trying and failing to swallow, Nick took a swig of water to loosen his vocal cords. "She pinned some of it up on the walls, the output from the plants. Now she's in there with Anton Prados—he took your place, you know."

Darrow nodded gravely. "But I'm not dead."

"That's just what I mean. It's wrong. It's lies. But part of it's true, maybe. The Quadi, they might have done what they said—cloned the human DNA here. We always thought so, but now they're claiming they constructed the planet, and that the Dassa don't know anything, that they're in the dark. But, sir, the Dassa *are* in on it. They always wanted our help—to release the human genomes. Into their keeping. See, they can't reproduce fast enough. The variums aren't efficient, they—"

Captain Darrow gestured for quiet. "Don't get yourself worked up, son. I can separate truth from lies. Zhen is doing the translating. *I'm* doing the thinking. And the Dassa bastards aren't going to win."

Nick closed his eyes. *Thank God. Thank God he isn't deceived.*

The captain's voice came: "Get strong now, Nick. I'm going to need you when I take back my command."

"*Take back?*"

The old man's face distorted into a grimace. "That's right, *take back*. And you'll be my right-hand man. Who else can I trust?"

The words were bittersweet. The captain needed him.

"My, my," Bailey said.

It was all so swift, following on the dreadful night of Nick's betrayal and Vidori's garden. Now, the stunning breakthrough. Anton couldn't quite grasp it, or hold the concept: hope restored, humanity restored—or so it seemed. Zhen hadn't finished translating everything, and a thousand questions remained. He swept them aside, saving them for later.

Some of the notes were pasted up on the wall, looking precious and insubstantial, as though at any moment the future of Earth could be blown away by a gust from the river.

Several hours ago, still in the middle of the night, Zhen had found Anton. She'd looked like a wild woman. Her hair stood out in every direction, matted and pasted into tufts, perhaps from too much thinking.

"Got it," she'd said. "We got it."

Anton had taken one look at her face, and believed her. She'd got it.

"*Codas,*" she'd said, taking him by the arm and hurrying him toward her work hut. "They're in what the Quadi call *codas*—little summations."

She'd pulled him along faster, almost at a gallop, down the palace halls, gesticulating as she went. "The decipherment was easy. They made it easy. It's a quadrinary system, not a binary one, because of the ATCG of the DNA base pairs."

"Slow down, Zhen. It's in the DNA, that's what you're saying?"

"Yes, I just said it's in the DNA. And get this—the four bases code for ASCII." She'd rolled her eyes. "Yeah, ASCII.

"I didn't believe what I was seeing in the genome at first. It was too big, impossibly so. I thought the program screwed up. But I modified the language program to specifically translate the quadrinary code. That took a while. When I ran the program, it didn't work, so I figured I'd made a wrong turn somewhere. Then late last night I finally figured out that I might be using the wrong plant variety. See, some of the varieties encode for different alien civilizations . . ." She'd waved Anton's questions away. "More on that later. Like Sergeant Webb said, we can't decode that stuff. But the next variety I tried, that was the one. It took the program twenty-five seconds to break the code."

Now, in the science hut, Zhen was rushing through further explanations, answering questions from Anton and Bailey, but impatiently. She wanted to get to the codas.

Of the DNA sequences.

The four-base-pair system yielded 4x4x4x4, for a total of 256 characters, the basis of ASCII code. Although a hideously inefficient coding system, it was instantly recognizable. The langva genome was engineered to store the entire archive of Quadi information—a gigantic DNA molecule that, if written out at four base pairs per millimeter, would stretch from the Olagong to its nearest planetary neighbor . . . and would extend even farther, except that the code sometimes read in both directions at once—a feat of incomprehensible complexity.

Through the river-side screen, a trickle of a breeze cooled Anton's face. Although without sleep this night, he was wide awake.

Bailey tapped at the radio transmitter. "Let's send this to the *Restoration*. It's too valuable to just be in our keeping."

Zhen snorted. "I already did that." She looked at Anton. "Begging your pardon, Captain, but I was too nervous when I couldn't find you."

Anton waved it away. "Well done, Zhen. That was well done." He was gazing at the notes pasted on the wall. "Now read it out loud again, the beginning part." Zhen had zoomed through her translation fast, to get to the part about human salvation. But now Anton wanted it slow and steady, so it could sink in.

Bailey rose from her seat. "Let the girl rest a moment. I'll read it." Zhen turned to frown at Bailey. It was Zhen's discovery. After a moment, though, she crossed the room and sank onto a low platform, not relaxing, still springloaded.

Bailey peered at one of the notes. "Some of this is technical stuff. About how to create life . . ." She turned to Anton. "It talks here about fulva. I'm not sure our people will like that."

Zhen snorted. "How else are we going to rejuvenate the genomes? Wave a wand?"

"Artificial insemination, perhaps."

"Well, the Quadi gave us instructions for a fulva process. Beggars can't be choosers."

Anton was still gazing at the wall. "Get on with it, Bailey."

"Start on the east wall," Zhen said. "That's the easy stuff."

Raising an eyebrow, Bailey went to the east wall. "Science wasn't my subject, Zhen my dear, but I wasn't exactly a bonehead." And she began.

Anton leaned against the corner pillar of the hut and listened with closed eyes.

Coda One. Uncommon Complex Life.

In this galaxy, complex life is uncommon. It can be surmised that in other galaxies, animal habitability of planets will be as rare, although no species endures long enough to traverse more than one galaxy. Worlds with climatically suitable environments for water-based biotic inhabitants are rare. Most critical is astronomical setting. A position away from the chaotic center of the galaxy is a prerequisite. Infrequency of extinction events caused by celestial collisions, hard radiation bursts, and supernovae is fundamental. Of stars, only a few possess the longevity to enable complex life to evolve over the requisite millions of years. Bright stars are short-lived. There are many bright stars. Only a zone of narrow tolerances around a star allows water in liquid form. In addition, a moon is needed at the right distance from a conducive planet to stabilize axial tilt. Also important is a massive planet at a conducive distance to clear cometary obstacles. Many biogeochemical factors are necessary for habitable planets. Susceptibility to extinction events is improved if diversity of body plans among animalia is high, an infrequent circumstance. Millions of planets harbor microbial domains, but sentient species occupy merely seventeen worlds in this galaxy, and in this time frame. Three are ancient, senile civilizations that will be extinct in your interval of existence. Of the fourteen remaining civilized worlds, six are/were victims of the galactic depletion event, including Earth. Some will not recover even with the data salvage and sequestration undertaken here.

Coda Two. The Galactic Depletion.
The anomalous dark matter structure continues its course through the galaxy, bound gravitationally, never to depart. Coda sixty-one describes its entropic fields in detail. Humans developed the technology of quasi-crystal that deflects the data transfer event, but even this strategy could not prevent the serious depletion of Earth's complex life. Quasi-crystal was an imperfect solution. There is no perfect solution. While extinguishing worlds, the dark matter structure has amassed two billion years of knowledge. Because of this cargo, we could not destroy it, nor could we deflect it from the path bringing it among the fourteen civilized worlds. We attempted to bestow saving technology on two such worlds. Both resulted in disaster and chaos because of cultural dismay and martial response. We fled, vowing to save some things, but in our way. We were the first galactic technological species, but the tenure of our civilization is ending. We never reckoned to leave behind an empty galaxy. Our purpose is to forestall such a circumstance.

Anton looked at Zhen. "How many codas are there?"

"I stopped counting at four hundred thirty-three," Zhen said. "Most of them are extremely long codas on microbiology, genetics, math, and chemistry. These first codas are the short ones—eleven of them. Some of the codas have mutations in the genetic code, introducing garbage into the messages. We can solve that by sequencing several individual genomes, mixing and matching to assemble complete codas."

Bailey frowned. "What about human genomes? If they're in there as well, what if they're messed up too?"

Zhen waved her off. "It's all in the codas. How to identify harmful mutations and fix them." She looked at Bailey with pity. "You think the Quadi didn't think of that one?"

Bailey shot back, "There are lots of things the Quadi didn't think of. Like how Earth is going to react to raising babies in ponds."

"They don't need to be *ponds,* for Christ sakes," Zhen snapped, "they could be cute little pink crèches, if you want."

Anton said, "Read, Bailey."

Coda Three. This Planet and Setting Modified.
We resolved to salvage the biological and electronic information of Earth on a conducive world, remote from the path of the galactic depletion event. In a delicate process of three hundred years, we siphoned off retrievable data from the dark matter structure. We modified this unsuitable world, creating a compatible one, adjusting atmospherics and chemistries that matched the habitable Earth. We removed two orbiting moons for planetary stability. We modified the astronomical setting, eliminating a gravitationally disruptive gas giant. The astronomical and terrestrial settings have been developed for ideal cosmic, biological, and cultural life cycles.

Coda Four. The Life-Forms Derived.
Life-forms were developed with modifications to assure procreation. Within the dark matter structure, the degradation of information was high due to radiation exposure. Some codes, if badly degraded, were abandoned. The human species is modified here. Humans may accept species modifications. We could not accept modifications for ourselves. Also developed and modified are the other domains of life from Earth to xxxxxxxxxxecological web. In ordeexxxxxxxxxxxxxxxxxxxxxxx xxxxxxxxxxxxxxxxxxxxxxxxxxxxxxxxxxxxxxxxxxxxxxxxxxx xxxxxxxxxxxxxxxxxxxxxxxxxxxxxxxxxxxxxxxxxxxxxxxxxxx xxxxxxxxxxxxxxxxxxxxxxxxxxxxxxxxxxxxxx

"There's a bunch of squiggles here," Bailey said.

"The code was garbled. Just skip it," Zhen said.

Bailey waved at the tronics station. "I thought you said we could piece it all together from several individual plants."

Zhen sighed. "I've only been working on this for a *few hours,* for God's sake."

Coda Five. The Custodial Duty.
We stayed as custodians to tend habitats and assure diverse species survival. Because our time was waning, we accelerated the number of possible procreations using birth cradles. The sentient population having reached a viable level, we departed, leaving little evidence of ourselves to avoid cultist religions. We left them to develop a natural culture, including an indigenous language. In ten thousand years they will rise up a civilization capable of knowing of us. This is more likely if the first humans of Earth establish contact with them, for we have left the record in the language we identified in the Dark Cloud. All information is sequestered in genome repositories, the only reservoir that would last with minimal disruption over millennia. The complexity of the information stored here requires resistant storage. Biological systems are such storage devices.

Coda Six. Redundant Storage.

Zhen interrupted Bailey's reading. "OK, this is the part about the other messages."

Other messages. They were prepared for this part. The Quadi were calling to civilizations in other parts of the galaxy. Not because their higher life-forms were revived here—the world wouldn't be chemically and ecologically suited to extraterrestrial biologies. However, along with cultural products, the foreign DNA codes were sequestered here in computational formats. As for the individual alien beings, the Quadi claimed to be working on recovering them on other suitable worlds. Perhaps, after the time these

messages were recorded, they had succeeded elsewhere in
doing what they accomplished on Neshar.

Zhen said, "The information on the other—what they
call *depleted worlds*—is locked into different varieties of
langva, not the staple food variety."

Anton looked up. It was riches beyond grasping, here at
dawn after a sleepless night, with the night's revelations and
lessons.

"Keep going," he told Bailey.

Coda Six. Redundant Storage.
We have provided redundant information storage mecha-
nisms. First, regarding Earth higher and lower life, these are
encapsulated as information in the genome of the staple food
organism occurring in the habitable biome of this planet. Such
a strategy is obvious and will be seen immediately by the first
humans if they achieve technology to respond to the radio mes-
sages. Also sequestered here, in other varieties of the staple
food plant, are the biological and computational coded infor-
mation of the other worlds depleted by the dark matter struc-
ture. This gathered knowledge has two purposes: to transmit
to first and second humans the life and culture of the techno-
logical worlds, and redundant safekeeping of the same. In
parallel efforts, the information of the depleted worlds is se-
questered on other planets as our terraforming progresses. Re-
grettably, several of these worlds falter, and may have to be
abandoned. Not all storage solutions are viable, nor all plane-
tary revisions. Therefore, on every terraformed world, we have
encapsulated planetary knowledge from all threatened worlds,
for the benefit of redundant storage.

Bailey stopped reading and Anton stood at the sound of
a screen sliding open. They saw Shim standing there.

He hoped that any business she might have could wait,
and would have said so but for the look on her face. In his
time among the Dassa he had learned to heed that too-
quiet, controlled expression on people's faces.

"Captain, thank you," she said. Her eyes flicked over the wallful of notes, but she didn't seem to disapprove of the defacing of the screens.

"Shim-rah," Anton began. He walked over to her. Perhaps this could wait. Then, looking past her shoulder, he saw Vidori. Shim backed out of the way, and Anton moved past her into the corridor. Some meters away a clutch of viven were gathered; the king was standing alone. Anton felt sick at heart. He could never again be in the king's presence without remembering. Without being aware that human and Dassa would forever regard each other as mistakes . . . *modifications,* to the Quadi.

Vidori's face was dark with some burden. Anton and Nick had left the telescope with the terrestrial eyepiece attached. Maybe Vidori had discovered this, and suspected what they'd seen.

"Anton," Vidori said. As Anton made his greetings, Vidori looked into his face with such compassion that a tremor of premonition touched Anton's skin. He hoped that the telescope was the matter at hand.

"I bear this news, Anton. But will you forgive me for what I have to say?"

I don't know. He couldn't answer out loud, but silently, he answered, *I don't know if I have that much forgiveness. If you're talking about Maypong.*

"Maypong is dead," came Vidori's words.

Anton turned aside. No, that couldn't be.

"This morning, so the Second Dassa has given me to know. She died in the varium."

Anton looked down the long polished corridor, full of people with their errands, with their lives. Inside his chest hotness welled up, tight, and virulent.

Then he had a thought, that perhaps the king was mistaken. "It's a lie."

Vidori's words emerged slowly. "I sent Shim, who has seen her. Maypong's body."

Maypong's body. He could say those words so easily, but

they were terrible words. Anton remembered Maypong on the dock. She was alive then, and Anton had a gun aimed at Oleel's forehead. "I should have killed her," he murmured.

"Do not say so, Anton. Not out loud."

Anton spun around to look at him. "Don't say so? Don't say that I had it in my power to save Maypong? Don't say that you also, Vidori-rah, had the power?" He held the king's amber gaze, saying, "Did you not?"

"No."

"You said Oleel would not keep her. You didn't honor Maypong enough to save her." The viven stirred, murmuring among themselves. He looked up, and saw Shim standing by the screen, tears falling down her cheeks.

"Anton," Vidori said. "Maypong took her own life in the varium."

Anton tried to make sense of what he was hearing, but it wasn't registering. Oleel killed her; surely it was Oleel. But then the king repeated the terrible news: "Maypong killed herself."

Another lie. Wasn't it?

Seeing the doubt on Anton's face, Vidori said, "Oleel would never allow blood in a varium. It is impossible for her. And she would never have killed her—in that way."

"What way?" Now Anton needed everything to be spoken. By the king. He needed to say it all. And he did. She was allowed her morning swim. She had a knife. She cut her stomach open.

When he recovered himself, Anton looked at Vidori with loathing. "You ordered her to kill herself. Part of the great plan, the royal timing?" *To force issues, to find a reason to move on the uldia?* he thought, but didn't say, because of the viven standing there.

"No," Vidori said. He hadn't moved from the place where he stood. He commanded the corridor from there. Indeed, he commanded the braided world from wherever he stood; he could order *thousands* to kill themselves, at any time. Maypong was expendable.

But, "No," the king said again, gazing steadily at him. There was pain in his eyes, but not shame.

"Why, then?" Anton said, waiting for the spin, the politics of denial.

"Maypong had her own reasons; but they were not my reasons." Vidori broke eye contact, summoning Shim.

"What reasons?" Anton kept asking questions he didn't want the answers to.

Vidori looked down the hall, anxious to be gone.

"What reasons?"

The king spoke softly. "I believe it was for you, Anton. Of her own volition. To deprive Oleel of her hostage." He went on, "Because of the bonds between you."

The bonds. Because of the bonds. Now it was Anton's turn to look away. Each revelation was a cut, slicing deeper. "What else?" Anton asked hoarsely. *Tell me everything. Don't parcel it out.*

"Nothing else," the king said, his voice a whisper.

As Shim came forward, Vidori said, "Shim will tell you of the funeral barge and what will happen next." Then he said, "I hope you will forgive me, Anton. I do hope so."

Anton walked away from him and his chancellor, back to the room where Bailey and Zhen stood at the open screen. By their faces, they had heard.

Bailey shook her head. "So young. Oh, Anton . . ."

He looked at her, and the grief welled up, almost spilling out. Bailey was a hard old woman, but she was a friend, too. "We need to go home, Bailey," he said. He turned from her as Zhen wandered back into the hut and began pulling the slips of paper off the wall, as though the task couldn't wait. He looked back at Bailey Shaw, saying, "Don't we?"

"Yes," she said. "Maybe so." She was watching as the king gathered his retinue of viven and walked away.

As Shim came up behind him, he turned to her. It might have been Maypong standing there in fine brocade and pulled-back hair. It might have been, but it wasn't. He couldn't bear to look at her. "Leave me alone for a moment, Shim-rah. I will walk."

"Anton," she whispered, "I will wait here for you until you have a peaceful heart again."

Then you'll wait a long time, Shim-rah. He parted an outside screen and stepped out onto the walkway, looking for a place to be alone.

TWENTY

Coda Seven. Messaging Satellites.
Our satellites orbiting this planet send radio signals to Earth
to alert the human species of preserved data stored here. The
satellites send redundant messages in case of radio failure.
Messages are also sent to the other five worlds threatened by
the entropic cloud, with the intention to disclose the presence
of the respective salvaged information. In our interval of exis-
tence we have not yet had complete success in reanimating the
biotic inhabitants of the depleted worlds, except on this
planet. All information is here for safekeeping.

Nick's blood reddened the twine. He had almost chewed
through the bonds, but he'd lost one tooth doing it. His
gums were too soft. To free itself from a trap, an animal
would gnaw through its own bones, wouldn't it?

The voice from the corner came to him. "I'd help you,
son, but I'm dead." Sometimes Captain Darrow didn't have
a positive attitude. That wasn't how Nick remembered him
on board ship.

Nick yanked his hands apart, breaking the last strands of

the cord. He had to hurry. Now that Anton had the genetic information, they'd be leaving, bringing home the deadly code that, once brought into living form, would mangle the human race. Because, contrary to what they were saying, it wasn't human genetic code. It was just Dassa, Dassa, Dassa. A trick to raise up more like themselves, absorbing the human race, altering it past recognition. Nick knew that his thinking was a little garbled. But he had the gist of it.

He slipped into an unoccupied boat. Captain Darrow knelt in front, gun drawn. They might need that gun when they confronted Oleel. He could imagine her gloating about how she had duped them. But once she admitted her schemes, Nick would be vindicated. Captain Darrow would witness her confession, since he couldn't count on Anton anymore. Nick paddled, trying to concentrate, trying not to think how much he loved Anton, and how he'd have given his life many times over to save the mission, to be of service.

And now he was dying on this hateful world, with its twisted morality and corrupt alterations. No one saw it, not even Bailey, who, more than any of them, seemed to love the happy natives.

He went in the back way, under the mangrove tree, into the tunnel, bright with green fire as the day stoked up.

"Secret doors, eh?" Captain Darrow said, impressed that Nick knew the way into the forbidden compound.

"Yes, sir. No one guesses what comes in and out of here. You'll see."

Because of the narrow confines of the canal, paddling soon became impossible, but Nick hauled the skiff along by grabbing aerial roots. Approaching the stone pavilion, he hesitated. Too crowded, with uldia leading groups into the forest, to their appointed variums.

"These where the monsters incubate, then?" Darrow asked.

"Quiet," Nick had to say. Uldia were close by, sniffing.

Nick continued pulling the craft along, passing Oleel's

lair, probing deeper into her realm, until they came to a region of empty variums.

"Let's tie up here, Captain. We'll have to go on foot now."

Darrow looked at him from the bank, frowning. "Where's your side arm, son?"

"Anton won't let us go armed."

The frown grew deeper. *"Anton,"* he said. "Not a real captain. That should have been you, Nick."

He was beyond caring who was captain. That contest didn't matter anymore. Nick secured the boat and scrambled up the bank. Through the bushes he could see the stone fortress in the distance. He thought he caught sight of Oleel standing in a high, open window. They'd have to be careful.

"This way. Stay off the paths, sir."

Nick led the way through the thicket, skirting the edges of several variums, empty, perhaps gestating, he thought. His foot slipped on the mud and splashed into the water. Freezing, Nick listened for the uldia.

Captain Darrow waded out into the varium. "Ever wonder what it would be like, to swim? You know, the sex? Don't try to pretend you haven't wondered."

"Don't go splashing, sir."

"We could strip off our clothes and give it a try, Lieutenant. Just one swim. Couldn't hurt. How long's it been?"

Captain Darrow was kicking up muck from the bottom of the pond. Nick looked at the pond, and thought about the enfolding waters, and how it might not hurt, just for a moment. The jungle was full and warm like a woman's arms, like a woman's musky self, the whole world was heavy with sex and languorous with time and permission to do anything, anything at all . . .

"Get out of the water."

Someone was talking to him.

"Shh," Nick said. Captain Darrow was disappointing him; he didn't seem to realize how exposed they were.

"Get out of the water, Venning."

Oleel stood on the bank.

Nick looked down and saw that he'd stumbled into the varium up to his ankles.

As soon as Nick set foot on the bank, a dozen hands gripped him and dragged him away from the varium and onto a path.

Oleel didn't look well. She shuddered, her glance flitting again and again to the varium. "Ruin," she said. "Oh, ruin."

The uldia were still holding him as Oleel looked at him with her usual expression. Loathing.

"Yeah, ruin," he said. "It's what you planned, right? Ruin of Nick Venning and all his people. Hop from world to world, spreading yourselves, right? Go ahead, you can talk freely now, in front of the captain."

Oleel looked at one of the uldia, the closest one, then back at Nick. "Captain Anton is here also?"

"No. Captain Darrow is here. Anton Prados was never really captain. We'll be taking orders from Captain Darrow." He looked around, not seeing him.

"Captain Darrow. This is the name of the dead captain, yes?"

"No, not dead. Not anymore."

Oleel stood for a very long time. Her attendants also stood, unmoving. Finally, she said, "Take him away and strangle him."

She turned to go, murmuring to her attendants, "Send word to the king we had no choice. Remind him it was his duty to prevent sacrilege."

It wasn't going to end like this, before he'd exposed her, before she confessed. Before his death meant something. "Wait." Nick staggered forward, dragging his uldia guards with him. "We know all about you, about your plans. We figured out the messages, and we figured out it's you."

She turned to face him. "You found your messages?"

"*Your* messages, *yours*. You think we believe that it's human stuff inside those plants? Think we couldn't figure out your schemes?" That damn quiet face—so good at hiding her thoughts. She was exposed now, but she wouldn't give him the satisfaction of showing any fear. He went on, needling her, "Oh, little ponds all over the place, all over the Earth, all over the galaxy. Yeah, we figured it out just in time, before we brought the langva home." He added, "*Thankfully*," in a parody of their expression.

"Oh yes? The plants have messages? The langva plants?"

Nick almost laughed out loud. "Yes, the langva plants. They aren't real plants, they're time bombs, and we know everything. How dumb did you think we are?" Any moment now she would admit to it. Captain Darrow was there, in the bushes, hiding, waiting to hear. If she would just say it.

But she and her women looked like they could wait forever. They *had* waited forever, for the humans to come.

He rushed on: "The part about the other worlds, calling everybody to come here, that's good, Oleel. But did you think we wouldn't be suspicious about that? It's how you seed the universe, isn't it?" He charged forward. "Isn't it?"

The uldia yanked him back, forcing him to his knees. He fell like a sack of meat, no life left.

Her deep voice fell over him. "Other worlds?"

Still pretending, the old hag. He began talking, proving what he knew, laying it all out so that she couldn't doubt him. Once he started talking, he couldn't stop. It was his court of law, with him the prosecution and Darrow the judge. The sweet day of reckoning.

When he finished, he saw that she was moved. Finally. Her face struggled to conceal it, but she was afraid.

"First the humans come among us," she murmured. "Then—other beings. How many creatures can the Olagong bear, how many mouths can the river lands feed?" She turned to her attendants. "And perhaps they are among us already, in the fields, ready to spring from their hiding places among the crops."

If the woman would just stop pretending. He didn't like her immovable face, her cold eyes. He was starting to shake.

Nick thrashed at the uldia, trying to rise. But it was no use. *No use*—that was the refrain he'd been running from this whole mission. He was of no use.

His throat was so dry it was almost glued shut. "Just for once, tell the truth, goddamn you."

Oleel pointed at him. "Do not talk so much." She looked at the varium, its flat waters catching a wrinkled image of the sun. Then she crouched down, level with him. She gazed at him, murmuring, "You are mistaken, Venning. I knew nothing of this. Until now."

Then she rose, smoothing her robe. Turning to her attendants, she said, "Strangle him. Throw his body into the Sodesh." As the uldia hauled him to his feet, she said, "You would have been sent back to the palace, because you are not worth the trouble of killing, except that you have ruined a varium."

He sneered. "I didn't swim, don't worry. Think I'd give you my seed?"

A small shudder overcame her. "But your body oils have polluted the birth pool." She pointed to his feet. "Wet."

Nick looked down at his feet, and saw his fatigues, soaked up to the ankles.

As Oleel disappeared down the path, the uldia pulled him in the opposite direction. He kept looking back for Captain Darrow, but the old man wasn't there. Fighting off a sickening fear, Nick considered the possibility that Captain Darrow was dead again.

At dusk, Anton stood with Bailey and Zhen on the little walkway outside their quarters where they could view the flotilla. A short while ago, Shim had come to beg him to join the king in the river room to observe the funeral barge. He had asked to be excused. Whether he blamed the king or not, he couldn't sort out right now—nor whether he blamed himself. But he wanted to be alone when he said good-bye.

The barge was just now coming into view around the bend in the Puldar. If Vidori had hoped for a great show on the river, Anton mused, he must be disappointed. Maypong was not mourned by thousands, but by hundreds. The skiffs of Maypong's kin followed the barge: brothers, aunts, uncles, along with grandparents and friends. Maypong's mother was deceased, but Shim had said Maypong's father would be among those paying their respects. But not Gilar, of course.

Bailey took his arm as they stood waiting. Nick had fled, leaving bloody ropes behind. Vidori had promised that his guard would seize him if they sighted him. Anton had almost said, *Look in the stone pavilion* . . . but of course, the king's guard weren't welcome there.

On the funeral raft, Maypong's bier was draped with a length of gold brocade. It fluttered in the occasional breeze like a butterfly with wet wings, unable to rise.

Anton still wasn't sure if Vidori would allow the barge to pause, would allow him to mount the platform and pay his last respects. Shim had said no, it couldn't be done, that Maypong belonged to the river and the river never stops.

But then, the barge did stop. It was some hundred meters away, out in the center of the Puldar.

Bailey said, "I'll come with you, my dear."

Anton shook his head. "No, if you don't mind, Bailey." She accepted this, holding the skiff steady for him as he moved down into it.

He paddled into the river, into a suspended day. The Dassa stood on every level of the palace, on every walkway, bridge, veranda, and arcade, and not one of them moved.

Approaching the barge, he was assisted from the skiff by Maypong's kin. He thought he saw Maypong's likeness in the Dassa who handed him up. But there was no one like her.

They wouldn't remove the drape. He wanted to see her face, but that was not to be. He knelt by her bier, one hand on the cloth on the side of the woven crib that held her. *For love, then, Maypong? To distinguish me from other lovers? Or for my people and my mission, because of me?* He pressed his forehead against the bier. No answers. *I love you, Maypong. All that you were. All . . .*

At the king's stairs, Bailey saw that the judipon were distributing Maypong's goods. She'd come down to pay her respects to the king, but the sight of Maypong's things being handed out to greedy hands in skiffs was more than she could bear. With Zhen already back at work, and Anton gone walking in the gardens, Bailey went looking for a skiff. The river would restore her spirits.

Finding a skiff, she paddled into the river. The sun was making a production of the day's end, staining the western sky a haunting rosy-yellow color. She found herself paddling in the direction she'd taken so many times: Samwan's compound. Since she was going to stay on this alien world, it was good to have friends. New friends. As for old friends—well, saying good-bye to them would be hard indeed.

With the night coming on, lamps outlined Samwan's pier. This time, she had to scramble from the skiff by herself, not easy given her long tunic. Voices came to her from the center of the compound, where the household was gathered for a meal. But the river itself was very quiet, with just a few boats upon it.

In the compound, children scampered, their hoda nursemaids playing with them amid the laughter of the household women. This was a world, she thought, of simple joy and great pathos. Not unlike Earth. She hoped Samwan would let her join their meal.

Anton was hurrying down the corridor, garnering looks from viven who thought it improper to rush.

He hoped the king would still be in the river room. That

would make it easier to intercept him, as he should have done hours ago. He should have told Vidori everything the moment he discovered Nick's escape, but there was Zhen reciting the ancient codas, and then Maypong . . . And now Nick had slipped away, to join Oleel. Where else could he go? That meant Oleel would hear about the langva.

Anton didn't know which part of the Quadi story Oleel would exploit. But if the woman despised humans, what would she make of yet stranger beings? Beings who were perhaps even now on their way . . .

He hurried into the river room, full of Dassa and hoda and uldia. On the other side of the great hall Vidori was just leaving, surrounded by nobles and chancellors.

Several viven approached Anton. One of them was Nidhe, saying that they shared a sorrow for Maypong, that it was very sorrowful news . . .

Yes, yes, thank you, Anton had replied, wondering what they thought of him and Maypong, or what they knew. But he merely excused himself, pushing past them. Meanwhile Vidori disappeared down the hall toward his quarters.

Seeing Shim, Anton called out, and then she was turning to him in consternation, looking like she couldn't handle more problems. But there *was* a problem, one the king had to hear.

"Shim-rah, thank you. I must see the king right away."

Searching Anton's face, she said, "What has happened?"

"It's Lieutenant Venning. He has damning information, and is delivering it to the Second Dassa. Hurry, Shim-rah." He took her by the elbow, pressing through the crowd. Up ahead, Romang had seen them coming, and alerted Vidori, who turned, frowning. As they marched forward, Shim said, "It is very bad respect to interrupt the king now, Anton. He cannot have an audience at such a time."

"It will be very bad respect for him to be deprived of information that Oleel has."

Vidori watched as Anton pushed forward.

"You have now changed your mind again, Anton," he said. "Whether you will be with us or not with us."

"Rahi, I bear news." He looked at the gathered nobles, at the war chief, at Shim and the king's brothers and all the hangers-on that Anton had come to recognize over the weeks. But he needed privacy with the king.

The king lowered his voice as much as possible. "News that cannot wait on a day when my chancellor has died?"

"No, Vidori-rah, it can't wait." It shouldn't have waited this long. "It's Venning," Anton said.

"We know that he has escaped confinement."

"Yes, rahi." He kept the king's gaze. "But it's worse than that."

Vidori looked at Shim, exchanging God knew what message with his eyes.

Shim collapsed. She sprawled on the floor, creating a commotion.

Romang hurried to her side, kneeling, as viven gathered around, sounding alarmed. Someone called for an uldia. One hurried forward, but Vidori said, "No, it is nothing but grief. Bring her to my chamber." As guards came forward to carry her, Romang ushered the viven back to the hall, and Anton joined the king in a rush toward the royal apartments.

Shim was managing a very convincing moan, and holding her stomach.

"I would not want to lose two chancellors in one day," Vidori said.

As the group approached the king's suite, Anton gathered the threads of his story—the story that Oleel had no doubt heard already from Nick, in the final and telling blow from his ex-friend, the former officer of the *Restoration*. Of course, Nick might have simply fled for his life, with no intention of telling all he knew. But Anton was assuming the worst. When lately had Nick Venning failed to deliver the worst?

As the screens slid shut, the only people in the king's

suite were Vidori, Anton, and Shim, who sat up now and smoothed her tunic.

The king turned a dark gaze on Anton. "Now it is your turn to give terrible news, I fear." At that moment he looked like a man well used to receiving it.

Anton began giving it.

Near a hut, Bailey noticed one of those dreadful miniature scenes. She tried to ignore it, but she was always drawn to the little wallishen. And sometimes, if they dealt with her people, she was inspired to change the figures inside them, just to answer back.

And yes, this particular scene was about her people, and not very nice. She looked for the figure with the big hat. There it was, the head no longer attached.

Suddenly Bailey noticed a very young hoda standing nearby.

Bailey said, "What do the wallishen accomplish? Why do the Dassa produce these?" It had never occurred to her to ask what they were *for*. She'd always assumed they were art.

The hoda signed, >The superstitious create them to influence the future.<

Ah. Well, that settled the matter of *art*, then.

Bailey crouched down to pick up the head with the hat. She thought she'd take the head and the body and just remove them from the little drama.

"Oh, but Bailey, do not touch the wallishen."

She turned. Samwan stood there with three of her sisters. One of them motioned for the hoda to leave, and the slave retreated.

Bailey rose. "Samwan-rah, thank you. But I must say, this scene offends me."

Samwan came closer. "But why, Bailey?"

She held the doll's head in front of Samwan. "Decapitated. Not respectful."

"But Bailey, it is not *meant* to be respectful."

A hot pause ensued. Bailey thought she might just have been terribly insulted by Samwan. "Samwan-rah, do you condone a wish to see me harmed?"

Samwan's face grew still, and her usual good nature drained along with the last of the daylight. "Did you care that Samwan was harmed?"

"I beg your pardon?"

"Oh yes, in the matter of singing in the forest."

Bailey thought back to that day. How had Samwan been harmed?

One of Samwan's sisters ventured, "The king issued a reprimand, and the judipon cut our ration. It was hard on us. Did you help us on that day?"

"What could I do?" Bailey was looking among the women for some sign of relenting, but they only grew more stony.

Samwan said, "You, who are the particular friend of the king, can ask such a question? Did you ever offer to intercede? Or ask if I fared well? No, Bailey, you did not. We wondered, then, if we were truly friends. And then the king declined to send us an engineer for my new river engine, and now we are the poorer for it. All because the king deemed that I am not a proper custodian of my lands." She interrupted as Bailey started to speak. "And then when you sang, the hoda began to see themselves as no longer vulgar. And many hoda have fled to the Vol, and in the fighting on the borders, two of my children have died."

She looked at the doll's head in Bailey's hand as though she had just separated it from its shoulders and was admiring her work.

"I see," Bailey managed to say. There was no point in discussing this; they had made up their minds. She slipped the doll parts into a pocket. "It is well to know who your friends are. But I see that I have been mistaken."

Samwan said, "We have had pleasure in seeing you, though, Bailey. All with weak pri are indulged in my compound, whether children or the very old."

"Weak pri?"

"Oh yes, Bailey. The very old are indulged in the Olagong. Like children. They can do no harm." Pointedly, she added: "Nor are they much effective."

Bailey had to smile at the depth of the insult. This Samwan was skilled.

It was time for a good exit. "That is too bad, Samwan," she said. "Where I come from, the aged have honor." Bailey turned and stalked off toward the pier.

As she left, Samwan's voice trailed behind her, "Oh but now, thankfully, you are in the Olagong."

Bailey felt like a fool. *No fool like an old fool.* Was that why she had been popular from the outset, because she was considered weak and no threat?

Bailey stopped on the dock, looking down at the Puldar. In the distance, a column of smoke rose over the jungle. Something was on fire. These people had to be wary of fire, with everything made of reed and wood.

As Bailey stepped into the skiff, she saw another curdle of smoke from the direction of the Nool River.

Samwan and her sisters rushed onto the pier, staring as well. Samwan murmured, "Best go home, and quickly."

In the last of the daylight, Bailey saw that the Puldar was completely deserted. She set out paddling as fast as she could, with a line of smoke drifting toward her, casting a shadow on the river.

TWENTY-ONE

Coda Eight. Temporal Setting.
All things exist in a natural and impermanent span of time.
All species one day perish. All settings degrade. All things alter
over time, complexifying, simplifying, and extinguishing. This
is the universal life cycle. A place, life-form, setting, or culture
has a natural tenure, or interval of existence. The galaxy also
has a life-bearing tenure. As the universe ages, radioisotopes
necessary for plate tectonics and temperature control of higher
life-bearing planets are more uncommon. New worlds likely to
develop complex life no longer form in the galaxy. The habit-
ability of the galaxy declines. The high golden age has crested
in our time. This makes all sentient organisms rare and wor-
thy of recovery.

It was a small thing at first. Afterward, Anton remembered the moment the braided lands began to unravel.

He had been telling Vidori and Shim as much of the codas as he could remember. There were eleven of them,
packed tight with information that changed everything for
Anton's mission—and just as much for the Dassa. Vidori lis-

tened carefully, gravely, as Anton struggled with the Dassa vocabulary. There were no Dassa words for concepts like *radioisotopes* and *terraforming*. Some concepts were impossible to convey in a short time: *dark matter* and *plate tectonics* and *gas giant*. Anton glossed over them, giving a quick translation. He could only guess what this astonishing information sounded like to the king and his chancellor.

Yet the Dassa knew—had always known—that the Quadi created them. In some ways, they lived in a more completely imagined universe than humanity did. The fact of the Quadi was immemorial cultural knowledge, even if only general and hazy. In the Dassa worldview, the universe held another sentient species more advanced than themselves. Humanity had received that same information with far less grace.

Now and then during Anton's narration, Shim glanced at the king, perhaps to assess his position, whether the revelations of the codas boded good or ill. But Vidori's face betrayed only intense concentration.

At one point the king had said, "So then, Anton, we are cousins indeed."

"Yes, rahi." It didn't trouble Anton as it had some of his crew. He suspected it had never troubled Vidori.

Then the king's posture changed. He turned in his chair, listening. Or smelling. It was at that moment that war came to the Olagong. But its roots were entwined with the circumstances of power—the fact that Oleel was leader of the uldia when an infirm old man commanded the judipon, and when an ambitious daughter hid under the love of a visionary king.

Shim rose, crossing the room and parting one of the hallway screens. Anton heard her murmuring to someone in the corridor.

But she had gone in the wrong direction. Vidori went to the great porch overlooking the Puldar, drawing open the screens. Anton followed him onto the veranda.

At first all he saw was the black river, defined by lighted huts along the banks.

"Vidori-rah," Anton said, "is something amiss?"

The king didn't answer at first, merely pointed off to the south. There, through the heavy screen of the forest, a flicker of light emerged, high and bright.

"Fire," Vidori finally said.

A curve of smoke drifted eastward on the light wind. The king murmured, "I thought she would come with boats and arms. She is bolder than I knew. Fire . . ."

"What is she burning, rahi?" No need to ask who *she* was.

"The fields," Vidori said. A noise behind them drew their attention. Standing by an open screen was Romang, and next to him, Shim. "Vidori-rah," Romang said, his voice deep and gravelly.

The king only said, "How many?"

"Thousands." Romang strode onto the deck while Shim closed the hall screens. He said, "Many of them are judipon."

Vidori turned back to the river, as though looking for judipon warriors in the blackness of waters and forest. "So people give belief to the transmissions."

Anton was losing track of the conversation, but he remained silent, surprised that he was allowed to remain, now that the war chief had come.

From the corridor came the sounds of people running and voices raised. The palace was awake.

Romang said, "They have been saying strangers will come in air ships and take the Olagong. People stranger than the humans. Worse," he said, as though that was hard to imagine.

Vidori took pity on Anton. Turning to him, he said, "The judipon are much accustomed to using radio to transmit their schedules along the braids. Now Nirimol uses it to transmit his lies."

Nirimol. Not Homish. Anton jumped to the conclusion that Homish had died—naturally or with a little help.

The king paused, looking back at the darkened river. "We did wonder, when the transmissions began a few hours ago, how they could claim there was danger in the stars."

"Vidori-rah," Anton said. "Such beings are not likely to come, nor to bear arms against you if they did."

The king stopped him with a gesture. "Oh yes, so I believe, too." He turned to Romang. "I have learned that the Quadi have honored us by leaving in our safekeeping the wisdom of the stars. Just as humans have found that our world contains remedies for their ills, left by the Quadi, so now it is discovered to be the case for several more such worlds without pri. They may seek our favors to help them, and if it is in accordance with the braid, we shall do so."

Romang nodded. If his king said so, it was so.

The king's face fell stern. "But it is a weapon in Oleel's hands. It is more of a weapon than I had hoped for her to have." He glanced back at Romang. "You are ready?"

"Yes, rahi." He cast a troubled glance at Anton. "Another matter, though." Clearly, he was reluctant to proceed in Anton's presence.

"He stays," Vidori said. He turned to Anton. "What I know, you will know, just as you have withheld nothing from me regarding the Quadi messages, thankfully." Implicit was the demand that Anton *not* withhold anything.

Vidori continued, "As you share our plans and goals, my hope is, Anton, that you will stand by me in what is coming."

Stand by him. But how?

"As you revealed the hidden messages tonight," Vidori said, "I was already thinking how to counter what Oleel would do. We can make transmissions of our own, Anton. We can, if you agree, put forward that strangers from outside worlds are no threat." He pointed up, toward the ceiling, toward the roof, and its collection of telescopes. "Because of your ship's standing in protection." Vidori lowered his voice. "That, however, would mean that you would not return home, but stay instead in the Olagong."

The size of this request stopped Anton cold. But he knew his answer. He hesitated to say it too quickly, lest it sound ill-considered. They would go home; of course they would. Earth was dying. They held remedies in their hands. They must go home.

There was almost a smile on Vidori's face. It hovered around his lips, but it held no humor. Only recognition that he had asked a momentous favor. Then he said, "I will free the hoda."

Anton was startled. The events of the night and the previous day were spinning around him. He had to juggle the implications of so many things, and now the king had just tossed another ball in the air. A flaming one. He wondered if Vidori was using the hoda's plight as a bargaining chip.

"Whether you stay or not," the king said, as though knowing what Anton was thinking, "my plan has always been that the hoda must be free. The prosperity of the Olagong comes from all our work, not just those who hold themselves proper Dassa. All are proper Dassa, just different, in ways that the world has made manifest. Just as the universe is differently manifested."

He turned to Romang. "I have said that the hoda must be free, Romang-rah. There will be no more clipping, nor punishments for hoda bearing children." That high-minded pronouncement was followed by a cynical one. "If they are spared clipping by us, they will not turn to the Vol. Is that not so?"

Romang nodded stiffly. "As you say, rahi." Here was a man whose vision went as far as king, troops, and strategy for war, but *As you say* would be his answer to all that Vidori ordered, and in that way his vision would be as broad as his king's.

The breeze brought the first hints of smoke to Anton's nostrils. Down the river, toward the confluence with the Sodesh, more fires blazed. Oleel was burning the copses of langva, to destroy the messages, not understanding that so much more was about to change than having unwelcome visitors. Vidori had planned many changes. His plans were intricate and patient, and all dependent on timing. And whether he was a liberator of hoda because of conviction or convenience, Anton would have to judge after considerably more sleep than he'd had in the last day and a half. For now, there was still the need to answer the king's request.

"Vidori-rah," Anton said, "one day, not so long ago, we stood on this deck and you pointed to the Dassa in their boats. You said that your rule depended not on control, but on devotion." He faced the man squarely. "It's because of devotion that my crew and I came here. And it's because of devotion that we have to leave."

Vidori straightened. "And the fields will burn, and the wisdom of the Quadi will be lost."

"No, rahi, some will remain . . ."

"But you said, did you not, that each foreign world is in a different langva variety?" Seeing Anton nod, he continued, "You must understand, we plant only one variety of langva in the Olagong. The others"—he gestured toward the forest—"are rare. They can be lost, Anton." When Anton remained silent, he murmured, "But you and I, we are not *devoted* to such worlds."

Anton felt the sting of the reprimand. This world was, as the Quadi said, a nexus world. Its treasures were unimaginably vast. How could one not be . . . *devoted*?

Romang interrupted, but hesitantly. "Rahi, we must speak."

Vidori nodded to him. He was still struggling to accept Anton's decision. He didn't look at Anton now, but out toward a new and heavy fog on the river. "Speak then, Romang-rah."

But Romang hesitated, exchanging glances with Shim.

Reluctantly, Shim came forward. "Rahi, the Princess Joon has fled the palace. She took her personal guard and chancellors."

Vidori's face went blank. After a beat he said, "There were no boats on the Puldar."

Shim's face contorted a bit. "No, no boats, rahi. They fled on foot, into the forest."

"Gone," Vidori whispered. He glanced over at Romang for confirmation.

The man stood silent, giving it.

Vidori said, "Oleel infiltrated her chancellors. My daughter went under compulsion."

Anton knew that the king was denying what he was hearing, knew how the mind struggles to find alternate explanations for truths too painful to bear. As he himself had with the news of Maypong: *Oleel's lying. She's alive . . .*

Romang had the grace to keep Vidori's gaze. "No, rahi, *Joon* led *them*. So my spies have said."

There was a very long silence, during which no one dared to speak. Finally Vidori said, "You have good spies, Romang-rah." His eyes darkened. "Even in my daughter's compound."

Romang raised his chin, justified by the event of Joon's defection. "Yes, rahi."

Then Vidori turned his back on all of them, walking to the rim of the deck, his feet on the very edge, his body composed, his tunic filling with wind and smoke. "Pursue them," he said.

And: "Shim, I will dress for battle."

She turned to arrange it, grateful for something to do, some service she could perform that was familiar, and proper.

Before Anton took his leave, he asked for, and received, a contingent of guards to accompany him to the shuttle. He would see Vidori once more before he left. Yes, when all was ready, the king allowed, he would say good-bye. There were no recriminations. But Vidori still faced outward, looking at the river.

Anton felt as though he were retreating from the field in some shameful manner. He would gather together his people and their botanical cargo and leave. Now that there was civil war, he owed it to his mission to leave sooner rather than later. Because of devotion. Behind him, he left a world in chaos.

And perhaps made so much worse by his having come to the Olagong in the first place.

On the ridge, by the light of a nearly full moon, Gilar could see the River Sodesh in the distance. Boats went up and down it, filled with fire.

Mim blacked out the biolume and stared with Gilar. *The river burns,* the older woman sang.

For hours, as they'd hidden in the forest, the acrid presence of smoke swelled and faded, according to the wind's direction. Here at the ridge, they finally saw where the fires leapt, in the fields along the Sodesh and in torches from the boats.

Something's happened, Mim ventured, stating the obvious.

Oh yes, much had happened. Maypong was dead in the varium, by her own hand. And in that moment, Gilar turned from the stone palace in horror that such things could be. Before leaving, in a parting act of defiance, she and Mim had slain the two uldia, the two that were twisting the knotted rope around the neck of Captain Anton's crew member, Nick. Gilar and Mim had stolen upon the uldia guards and killed them, freeing the human. They fled in a skiff, but realizing the river would be the first place Oleel would search, they abandoned the boat, making their way into the wild hills on the southern bank of the Sodesh.

Gilar coughed, fighting off the bitter smoke. *It is the Vol, perhaps.*

Mim looked hopefully at Gilar, expecting her to take advantage of this event. As though Gilar were a strategist. But she wasn't. Why did the sisters expect her to know something that generations of hoda didn't know? She had no plan. But she couldn't admit that to Mim, not with that expression on the old hoda's face.

They continued to watch the fiery scene on the river. It was astonishing to see torches in boats, as though the great river were inhabited by fire beings, their long hair trailing orange in the night wind. Gilar's eyes blurred, and the river scene vanished, replaced by the red water of the varium. . . .

Mim placed her hand on Gilar's forearm in warning. Something moved below them, in the ravine. Shapes wound through the forest. Gilar and Mim lowered themselves to the ground. But no one rushed up the hillside or raised an alarm. This group was headed in the opposite direction from Gilar and Mim. Toward the Amalang.

After the band passed, Gilar signaled for Mim to follow her, and they crept along the ridge, keeping the group in sight. By their dress and aspect, these weren't Vol, nor the king's soldiers, but highborn Dassa.

Now, directly below them, the group had stopped to reconnoiter, their voices carrying up the hill.

>I'm going down,< Gilar signed. >Wait here.<

Mim acquiesced, and Gilar crept into the ravine toward the voices.

The Princess Joon stood in the clearing, her attendants bearing biolumes that iced the scene with greenish light. Despite the obvious stealth of her small force—heavily armed, Gilar noted—Joon herself wore the brightest blue. Her short jacket was shot through with silver threads, and at her neck was an inset of dazzling white. She wore heavy boots and a slit skirt made for hiking. Around her were gathered her chancellors, including Gitam, and a contingent of hoda bearing gear. At least forty palace soldiers milled about, wearing the colors of the princess now.

". . . and we will come in from the south," Joon was saying.

Her captain motioned for his people to form up. "We will move within sight of the river, with luminaries. That should draw them."

Joon was looking past his shoulder, her face tense. "No, too obvious. Let Romang track you. It will be dawn soon, and easy to do. I will take Gitam on the southern path, with too few of us to notice."

"Yes, Lady."

"Hand off my standards to the slave."

The captain did so, giving one of the hodas two long poles, with blue and silver pendants furled.

Gitam was shouldering a pack, an odd sight for a noblewoman. But Joon would be traveling with a small retinue now.

As the group divided in two, Joon bid farewell to the larger contingent of her force. In the smoke-hazed air, the biolumes created a nimbus of light. She spoke to her captain. "Kill Romang if he pursues you. In the new braid, I would not be troubled by his face. If you wish to please me."

"I will please you, Lady."

"Oh yes," she said, "you have done so, many times. But now it is war, and you must see me with new eyes. As your queen." Joon went on, "When we meet on the Amalang, Nirimol will be present, standing at my uldia's side. But neither one of these is your commander, neither one is the First Dassa. Remember that, Captain."

The captain murmured, "I need no reminder to be loyal, rahi."

Joon held his gaze. "This Nirimol has ruined Homish with medicinals. Who could trust him, if he is a poisoner? So then, Captain, he will not lead our combined forces. If you please me, you will."

The hoda was unfurling the blue standard.

Joon swung around to stare at her. "Hmm. I wonder if I have employed a fool. You don't look like you have water for brains. But perhaps I am wrong. Do you think banners will keep us invisible?" She waited for an answer.

The hoda could not respond, her arms being full. Finally she managed to sign, >No, rahi. Forgive me.< She hastily rewrapped the banner, and stood trembling.

But Joon was in an evident hurry, and gestured her chancellor and the hoda to follow her as she strode from the clearing into the deeper forest. The larger group set out as well, in a different direction. Gilar watched as the bright silks of Joon's garment wove into the forest and the last of their passage became inaudible.

Gilar knew where they would eventually meet, unless Romang prevailed: Oleel's pavilion. Joon had abandoned Vidori. She had abandoned the braid, the world of the Three that was led by the king.

So then, the Vol had not attacked. Oleel had.

Gilar lay on her stomach in the rich humus of the forest floor, trying to absorb this event. Oleel had ever been Vidori's enemy. But to openly contest the king, that was a new thing in the Olagong, never seen since times of legend. The Princess Joon, it seemed, could not wait to be queen.

The junction of events brought dangerous waters. Dassa fighting Dassa. And in this convergence was Gilar's opportunity. She could sense great things on the move, could almost see her own form moving among the shadows, in the tumult. But what *was* her opportunity? To fight for hoda freedom? How could this be?

From the ridge, she heard Mim sing, Gilar, my sister?

Yes, coming, Gilar sang back. As she stood, a bird flapped in the bush, rising past her and causing her to stagger. Her heart pounded, and she stopped, listening for what might have caused the bird to flush from cover. But the stand of trees remained empty of all but her and the bird. Calming herself, she thought of the bird of legend, the ashi, and how when the rivers fell, their nests were easy prey. *May the rivers swell,* the saying went.

She stood very still, waiting. The forest was silent, smoke-filled. She listened, waiting for something: for the smoke, moving like a gray ghost, to take its voice, or for the nearby river to speak. Something was emerging, the thing that she had been looking for: her true vision.

What would it mean, she wondered, to be free among the Dassa? To keep their tongues? Perhaps to own land, to have occupations as hunters or chemists or soldiers? Simply allowed this freedom or that one. But all the while the hoda would remain beholden to their mistresses and the Three, and so would never rise high. And what could be given could be taken again. She didn't dare move, lest the thought fly away:

It was not enough to be free. To rise high, they must be separate as well as free. Because they were the fourth river. There had always been four rivers, despite what everyone said. There were the Puldar, the Amalang, and the Nool—the three, plus the greatest river, the Sodesh. How strange that the braids were always called the Three, when there were manifestly four. If there were four rivers, there were four powers—if the hoda dared to claim what was theirs.

So freedom wasn't the song. Power was.

She scrambled back up the hillside, her heart pounding anew. Yet something nagged.

As she topped the ridge, she stopped, gazing at Mim, a hoda these forty years. What would old Mim think of getting children the way it must now be done in the fourth realm? Because that was the price of hoda power: to grow children of their own bodies. There was no other way. *So be it*, she thought. They would find men willing to try a different sarif. This was no time to be squeamish.

Mim stared at her. What, Gilar?

Gilar looked east, in the direction the sun would rise, in the direction of what might be an empty stronghold right now, if Nirimol was away fighting. She and her sisters needed a gathering place, one that could be defended. One that had a radio.

We'll take the Nool, Gilar sang.

She would worry tomorrow about the growing of children.

*   *   *

Bailey watched the Dassa calligrapher write out the words. The king's secretary held the writing implement in his left hand, while with his right hand he regulated the flow of ink down the tube, tracing the flowing script of the Dassa onto the paper.

As Anton had requested, Bailey was reading out Zhen's notes relating to the eleven codas, so that when the ship left, the Dassa would possess a translation.

"That will do for now, Isda-rah." Bailey rose, folding Zhen's coda printouts into a small shoulder pack she'd borrowed from Shim.

The king's secretary looked surprised. He expected eleven codas, and they weren't finished yet.

Bailey smiled. "Come back in an hour," she said, implying they'd finish then. She wouldn't be here when he came back. The copying task was for appearances, because Anton had ordered it.

Reluctantly, the secretary left, leaving behind his ink and paper. But he needn't have worried. The Dassa would have the codas. They were staying on Neshar with Bailey.

Isda had just finished copying the coda on Messaging Satellites. This planet was the nexus point. What better place to end her days than here, at the center of the universe? Culturally speaking. Even without the grand vision of the Quadi, she would have stayed. But the codas lent an extra dimension to her decision, folding her into something vast and old—the custodial duty. Though she didn't know how she could foster higher life in the galaxy, she liked seeing herself as doing her best for the hoda, with whom her destiny seemed linked by song.

Reassured by these thoughts, Bailey stopped by the crew quarters to say good-bye to Zhen.

Botanical samples and disassembled equipment lay in scattered piles, ready for boxing up. Zhen was packing, cramming her few personal items into a stuff sack. The woman was in a frightful mood, grumbling to Bailey and to herself that it was not time to go, with so much left to do. To Zhen, the war was highly inconvenient.

Bailey put a stop to Zhen's rant, saying mildly, "I want you to know, Zhen, how steady and invaluable you've been on this mission. I see that I chose well."

Zhen frowned at this interruption. "Talk to Anton, then. Tell him to delay."

"Zhen, my dear, the Olagong is on fire. It's time to leave. Earth can send more ships. You can come back."

A rude stare answered this pronouncement. "It will take *years* to get back here. I'll be past *thirty*."

"Ah," Bailey said. "Over the hill."

Zhen saw her mistake, shrugged. Returning to her packing, she said, "Anton's out in the compound making one last search for Nick. In case he's drunk somewhere under a palm tree."

It was Bailey's excuse to leave. "Good-bye, Zhen, my dear." She turned back at the door screen. "My bet is that you've already made your scientific reputation. A formidable place in your field, the envy of your peers." Bailey sighed. "I hope you find celebrity more enjoyable than I did." She looked at the woman with a growing lump in her throat. Then she smiled brightly and hurried off.

She wouldn't miss Nick, but Zhen and Anton were different matters. Especially Anton. Oh yes, a son to her in all the ways that mattered. She would have been proud to have him as a son. He'd come into the captaincy and grown up all at once, and she did love him—as much for the ways he'd stumbled and gotten up again as for the ways he'd so wildly succeeded. She really wasn't looking forward to this next part.

Out in the palace corridors, she made her way among hurrying Dassa, nobles, chancellors, and soldiers, each intent on some purpose of the king's. As she exited onto a covered walkway overlooking the plaza, she saw the king's guard forming up, bristling with weapons and milling about in orderly chaos.

Bailey looked up to the king's veranda. It was empty. But above that, above the third story of the king's quarters, the great lightning rod still commanded the roof. Bailey wondered if any Dassa could ever look at it again without seeing a girl bound to it. Gilar had good instincts for drama. It was one reason Bailey thought they'd get on well, if Gilar would accept Bailey's planned offer of singing lessons.

Once in the courtyard, Bailey couldn't see over the soldiers' heads. Nevertheless, she threaded her way toward the other side of the plaza and its covered walkway. From there, it was a short walk to the palace gardens, where Anton might be found.

The crowd parted for new arrivals to the plaza. By the topknots on their heads, these were judipon. Bailey felt a momentary alarm, seeing the group that betrayed the king, but the soldiers let them pass, casting them sidelong scowls.

One of the judipon was old and stooped over, his skin waxy gray and his hair pulled up onto his head in a futile effort to create a bun. On each side of him two judipon supported his faltering steps. He tottered by, then stopped, despite his attendants' efforts to keep him moving.

"Leave off! Leave off, you excremental toadies!" He yanked himself free with surprising force and turned toward Bailey, staring hard at her.

He grinned, terribly, his teeth browned and sharp. "Thought I was dead, did you?"

Bailey shut her mouth. Yes, she had. By Anton's description, this could only be Homish.

The deposed leader of the Third Power continued to smile, his eyes alight with more life than his body had. "Rumors and lies, old woman, rumors and lies. Thankfully, I still swim every morning, even if someday I sink and drown in a varium." He took a step forward, looking as though he would pitch forward, but his assistants rushed to help him. He whispered: "You know what happens when an old man dies in a swim? They fill in the pool with dirt. Leave you like a potted plant!" He shook with a silent laugh.

Sobering, he looked Bailey up and down. "I thought you'd be taller."

Bailey shrugged. "Old people shrink, I guess."

He threw back his head, cawing with laughter. "Yes, yes, I used to be as tall as Nirimol, the great turd of the Nool!" In a darker voice, he continued, "You can tell him I've never felt better, now his poisons are gone."

Bailey said, "I don't plan to talk to the traitor."

Homish danced a little, unless it was palsy. "Good, good. You foreign hoda are catching on." He waved at her as he turned away, muttering, "Oh yes, we'll stay in the palace a while, until the river spits Nirimol out." He squinted at her. "How did young Anoon like the cloud country?"

Bailey smiled. "Very well indeed, Homish-rah." She wondered just how crazy Homish had been that day that he warned Anton against the judipon and urged him to go up-country.

"Eleven! I knew that was his numeration," the old judipon said. "The climbing number, for someone who will be raised high. Oh yes, I liked Anoon well enough. Too young to be a leader, though." His judipon closed around him as he turned away.

Bailey answered to his back, "No, Homish-rah, I don't think so. Not at all."

But Homish and his retinue had moved on. For a moment the plaza was less crowded, and a clear view opened up toward the far side, where a dark-haired man stood on the covered walkway.

He stood alone, but surrounded by an aura of power, by his stance, by his expression. *No, Homish,* Bailey thought as she walked toward Anton, *not too young at all.*

As she looked up at him from the plaza level, she said, "Did you find him?"

"No. He's run to Oleel." Anton's gaze swept over the courtyard, taking in Vidori's mobilization with an unreadable expression.

Bailey looked at him and guessed that he was saying

good-bye to the palace, to an era in his life. His uniform was faded, his hair falling forward over his forehead. He didn't look like Captain Darrow, but there were planes in his face that the weeks here had sculpted, and a new depth around his eyes.

Bailey knew that some of that depth came from sorrow. In time it would become lines, and finally wisdom. She envied him his journey.

"Anton," she said, and then stopped.

He looked down at her, glancing at her shoulder pack. "What's in the little backpack, Bailey?"

She wanted to climb the stairs, to stand next to him, to be eye to eye. But now that she had started, she had to finish saying what she'd come to say. "The Quadi notes. I thought they should stay here." And to make it quite clear, she said simply, "I'm not going back, Anton."

He broke off eye contact, and looked over her head again to the troops, to the covered porches surrounding the plaza.

"Don't do this, Bailey," he said softly.

She shrugged. "I'm an old woman. I don't like to travel." It's not what she'd meant to say. She'd meant to talk of Gilar, and her intention to help her. She'd meant to say that she'd give something of herself. But Anton knew that she was settling in to the Olagong. He could fill in the blanks. That's what Anton had done from first setting foot on this planet: fill in the blanks.

He met her eyes again. "You'd be in danger here. It's the worst possible time to be a human in the Olagong." He crouched down on the porch, coming closer to her level. Leaning against the porch post, he said, "And Bailey, I'd miss you on that journey."

She didn't trust her voice for a moment. Instead, she closed the gap between them, and reached her hand up to his.

"I'll miss you, too," finally came out. She snapped her eyelids up and down trying to stay firm.

He looked into her face, and he seemed so vulnerable. "Why?" he asked. So he had asked her, after all, to give the reason.

And out spilled, "Because I've been happy here."

A smile cut into his face then, the kind of smile that would leave lines, eventually. "Yes, I know." He looked past her, into the plaza. "I know what you mean."

A commotion down the walkway, and both Bailey and Anton looked up. Vidori was approaching. Come to say good-bye.

Bailey said, "The king's given me permission to stay, if you approve."

Anton stood up to meet the king. He murmured to her, smiling as he said, "Who ever stopped Bailey Shaw from doing exactly what she pleased?"

And then Vidori was standing there, and as Anton greeted him, Bailey stepped back among the milling Dassa and, rather than say good-bye and ruin an exit with smeared makeup, disappeared into the milling crowd.

TWENTY-TWO

Coda Nine. The High Work.
As we conceive it, in the tenure of our species, the high work is
to preserve and reanimate the creations of the civilized worlds.
Our reasons are recorded in Coda One. We were the first species
to attain civilization. Three others coexisted with us for a time,
but fell into senility before making contributions to the high
work. Because the galaxy grows old, you who come after will not
have time to naturally accumulate profoundly useful knowledge.
Thus stored here is all that we know and all that others know.
This is the nexus point for knowledge. If we are able, there will
be other repository worlds, but this is the first successful one. It
may be the only one, due to unavoidable failures. The cycle of
our existence comes to the end, but overlaps with the intervals of
existence of other sentient species who may carry forward the
custodial work. Though assimilation of the nexus world
knowledge may take many generations, there may be time to for-
ward the work. What else is the reason for all we have done?

The river was a moving battlefield. Amid the twisting
smoke of the fires, Anton could see the armed boats scat-

tered on the Puldar, filled with Dassa fighting under the silver standard of Oleel or the black of Vidori. Some, not bothering with standards, simply wore shreds of dyed cloth as headbands.

Anton's two war canoes flew the black banner, but the soldiers on board made no challenges to the silver, only powering the canoes onward with hard, steady strokes. Vidori had put his guards under Anton, and they knew their mission: Bring the humans safely to the islet of Huvai, the resting place of the shuttle. Bring both canoes, if possible, but bring one of them at least, the one with Anton or the one with Zhen. Each canoe had half the botanical cargo. All that was needed. With painful exceptions: Bailey. Nick. Maypong.

Anton sat in the second canoe, his gun resting on his knees, as he peered through the smoke, watchful for attacks from Oleel's supporters, whether uldia, judipon, or common Dassa. Ash particles, bits of the Olagong, were born aloft by each new breeze, creating a boiling smoke.

The king's officer, Moshani, deftly commanded the first canoe, where Zhen rode. Fires from burning huts and docks brightened the shores, jumping out of the murk of drifting smoke. Oleel had begun by burning the fields, but there was no stopping the fire once it got a taste of thatch and timber. Anton had given Zhen a gun, and also Moshani, taking three minutes to teach the Dassa how to shoot a pistol with underbarrel laser sight and thermal imaging. Zhen didn't need the lesson, and clutched her weapon with something like devotion. Anton thought she would single-handedly mow down Oleel and the judipon to get her langva samples to that shuttle.

He would have liked to have had Nick by his side. The old Nick. Anton had failed to make him his confidant and right-hand man, and Nick hated him for it. But even before that, Nick had wanted him to fail. It was an intuition, and Anton had acted on it, driving a wedge between them, a wedge that became sharp-edged and fatal.

Still, Anton kept a watch, peering through every tear in the curtain of smoke, hoping to see lost things come back to him. The fire was making such retrievals doubtful. They were just passing Samwan's islet, where outbuildings were engulfed in flames. Worse yet, the fields were smoldering.

On the islets, householders like Samwan cultivated several varieties of langva. Folded within some of these was a world. It was ambiguous as to whether alien beings' DNA was truly preserved there. The codas said the varieties contained information, cultural narrative, which Nick and Oleel saw, or pretended to see, as a threat. Though alien creatures wouldn't spring from the forest, they might come in search of what they had lost. If these events had played out on Earth, the reaction might not be so very different. *Cultural dread*, as the Quadi termed it.

Their canoes swept into the confluence with the Sodesh, the sterns sweeping awry in the crosscurrents. Paddling with strength and skill, Moshani's soldiers brought the canoes into the center of the great river. They maneuvered the craft among smaller skiffs, beating a swift path upriver. Some of the Dassa hailed the sight of them.

Moshani brought the canoes nearer the shoreline, where he judged they could only be set upon from one side. This course was taking them past the wetland grasses with the network of canals, the swamp where Vidori had hunted that day, when the woman had fled with her outlaw child in her womb. The woman's bones had been left in the stand of trees where she died, with no burial given, and no respect to her unborn child. Killed by Maypong's knife, at Vidori's order, for Anton's sake. All his purposes that were so right, all the outcomes that were so wrong. It was a gray landscape, truly. Except that now they were bringing the Quadi's legacy to Earth, bearing it up the Sodesh, bearing it home.

They were leaving the sounds of battle behind them. Shouts still came to them, but fewer and dimmer. Now, as they moved through the heavy smoke, the sound of the soldiers' paddles was all that anchored them to the world.

It was in that momentary peace that the barge came down on them from the confluence of the Amalang, where it had been waiting. They heard it before they saw it. The sound of splashing poles, in unison, setting up a rhythm that could not be natural eddies. It was only a dark blur, still a hundred meters off, when Anton hissed to the paddlers, *They're coming.*

He didn't know who was moving in on them, but he quietly urged the soldiers to redouble their pace, and as they passed Moshani in Zhen's canoe, he signed the warning to him.

Anton turned to face what was coming.

It was an uldia barge. Anton could see that it was moving in front to cut them off. The uldia had exchanged their robes for wide trousers and vests crossed with weapons. There were many of them on the platform. But the barge would be slow, for all its firepower, and Moshani directed the canoes close to the bank, forcing them all to duck under the overhanging branches.

Roots slapped Anton's face as he took his first shots, toppling a few uldia holding poles. He heard Moshani firing as well, and it had an effect: The barge poled off farther into the Sodesh. Anton's canoe crept slowly through the roots along the bank, but it was only a temporary respite, and only effective as long as the fog kept them hidden. Just ahead, Zhen had grabbed a paddle, and was stroking like a madwoman.

Both canoes broke free of the overhang then and churned upriver. "Watch for their canoes," Anton shouted to Moshani and Zhen.

Next to Anton, one of the soldiers rose up for a better aim, and paid for this by taking a shot full in the chest. Without a moment's hesitation the paddlers threw him over, lightening their load. Then they began paddling fiercely again.

The barge fell farther behind. Then a war canoe came out of the haze. It was fast, using most of its space for paddlers, but in the prow were two uldia with rifles. Lying athwart the gunwales, Zhen picked off one while the second uldia took clear aim at Moshani. But the king's man sent a knife into her.

Anton took aim and picked off two more, but still the canoe rushed toward them, and in the next instant Anton's canoe shook from the impact of the enemy prow.

Now, knives drawn, Anton's men turned to face the uldia canoe. He found himself facing an uldia with slaughter in her eyes. He blocked the first thrust, as the canoes rocked and the two sides clashed.

Meanwhile, Zhen's boat was grappling with an uldia canoe as well, and both Moshani and Zhen were firing point blank into their attackers.

In the midst of this carnage, the river brightened behind Anton's canoe, leaving a hole in the smoke. There, the uldia barge was in full view, some fifty meters downriver. They weren't firing, being out of range of Dassa weapons.

A woman stood on the forward end. She wore robes, and stood taller than her entourage. By her build, and the stance, it was the stone woman herself. Her gaze might have locked with Anton's; it was too far to tell. But when he saw her through his gun's scope, her square face looked directly into his.

She had made such a simple mistake. Thinking that his gun had only the range of hers.

Not hesitating this time, he fired. As he should have done that time, despite Maypong's plea, that one time, on his dock, when she had been so terribly wrong.

Oleel fell with a look of bafflement. A cry went up from the barge.

At the same time his canoe pulled forward, away from the uldia canoe, which fell away, bearing a cargo of dead.

Peering through the scope at the scene on the barge, Anton saw a huddle of uldia around their fallen leader. And toward the back, a very tall man with his hair rolled on top of his head.

Anton aimed, but missed in the wildly pitching canoe. Then the smog came rushing back, closing off vision.

"Zhen," Anton called, wanting to hear her voice.

"Sons of bitches," Zhen yelled back.

"Daughters, actually," Anton said. His heart was still pumping hard, his senses acute. He drew up closer to Zhen's canoe, saw her sitting upright, unscathed.

Moshani turned back from the prow to meet Anton's gaze. He was holding the pistol Anton gave him by the muzzle, having used it to bludgeon the attackers. Anton nodded to him, conveying, *Well done.*

And then, exhausted, they made their way upriver. Anton took a paddle from the man in front of him, and they went forward as best they could, coming into the landing site on the last of their adrenaline.

Huvai's islet began with a tangle of undergrowth by the bank. Once through, the group climbed the path leading up the long slope to the landing site, a flat rock formation, scoured of trees, jutting above the forest. As some of the soldiers stayed on the bank to care for their wounded, the rest of them carried the contents of the canoes up the long slope. Vidori's guard met them partway down, helping them with their loads. That boded well; the ship was still under guard.

At the top, he saw the bivouac of Vidori's soldiers, who had held this place secure in the weeks since their landfall. And there, the shuttle craft, looking denuded and sterile, amid the liana vines draped in the background.

The leader of the king's guard said that before Anton entered the craft, he must see a prisoner confined in a nearby thatch hut. So, after being led to a makeshift brig, Anton finally found Nick Venning.

The Dassa soldier said, "He claimed the air barge was his, and he must take it."

Securely bound with rope, Nick looked up at Anton, his eyes flat, with no flicker of recognition or even surprise.

"Shall I kill him?" the soldier asked.

Just what Anton was asking himself. Here was the man who had tried to abandon his crewmates, and scuttle the mission. He searched Nick's face for some sign of the old officer, but the man had fled. "No," Anton said. "Carry him on board."

Then he and Zhen turned to their hard-won cargo, stowing it securely on the shuttle.

Excusing the king's soldiers, and waiting for them to vacate the rock plateau, Anton began prelaunch procedures. They were going home. Finally, and at last.

Some of them.

Bailey was in the river room when a pillar of light lit up the western sky. She hurried to the steps of the great room where it joined the Puldar, and watched the shuttle rise from the forest. In the clotted air, she couldn't see the craft itself, only the torch of propellants on which it rose.

It took her by surprise, how hard it was to watch it go. Her throat cinched tight as she followed the shuttle's path up from the Olagong. After the roar faded, a quiet descended on the river, as though the Dassa along its length had stopped fighting long enough to note this event, the departure of the born to bear. She wondered what they felt, whether relief or dismay.

She had gone down the river steps, and found that she now stood up to her knees in the water, to no particular purpose, but still watching through the smoke for the pinpoint of light that was the human craft. Leaving. Well, of course it was leaving. Silly old woman, to find tears at such a moment.

She leaned down and dipped her hand in the river, splashing her face clean.

Deep in the forest, Gilar's band was effectively blind. They had no view of the river or the horizon, so when the thun-

der came, they stopped and looked at each other in consternation.

One of the three dozen hoda who had joined them as
they made their way through the outskirts of the nearby
compounds sang, The human captain flies up to his great
barge. Then, seeing the expression on Gilar's face, and mis-
taking it for confusion, she added: He is going back where he
came from.

As they made their way toward the Nool, Gilar and Mim
found scattered hoda who had run away from their mistresses. Many of them made common cause with Gilar.
Others were running west, to the Vol, despite rumors that
Oleel had a blockade on the Sodesh to prevent them.

She looked up, past the treetops, expecting to see the
ship fly right over them, so loud was the noise of Anton's
craft.

Are you sure? Gilar asked.

The hoda was sure. She'd been on the river, and had seen
Anton's boats racing up the Sodesh.

Gilar was still gazing up. Closing her eyes, she held on to
the receding thunder of the craft. It seemed very long ago
that she had been a young girl dreaming of Erth. But the old
longing still held power, as old things often did. Like having
a mother of the Olagong, who'd taught her how to live with
courage and die for something worthwhile.

The thing that made her saddest of all was that Maypong
was not on that ship.

After a moment, someone sang, Bailey stayed at the palace, though.

Gilar looked at the woman for a long moment. Why had
they not told her this before? And why should it matter,
when it was only an old woman with a good singing voice?

Her smile, when it came, was broad enough that everyone in the group caught it.

Bailey stayed.

* * *

On the *Restoration*, the hum of the ship surrounded Anton, louder than he remembered it. The bulkheads seemed closer now, too, with their systems pulsing just beneath the metal plates. A strange place—tight, and colorless. The faces of the crew, many of them haggard, seemed new, too.

Webb had been a welcome sight. After a lengthy debriefing with the sergeant, Anton had gone to the medical suite. Of the crew of nineteen, five remained unfit for duty, but were recovering on a cocktail of drugs designed for each crew member's particular gene patterns. The therapy was only possible because the virus was in a stable consensus sequence, not creating new versions. By Anton's side was the burly medic, Spence Norval, one of the hale ones. But all of the patients, no matter how weakened, wanted to know the story of the genetic sequence and what they were bringing home from this world. Anton repeated it, down the line of beds.

He looked down at a patient, Ensign Petry, once a strapping boy of twenty. *Boy.* Anton could call him that, being four years his senior, and his captain.

Spence said, "Petry held down engineering for the past weeks, Captain."

Petry nodded at Anton. "Welcome back, sir."

"Good work, Leo," Anton said. "We'll need you back on grease detail, as soon as you can stand up."

"I'm ready, Captain. Let me at 'em." He grinned, showing reddened gums.

"We could fit Nick in here, Captain," Spence said as they continued down the line of beds. Corporal Norval was a friend to Nick; a friend to most of them on this ship. A likable man, and competent. The *Restoration* had been lucky to keep this one upright.

Nick was isolated and bound in an end cabin, where he was improving with the help of a tailored pharmacogenomic concoction. But it would be a slow recovery.

The tour completed, Anton faced Spence in the middeck corridor. Clean-shaven and pasty-faced, the man looked fresh compared with Anton, who, despite a shower and a new uniform, was haggard from lack of sleep.

"We got what we came for then, I guess," Spence said.

Anton nodded. "It's in the hold, as much as we could gather."

"Zhen said it's a food. Like a tuber. And all wrapped up in the DNA. That about it?"

"Yes, that's about it." Through the cabin door, Anton could see the rows of his crew, lying amid sheets and tubes and blinking monitors. All that they had endured on this ship had come to mean something. He was thankful to be able to say so. Leaning against the bulkhead for a moment, he took a moment to let Spence know that it *had* been worth it.

"It's a legacy," he said. "Might take us a hundred years to read everything that's there, and then do something with it. The technology is far beyond us—*how* far, we don't know."

"And there's stuff from other worlds," Spence said. "Have we translated anything?"

"We don't even know if we *can* translate it." Anton paused. "But if we succeed, then it's a back-door chance to learn about other beings, what their civilizations are—without the space voyages that the Council opposes. Without the risks of space travel." He didn't need to elaborate on *risks*, not to this man who was lucky to be walking under his own power.

Nexus world was a concept they had barely had time to discuss, much less assimilate. Neshar held a priceless inheritance, one that would challenge Earth culturally, scientifically. Anton thought of the ways that Earth had to change. He'd fled from some of those things, fled to the haven of military service. Now the *Restoration* would bring back more than human diversity. Maybe too much diversity. He was looking forward to it.

Spence said, "Call themselves the Quadi, then? Is that what I heard?"

"Actually, they never named themselves, in what Zhen has translated so far. That's the name the Dassa gave them."

"And maybe they haven't even survived." Spence shook his head, as though being both *advanced* and *dead* seemed contradictory. "That's what Nick said."

Anton cocked his head. "Nick?"

"He's dying. And raving. I stopped in, sure." Spence looked away. "I wish I hadn't."

Anton remembered how small a ship this was. "Post a guard, Corporal. Outside his door."

Spence raised an eyebrow. "A guard? We don't have anybody extra for a guard." And then, at Anton's continuing gaze, "Yes, sir."

Anton clapped a hand on the man's shoulder. "A tough duty. You've done well, Spence. Just a little longer now."

He was continually urging people to *hold on*. From the look in Spence's eyes, he thought some of them were damn tired of it.

Webb turned to greet him on the bridge. The big man had a comforting heft, and a stolid demeanor—indeed, he'd brought the crew back from the brink of mutiny during the bad weeks of Anton's absence.

Beside Webb, Lupe Rodriguez ran the linguistic sequences, checking the satellite broadcasts. The ones they'd once thought were noise.

"Corporal," Anton said, returning the salute.

Lupe gave a nod, a coldness in her eyes. She was one who had voted to go home. But then, to be fair, they had *all* voted to go home. Except Webb.

The room, kept cool for the main on-board tronics, made Anton shiver. Or perhaps it was from seeing the bridge, formerly with a component of six, now stripped to two.

Webb said, "Lupe's been working on the radio broadcast codes, sir."

She looked up from the screen where she sat. "True,

Captain. They've got a grammar, at least the two I've been working on."

Webb shrugged. *"Come find what you have lost."*

"I don't know if this is right," Lupe said, "but some of these are diverting to Kardashev tunnels, and it could be they're packeting through them. As radio waves. Don't ask me how."

Anton considered this. So perhaps aliens would show up sooner than he'd thought. Perhaps Oleel did have reason to worry—not that her revolt could stop any of it.

Lupe busied herself at her work screen. Webb had shown good sense in having crew involved in these translations, enlisting them in the work, the cause.

Looking at Anton, Webb urged him to sit down. Anton hadn't slept for two days, and by now he knew it showed. He sat next to Lupe as she keyed the board. There were three satellites, broadcasting in two directions each. While she worked, Anton gazed out a portal, where the stars burned, near and far. It was a view he'd often used in the past to let his mind wander. With no wandering moments for many days now, he longed for that state, with nothing to decide or unravel. So when his thoughts went to Maypong, Anton let them. His thoughts went so far as to bring Maypong onto the bridge, where she would be looking out the very same portal as he was now. Where she would perhaps join Webb and him in thinking, *All those worlds . . .*

As Anton made his way back to his cabin for a much-postponed sleep, he realized how carefully he had avoided looking out the other portal, the one that held the view of Neshar.

Gilar stood in the great wood hall. It was the river room of the judipon, with the Nool River flowing over its steps. Incredibly, not a single person defended the compound, now lying nearly empty of judipon. Nirimol had required his people to leave their ink pens and take up arms instead. The few old men remaining behind looked surprised to find a group of hoda entering the place, led by a young hoda wearing a headband of yellow.

Now the sisters possessed a great pavilion, one with stores of food, and even a few guns and dart tubes left about. Through the halls, smoke drifted, causing a scrape in their throats, and a murk even with the luminaries blazing. Floors strewn with paper rounds gave evidence of records hastily bundled away, those numerations the judipon deemed crucial to the business of the Olagong. Gilar smiled to herself. She didn't think Nirimol understood the real business of the Olagong. How his spindles must record a new power, and a new world.

Gilar still felt like an imposter, leading the hoda. Mim was of an age that might command respect, but she was content to stand behind. So here Gilar was, striding through the judipon realm, commanding her thirty-two soldiers. Although she knew nothing of fighting and tactics, nothing of leading people, Gilar had begun to accept her role. Because of one thing: her vision in the forest ravine, that the hoda were to be the Fourth Power, with their own pavilion. That their color would be yellow, for Maypong.

A commotion in the hallway. Gilar turned as a sister hailed her, singing: The radio, Gilar!

As Gilar ran to join them, the sister showed her down the stairs and then into a room where Mim and several others were standing, surveying a place of electrical machines. Among tangles of cords, machine parts, and denuded paper spindles, a long empty table commanded the center of the room.

A judipon cowered in the corner, subdued by a sister twice his size. "Oh, he took it, yes, mistress," the man blathered. "Nirimol took it. The transmitter. He had use of it, he said."

So did we, Gilar thought. So much for the judipon's vow of river hands.

She had little time to consider this setback, for a new

person had entered the radio room. In the company of several hoda, there stood the human woman, Bailey.

"I'm so sorry about Maypong, my dear," the old woman said.

Out on the Puldar in a skiff, Bailey had found groups of hoda huddling on piers, watching the river. None of them knew where Gilar was, until Bailey had happened upon Osa, a lone hoda in a tattered skiff. The woman was a scout Gilar had sent out to look for trouble. Bailey had hoped she didn't fit that definition.

Osa had brought her to Homish's pavilion, where Bailey half expected to be spindled on one of those great storage needles. The judipon were the king's enemies, of course. But she'd braved it out, and now stood with the youngster in charge of one of the Olagong's revolutions.

In this cluttered room with abandoned cords and dusty radio tubes, Bailey asked for a riser to sit upon. She had no business asking for favors, but it was late, and her old legs felt as if she'd walked from the palace, not ridden in a boat.

Seating herself, Bailey began, "I've made mistakes." Several dozen hoda were watching her, warily, bristling with arms. "I haven't been paying attention as I should have. But I mean to do better."

Gilar looked at an old hoda standing nearby, one Bailey took for an officer, or some such thing. The ragtag group was at least organized enough to have taken the judipon pavilion. Still, they remained silent.

Bailey continued, "I have some influence with the king. I'll help you, if I can. If you're willing to trust me. And," she added, "if he's still the king after all this fuss settles down."

The hoda were singing among themselves, an annoying little hum, just when Bailey felt they should be paying attention to what she was saying.

Finally, Gilar signed, >Why did Captain Anton leave you here?<

"Because I refused to go home. It's late in my life for long voyages."

>Will other humans come here, after he has gone? And will there be other beings, with other ships?<

"Gilar, I don't know about other—beings. I shouldn't think they'd be showing up anytime soon. And as for other ships from Earth, well, that is years away, if ever."

The girl seemed to absorb this, watching her, no longer the waif she had been that day in the skiff, desperate and bedraggled. No, this was a new Gilar. She was surrounded by hoda who watched out for her. How many followed this girl with the fine soprano voice?

"When this fighting is over," Bailey said, "I'd like to teach you a song or two, if you're still interested." She looked at the girl's hand, bandaged, reminding Bailey of the penalty for songs in the wrong place. But still, she would teach her.

Gilar's face softened. >The song of the palace? That you sang for the king?< She looked around at the other hoda, and by their expressions, Bailey thought the suggestion went over.

"You know," Bailey said, "we could all get in a dreadful lot of trouble."

Gilar smiled. >Yes. But we rise, Bailey-rah.<

One thing they had to get straight was that Bailey would not undermine the king. "You should know, Gilar, that I won't help you harm Vidori."

Gilar raised her chin. >He won't die of a song.<

Well, the girl was bold, indeed. The hoda watched Bailey, waiting for something.

Finally, Bailey stood. *When in doubt, follow your impulses.* The maxim had served her well in the past, even if it had gotten her into a world of trouble at times. It did appear that they wished to start their singing lessons forthwith.

She uttered the first, glorious notes of "Sempre libera." Verdi, for the revolution.

TWENTY-THREE

Coda Ten. Cultural Opposition.
It is necessary to set aside cultural dread. Conflict and avoid-
ance of contact are barriers to the progress of civilized worlds
and the custodial duty. Coda One describes how ours is not an
enduring and safe universe. Higher life has a narrow temporal
and spatial range. The universe needs no assistance to deplete
complex life. What is required is to overcome xenophobia and
endeavor to further the prospects of sentient species. The cul-
tural records stored here and elsewhere may provide familiar-
ity and interest in diverse sentient populations. Species and
cultures may undergo change as a result. In approaching con-
course with other advanced species, avoid fear and consterna-
tion. We are not immune from such states of dread. While
accepting the custodial duty, we could not accept ourselves
changed or our culture altered. It is a barrier to our survival.
We do not survive.

Anton awoke, overheated, sweat slicking his body.
Checking the time, he saw that he'd slept a full shift and
more, pursued by disturbing dreams: the judipon lowering

the wire cage over a girl's head; Maypong walking, red foot-prints on the path.

Anton dressed, then sat on the edge of the bunk, dreams lingering. On a day when he should have awakened thinking of what lay ahead, he was beset by things that had passed. The people he must put behind him: Maypong, Bailey, Vidori, Gilar, Shim. And Oleel. Today the *Restoration* would leave orbit, beginning the run to the Kardashev tunnel, the journey back.

He found himself going in search of someone to talk to. That would be Zhen.

She wasn't in her cabin, but he soon found her. She was with Sergeant Webb, sitting in his compact cabin, a flask of whiskey on a table between them.

Webb stood. "Busted," the older man said. "Begging your pardon, Captain."

Anton said, "I hope you have another glass, Sergeant."

Webb's mouth curled into a smile. He rose to accomplish the task, then plopped down a chipped mug and splashed some amber liquid in it. Given the ship's space and personal stowage limitations, Webb was rumored to have nursed three bottles of fine whiskey through the entire voyage. Captain Darrow had taken a glass or two with the man, but this was Anton's first.

Zhen smirked. "I didn't think you broke the rules, Captain."

"Sometimes you have to," Anton murmured, and got a rare smile from her.

They drank in silence for a time. Webb watched Anton with a steady gaze. He leaned forward to top off his captain's drink.

Webb refilled his own, waving the bottle at Zhen, who demurred. He sat back with his drink, saying, "We're about done with systems tests, Anton. Could fire up anytime." It was time for that, of course.

Anton rolled the whiskey over his tongue, swallowed. And again. It cauterized the bad taste in his mouth. The one that came from his misgivings, the misgivings that now, after a bit of whiskey, were becoming clear to him. The bad taste came from abandoning Maypong's world. Even though he had to.

Though he had a clear responsibility and mission, and there was no possible dispute of what he had to do, he had been fending off an errant thought for days now. The unwelcome knowledge that his mission, so extraordinarily successful, was yet a failure. In a moment of cynicism, the entire endeavor could be summed up in a few cold words: *We came. We took. We left.*

"Captain?" Webb leaned back, cradling his drink. In a tone both straightforward and muted, he said, "It might help to talk."

"Yes, I think it would." Anton floundered for a beginning, but Zhen and Webb weren't in a hurry, and there was half a bottle left.

Anton said, barely audible, "Feels like hell. Leaving." He took a drink. "That's the short of it."

Webb raised an eyebrow at Zhen, then refilled all of their glasses. "And the long of it?"

Anton tilted his chin in the direction of the portal in Webb's cabin. "That world below us, Ethan. It's the repository. We're leaving it to a raging tyrant, a woman who can depose a decent king."

Zhen said, "I thought you killed her."

"With luck. But Nirimol could carry on." After a pause he said, "But it's not just the Olagong on my mind."

"No," Zhen said. She took a drink, murmuring, "It's worlds within worlds."

Webb frowned. "But we've got the code."

Zhen murmured, "Some of it."

Anton had the sudden, gladdening thought that the woman just might be walking down the same logic path he was. He turned his attention to Webb, the man who might have missed Captain Darrow, but who'd remained loyal to the new captain.

Anton decided to trust him. He had to say this thing before his better judgment quelled the thought, much less the words.

He said, "What if we stayed?"

The sergeant was gazing at him, betraying nothing.

For a moment, Anton thought of Vidori. When they had first seen the fires on the river that were meant to stamp out the Quadi legacy, Vidori had said, *You and I, Anton, are not devoted to such worlds* . . . Leaving unsaid, *We are devoted to more narrow concerns. You for Earth, I for my power in the Olagong. And this is not a good thing.*

Zhen was staring fixedly at her glass of whiskey.

Finally Webb said, "Earth needs what's in those holds, Anton." He locked gazes with his captain, not with hostility, but immovably. To someone like Webb, the mission goal was not for tampering with.

Anton wanted to say, *Sometimes the goal changes.* But he thought better of the direct approach. Rather, he said, "Earth could still have it. We could send word back about what we've found. Let them decide to come for it."

Webb hadn't moved. "That would take years, Captain."

Years. Three years for the mission's report to reach Earth, if borne by a drone craft through the subspace tunneling. Given Earth politics, it could take considerably longer.

Anton said, "They have some time." It was a risk to say so. It sounded like he was consolidating his position. And so he was.

"Look, Ethan," he said. "The Olagong is more than it appears. That war down there is not just about which petty ruler wins. We have a stake in it. Oleel and Nirimol mean to destroy much of what the old race worked to save." He looked at Zhen. "Worlds."

Zhen put her glass on the table, sitting upright. "There are varieties of that plant that have been thriving in narrow ecological niches for ten thousand years. The loss is . . ." She shook her head. "It's unthinkable." She looked up, noting

Webb's confusion. "The other worlds are folded into other subspecies of langva. On board here we only have the few species I was working on, that I had in the lab this week. What we have in our hold represents a damn narrow goal."

Anton said quietly: "The mission can change its goal."

Webb took a long pull on his drink. Staring into the glass, he said, "The crew might not last the ride home. It's not what anybody wants to say, but the radiation pounding is making hash out of our resistance. Maybe the virus reservoir is right here, in our own crew. It could break out again. With our luck, it will." His shoulders relaxed then, and he turned to Anton with a more open face. "I don't know about other worlds; that goes beyond what's in my keeping. But the lads and gals are mine to see to, begging your pardon, Anton. They've been in my care. I put half of 'em in shrouds. I don't care to do that again." He stopped then, not giving an aye or nay to the matter, but leaving room for Anton to do so.

And he did. "Here's a proposal then. I won't make this an order—but I'm not putting it to a ship vote, either." He clearly remembered Bailey's acid words: *This isn't a union ship. We don't whine, and we don't vote.* "We send our report to Earth. Tell them everything, urge them to come. But out front, tell them about the Dassa: what they are, and why. And why it's hard—sometimes impossible—to accept. Tell them there are varieties of worlds. Varieties of human. So they can get used to the idea."

And whether they came or not, his crew would also have to accept changes. Their future was with the born to bear. If Maypong had lived, she would have insisted that he have sarif with those most like himself. He was sure that she would have. And in like manner, she would have claimed full sarif expression for herself. They would have worked it out, somehow.

He closed his eyes, thinking of her.

"Captain?" Zhen was frowning. "Are we going to do this or aren't we?"

Anton looked up. For this to work, he needed Webb's support. His firm support. He locked gazes with the man, and Webb understood what was being asked.

Webb gave the slightest dip of his chin as an answer. "God help me," Webb said.

"God help us all," Anton murmured.

"Was that a *yes*?" Zhen snapped.

Anton thought of the small band they would form, when eventually everyone came down to the Olagong. They would be immigrants, and would very much need each other. He realized that he had always liked Zhen, despite her quick temper. She always said what she thought, and that would be a relief in the Olagong.

"Yes," Anton said. "That was a yes."

He reached for the whiskey bottle.

Nick took a deep breath, looking into Spence Norval's face. Spence was loosening his bonds. But was he really? Nick knew that he sometimes saw things that weren't real. It was the stress, the stress of the universe's unraveling.

Spence was saying that the *Restoration* wasn't going home after all. That Anton had decided to stay. For a moment Nick was relieved that they weren't going to bring the infected DNA home. But a problem still remained: the drone and its packet of information about the riches found, the answer to Earth's problems. So Earth would send another ship, and then it would begin all over again, the nightmare. No, the folks back home needed to remember that the *Restoration* had pursued the signal and never been heard from again.

Spence was swearing under his breath, fumbling with the code on the restraint locks that bound Nick to the bunk.

"Who's with us, then?" Nick asked.

"Lupe for sure. She'll meet us on the flight deck. First we commandeer the arms locker. By that time she'll have more people with her. The ones who want to go home."

"Where's Anton?" Nick asked.

"On the flight deck with Webb." He stopped for a moment, searching Nick's eyes. "You said Anton has got to be stopped, right? You're with us on this, Nick?"

He hated to lie to Spence—the man meant well. But he didn't know the things Nick knew.

"We'll stop him," Nick said. "Stop him cold. It's what Captain Darrow . . . would have done." He didn't want to discuss how Captain Darrow was still around. Unless he was a phantom. It didn't matter, though. The rest was true, about how once the genomes were brought home, were cloned, they'd revert to Dassa form.

"Give me a gun, Spence."

The restraints sprang free, and Nick was struggling to his feet. A small pistol came into his hand. Spence looked at him. "Don't fire on the crew. Just Webb and the captain."

Nick nodded. *Just kill the fat sergeant and the thin captain. Got it.* Spence turned to the cabin door to check the ship corridor.

Behind him, Nick brought the gun up and hit Spence on the skull. The man crumpled.

At the door, he listened for sounds in the corridor, then slipped out, moving quickly, with more energy than he'd had in weeks. It was finally coming to the point—the point of his life, of his death.

Scrambling down the ladder to mid-deck, Nick thanked his luck that there were only a handful of able-bodied crew walking the decks. The ship was big and empty now, big as a mausoleum with the dead and the near dead aboard.

At the hold, he yanked a release, then pulled up the hatchway from the floor and slipped down onto the bulkhead ladder. He pulled the hatch shut, and descended.

There was the science module off to starboard, and to port, the hold, now pressurized, Nick knew, holding Zhen's samples. But it was cold down here, or else Nick was sweating and shivering on his own.

His hands shook as he touched the keypad by the hold

doors. Now that it came to the moment, he trembled. He
was afraid. Wet spots from his fingers lingered on the keypad as he programmed in a sequence that would open the
doors and lock them in place, bringing the ship in contact
with the vacuum of space.

But not yet. He slipped into the hold as the doors closed
behind him.

Around him the bagged samples huddled among the
canisters and sealed cartons of the ship's stores. The samples with the little tags dangling from them, showing Zhen's
system of collection: time, place, descriptors. Like tags on
the toes in a morgue. Nick didn't blame Zhen. She was trying to save her people. The whole mission had begun that
way, but the lie couldn't hold up.

He finished coding in the sequence on the outside bay
doors. They'd open in . . . what, four minutes? OK, four
minutes. Because anything less wouldn't give him time to
say good-bye. Even after all that had transpired between
him and Anton, Nick still wanted Anton to know that good
men could disagree. For in the end, Nick still loved Anton as
a friend. Past rage and hate, he'd ended back at friendship.
Now that he was going to kill the ship, it was calming to
know it was for love.

He turned to the comm node. Punched in the flight
deck. He hugged his sides with his arms. So cold. His body
seemed to be turning off a few minutes too early, going to
zero. Preparing for annihilation. It aided his feeling of calm.

But when he linked with Anton on the flight deck, a stab
of warmth came back.

"Anton," Nick said. His voice wobbled. He coughed to
clear his throat. "Anton."

"Nick? Where are you?"

"Far away."

A muffled voice. Anton sending someone down to the
brig, no doubt. Nick didn't have much time. He looked at
the chronometer on the outside bay doors. 3:26, 3:25, 3:24.

"I just wanted to tell you that I know you meant to do

the right thing. I was against you. But I know you tried to do it right." He coughed. "You were wrong, though, Anton."

"Nick, where are you?"

"I'm dying. Leaving now." Anton's voice was stabbing at him. His old friend. They were both so young. Had tried to do it right. Failed. But he did love the man.

"Anton. I'm sorry. You get ready to die now."

2:05, 2:04.

Nick could hear running on the mid-deck. They'd found Spence, maybe.

"Let me help you, Nick. I know you've been hurt. Let's talk. Will you talk to me?" Muffled voices came through the comm node. The flight deck was astir now. They were wondering where he was. Mustn't say.

Nick said, "Remember how we played cards until we were stupid? How we bet ourselves into debt?" Nick tried to laugh, but couldn't conjure it. "I think you owe me 'bout a million, don't you?"

"I do owe you, Nick."

1:16, 1:15, 1:14.

"Forget it. I forgive it all, Anton. I'm leaving. We're all leaving, and every one of these bags."

Nick turned to look at the hold. It would all blow out the bay doors within seconds. A quick way to go, by God, not the slow slide he'd been on . . .

"Anton?" He waited. But there was no answer. "Anton?"

Nick swore. The bags. He'd given away his position. Oh, Venning, you screwed up again. Again and again.

Then, gathering his wits, he started keying the pad. There was under a minute to go, but it was too long. He had to shorten the sequence. Only it was locked. That would take a while to undo. His hands shook as he punched in a maneuver to instantly open the bay doors and the interior ship doors opposite. To open both doors, to blow out the ship.

For love of duty.

*   *   *

Anton was dashing for the flight deck door. "He's in the cargo hold," he shouted at Webb. "Override him. He's going to lock open the bay doors."

He ran. Behind him, he heard Webb shouting for backup. Anton pounded down the short passageway from the flight deck, to the forward ladder, sliding down it and hitting mid-deck with both feet.

Webb was on the ship intercom, saying, "We're trying, Captain, but he's got us locked out. You've got thirty seconds before he blows it."

Anton raced to the hatchway in the floor, unlocking the arm and swinging the hatch door up. Sliding through, he found the bulkhead ladder and slid down to the lower deck.

The instrument pad by the side of the cargo bay doors was blinking orange. A Klaxon had come on sometime during his race to the hold, blaring in tandem with the pulsing of the light.

Anton was at the keypad, pressing Override. Override. But the light still pulsed, turning his fingers the color of fire. Override. The counter was showing twenty seconds. Nineteen. This couldn't be.

Anton activated the comm node on the door. "Nick. Release the inner door. Take the cargo with you. Let us live. Your last act of honor. Do it, Nick."

Nick's voice came thin and reedy through the intercom. "Good-bye, Anton. See you soon, old buddy."

Anton drew his pistol and fired point blank into the keypad. The electronics flared blue.

Then a rumble grabbed the deck, a tremor and a double-punch explosion. Nick had blown the bay doors.

But the inner doors held. From behind them came the crashing of materials blasting toward the open bay, the chaos of every loose part, tool, and shred of exploded equipment whirling in a frenzy to reach the gap and jettison into space. Among them, one Nick Venning, lately of the starship *Restoration*. Once of sound mind. Once a friend.

Anton lay his head against his arm along the bulkhead, catching his breath.

In the next moment, Ensign Petry was crashing down the ladder, armed and with a wild look in his eyes.

Anton turned to him. "Doors held," he said, wonderingly.

Petry's eyes widened as it sank in that the cargo hold was blown. He held his pistol, pointing it at the door as though hell itself was likely to throw open the doors and come charging though.

Petry looked up as Webb lumbered down the ladder. Then he holstered his weapon, murmuring to Anton, "The crew was with you, Captain. We were never going to . . ." He looked at the cargo hold. "It was only Spence and Lupe."

Anton nodded, clapping him on the shoulder. "Thank you. Stick with me, will you? I'll need you."

Petry gave a crumpled smile. "Yes, sir." Then: "We want our feet on real ground. We'll stay, Captain."

Webb looked at the hole in the bulkhead where the control pad had been. "Not elegant, Captain." He grimaced at the damage. "Kind of like going through the hut wall that time?"

Anton shrugged. He was developing a style. Not a great one, but it was better than none at all. "Yes, Sergeant," he said. "Kind of like that."

TWENTY-FOUR

Coda Eleven. To Leave the Galaxy.
In two billion years the dark matter structure will return.
That is the next cycle of its journey. Though now it grows sa-
tiated, having nearly reached equilibrium, by then its data will
have dissipated, renewing the gradient between itself and the
life-bearing planets it encounters. Then the sentient species
that remain here must leave the galaxy. In that epoch, if you
survive, you will have surpassed us in knowledge, using all
that is stored here. What the other galaxies hold, we have not
assayed. You may do so. You may encounter other custodial
species even more advanced than yourselves, or none, given the
factors naturally contributing to the paucity of complex life.
You may write the codas of the universe.

For a landing place, Anton selected a cultivated flatland
near the palace. No fires burned nearby, so he judged the lo-
cation a safe place for the shuttle.

At the controls, Anton put the craft down with a sure
touch, his crew ready and briefed to deploy outside the craft
and defend it. With just five others on board, Anton

wouldn't be bringing firepower to Vidori—though he realized it wasn't physical weapons the king wanted, but psychological ones. Anton also knew that the crew needed to stay segregated for a quarantine period, to be sure they weren't carrying disease. Of course, he could be infected, too. But his immunity had held this long, and he'd only been exposed for forty-eight hours. Besides, there wasn't much choice.

He'd told the shuttle crew what to say to any of the king's guards who approached the ship. Later, when the sick did come down in the shuttle, they'd need a pavilion to themselves. Zhen said one of the codas, a long information dump on biomolecular engineering, might offer a breakthrough for effective antimicrobial agents. Perhaps, even with their limited equipment, they could make use of this, should the virus erupt again. But that was tomorrow's issue. Today, there was a war.

Anton shut down the systems. Assembling with his people at the access hatchway, he saw the looks on the crew's faces, especially the youngest among them. It was a foreign world, a planet they'd have to call home, and that wouldn't welcome them, not entirely.

And, they would soon find out how the aversion went both ways.

Anton would have welcomed an encounter with Vidori's soldiers, but he hiked toward the Puldar unchallenged. In the early dawn, the area was quiet, with heavy smoke obscuring any sight of the river or glimpse of the king's pavilion, which must be nearby. Distant gunfire gave evidence of fighting upriver, perhaps all along the river system. He hoped that Bailey would be safe in the king's pavilion—if she stayed there, managing for once to stay out of affairs in which she had no business. The chances of that were slim, he figured.

Moving downslope toward the river from the landing

site, Anton chose to travel light, with a handgun and a rifle, a vest bulging with power clips to recharge his weapons, and one small drone. A combat knife hugged his lower right leg. Goggles lent thermal and low-light vision in the miasma of smoke, and a radio node on his collar established a link with the shuttle. He would be an easy target; no one could mistake him for a Dassa. At the same time, visibility was what he brought to this fight. To be seen at Vidori's side.

But first he had to find him.

Impenetrable brush along the Puldar separated him from the river, forcing him to beat his way west along the overgrown shore until he found a dock at a small compound. The residents had fled, leaving the place inhabited only by drifting smoke. Anton strode onto the pier, scanning the river. A few empty skiffs drifted on the current and several were pinned against the dock by the river flow. He chose the sturdiest of them and, grabbing a paddle, headed downriver.

Vidori would be looking for him. The whole of the Olagong must know that the shuttle had returned. Some would be glad to see him. In truth, Anton would be glad to see one of them himself; he had a friendship of sorts with the man. But he also had a proposition and a bargain to negotiate, and friendship notwithstanding, it was a negotiation he intended to win.

He paddled onward, his pistol on the floor at his feet, keeping a rhythm, dipping and pulling. In the near distance on the river, he saw skiffs, ghostly in the smoke, but no one yet took note of him. The dip and pull of his paddle came louder to him, magnified by the strange acoustics of the river.

A growing sense of something amiss made him change his rhythm. Behind him, the old rhythm remained. Someone was following him. With a deep lunge of his paddle, he moved to the shore, wedging his skiff near an enormous dead tree that leaned out over the river. He braced himself in the boat, and unslung his rifle. Activating it, he aimed at the splash of paddles. Through the scope, he saw a boat, with five people in it. Farther off, he saw a second craft.

A war canoe hove out of the murk, flying the silver banner, caught unawares by Anton's sudden stop. It took only a moment for its paddlers to spot him by the shore. By that time, however, Anton had sent a barrage of fire into the craft, creating mayhem but also alerting the second boat. The last man left upright in the first canoe was firing at Anton, but his aim was ruined as his boat, with its dead paddlers, fell away on the current.

Anton turned to the second craft, picking off a few Dassa while they were still blind to him, aiming at the hot images revealed by his goggles. The canoe moved swiftly in the direction of his fire. Anton easily cut down the occupants, lined up as they were in the canoe, and lacking the stability of the platform from which Anton was aiming.

The second canoe and its load of dead drifted back down the Amalang, retreating into the cloak of gray.

Anton stared hard into the river, primed for more boats. It was calm, the only sounds those of the river and the distant gunfire.

But suddenly, the rules of engagement changed.

A branch along the riverbank bent down. In the next moment he saw shapes moving behind the screen of brambles. Too close to the bank to use his rifle, Anton seized the pistol and fired.

Shots returned his fire, pinging into the water near him. There must have been a third boat that pulled ashore. Anton knew he should move out, but he was trapped against the horizontal tree, with its great trunk and branches. He clambered out of the skiff, splashing through waist-high water, shooting as he went, hearing screams from the bank as his shots found their marks. Anton crouched low, up to his chest in the water, aiming toward the shore. He risked maneuvering his rifle into position, and then raked the bank with fire. After a time he thought they might all be dead.

A flick of wind by his cheek. Something was bobbing in a branch in front of him. A needle-thin dart. Anton swung around.

There on the tree, hanging out over the river stood someone just raising another dart into a tube. Anton lunged sideways into the water. He tore off his goggles, now useless, and swam for the protection of the leaning tree where his assailant stood, still blowing darts into his path. He was below the tree trunk now, screened. The tree creaked as the soldier walked along its wide expanse until he was directly over Anton's hiding place.

From overhead, he heard a familiar, lilting voice: "Oh yes, I had forgotten that humans are good swimmers." The tree creaked again, and the trunk pushed slightly down on Anton's position. "But do your guns fare well in water, Anton?"

They did, but he wasn't about to tell the Lady Joon this.

"Come down and find out, Lady." He saw her reflection, cloudy and broken in the river's current. She wore trousers and her hair was knotted on top of her head.

Again a creak of the tree. He thought she might be crawling out on a side branch to get a clear shot at him. "Hmm. Perhaps we should meet on top instead."

For a moment Anton saw fine leather boots jump from one branch to another. She was on the upriver side, but he couldn't get a shot at her without moving into view.

"Now that I've come to stay, Joon, you should rethink whose side you're on."

"Perhaps you are right. I had not thought of that. Let us think: We have the uldia and the judipon against the king and one human fighter with two useless women. Hmm. One must think about where to turn next."

Suddenly she had hopped to a lower branch, and crouching, sent a dart into the shallows, missing him. As Anton returned fire, she jumped back up onto the trunk, crunching the massive length down on him, pushing his head into the water.

He moved to the opposite side, coming back to the surface. "This might be a good time," he said, "to tell your father you're sorry." He hoped that would keep her talking for a time. Making his way through the water as quietly as he could, he approached the shore, where the shallow water would ease his way to the top of the trunk, and a clear view of Joon.

He heard her throaty laugh. "Oh Vidori-rah, please excuse my mistakes," she said in a parody of contrition. "It might appear that I would be queen, but now I am suddenly loyal." She paused, loading her dart tube again by the sound of it. "Now what shall my father say to that, Anton?"

Anton sprang up on a lower branch, and then to the top of the trunk.

Joon stood in brilliant blue silks, her trousers bloused over sturdy boots, and her jacket bristling with darts. She blew on her pipe just as Anton's wet boots slipped on the smooth bark, sending him forward into a hard fall. Plucking another dart from the strap on her vest, Joon had just begun to aim again when the world went sideways.

A blistering crack came from behind them, and suddenly roots of the tree that had been holding it to the muddy bank sprang free and the massive trunk plunged into the river.

Anton, on his hands and knees, had better purchase, and watched as Joon lost her balance and, flailing, fell. She slipped between two large branches, and then the tree toppled over her.

Left on the sloping trunk, which had now found a new stability, Anton crept down its length, pistol aimed at the submerged crown of the tree. But Joon was not coming up for air.

She could well be swimming underwater, moving to the shore.

Anton watched for any deeper flash of blue from the river. Then he went in after her.

The great branching head of the tree formed a maze in the cool waters. Anton pulled himself down, using branches for handholds. A fish swam under him, its eyes on top of its back, staring up at Anton. As it passed, he saw a blue hole in the river, a deeper blue, more of silk than of water.

He saw a slender arm pushing among the branches. Ineffectually. Joon was trapped.

As he swam nearer, he saw just how trapped. On the shallow bottom of the river, Joon lay on her side, pinned down.

Breaking to the surface, Anton took another gulp of air, and dove. As he approached Joon, he saw that the tangled branches of the tree had pinned her hair—now all unbound and surrounding her like seaweed—into the thick mud of the river bottom. He yanked on the branch, but it was immovable. Then he pulled on her hair. Her face was pale and flickering with the sunlight that came twisting through the two meters of water. Anton withdrew his knife from his leg strap. Smiling at him, Joon lifted her chin, exposing her neck.

But Anton began cutting her hair, slashing it away from the branches. It floated up past him as he worked, ever more hair, threaded into the tree in a thousand places. He went back up for air, and down again, slashing furiously, shearing her head of its thick growth. Anton had come up onto the trunk to kill her, but now it became important to save her. He didn't know why.

With a last slash of his knife, her head bobbed free, but she was still trapped in a cage of branches. These Anton tore away and broke, using strength he didn't know he had. Finally, he cut away all her bonds, and she floated free, but limp. He pulled her up from the river, gulping for air as his head came free.

He dragged her to the shore, forcing his way past the enclosing thicket, laying her on the bracken, her head to the side. Water poured from her mouth. He knelt by her side and blew air into her lungs, catching his own ragged breath at the same time.

Her lips were extremely cold, but her eyelids moved. Then Joon opened her eyes, and grabbed his hand, pulling it to her chest, holding him in a strong grip. Any lesser being would have been dead by now, submerged so long under that tree. Joon, however, was of a different sort, she had pri of the royal line. But her face was bluish silver, and she was dying. He didn't know why it mattered to him. She had tried to kill him, had betrayed her people.

He leaned closer to her, murmuring, "Rest now, Lady Joon."

And she did, closing her eyes, and relaxing her face, still beautiful.

She had no pulse, or breath. Exhausted, he sat back on his heels. A spot of sun came through the branches and warmed his head. He stayed by her side for a time, remembering her as he'd first seen her, in her father's chamber, and then on the roof of her pavilion, looking out on the Puldar, teaching him what was in her to teach. Perhaps he had not listened well. But that was all past now.

Eventually, he climbed out onto the trunk of the tree, and sat. He stared at the river, still shrouded in smoke. He would have brought Joon to Vidori for justice. He wished that he could have. He wished that many things had been different here, but the river did what it would. By God, he was starting to think like a Dassa. He thought Maypong would have liked that.

From upriver, he heard an odd humming sound. No, it was something else . . .

The distant sound continued to travel down the river, garbled by the water. And soon he was sure he knew what it was. It was the sound of singing.

By her latest count, Gilar had sixty-eight boats. They were small skiffs, not great war canoes. But these skiffs carried a hundred warriors up the Sodesh toward the coming battle. With Anton's return, Oleel would have to move quickly to consolidate her rebellion. Despite her wound, the big woman's voice was stronger than ever, now that she had the judipon radio. Her voice carried to the huts along the Sodesh and its tributaries: *Strangers will come from the stars; like the Vol, they will demand the Olagong, where children grow best.*

Perhaps Anton's return in the fiery air barge only lent credibility to Oleel's claims. Gilar hoped that sixty-eight boats would also have credibility. With the king.

Her people were still singing Bailey's song. As the flotilla grew, the song came on stronger, drawing more hoda from the compounds, and from the jungle, where many had been hiding, wondering whether to run to the Vol.

Mim, paddling close by, herded the boats along, urging the hoda to sing. Gilar smiled at the old woman, who was proving more resilient than many of the younger ones. Mim gestured for Gilar to sing.

Gilar had sung until her throat was hoarse from the caustic air. But every time she paused, she remembered the taste of dung behind her teeth, and the effluvia trickling into her stomach. And she began again.

When she saw the metal bird, Gilar knew it for Anton's messenger. It had no wings, and its dark sides were sealed with bolts. It was no ashi of fine plumage, but it was a glad sight to her. She turned her skiff toward the center of the river and, signaling the boats to follow her, let the messenger guide her.

If she thought the metal bird a strange sight, she was soon greeted with one even odder: Anton Prados, the great captain of Erth, sitting on a log in the river.

He wasn't surprised to see her. He had sent for her. The metal bird came back to his hand, and several struts folded together, creating a smooth surface all around. Anton slipped it into a pocket. "I heard your song," he said.

Gilar savored the moment. Not so long ago she had imagined being in the presence of Anton Prados, talking with him in the palace, learning about the world of the born to bear. Now she must be wary. He was allied with the king, and the king was not necessarily for Gilar.

She looked up at him as he sat on the giant trunk of a fallen tree. >I have sixty-eight boats,< she signed.

A small smile crept onto his face. "Good. You'll need them."

She wasn't sure what to say next. But suddenly he was getting to his feet and offering her a hand, and she was accepting it, and then they were both standing on the trunk of a tree that had toppled into the river.

>I thought you were going home,< she signed.

"So did I."

The hoda skiffs were tying up along the bank, the sisters using this break to sharpen knives and share food.

He gestured for her to sit next to him. When she did so, he said, "What would you think, Gilar, if I stayed?"

She looked at him, trying to absorb the idea. >They don't like the born to bear around here,< she signed.

"No. But I might not have much choice."

They sat in silence for a few minutes. He looked so strange, with his light skin and hair black as mud. Oddly, his clothes were wet, as though he'd had a dunking in the river. >I don't mind if you stay.< If he was asking her permission, she was happy to give it, with all the authority of her sixty-eight-skiff army.

He turned to her, holding her gaze. "Maypong loved you, Gilar."

She nodded slowly. Of course they would begin with Maypong. Where their lives intersected.

Then he had a story to tell her, of his trip with Maypong to the canyon lands. About Maypong's journey to sorrow. While he did so, Gilar turned away to watch the river. Her sisters in the boats below were watching her, and Gilar didn't want to be seen just now.

When he finished relating the story of the paths, and the bridge, he wanted to hear her story. She knew he was collecting information for the king. That matched her own goal, that the king should know that the hoda had risen. So they sat on the trunk of the tree, and she told him about running away from the stone pavilion. Of her resolve about a Fourth Power. He nodded grimly, hearing that Oleel had been wounded, but that she still preached.

After their stories were told, she thought that there was a confluence here of the things both of them had to do. She had always known that this man would change her life; she just hadn't realized he would change the whole Olagong.

Mim signaled Gilar that she was anxious to be on the move.

Gilar rose. >Soon Oleel will bring her boats against the king's. So I will bargain with him. To bring the hoda to his side.<

"Vidori will bargain hard," Anton said. "You might not get all you want."

Gilar thought that perhaps Anton did not quite understand her strength. >The judipon have carried much of the fight so far. But when Oleel brings the uldia to battle, many of the king's soldiers will refuse to kill them. They are bound by ties of the birth waters.< She fixed him with a direct gaze. >My sisters and I have no such ties.<

He smiled at her. "A good strategy." Then: "I'd like to help, Gilar."

She had the bitter thought that perhaps he might have helped before. But she let it drift away. She'd take help where she could get it.

Mim paddled forward, signaling Gilar to hurry.

Anton looked at the skiffs. "A larger force of your sisters would be helpful."

That she knew. >Oh yes, but I need the radio for that.< She prepared to jump into her skiff.

"I'll paddle," Anton said.

Gilar considered this startling offer. Accepting him into her boat, she gave Anton the paddle. He propelled them into the river, with the sisters following, amazed.

* * *

It was on that trip up the Sodesh, while Gilar and Anton shared a skiff, and made what plans they could, that the main forces of king, judipon, and uldia met in the great river.

Anton could hear the renewed din of voices and gunfire. As he and Gilar's force approached the confluence of the Amalang and the Sodesh, the battle scene spread out before them, clogging the river with barges, skiffs, and smoke.

Somewhere in that chaos was the man they must find.

Anton and Gilar reconnoitered on the north side of the river, tearing lengths of cloth and smearing them with black mud, in an attempt to be identified with the king. But black banners would not guarantee a positive Dassa reaction to seeing hoda with weapons.

As a canoe filled with black banners paddled by, Anton hailed it. The soldiers frowned, and might have fired on him, but one among them thought better of it and said he'd bear a message forward to Romang, who was close by.

On the muddy bank, Anton and Gilar took a quick meal among her band of hoda. Watching them, listening to them, Anton learned that they had more than one way of speaking. They had a tonal language, one that, remarkably, they had kept secret. His first thought was to tell Nick. Why he couldn't, all the reasons why, darkened his view of the river for a time.

Before they could set out again, Romang appeared out of the murk of the river, his great war canoe expertly guided by warriors. It sliced into the bank, and Romang debarked, his face covered with soot. He scowled at the sight of this force of hoda. But he agreed to take a message to Vidori, who was now engaged with Nirimol on the upriver front of the battle. Anton's message was that he was back, and wished to discuss whether he should stay, and under what terms.

As Romang's face darkened to hear things put that way, Anton hastened to add: "The hoda will fight for the king."

It was Gilar's choice. Before they could expect the king to make concessions, the hoda had to prove themselves. Gilar had chosen rightly; Romang and his soldiers needed to see a display of loyalty.

"How does the king fare, Romang-rah?" Anton asked.

The war chief paused, considering. "He is outnumbered by the judipon and uldia." Then he added, in a low and feral tone, "And my soldiers will not enter Oleel's palace."

"Romang-rah, we will do so." He let that sink in with the man, who warily eyed a nearby hoda. "But," Anton added, "you must tell your people that it's proper that the hoda fight the uldia." Romang's look was a weapon by itself.

Anton pressed on: "We'll take Oleel if we can. But it can be no disgrace for us to strike her down, or her uldia. Do you agree?"

After a moment, Romang nodded. "Do it." And this was all the promise Anton got, or was likely to get.

Romang didn't tarry, but settled into his canoe then, slipping out into the Sodesh, to bear all the news to Vidori, including the tidings of the Lady Joon, and where her body lay.

Together with three dozen hoda, Anton and Gilar entered the realm of the uldia: Oleel's pavilion. Cool and quiet, it gave no evidence that it was even occupied. If Romang had the full picture, the uldia were on the river, attacking with impunity among a demoralized royal force.

Gilar knew the pavilion well, and so did Anton, from the layout Nick recorded in his notepad, particularly his sketches of Oleel's courtyard and gallery. As the group split in two, one followed Anton to the courtyard, and the other Gilar to the second-story gallery.

Short of the courtyard, Anton signaled for the women to wait, then brought out the point drone. He watched his palm screen as the drone flicked around the corner, sending images back to him.

The drone revealed an empty courtyard streaming with sunshine, and with the edges in shade from an overhanging mezzanine held up by pillars. Also relayed was the sound of fighting from the river, which Anton hoped would cover the whir of the unit's motor. Moving higher, the drone captured a view of the gallery. A lone figure sat across there, in a section of the gallery opposite where Anton stood. He recognized Oleel, sitting next to a machine.

Recalling the drone, Anton turned to the sisters, as they referred to themselves. After they'd conferred they climbed to the mezzanine from the nearby stairs and waited there for his signal. Then Anton crept forward, his rifle in his arm, into the courtyard, hoping to be able to take dead aim at Oleel. But her position was set back from his line of fire.

She was speaking to someone. After a time the sense of what she was saying came to him, and the realization that she was using a radio transmitter. She was rallying the Dassa, those who sat by receivers along the rivers trying to fathom what was happening to the Olagong, and whom to fight for. Oleel was answering that question in no uncertain terms.

Crouching, he braced the rifle on his upraised knee. He would make a noise, and then she would came to the edge of the mezzanine.

Her voice, when it came, startled him. It was resonant and full.

"Venning promised that you would not stay, yet here you are."

Anton had heard her voice only once before, but he hadn't forgotten it, and probably never would.

Her voice commanded the hall. "He lied. We see how you deal with us."

Watching for her in his scope, he responded, "If you wanted to know my plans, you should have asked *me*."

He saw her head for a moment, her square head with its gray bun of hair. But then she retreated out of sight. "Have you come to kill my ladies for the sake of the king?" She didn't wait for him to answer. "Oh yes. But have you thought, Captain, what you will do if I win?"

"You won't, Oleel. There are more set against you than the king."

"Such as you?"

"Yes. And the hoda. They are here with me."

A pause. Then: "Venning said you liked outcasts." Her voice was smaller as she added, "But they are few."

"You are fewer now too, Oleel. Joon is dead. I saw her die."

A strange sound came from the gallery. It was the sound of a moan, amplified by a large frame.

"Saw her die?" the voice came, splintered.

"She drowned in the Sodesh. An accident."

Her voice rose again. "No, not my sweet Joon." She came forward, but remained hidden by a pillar. "Not, not Joon . . ."

"Consider that you killed her, Oleel. Her tie of birth waters meant she would do all for you. And she has."

Though her voice was soft, it carried with surprising fidelity in the stone hall. "You say the river took her with its hands?"

His silence answered her well enough.

Then Oleel emerged from her hiding place and walked into full view at the edge of the deck. Anton had her in his sights. But she just stood there, exposing herself, like a noncombatant. And Anton hesitated.

She looked down at him. Her voice thinned, but its whisper carried. "So you have brought us all to ruin after all. Was not one world enough, that you must take mine as well?"

Behind him, a murmur rose from the sisters, impatient to have him shoot. But Anton paused. "There is room enough on this world for twenty humans, Oleel."

"Room enough?" She gazed over his head, at the window on the opposite side of the mezzanine, as though looking beyond it, to the variums. "Oh, enough room for born to bear, do you say? Enough room to cast away my world and all that we were?" She looked down at him suddenly. "And you as leader of the degenerates. Is it so?"

For an answer, Gilar moved out onto the gallery from the stairwell nearest Oleel.

"Oh yes," Oleel said, "the slave again."

Gilar walked forward. Behind her stood the sisters, all armed, quietly armed.

The big woman's upper chest was wrapped in bandages. Over this dressing she wore an open robe. For the first time, Gilar noticed she leaned heavily on a staff. The woman's pri was weak, yet she stood like a monument. Nearby sat the radio transmitter the chief uldia had been using.

Oleel looked at Gilar with the ghost of a sneer. Her face, never expressive, still had room for contempt. "We knew about your singing language. It was how we kept track of hoda schemes."

By way of answer, Gilar sang, We killed your guards.

Oleel's gaze flicked over to a place where she might have expected reprieve. Her face hardened.

From the courtyard came Anton's voice: "Ask the king for mercy, Oleel."

"Do you think I care for Vidori's mercy? I will follow Joon, of course. Despite what the Olagong made her, I forgave her everything. The palace, her father, her state—nothing stood between us, nor ever will. I forgave it all."

Gilar knew that Oleel was right. She must follow Joon. Jump, then.

But Oleel was already looking out over her courtyard, her realm. Then she took one step into the air, and fell. On the stone floor below, her bones shattered, and her skull.

Gilar stood at the edge, looking down on her. Blood was pooling on the stone floor, at the place where one floor stream came out from the west and joined another from the south. An analogue of the Sodesh and Amalang confluence. The two streams began running red.

TWENTY-FIVE

The haze-filled air fed a purple sunset. Through the bruised smoke, Anton sped along in the royal canoe, attended by the king's guard. Once Gilar's skiff carried Oleel's body into the river for display, the uldia put down their arms. The battle was over.

Anton's craft passed boats, skiffs, and barges full of supplies and soldiers, many of them wounded. Then, approaching a pier surrounded by boats, Anton's canoe plied its way to the dock. A figure waited there, his hands clasped behind his back, and dressed in black and gray.

Vidori was alone on the pier. Behind him, in a makeshift camp, thousands of soldiers thronged among pitched tents. The guards sprang from the canoe. But it was Vidori's hand that came down to help Anton onto the dock.

Anton took the offered help, the first time he'd ever actually touched Vidori. It was a human gesture, that hand-to-hand. It seemed a good beginning for what came next.

As always, Vidori was scrupulously shaven, but the signs of battle lingered in his clothes, covered as they were with soot. His face brightened at the sight of Anton standing next to him on the pier, empty save for the two of them.

"Anton-rah," the king said.

Anton raised an eyebrow. Here was an early concession. "Rahi, I am glad to see you."

Vidori didn't lead him from the dock, where they were most likely to have privacy.

After a moment Anton said, "Joon drowned by mischance on the Sodesh, Vidori-rah. The tree fell, and pinned her. I'm sorry." He'd told Romang the details. That he hadn't killed her, but would have, if his aim had been better.

"The braid took her," Vidori said. He stepped past Anton to the very end of the dock, looking out on the great river. "Do you know what we say, Anton, about those who have no burial?" He went on without waiting for a reply. "That they have no rest, but swim until the braid releases them. Sometimes never."

"Rahi, I did bring her from the river. I told Romang where her body was."

Still facing outward, Vidori said, "But he put her into the river again, where she will swim, thankfully."

It chilled Anton to hear him say that. The cost of the retribution chilled him. He heard the cost in the man's voice.

Vidori turned back to Anton. "She wanted to die."

No, she wanted to be queen, Anton thought, but withheld saying.

"She was bearing a child within her."

Now Anton was truly speechless. And just as the idea was taking root, Vidori added one sentence too many:

"It is sometimes the result of human sex, I believe."

Anton felt the words hit him, and then press down, seeking some kind of perverse entry. "I . . ." He couldn't finish. Vidori was saying it was Anton who had impregnated her. Joon was born to bear? Joon?

Vidori looked at him with what might have been compassion. Or compassion for himself. He said: "I knew what she was. I couldn't give her up. I begged her to dissemble.

Oleel agreed to help, and hid her nature. We both loved her, perhaps Oleel even more than I. Sometimes, I have come to believe, the reason Oleel hated all other hoda so was her rage that Joon was thus defiled."

The image of Joon's death came to Anton's mind, when she took his hand and brought it down to her chest. But she had meant for him to touch her belly. What this child meant to her, he would never know. But he did know that she was trying to tell him. Perhaps she'd hoped to tell him several other times when she'd tried to see him. Even as he avoided her. His eyes grew hot.

Vidori was saying, "After a time it became impossible for us to think of Joon as hoda. She was beloved of us, nothing more. So you see, her interest in the hoda was not a trap for you. She might have been a good queen. But she thought that I had no vision for the slaves, and so betrayed me. I kept her out of my true plans. I was foolish."

"*I* was foolish, Vidori-rah. Very foolish."

If he had observed Dassa customs in this Dassa world, Joon would not have been pregnant. All that had been required of him was that he observe sarif, in their way, a way that worked here. If he had observed Dassa custom, Joon would never have had reason to hope that a pregnancy would bring her power, align her with Anton against her father . . . if that was her plan. He felt it was. And she was not wrong—it would have put her in a different light for him. He thought of that unborn child, and the emotional cost in Joon's decision to show herself as a hoda. Or had she been a visionary, one who would have reveled in being a hoda queen?

When he put his attention on Vidori once more, Anton saw the man's resolve returning to his face, that calm facade that was his refuge. "But Anton-rah," Vidori said. "I will not speak of her again. I will not speak of my foolishness, or hers. Or yours, ever again."

Anton knew that he never would. So he was left with the king's words coiling around his heart, leaving him with a terrible ambiguity. Here in the Olagong, the braid chose Joon for him, instead of Maypong. And then took both of them.

Giving Anton this moment alone, Vidori walked down the pier toward camp, where he was immediately importuned by his lieutenants. When he finished with them, he waited for Anton to join him.

It was a long wait, but Vidori stood quietly, staring at the river, and no one dared interrupt him again.

At length, Anton did, glad for the cover of the acrid smoke, which left everyone's eyes raw. Vidori led him through the encampment. Anton followed, wanting to say things to Vidori, wanting to talk about what would never be discussed again: Joon, her hopes, her child. It saddened him beyond measure that at the last, she might have wanted to die, as Vidori said. Because she had lost Anton's support. And it was too late to not be pregnant.

Finally, he forced himself to set it aside for later. There were other things he'd come to say to Vidori that needed saying.

Vidori was winding his way through what he called a *staging ground* for the wounded. The Dassa had no word for *hospital* or *infirmary*. Many fighters, both male and female, were lying on pallets, their wounds bound. Helpers applied ointments; but for surgery, they would have to rely on the uldia.

And, surprisingly, there were a few uldia present here. And more arriving every hour, having heard of Oleel's death. Vidori's strategy, he said, was amnesty for any uldia who came freely to him. By what Anton was observing, it was the right decision, for these Dassa soldiers were deferring to the uldia, grateful for their medicinals and ministrations.

The king stopped to talk with the soldiers and conferred with the uldia who tended the most critically wounded. He had all their names, and used them. But soon Vidori was leading Anton away from the tents, along a path by the river, toward somewhat higher ground.

As they walked, Vidori told him that the judipon under Nirimol had fled up the Sodesh, perhaps to take refuge with the Vol. The fighting, he believed, was over, at least for now. He had set his army to putting out fires, and thousands of Dassa—whichever side they had been fighting on—had put down their arms and begun to attack the fires instead.

Anton knew that Oleel's death was not the end of the conflict. All the problems were still before them, and even worse than before. The hoda had risen up; Dassa had killed each other in civil war. These were scarring wounds. And, as well, there were the alien cultures supposedly hidden in the forest, in the langva, and they—or the rumor of them—would need to be quelled.

It was all far from over.

Emerging from the forest at a bend in the Sodesh, they came to the king's command tent, with views of the river to both the west and east. A unit of guards made way, and the two of them entered the open-sided pavilion. Shim, conferring with several viven, dismissed them as the king entered.

"Anton-rah, thank you," Shim said, beaming.

Anton returned her greeting, just as happy to see her.

A tray of food and drink appeared. They took the meal in silence, and while they did, the sun set and servants lit oil lamps.

As Anton prepared to speak, he met Vidori's eyes. There he saw all the unspoken things that formed the powerful undercurrent to their relationship. He hoped it was a current of trust and shared grief, and not one of resentment. Perhaps even Vidori wasn't sure.

"Rahi," he began. "You asked me a few days ago to stay on your world. To stand in protection of the Olagong against what the stars might bring." He paused, then added, "I'm not sure the stars will bring any further trouble than a new batch of humans. And I'm not sure more humans *will* come. And if they do, you must know, we aren't a warship."

"But you have weapons." Vidori sipped a drink, falling back into his easy manner of playing the game of words.

"Some. But we aren't much of a force if conflict comes." He sat back from the table, preparing to be as tough as the king. "But there is the appearance of protection. A political statement. Yes?"

"Yes."

"If that's the goal, then we can discuss what's best for your people, and best for mine. They're mixed together, though, rahi. I have to tell you that they are mixed together. Because of Gilar."

The king tossed back, *"Mixed?"*

Anton shifted in his chair, saying, "The hoda are human." Joon was human. The king's elaborate plan to soften hoda conditions was not, as Anton had once thought, solely to prevent them from defecting to the Vol. It went much deeper than that—to the heart of things, to his beloved daughter.

The king took a piece of fruit and chewed thoughtfully. He gave no sign that the subject disturbed him, but his control was too perfect. Anton had learned from Maypong to interpret stillness and calm.

"I have said I will free the hoda," Vidori said.

Shim looked at the river, saying, "It would appear they are already free. Some of them."

The king flicked an amused expression at her. She had told the truth, but it was surprising, coming from the quiet Shim. Well, she had been out in the field during conflict. It did change people, as Anton well knew.

"And *free* is only a word," Anton said.

Vidori's words came quietly. "What words do you like better?"

Anton had the words straight from Gilar. "Land. Respect."

"Every islet belongs to a lineage. This is a thing, Anton Prados, that cannot change in the Olagong."

Anton said, "Outside of Lolo, far up the Sodesh, there is

unclaimed land. Land not well suited for variums. It would serve well for the hoda." *Who have no need of variums,* he left off saying, it veering too close to the topic that would never be discussed again.

Shim glanced at the king, to see if he was angry.

He was. Vidori stood, staring down at Anton, his eyes taking a glint from the oil lamps. Then he turned away and went to the corner of his tent where a radio receiver sat on a low table. He turned a knob. Through a hiss of static came garbled words. He tuned the radio. Gilar's voice was clear: still transmitting from Oleel's pavilion, still calling in song to her sisters in the households along the rivers.

"Is this growing army of hoda my next battle? Is this whose side you've come to defend?"

Shim was staring intently at her hands, folded in her lap.

Anton rose. "No, rahi. The hoda have already fought for you. They took Oleel's compound in your name. It's yours." He looked at the king. "I won't fight here again. I won't kill Dassa again. Whatever happens among the Powers—and the Vol—it will happen without me. So it's not a matter of arms, but of—politics. And yes, in that I side with the hoda. Because they're my people more directly than any highborn Dassa. They're my only future if I stay. My crew and I will live among the hoda, where our welcome is clear. By your pardon, Vidori-rah, if we stay, we must go with the hoda."

In the glaring silence that followed this pronouncement, Shim rose and directed servants to clear the food and bring wine. Then she poured the wine, clearly with high hopes that it would help. She held out a glass to Anton, who drank, because it was custom that the guest drank first. Vidori ignored his glass and strode from the tent. Shim's look warned Anton to go slowly, but that was just what he couldn't do. Now was the moment in which the right thing could be done, and the future imagined anew.

Handing the cup of wine back to Shim, he followed Vidori outside, where torches were dug in along the bank and around the tent.

Sensing his presence, but not turning around from his stance facing the river, Vidori said, "So now we will have the bearing of children in outlandish ways."

Anton replied, "Unless you pronounce it normal."

The king threw him an annoyed glance. "And the households that rely on the hoda for care of children? Who supplants the hodas' place in our households? Do you have a word for that?"

Anton did. "Uldia."

The corner of Vidori's mouth turned up. "Well, they do need something productive to do, it would seem."

"And some hoda will prefer their familiar households. The uldia will have help."

"Oh yes, the uldia will be happy to clean soiled babes and cook meals."

Anton ventured—and this was Gilar's idea too: "You might consider reducing the uldias' receipts from the tithe, and increasing the householders'. The mistresses of the compounds could then pay the uldia for their services, bringing all into balance again."

After a very long silence, the king's voice finally came to him. "You have become a harder man to deal with, Anton-rah."

"Yes, rahi."

Several minutes passed. The river flowed on, changing, and staying. Shouts came from those Dassa still moving upon it in skiffs and canoes.

Vidori turned to him. "Here is what I say: The hoda will be an extension of the king's power. They will be on the Sodesh, but that cannot be solely *their* river. It belongs to all."

"But, rahi," Anton said, "they must have their own chief."

"Yes, granted. But there will be only three Powers."

"Yet four chiefs?"

Vidori waved this away. "I will set the judipon to numerations. They are good at it." He started to pace along the riverbank, thinking out loud. "If the hoda occupy lands up-river, so close to the Vol lands, then they will maintain a fortress there. They will defend the Olagong from Vol intrusion, as a first line of defense. They are aligned with me, or they cannot stay."

Anton thought that might suit Gilar. It wasn't as though she believed she could avoid compromises. "I'll ask her, rahi. It's a good plan."

Vidori raised an eyebrow. "You say so? Thankfully I have not lost my powers of strategy, then."

Anton didn't rise to the bait. "I would never think that, rahi."

"Do you not, Anton? Did you not return and conclave first with the hoda before turning to me?"

Anton gazed back at this man he might call *friend*. "You've given me your courtesy and your protection, and I owe you much for that. But the hoda are my people, just as the Dassa are yours. Nothing alters that. I think we're both anchored, Vidori-rah, by our devotion."

"Oh yes," came the voice. This time it was Shim who answered. She stood beside them holding two cups of wine. "By devotion," she said, turning to the king and holding out a cup of blue wine.

Vidori looked at her, and at last accepted the cup. Anton took the other one.

Without coming to a conclusion about everything, they drank. It was a beginning. And they hadn't killed each other. Shim fetched her own cup, and drank deeply, her hands shaking a little.

It had grown very dark. Shim had left the two of them with a fresh jar of wine.

They were seated on the bank of the Sodesh, watching the river bearing yet a few more boats on its broad back. Many of the fires were abating, and the forest had resumed some of its healthy chatter. The sound was comforting, after so much silence from the creatures of the Olagong.

Vidori had been talking about the codas. He'd been thinking about them, although when he'd had time to think in the last four days, Anton didn't know. But Vidori was a thinking king, above all else. He was a man who had just learned that his world was the center of things. Then again, in some ways this squared with what he had always thought.

The idea of sharing this world was where he surprised Anton. Because Vidori was not troubled by the possible visits of other beings. Perhaps he took comfort in Anton's opinion that it would not happen in his lifetime. It hadn't happened in ten thousand years, Anton had pointed out. But with the passing of time, he'd pointed out as well, such visits became more likely, as messages had time to reach home worlds, and ships had time to come looking. And though Anton had said the *Restoration* was no warship, Vidori also had faith that the ship would be a protection should the aliens, if they came, be more Vol-like than Dassa-like. But some things did give him pause.

"How many humans are folded into the Olagong?"

"We don't know." He didn't want to say, *Millions.* But the king already knew.

Vidori said simply, "You will not outnumber us. Then it would be your world, not ours."

So they were still negotiating. And in this, Anton had no authority. What would the ships from Earth do, if they came? Would they take the legacy back to Earth? Or stay?

Well, they must not stay. This was the Dassa's world. If the hoda reproduced and became more numerous, of course, the result would be the same. But the bearing of children seemed to Vidori a small and gradual thing. He wasn't alarmed by the prospect of hoda children being fathered by Anton's crew. There were only a few human men, after all. But the condition was clear: *You will not outnumber us.*

Thinking of his crew of eighteen people, Anton didn't think it would go against Vidori's wishes.

"It is a fine line to walk, rahi," Anton said. "But we'll have to walk it."

That seemed enough for now.

Vidori reached into a pocket, bringing out something and pressing it into Anton's hand.

It was a small piece of golden cloth. In the flickering torchlight, it caught glimmers in its folds.

Vidori said, "I retrieved this."

Anton clutched the bit of cloth, and was surprised at what he felt. Not sadness. But a bittersweet joy. To have a piece of that fabric she loved so well. "Thank you, my friend," Anton whispered.

Then Vidori said, although he was looking at the river, and it might have been just a stray thought, "You could stay at my pavilion and be my chancellor, Anton."

It was so like the man to use every advantage. But it would be very like their new friendship for Anton to say no, and not hesitate.

"I don't think you need another chancellor, rahi." Shim was entirely up to the task; he'd always thought so. Anton added: "If ships come from Earth—*if* they come—I'll be at your side to help you, Vidori-rah. I promise you that. But you don't really need me."

"Do Gilar's people need you?"

Anton paused. "I think they do." Then, mindful of his crew, of Zhen, and Bailey, and Sergeant Webb, and Leo Petry, he said, "But we certainly need *them*."

"So the hoda will have their own pavilion," Vidori said softly, as though trying out the sound of it. "It is not our tradition."

Anton smiled. "Perhaps it should have been."

That brought a look from Vidori, but he settled the matter by saying, "Well, there were always four rivers."

EPILOGUE

Bailey was packed and ready to go when Anton came for her at the palace. Everything that she owned lay in a small pack at her feet, as she waited at the steps coming up from the river.

With Anton were three canoes of the king's guards, and three crew members from the *Restoration*. The shuttle had gone back to the ship for safekeeping, even though the fires were gutted after the night's heavy rain, and Nirimol had fled to the Vol, too weak to confront the king and his new allies.

Anton handed Bailey down into the canoe. Behind her, Shim bustled with packages to send along, and urged them on Bailey, who took them, hoping they were gowns.

Shim waved brightly as the convoy set out in the morning light, diffused by a thin haze. Acrid smoke smells gave way to the char from Lolo's fields and compounds. Still, the day promised to be fair.

Bailey had spent the three days since the battle on the Sodesh writing up a brief report to accompany Anton's radio message home. She hoped it set the right tone, but in any case, the report was more to bolster Anton's credibility and inform her fans that she had taken up singing again.

She had also taken time to request that the king give Samwan engineering help on a new generator. Vidori had expressed his opinion that Samwan didn't deserve such help. Bailey had replied that she'd take it as a personal favor if he changed his mind. Shim cast an acid glance at Bailey, murmuring that favors should not be directly sought, but must go through a chancellor. And Bailey had simply turned a dazzling smile on the woman.

Vidori had finally pronounced, "Samwan shall have a generator." And then, extracting his payment: "I hope I may present your singing in my palace sometime soon, Bailey-rah."

But of course.

Now, Bailey sat just behind Gilar as the girl stroked the paddles with an energy Bailey could only admire. But she was paddling for the new land, of course, and a new life. Quite a girl. Bailey blamed herself for not seeing Gilar's potential at the beginning. But they both had a lot to learn.

Zhen was still on board the *Restoration*, but would be coming down in a later flight. The woman would be the only modern biological scientist on the planet. Singlehandedly, Zhen could hardly expect to make much progress on bringing humans forth from genetic code. Perhaps their main issue would be to raise up the next generation to continue the work. Their schooling would begin with the knowledge stored in the *Restoration*, and move on to Quadi things. But Bailey, however, didn't see herself as a schoolmarm. Instead, she saw herself enjoying morning tea in private apartments, then giving singing lessons to two or three gifted students in the afternoons . . .

But in truth, there were other things the hoda might ask of her. *How do we have children? How do we form families, Earth style? And should we?* Bailey thought they would figure it all out, and that she could help in that process.

Though the battle was three days past, the river still bore

a few bodies. Dassa pulled the fallen into skiffs, bearing them away for burial. At Vidori's command, they made no distinction among judipon, uldia, king's guard, or hoda. But once past the confluence of the Amalang, where the uldia pavilion lay hidden up its smoggy length, the fleet broke free of these mortal signs of conflict. They passed the hospital camp and soon approached the region where Anton meant to make a brief stop.

Most of the boats proceeded on, but Anton, Gilar, and Bailey, along with a few soldiers, pointed their canoes into a region of tall grasses where hidden canals plied their way into a marshland.

Nidhe, the king's brother, had a sure memory of the route, and he led the way. Behind him came Anton's boat and one empty boat in tow.

The day was clearing of smog. The fires had not come so far as this, and Bailey allowed her eyes to rest on the apple-green grasses, leaning over on the breeze. Clear of trees except for one nearby stand, the land lay flat and broad, with the sky arching over them in an unaccustomed swath. It was a glorious day, and one that made her thankful for life and sky and water. The thread of memory, of Remy—her sister and daughter—came to her. She didn't shoo it away. That undercurrent would always be there. She let it flow through her, graying the day a little. But before long the day brightened again.

After a time, Anton and Gilar returned from where they had gone. They carried the shroud between them, and placed it in the extra boat. Bailey looked hard at the bundle of bones. *Oh, my dear,* she thought. And said it for so many reasons, not all of them having to do with Remy.

They retraced their path through the marsh. The hoda's bones would be the first laid to rest in the new burial grounds, the one in the fourth pavilion that the king's engineers and workmen and hoda would build. Here would be a burial ground for the born to bear, and someday soon Bailey would lie down there, too. They all would. And that was just fine.

Back on the Sodesh, the sun fell harshly on their backs. Bailey donned her hat. In front of her, Gilar did the same, having fashioned one in imitation of Bailey's. Gilar had stopped taking the cleansing broth in the mornings, but her hair was still missing, and her bald head remained sensitive to the sun. She was the newest hoda, the last to be clipped. Soon the hoda would have to pick a hairstyle, Bailey thought. She set her thoughts to it.

Ahead of them, they could see the rest of the fleet just turning a bend in the river. Bailey's group paddled to catch up. By her side, Anton was instructing the three crew members in Dassa-style paddling, and they looked like boys on an outing. Well, she felt the same way herself. Noting her gaze, Anton waved a paddle, and it glistened in the morning sun before diving down to the river again. She saluted off the brim of her hat. Thank God he had made it back to her. Someone had to carry on in the long run.

Meanwhile, Bailey felt that the day warranted a song. She wasn't sure if it should be a finale or an opening. But certainly, a song might do.

As Bailey tested out a few bars, Gilar turned around, paddle in hand, and smiled, showing teeth, in the human style. She raised an eyebrow, inquiring.

Smiling back, Bailey answered, "A new song, Gilar. Puccini this time." She would sing a song about a child, "O mio bambino caro."

Bailey added, "Time to expand your repertoire, my dear."

ABOUT THE AUTHOR

Kay Kenyon began her writing career as a copywriter at WDSM-TV in Duluth, Minnesota. She kept up her interest in writing through careers in marketing and transportation planning, and published her first novel, *The Seeds of Time*, in 1997. *The Braided World* is her sixth novel. She lives in Wenatchee, Washington, with her husband.

Visit her website at *www.kaykenyon.com*
Or email her at *tko@kaykenyon.com*

KAY KENYON

THE SEEDS OF TIME
____57681-X $5.99/$7.99 Canada

RIFT
____58023-X $5.99/$8.99 Canada

TROPIC OF CREATION
____58026-4 $5.99/$8.99 Canada

MAXIMUM ICE
____58376-X $6.50/$9.99 Canada

THE BRAIDED WORLD
____58379-4 $6.99/$10.99 Canada

Please enclose check or money order only, no cash or CODs. Shipping & handling costs: $5.50 U.S. mail, $7.50 UPS. New York and Tennessee residents must remit applicable sales tax. Canadian residents must remit applicable GST and provincial taxes. Please allow 4 – 6 weeks for delivery. All orders are subject to availability. This offer subject to change without notice. Please call 1-800-726-0600 for further information.

Bantam Dell Publishing Group, Inc.   TOTAL AMT $_____
Attn: Customer Service   SHIPPING & HANDLING $_____
400 Hahn Road   SALES TAX (NY, TN) $_____
Westminster, MD 21157

      TOTAL ENCLOSED $_____

Name _____

Address _____

City/State/Zip _____

Daytime Phone (_____) _____